Talk Dirty to Me

Immy Keeper

MINDLESS MUSE PUBLISHING, LLC

This book is a work of fiction. Names, characters, places and incidents either are products of the author's imagination or are used fictitiously. Any resemblance to actual events, locales or persons, living or dead, is entirely coincidental and not intended by the author.

TALK DIRTY TO ME

Dirty Series, Book 1

MINDLESS MUSE PUBLISHING, LLC

www.MindlessMusePublishing.com

Copyright © 2019 Imogen Keeper

All rights reserved.

The right of Imogen Keeper to be identified as the author of the work has been asserted by her in accordance with the Copyright, Designs and Patents Act of 1988.

This book is sold subject to the condition it shall not, by way of trade or otherwise, be circulated in any form or by any means, electronic or otherwise without the publisher's prior consent.

Contents

	VI
	VII
1. 1 - get ready to read with one hand	1
2. 2 - a stranger named stranger	11
3. 3 - day glow panties	22
4. sex on the brain	28
5. and so the lying begins	50
6. everyone lies	64
7. I want to ruin your panties	71
8. trust corroded	84
9. one-eight-hundred-hit-4-you	97
10. my ovaries are blue blue blue	108
11. a big pink dildo	127
12. a dick pic	141

13.	that hot guy with the everywhere tats	162
14.	he's a stranger to me	180
15.	15 half gross, half hot	190
16.	jacks don't always beat threes	202
17.	your thong is neon pink	207
18.	what if I say moo?	222
19.	I've always been a coward	228
20.	20 - I trust you	234
21.	21 - heaven smells like peaches	244
22.	22 - what's your real name?	257
23.	23 - maybe I can be that guy	271
24.	24 - the life I want	277
25.	25 - garden vomit	283
26.	26 - you planned it this way	289
27.	27 - an arm on her	299
28.	cherry on the misery cake	305
29.	29 - pony up	316
30.	30 - be selfish	322
31.	31 - the orange dot	327
32.	32 - what about Wet Panty?	331
33.	33 - rocks	339
34.	34 - who is this guy?	346
35.	35 - too many things	352
36.	36 - we all have secrets	362

37.	37 - a kinda hot ex hitman writer guy	365
	Want more sexy dirty stories?	371
	Fight Dirty with Me Sneak Peek	372
	Fight Dirty with Me Sneak Peek	384
	Chapter	399

For the girl at summer camp who handed over a wrinkled-up, pilfered-from-her-mom novel with an arranged marriage, a mistaken identity, a fake duchess and a secret Romany duke.

You began my life-long obsession with capital R Romance. I don't remember your name or the author's or the book's title, but I'll never stop hunting for that story, I'll never stop reading Romance, and I hope I never stop writing it.

Sometimes a single moment can change your whole life.

Sign up for Immy's VIP room for a FREE BOOK and to be the first to know about giveaways, sales and new releases:

https://www.imogenkeeper.com

1 – GET READY TO READ WITH ONE HAND

STRANGER

Most people don't go around hiring killers. They don't even know how. So, if they get around to deciding they want one, they go on the dark web, find a local hack, pay a few thousand dollars, and the vic gets knifed down or bludgeoned in the streets.

That's not me.

I go in at night. They never wake up. Nobody sees me, hears me or even knows I was ever there. I'm a ghost. Nothing more than a shadow in the wind.

And I don't work for normal people. No housewives or lawyers. Which makes this next job … strange.

> Ender9551: Her name is Mia Whitten. It has to happen in March. Not before.

Usually, I have a month or two to vet the client, study the target, cover my back.

But March is a long time away.

It's barely September now, the sun still hot, the trees thick with summer leaves, still in their brightest stage of green. Who takes out a hit for seven months in the future? And why? Someone either dangerously deranged or meticulously organized. Or both.

"New contract?" My brother, James, shifts on his wheelchair, the vinyl seat making a sound like a fart under his ass. From this distance and angle, no way can he see the screen.

"What do you mean?" I turn to face him.

He tosses his book at the coffee table, his nostrils flaring. "You just got a new target, right?"

I make a non-committal face. He doesn't know what I really do. He thinks I run private security hacks, probe protective service plans for flaws. It's what I tell everyone who asks.

Right now, he's either fishing. Or I'm projecting.

He rolls his chair closer to me, his thumbs on the rims, and I minimize my screen just in case.

"Who are you going to kill this time?"

My stomach tightens instantly, and I draw a long, slow breath. From the set of his shoulders, he's not fishing. I'm not projecting.

"How long have you known?"

"Since the last time. I read the news."

I meet his eyes, hazel like mine, like our mom's before she left us. Shadowed by dark brows, thick and black like mine, like our dad's before he left us, too.

The silence between us is loud. I have no idea what to say. Yes, James. I'm a killer. I kill people. That's what I do.

Gogo—don't ask, I didn't invent that monstrosity of a name—a hound dog, groans from her spot on the floor by his feet. She showed up here a few weeks after I bought the house, skinny, tail wagging, those soft liquid eyes staring up at me, no identification beyond a single blue tag with her name on it. A ridiculous name for a dog with a face that looks eternally unimpressed. She looks bored, but acts like a live wire.

Somehow, I started feeding her, and she never left.

Her tail thumps when I glance at her, but she doesn't rise. No support on the canine front.

I glare at her.

Her tail thumps.

The silence thickens.

"You don't have to do it," he finally says.

I push up from my chair and cross the living room.

I stop at the windows overlooking what I've come to think of as my mountain. "Tell me then, go on. What am I doing?"

The leaves haven't started changing yet, but the green has darkened. The colors will come soon.

"I'll have the prostheses soon. A few months. Then I can start working again, get a place of my ow—"

"This is your place." I bought it for him, two days after he was injured. I have no use for all this furniture. Rugs and chairs and pillows and shit. Houses and cars and mountains are for normal people.

I'm not normal.

"No." His voice comes out loud, maybe louder than he expects because he pauses before continuing. In the six months since his accident, I've barely heard him speak in more than a hush or a whisper, as if he's eternally trying not to be a burden. "This is your home, Stranger."

"I have no home." Don't need or want one either.

He tosses out a hand, like he's physically rejecting my words.

"Then make one. Start writing again. Stay—" He breaks off sharply, like he's trying to pick his words carefully. "Stop, before you get yourself killed, or arrested, or become a sociopath."

I'm probably already a sociopath. I slide my hands into my jeans pockets. "I'm happier alone."

"You're not happy. You're a robot."

It's true.

"I don't blame you, Stranger. I never did."

The surge of anger, unexpected and hot, has me turning to face him, my fists clenching. "This has nothing to do with Mom."

He tilts his chin back, surveying me. "I didn't bring her up. You did." He glares at me. "You still think that was your fault?"

I don't think it. I know it. She wouldn't have left if I'd been different. I could have gotten a job, helped out. Instead all I did was get myself kicked out of school, get arrested, land my ass in and out of juvie.

"This has nothing to do with her," I say again.

"Then why bring her up?"

"I shouldn't have left." He'd been barely fifteen, with peach fuzz on his upper lip, and I left him in a group home filled with a motley assortment of drugged-up bullies and budding criminals.

"I got it then. I get it now. I'd have done the same thing. I did the same thing as soon as I could."

That sends a fresh wave of pissed-off racing through my blood. If he hadn't joined the Marines, he'd never have ended up in that chair.

He rocks his chair toward me. "Stop punishing yourself. Move on with your fucking life."

"There's no 'punishing'. Just want to get you set up so I can move on."

And I'm close. I'm a hundred thousand shy of the eight million mark. A conservative 4% return would only net 240K per year—a secure living. Enough for someone with ongoing medical bills, and who knows about inflation. That would set him up for life, with a little left over for me.

He can live here in comfort with a roof over his head, a soft bed, and a nurse to wash his stumps until he's old and gray.

And me? I'll be far away. Where I can't do any more damage.

His mouth forms a tight line. "I won't take your money. As soon as I get the prostheses, I'm leaving." He wipes his hand over his mouth, and his biceps bulge.

He's gotten big in the months since the accident. The constant physical work of lifting his body, the obsession he's developed with weight training, it's paying off. Where once he had the same rangy body-type as me, now he's thickly bound. Like a reverse Pop-eye, his biceps are swole up, thick as bowling balls.

He rotates one rim and spins his chair so I can't see his face. "Don't you dare kill someone and tell yourself you're doing it for me."

I can only see his face in profile as he stares at the empty mountain.

I say nothing.

Gogo rises and, toenails ticking, goes to stand by the door, panting pointedly. She wants a walk.

"Who's the target?" James asks, voice quiet again. The apologetic tone is back.

I open the door, and Gogo races out, her tail waving like a pendulum, her black and brown fur shining under the blinding sun.

The target. I tug on my earlobe. What do I know about her?

A lot, actually.

Mia Whitten.

Providence, 27, wealthy family, engaged, went to an expensive private university where she met the man she plans to marry. Pretty. Really pretty.

Thanks to the combined efforts of social media and wedding websites, everything I wish to know about this woman is online, easily accessible. I even know that she has a penchant for insanely colorful things, judging by her registry. Pink platters. Tea saucers with turquoise, yellow and hot pink flowers. A cookie tray painted with every color under the sun. Napkins embroidered with bold birds, leaves, more flowers. Her registry is like a fucking walk through a fake rainforest, full of fake fancy flowers. Expensive, useless shit, all painted up and pretty.

I also know who her bridesmaids are, her parents, her siblings.

Stalking gets easier every day.

I would know.

She's a writer too, who writes under a pen name, Mia Reed.

That made me laugh. It's too damned perfect. Like fate dropped me down the easiest mark. No security. In country. No passports needed. No struggle to get weapons under a foreign government. And she's annoying. I don't know her, but already the colors and the flowers and the birds are spinning in my head like an overload of rainbow-bright noise. And she's a writer.

Motherfucking perfect.

I've been writing for about as long as I can remember. Stupid ass journals and angsty poems as a kid, but later, in the Marines while posted up, real stuff. Stuff that helped me forget, let go, move past all the bad shit I've done.

She's not just any writer. She's a sex writer.

One review read, "so smokin' hot, you'd better get ready to read with one hand, and the AC jacked down as low as it goes."

She's the job that'll end this all.

It's got to be fate.

So what do I tell James?

Her face is sweet, classic, not flashy. Her photos speak to a cushy, easy life, as if she's floated above the shit pile of poverty, terror and pain the rest of the world experiences.

I've lived in that shit pile, clawed my way through it and killed some of the worst pieces of shit inside.

"Just a woman," I say, and instantly regret telling the truth. He'll be pricklier about killing a woman.

Mia Reed, what did you do to piss off Ender9551?

He blows out a long puff of air. "Who is she?"

I lift a shoulder, scratch the back of my neck. "Just a woman somebody wants dead. Doesn't matter who she is. You hungry?"

Because I want this conversation to be over yesterday, I head for the kitchen.

James doesn't follow. "I can make my own sandwich."

He can, but it's easier for me to do it. So, I make two anyway. Whole wheat bread, muenster, sliced turkey, spicy mustard, apple slices, with carrots on the side. Just like our dad used to make.

When I bring them back in, I slap the plate down on the coffee table in front of him, and sit beside him to eat.

He doesn't touch it. "I don't want to be your reason to kill a good person."

The apples crunch as I take a big bite out of my sandwich. "Who says she's good?"

"You did." Reluctantly, he takes a bite of his own.

"I don't know she's good." She has terrible taste in decorations.

"I can tell from your tone, the way you sighed, how you won't talk about it, that something bugs you about her. Which means she's not some foreign dictator or terrorist."

"Maybe she's an asshole."

His lips curl. "You kill people just for being assholes?"

I shrug, take a big bite of my sandwich and speak around the words, "Maybe she's a really big asshole."

He doesn't laugh. "You don't have to take care of me."

He's wrong. I do, so I look away. "Who said I was doing this for you?"

"Show me."

"Show you what?"

"Her picture."

"No."

"Why not?"

I finish my sandwich.

Finally, when I can't really come up with any good reason not to, I go get the laptop. This is surreal, really. Showing pictures of a woman I will kill to my brother over sandwiches like it's no big thing.

He stares at her picture for a while. "She's pretty."

"What difference does that make?"

"None. Can I talk you out of this?"

On screen, the woman stares back at me, that almost-lazy smile, the honey-gold hair.

James rests his elbows on his knees, leans in close. "Just... find out why they want her dead. What she did, if she did anything at all. Just one thing that makes her worth killing."

I tug on my lower lip. "I don't care what she did. I don't want to know some woman I'll have t—"

"What do you do? Spend a week on recon, getting to know the target? Seems like it wouldn't be a big deal to spend a day trying to figure out why you're doing it in the first place."

I could tell him to fuck off, ignore him. We were close once, but that was a long time ago. We barely talk anymore. It would be the end. A clean end to this pretense of family. Then, on the day he first walks on his prostheses, I could just leave the money here, the deed to the house in his name, take off, sever the final cord in this world that connects me to anyone, to anything, disappear like a ghost in the wind.

Instead, for some unknown reason, I find my lips forming the shape, and my throat making the sounds. "Fine."

I pick up my computer and disappear into my bedroom, hole up, stalk her some more.

The writing is the way in. Best way, unless I want to pose as a salesman for flowery junk.

She mentioned a writer's website in the foreword of her latest book. WritersWrite.com. That's the key.

So I sign up myself, and I become its newest member. Stranger Lowe.

I dig out my latest scribbles.

Not half bad, actually. That's a relief. I haven't looked at my work in a couple years, so I see it fresh, almost get caught up in the reading of it.

It's important that it's good, so I rework it several times. A woman like her is unlikely to be interested in chatting with a man whose professional work she can't respect.

If I'm going to pretend to be a writer to flirt with a pretty girl so she'll tell me all her secrets, I'd better be a damned good one.

And I need to think up a good opening line. One a writer can't resist responding to.

Simple, I decide. And complimentary.
Writers love compliments.

2 – A Stranger Named Stranger

MIA

> Mia: Check it out! Just passed 1K sales!

> Annie: Ahhhhh… Nice work my smug friend. Got my copy. I'll leave a review in a few.

> Mia: What! I'm not smug.

> Annie: You are the smuggest of the smug, but I love you anyway.

That makes me laugh as I text her back. Annie's my closest friend, and my fiancé's sister.

> Mia: Okay, fine. I'll admit it. Maybe I am just the tiniest bit smug.

I can't help it, though. I'm just so happy.

> Annie: You deserve it, friend. Enjoy the smug while it lasts. Kisses and hugs. Congrats on the release. Let's pop bubbly with the guys soon.

> Mia: Done! Give those babies some kisses for me! Hugs!

I set my phone down and push around the clutter on my desk to give it at least the appearance of order. The diamond on my engagement ring flickers and I smile. Sigh.

Yeah, I know. I almost annoy myself.

But not quite.

It's release day of my seventh book. By all reasonable projections, by day's end I'll be able to pay off my initial investment. That's huge. I'm making money!

I have the first act of my current work in progress to upload to WritersWrite.com. I'm engaged to my best friend's brother, Jeremy Dixon. I love his family. And he's the perfect man—even if he works so much, we almost never see each other. Actually, that's perfect too, because it means I spend most of my time writing. A solid two-karat solitaire sits on my ring finger, gleaming away—I'm still not used to it!—my parents are incredible, and my best friend had twin babies two weeks ago. They'll call me Aunt Mia.

I'm this close to being successful.

In a few months, I'll walk down the aisle for the perfect winter-white, pine-tree-studded, glittery and perfect wedding, and become Mrs. Dixon.

This is the life I've always worked toward.

So, yeah. Maybe I am a little smug. I do try to hide it though.

No one likes a smugface.

I sip my coffee from my favorite monkey-shaped mug—complete with a big green palm frond and a silly yellow banana. Annie got it for me on her honeymoon. It always makes me laugh. I scroll through the writers' forum. There's a fight about adverbs, a discussion about the role of gender in media, a cat thread, another about fantasy wizards, one about cursing, one about how only snobs use semi-colons.

At the top of the screen is a red circle with a number 1 inside. I click on it and find a new message from a writer named Stranger Lowe.

I've never heard of him which means he must be new.

> **Stranger: I read Wrecked. It's good.**

Wrecked is my current work in progress.

It's about shifters and love and sex. Okay, it's mostly about sex.

I lean back in my chair and tuck my feet under me, tap my nails on the desk's pink surface.

Sometimes guys hit me up because they think the fact that I write about sex is an invitation. I could just ignore him. I usually do, but it's a nice compliment, simple, open, non-creepy.

I click on his profile page. Not much to see. Hard jaw. Good nose. He's standing in front of a mountain somewhere, wearing a baseball cap, sunglasses and a thick fleece, rolled up to his elbows, revealing brightly colored tattoos, fit arms. I won't lie, he's pretty attractive, not like the type who needs to harass women online.

And he just read a book with vivid, graphic sexual content, written by me.

Not sure how to feel about that.

He's got only one chapter posted. I start to skim and get caught up reading it.

The opening scene is of an assassin preparing to kill a corrupt politician in Africa. Stalking his prey, learning his habits, covering his tracks. Something about the narrator scares me though. He seems dark, cold, inaccessible. I can't help but wonder at the person who can create that character. Even though I don't love horror or mystery, I can tell it's good writing.

And... he likes my work.

So now I'm extra smug!

And I can't not respond, so I type back:

> Mia: Really? Yay! That's so nice of you. Thank you!

He responds almost instantly:

> Stranger: I'm never nice. Just telling the truth. Where's the rest?

> Mia: Of Wrecked? So far, I only have the first half posted.

> Stranger: I know. Do you have more?

Is he serious? Why would he want to read romance? Few men do.

> Mia: Definitely. Sure. Yeah. Give me ten, and I'll post a few more chapters. It's a little weird though. Kinda kinky. Just warning you. Seriously, don't judge me! I swear I'm not a sex freak.

I get busy uploading my new work, and when I'm done, that red circle is there at the top of my screen.

> Stranger: Hmm… Do people call you a sex freak often?

> Mia: No! It's just… sometimes people get the wrong idea. They think I'm like my characters or something. And I'm not!

> Stranger: Nothing wrong with sex. What kind of kinky are we talking about?

> Mia: I mean, I write dark romance, so… you know.

> Stranger: I do not know.

> Mia: Have you ever read a dark romance?

> Stranger: I've never read any romance at all.

> Mia: It's a little twisted.

> Stranger: How so? Be specific.

I catch my lower lip between my teeth, and tell myself to be honest, not to be ashamed of what I write. It's hard though. Only five people on earth know what I really do. My two closest friends, Annie and Erica, and their husbands. Plus Jeremy. Well, and a whole slew of internet people on WritersWrite.com. But my whole family, and all my other friends think I work in accounting.

Seriously.

I lie to them all the time. Jer helps me lie because he thinks my romances are embarrassing too. But right now, online, I don't have to hide.

> Mia: Ummm… Some pretty aggressive dub-con, rare but occasional anal play, random spankings, a few buckets of cum. You know… the usual.

There's a pause. A long one. Long enough to make my cheeks get so hot all my smug just melts away like a snow cone in the summer sun and slides straight on down to the floor in a great big slushy puddle of shame.

I go get water from the fridge, replaying the words, hoping he'll know I was kidding—sort of. Ugh. Why can't I write something nice? I hate talking about my work with non-romance writers. I wish I could have have gone for cozy mystery or fantasy or something normal. Not dark erotic shifters who have constant intense angry sex. But this is me. It's what I love.

Everyone just thinks it's porn. And they're not even entirely wrong. Now I hate that he read it.

As I pass the dining table, headed back toward my desk, I bump into a chair which hits the table, shaking the candles in the candle-holder so hard a candle falls off, rolls into a pile of things I keep meaning to go through. The heart-shaped photo frame I made in grade school crashes to the carpet with a dull thud, and the splits in two right down the center.

Great.

I pick it up the broken heart and hold the two pieces together. A little glue should fix it? Maybe?

When I sit down, there's that red circle winking at me at the top of my screen again.

> Stranger: Buckets of cum? That's "the usual."
>
> Mia: Yes. Buckets. And I refuse to be embarrassed. (butIstilltotallyam)
>
> Stranger: Lol. Don't be embarrassed. Sounds good.

Is he saying "sounds good" the way I say it when someone sends me a new chapter to critique? Just all normal. *Sounds good.* Or does he mean it like he likes the sound of cum buckets?

I click on his picture again. Green mountains, white misty sky. Northwest? Appalachia? South America? *Take off those glasses, Stranger Lowe. What color are your eyes?*

The red circle is back.

> Stranger: Do you mean buckets literally? Like a pail? A whole pail full?

> Mia: No! Of course not. Gross.

> Stranger: It's a thing. A porn thing. It would be okay if you did. What are cum buckets then?

> Mia: Ohmygod. It's just... it's just a term I use because there's a lot of it. It's a trope of the genre. The guys are extra (ohmygodthisconversationisawful)...productive.

> Stranger: So this is what you meant when you said your characters like stuff but you don't.

> Mia: Exactly!

> Stranger: Yeah. Okay.

I close the screen but something about the exchange keeps pulling at me. I keep opening the message's window and staring at the black sans-serif typeface.

> Mia: It's just part of the genre. It's what's expected. Like how you write about killing

> people and stuff. You don't actually kill people, I'm assuming.

I hit enter. And instantly regret it. That sounded so defensive, so rude.

I should apologize. That would make me look weirder, though.

I force my hands to get to work, my fingers to type, but the scene I build is weak. My heart's not in it.

I sigh. Open the website to apologize. There's that red circle. Click.

> Stranger: Tons. My body count is deep.

> Mia: Ha. I might almost believe it the way you write.

> Stranger: It's not the same thing. Writing sex and writing killing are different. Killing people is inherently wrong. A person like that...there'd have to be something wrong with them. There's nothing inherently wrong about you being into weird sex shit.

Weird sex shit makes me picture handcuffs and whips, chains and hot wax, spankings and ball-gags, people putting food in their vaginas. None of that stuff even remotely turns me on.

Well, maybe spanking. A little, but I'm not going to tell him that. My last male lead spanked the female lead, but that wasn't formalized or anything. He just did it, and she liked it.

I liked writing it so much I asked Jeremy to spank me the night after I wrote it, and he swatted at me awkwardly.

It made us both uncomfortable.

I toy with my ring. I never know when to share personal information online. It makes me uncomfortable for myself. Privacy on the internet is an issue, as is trust, so I don't want to pry or push or overshare. And he's a man and we're talking about sex... But still, he seems so blasé, so non-threatening.

> Mia: But I'm not! I don't want to be whipped or tied up. Or treated like a pet. And I definitely don't want to be strung up in a sex swing or pooped on. Ever!

> Stranger: Poop? Who said you did?

I did.

I said poop.

I bury my face in my hands. What am I doing? Am I flirting with him? If so, I'm terrible at it. I shouldn't be flirting with anyone.

> Mia: You said I was into weird sex shit! Aaaaaand... it was ME. I said poop. Head-desk.

> Stranger: I didn't say you were into weird sex shit. Reread our convo. Aaaaand I said shit before you said poop. Relax.

> Mia: Oh. That's true. I guess it's just awkward. People always think I'm a pervert.
>
> Stranger: Who thinks you're a pervert?
>
> Mia: You should see my mom's face whenever romance novels come up.
>
> Stranger: I mean… did you tell her about the buckets of cum?
>
> Mia: Ha! No. She doesn't even know I write. Let alone romance. She thinks romance novels are for the recklessly stupid and the dangerously perverted. Anyway, the next act of Wrecked is up if you're interested. But no pressure. And go away now. You're distracting me, and I need to write.

I wait, but he doesn't respond. Nothing. Because he's letting me focus? Or because I offended him by telling him to go away? Ugh! I shouldn't care. I don't care. He's a stranger named Stranger, and I'm engaged to the perfect man.

I shake my head, close the browser, open my document, finish my crappy scene, which will need to be gutted and reworked later, and go to meet with some lawyers to make the man I love sign a pre-nup he really doesn't want to sign.

I can't help myself though, I keep looking at the top of my screen, dreading and hoping for that blinking red circle to appear, and amassing a mental list of questions about this stranger that keep on growing.

3 – DAY GLOW PANTIES

STRANGER

She lives in a brick townhome in a trendy neighborhood in downtown Providence. The lighting fixture above the front door was clearly designed for the light bulb to be easy to change. No problem to reach up with one gloved hand and twist it until lights out.

And I am shrouded in darkness. No one can see as I feeler pick inside the lock.

A second later, it snicks, and I slide open the door.

I freeze, listening. The fridge hums, the air conditioner whirs. But otherwise, silence reigns throughout the house.

The air moves with something sweet. Peaches.

No doorbell camera. No security alarm. The lock's a joke.

I shake my head, standing in the darkness, invisible to passersby, as I tuck my lock kit into my ass pocket and take my first step inside.

A staircase sits on the right, a living area on the left, with a kitchen at the back. A rear exit that leads to the private courtyard I scoped out earlier.

She left a light on for me.

Handy.

Thanks, Mia.

It illuminates the space well.

And what I see... gives me pause. I think I'd expected normal, traditional, based on her photographs, what I know about her, the soft, slightly-awkward banter we exchanged earlier. Safe beige or gray, navy maybe. Classy.

I should have known because of the crazy shit on her registry, but still, it's so at odds with the personality she's revealed to me so far.

This is... loud.

The rug is pink. Not the pale pink you see on baby commercials or wedding magazines, but bright stripper pink. The sofa and chairs are piled in those dumb pillows women like, a rainbow cacophony.

The walls are stacked with bright paintings, the tables and shelves are stuffed with books and what my friend Lex calls tchotchkes. A zebra sculpture, a Chinese waving gold cat, picture frames, vases, bowls, clocks... crap fills every space.

So much crap.

It's the exact opposite of the farm house, with its empty shelves, and scant furniture. It's not messy or dirty, or overbearing like those hoarders you see on TV, but it's definitely packed.

I prowl to her purse, tossed lazily across a dining table I can tell she doesn't use to eat. She uses it to store more of her crap.

I've never been in a space like this. It's like she's got something from every single place she's ever been, a tether binding her to this place, this time in her life, weighing her down.

What does she do with all this shit?

I paw through her purse, but there is nothing too interesting inside. I take pictures of all her credit cards, ID, a check. The routing number might come in handy later.

A bulky red ceramic picture frame, the kind kids make in kindergarten, sits on the table next to her purse. Two half hearts. I push the pieces together idly with a gloved-finger, building a picture of this nervous, bubbly, Mia Whitten woman in my mind. Writer, collector... what else? Why take out a hit on this happy fluttery woman?

I move closer to the shelves. There are so many photos it makes my head spin. Smiling people. Laughing people. Old people. Young people. Babies. Happy people. At the beach. In the mountains. In front of the Eiffel Tower, the Taj Mahal, the giant Buddha in Hong Kong, on safari.

Mia is in most of them, that same warm, open smile. As if she's never been hurt. Not once in her whole entire life.

So much stuff. So many people.

She's the anti-Stranger.

I seek privacy, she seeks people.

I seek emptiness, she seeks crap to fill it.

Her computer sits in the center of a loud pink desk. The chair looks suspect at best, flimsy with legs like twigs and elaborate carvings in an aggressive blue. I don't want to risk it snapping under me, so I just lean over it. There's no password.

Ah, Mia.

Her search history is hilarious, though unsurprising given what she writes, and I take a moment to amuse myself skimming through her latest searches.

Description of a vagina?

What's so great about anal sex?

Are blue balls real?

The last one makes me laugh silently.

It takes a few minutes to download the software that will allow me to screen share without her knowing.

There's nothing else to find on her computer.

Nor on this floor.

So, I make my way silently upstairs, placing my feet on the outer edges of the steps to avoid creaks.

There's a hall bathroom, two bedrooms. I shine a penlight inside. They are also filled with color, packed with paintings, and more books and sculptures and trinkets—this woman's got more shit than anyone I've ever seen. I pity the sad fool who has to help her move at some point.

At the end of the hall is an open door that can only lead to her room.

There's no light in here and I can't risk waking her with the torch on my phone, so I wait for my eyes to adjust, breathing in the honey-and-peach smell.

Scant light spills in from the street lamps outside, soft and rosy through sheer drapes.

She's breathing, soft, steady, even. I listen for a moment to make sure she hasn't sensed my presence.

This room is no different from the rest, full of hothouse colors so bright even the darkness can't dilute them beyond recognition. Pink and green wallpaper, pink carpet, a floral bedspread. And the lamps on her bedside tables are—I'm not kidding—gigantic parrots in green, orange and turquoise.

What is with this woman and color?

I creep away from the warm body on the bed and down the short hall to her bathroom. Some evidence of a man in her life is at the second sink, an extra toothbrush and a razor, men's deodorant. But mostly, this is as much a woman's world as the rest of her home.

The walk-in closet is a surprise. Based on the rest of the place, I expected it to be full of hippy shit, flowered scarves, annoying belts, loud necklaces, bold shoes, a jewel-box of colors, but it's the opposite. Mostly white, beige and black, a bit of navy blue. Simple solid colors. The air is thicker with her smell in here, her clothes saturated with it. Not just the sweetness of peaches and honey. More. A deeper smell. The smell of a woman.

A slim drawer holds jewelry, mostly simple gold. A larger drawer houses a kaleidoscope of lacy panties and bras. I pick up a thong—naturally day glow orange between my thumb and forefinger, let it drop back into the drawer.

I'm building a bizarre impression of a woman who shows herself to the world as prim and classy, but inside revels in the bold and the bright. Her place is vibrant just shy of garish, like her underpants. She's flashy, but only when no one can see. Like the stories she writes in secret.

I leave the closet and cross to her bed, moving slowly so as not to disturb the air around her.

She's on her back, an arm tossed over her head, the covers loose around her waist, her hair curling across the pillows, lips slightly parted.

Her phone sits on the table beside her, next to one of the bizarre parrot lamps, on a stack of paperback books. Again, no password.

Making my job so easy, Mia. Even a baby would cry if you stole its candy. She doesn't even offer up that much defense.

It takes me two minutes to activate an app that will allow me to track her movements, and a second that will give me access to all her activity.

I can go now. I've done what I came to do, but instead I find myself standing there, staring at her.

My eyes have adjusted to the dark. I can't see her perfectly, but enough to get a feel for her.

A narrow nose with a slight arch to it, soft brows, pretty lips. The blanket is pulled up to her ribcage. The soft curves of her breasts are visible in the dim light, the shadows of her clavicle, her slender throat, fine jaw. An elegant face.

She makes a noise, a soft hum in her throat and rolls onto her side. But she doesn't open her eyes, and I feel a moment of regret.

She'd have screamed if she had. She'd have known she wasn't safe. She might have been prepared. Not enough, but maybe enough to make it at least a challenge.

Tomorrow, I'll know all her secrets.

SEX ON THE BRAIN

MIA

For two days, I check in religiously on WritersWrite, but there's nothing from Stranger. I try to tell myself I don't care, that I wasn't looking forward to hearing from him, but it's a lie. Maybe I offended him.

On the other hand, my sales are going great. Just passed fifteen hundred. I'm in heaven, and I want to celebrate with someone.

I need someone to share this with. So I text Annie.

> Mia: Can I bring over some Chinese and hang out?

> Annie: YES! I've got bubbly, but only if you swear to watch the babies so I can nap in the shower for an hour.

> Mia: Uhhh… NAP in the shower? Whatever you need, crazypants. I'm yours for the night.
>
> Annie: It's warm in there and no one bugs me. Greg will probably do the same.
>
> Mia: Lol. Fine by me. Can't wait to see you all! Be there in an hour.

Annie and Greg bought her parent's house a couple years ago when they decided to retire to Florida. It's thirty minutes out into the country, with few neighbors, rolling green hills, and a massive, winding up-hill drive that Greg hates whenever it snows, but loves whenever they have big parties because it's so impressive and there's so much parking.

The house is an estate. Tons of land, empty acreage, a big pond, and a massive three-story home built about two centuries ago.

I love coming out here. It feels like the start of some wonderful and mysterious story to me. I can so easily picture I'm the narrator of *Rebecca* coming to Manderley for the first time, or going to meet some mysterious recluse, or a weekend party complete with a whodunnit.

But when I arrive, it's just the pair of them. Greg's wearing a wrinkled shirt that's way too small for his bulky muscled form, and a pair of plaid flannel pants. He's a good-looking guy—in a sort of testosterone-fueled, jock, meathead kind of way. Normally. Right now, he looks haggard. And so does Annie, in a stained nightgown, with greasy hair, and I'm not sure, but I think the sour, garbagy smell might be coming from one or both of them.

They look happy though, with matching loopy grins.

"You came!" they say at the same time, looking way too happy about my arrival, as if I'm an exotic and exciting dignitary come to visit.

"You should get out more," I say, wrinkling my nose at them.

"Seriously. But how?" Annie grabs me and hugs me—the smell is her—and drags me into the living room. "Here you go. You sure about this? They're both up."

Hart and Hadley, the babies, are lying on their backs on little pink and blue blankets, side by side on the oriental carpet, kicking their feet. It's not the first time I've seen them, but as always, I'm amazed by just how insanely tiny they are.

I set the bag of food on the coffee table and sit down on the floor next to my godchildren. "I don't know what you're complaining about. They're angels." I gesture at them. "Tiny little angel babies."

Annie blinks a few times. "They are now. In the middle of the night sometimes..." Her voice does a little waiver. "I want to tear my hair out. But for the moment, you're right, they're perfect."

Greg rubs her back, glancing at me a little hesitantly. "She's emotional. I think it's the lack of sleep."

Annie elbows him in his gut. "I'm right here, Greg. Don't talk about me like that."

He makes a *what-did-I-do* face.

"Oh! I almost forgot!" Her brows snap together as she turns back to me. "Did you hear about Amy Jekinsky?"

"Who?"

"That girl in college who didn't like you?"

I frown. "Everyone likes me."

"Not her. She hated you. Come on. You remember. The one with bad breath? "

I shake my head. Honestly, everyone likes me.

"Funky Amy. From that class on 20th century lit."

Oh! "Onions?"

"Yes."

"Her. Yes. Okay, okay." I do remember. She was a few doors down from me freshman year. "What about her?"

The corner of Annie's mouth tucks in like it does when she's sad. "Her husband died of brain cancer. She took over his business or something. He was thirty-seven."

Thirty-seven. I sigh. "That's so young."

Greg shoves out his lower lip. "She's got a net worth approaching a bill. So... you know. I'll save my tears."

"Greg!" Annie's jaw drops.

"It's true." He makes a placid face. "Talk to someone with a sick kid. They'll tell you how bad they feel for the woman who married a filthy-rich guy who died pushing forty."

I can't even begin to figure out how to respond to that, so I say, "Go sleep in the shower or whatever it is you want to do. I'll be good for an hour."

They hesitate, staring at me all shifty-eyed, like they've been caught stealing.

"At the same time?" Greg asks.

Annie just blinks some more.

"Yes, at the same time. Go!"

"Come get me if they start screaming." Annie's already tugging her lank, brown hair out of its messy bun. It's the same exact shade of auburn brown as Jer's when it's clean, and with that look on her face, all furtive and doubtful, she looks just like him.

"I'll be ten minutes," says Greg. "Seriously. Just ten."

"Get out of here. Take as long as you want. I'll be fine."

They take one look at each other and bolt up the stairs.

The babies don't move.

"You guys aren't so bad." I lie down in front of the old stone fireplace next to the babies and wonder if this is my future. Crazed to the point of tears for a few minutes of peace in a dark shower.

They're pretty cute with their tiny, wrinkly faces, their itty-bitty fingers, their sweet baby smell. Annie generally acts like all they do is scream and poop, but at least for now, they're just waving their arms in the air, sticking out their tongues and punching ghosts only they can see.

I make faces at them for a few minutes, dangle my keys, sing badly for them. They don't seem to care.

So I shrug, let Hart wrap his tiny fingers around my pointer finger and check my phone.

Nothing.

I shake my finger free from his impressively strong grip and make myself busy for a few minutes, tidying up the kitchen.

Hadley fusses. So I change her doll-sized diaper, moving carefully because even though Annie keeps saying they're stronger than they look, they look as fragile as cotton candy. When she's changed, I set her in a bouncy swing with a mobile of sleepy lambs and ducks hanging over it. I change Hart too and set him in a second bouncer by his sister's side.

They're like a pair of living dolls. For a second, I can feel it, what Annie must feel all day, every day... the oppressive responsibility of having two tiny humans to raise.

Greg comes down, looking much more like himself, dressed in jeans and a tee, his blondish hair combed. He's a few years old than Annie and me. She met him when she was working as a journalist. She interviewed him for a column she wrote on some senator Greg's firm represented.

"Annie says we've got something to celebrate. Champagne?"

"Always."

He comes back a few minutes later and hands me a glass full of golden bubbly happiness. "Thanks for watching the babies and for cleaning up. That was nice. How are sales?"

"So good!" I beam. "It feels like it's working. Finally, after all this time."

"That's good. Real good." He settles into a wingback chair near the babies. "How's the stalker?"

I roll my eyes. "Nonexistent."

"Annie says tha—"

"I know what Annie says. It's not a stalker. Just some idiot who sometimes writes stuff on my social media accounts. It's harmless. I delete the comments and move on. It happens to everyone."

Hart lets out a chirp, and Greg lifts him gently to his shoulder. The baby looks about the size of a gerbil in his hands. "What do you consider harmless?"

I tap my leg and refuse to tell him just how graphic some of the comments have been. "It's the internet. I mean... have you seen what people say on YouTube? It's just anonymous jerks. Doesn't mean anything."

"Yeah... but..." He tilts his head to the side the way people do before they say something I'm not going to like. "You've got a pretty face."

I have to close my eyes and suck in a long cooling breath. This is why I don't want Jer to know. Every argument anyone makes just makes me mad.

"And what? What has that got to do with anything? If I had an ugly face it would be okay?"

He pats Hart's back in a steady beat. "That's not what I meant. I just mean... people online are crazy. They see a pretty girl who writes the kind of stuff you write, they get ideas. Not saying they're right to get them. Just saying, be careful."

"I am careful." Sort of.

"Have you told Jer yet?"

"Why? So he can worry?"

The shower upstairs turns off. Annie will be back soon.

"It just seems like something I'd want to know." He chews on his lip. "If Annie were writing the kind of stuff you write, using her face on her website, and had people making sexual comments, I'd want to know."

That makes me think too closely about my new Stranger, so I ignore it.

Hadley fusses in the bouncer, so I bend down and lift her. Her tiny head rests on the dip where my collar bone meets my neck, her silky hair tickling my skin like the feathers of a baby duck. "So he can do what? Protect me? I don't need protection."

"You sure about that? What if one of these people is able to find you? Reverse track your photo or something, figure who you are, where you live. You don't even have an alarm on your house. You don't have a gun or know self-defense."

"Neither does Jer," I point out irritably, and we sit in silence until Annie comes back.

When she does, she looks happier than I've seen in a while. She babbles about my sales, full of questions, and I'm happy to let the stalker conversation go. Greg casts me an uneasy glance, but lets it drop.

An hour later, after too much moo shu, I head home.

I try Jer, but he doesn't answer, probably still mad about the prenup.

I sit down at my desk, and check in on the website, unable to stop a smile from spreading across my face when I see I have three critiques from Stranger Lowe and a message—also from Stranger Lowe.

> Stranger: Hello Mia Reed,
>
> I read more of Wrecked. The pacing is solid. I like the female lead. She's cute. The guy's a little soft. If he's such a badass, why does he bother spending an hour explaining to her why he kidnaps her? I think he'd just do it.
>
> Also, the use of the word fisting threw me. I know what you mean. He's jerking off, but it made me think of real fisting, you know?
>
> I sliced some dialogue. You tend to be long-winded there.
>
> And I think he'd be looking at her eyes while he jerks it. He wants her to feel that penetration. Know she belongs to him.
>
> And, I'd probably want to cum all over her face, not just her tits, and… maybe… push it into her mouth with my cock, feed it to her, make her lick it, watch. She could be on her knees. The angle works better that way.
>
> I'll finish the rest tomorrow.

My hands come up to cover my mouth. This weird little whimper comes out of the back of my throat. Like a breathy yelp.

I was not expecting that.

I lower my hands now and blow out a long breath.

It's still hot outside, muggy high summer heat that lingers. It's not even 8pm. and the sun is only beginning its descent, but my skin raises in goosebumps.

People have made comments on my work before about sex stuff, but I rarely get male critiquers and when I do, I think they feel weird reading sex scenes. Usually they stay quiet.

Not Stranger. He just laid it all out there. So bold. So raunchy. So inventive.

Now it's there, he's in my head, the scene he described.

I have this image of a man, a dark, faceless Stranger, nothing but that hard jaw, that Roman nose, and those vibrant colorful tattoo-covered forearms rippling with every jerk and flex. And it's not just any face getting covered. It's my face. I can practically feel it, hot and sticky. It's like it's burned into my retinas. I press my hand to my lower belly where everything is hot and tight and so empty.

I'm suddenly luridly curious about his body. How he smells. The sound of his voice. The shape of his thumbs.

I sit down in front of my keyboard.

> **Mia:** Oh. Wow. Ummm... That's good stuff. Thank you! Can't wait to read your crits. I'll try to hit you back this evening.

I reread the message, jiggling my leg, distracted by my own throbbing body. I've never fantasized about a real man though. Not even Jeremy. But now I am, oh man, I am. A little simmer of guilt niggles at the back of my mind. This is going no place good.

I reread the words again.

I'd feed it to her. Tell her to lick it. Watch.

I make that noise again, that pathetic breathy moan. Thank god I read it now while I'm alone, not in front of Greg and Annie. I'd never be able to explain that moan.

I need wine.

I can't help myself. I check my phone. He's responded already.

I make myself wait until I have a big glass of icy Sauvignon Blanc in my hand, push aside my throw pillows and make a nest in the sofa. Then I pull up the site on my phone, click that red circle I'm learning to love and hate at the same time.

> Stranger: Anytime. I don't venture into sex writing often. It was a fun couple hours.

Is there innuendo there? I narrow my eyes. It's so hard to tell.

> Mia: It's definitely fun to write.

Oh, no. Wait! I wish I could take that back. That sounds like I spend all my time writing sex and masturbating.

I take a big sip.

> Stranger: Writing is best when it's fun. I finished editing another couple chapters today. Feels good.

> Mia: Did you post them?

> Stranger: Yeah.

> Mia: Fun! Can't wait to read. What's it about?

> Stranger: The guy leaves Africa. You'll like it.

> Mia: What happens next?

> Stranger: He ends up getting hired to work for a senator. Doing security. But the senator's depraved.

> Mia: Depraved how?

> Stranger: Weird sex shit. You inspired me.

> Mia: Lol. Like what? Bondage?

> Stranger: Maybe. The narrator ends up falling for a girl with a thing for getting choked in bed. And then she gets strangled, and everyone thinks he did it.

> Mia: But it was really the senator, right?

> Stranger: No. But it could have been.

I pull my feet under me, kicking my sandals to the floor. They bounce off the carpet under the sofa. Jeremy would sigh if he were here. He hates when I leave stuff lying around.

I take a long sip. What am I supposed to say to Stranger? Does he like choking people in bed? I imagine big hands closing around my neck, tightening until I can't breathe.

Has he thought about doing that to me?

This Stranger, is he dangerous? Am I stupid not to be afraid?

I glance at my photo at the top of the screen. I hadn't thought about it this way before, wondered what a man looking at it might think. What does he see?

It's me by the water in Watch Hill at my grandparents' beach house. My hair's out behind me, blowing against the gray sky. I look pretty enough. My neck looks long. It's a good picture of me but I'm not anything special. There's no real clue about my body, though I guess he can see I'm not overweight.

I enlarge his picture on my phone's screen. There's some stubble along his jaw. Maybe a hint of a dimple.

I like dimples. I like them a lot.

And apparently, I like tattoos. I never knew that about myself.

I go back to my own picture, enlarge my face. Has he done that? Stared at my photo, big thumbs moving over the screen, spreading the pixels apart. What would he think when he saw it? Does he like how I look? My eyes are the same honey color as my hair. Maybe I should change it to a picture where I look prettier? No, I'd look desperate then.

I should be focused on planning my wedding. Not wondering what a total stranger thinks about my photograph.

I'm pathetic.

I text Jeremy.

> Mia: Hello, fiancé mine. Are you ignoring me? I saw Annie and Greg tonight. They seem stressed. What time are we having dinner tomorrow?

No answer.

I jiggle my knee, sip my wine, text my second closest friend, Erica. No answer.

Turn on the TV.

Nothing's interesting.

I chew my lip, tell myself not to check for the red circle, but do anyway. There isn't one.

I give in.

> Mia: So, who did it?

> Stranger: You'll have to read it to find out.

> Mia: Ha.

> Stranger: What are you doing right now?

> Mia: Nothing, you?

> Stranger: Not nothing. I'm outside. I live in the middle of nowhere. The trees are just about to change. It will be full dark in twenty minutes, but I'll be home in ten.

> Mia: What are you doing out there?

> Stranger: Coming back from a hike with my dog.

> Mia: Texting and hiking. Don't trip.

> Stranger: I never trip.

> Mia: What kind of dog?

Stranger: Gogo. Answer me. Exactly what are you doing?

Mia: Gogo? Is she a Pomeranian? Sigh. I'm having a glass of wine. Talking to you.

Stranger: A hound dog. Where? Be specific. I want to picture you.

Mia: My house. Sitting on my sofa. I'm wearing a blue sundress. Hound dogs are pretty.

Stranger: She's beautiful. What position? Leaning against an arm? Feet on the coffee table? Shoes? What color is the couch?

Mia: No shoes. Feet ON the TABLE? Never. Alright, you want details? Sofa is tufted white velvet with magenta and kelly-green accent pillows my mom needlepointed for me. I've got my feet tucked under me. Fuzzy throw blanket.

Stranger: Magenta? Kelly-green? Are these friends of yours? What is needlepoint?

Mia: The hottest of pinks. The brightest of greens. Needlepoint... is kinda like embroidery but in a grid.

Stranger: Music? TV?

> Mia: No music. No TV. Just you.

> Stranger: I like it. Sounds… cozy. PM me in an hour. I'll pour myself a beer. We'll have a drink together, I'll flirt with you in a confusing way, and you can pretend you don't like it and that it isn't weird to be talking to a guy you've never met about buckets of cum. It'll be fun.

> Mia: Are you always this bossy?

> Stranger: I just want to know what makes you tick, Mia Reed. I bet you're smiling.

> I am.

> Mia: How did you know?

> Stranger: One hour, smiley Mia.

I toss my phone to the side. I could write. But I'm tired. I check my sales. Another three hundred. I might pass two thousand.

Amazing.

Jer still hasn't responded. We've barely spoken since the pre-nup.

He didn't want to sign it, but it's part of the deal. My parents are insisting. My trust is protected so Jer can't get the money, not even if I cheat or divorce him, but my parents want it locked down anyway.

They adore him, but they adore me more. If I'm alive, the money is mine.

Jer spent the entire time biting his thumb and worrying. I think he sees it as a recognition that we might get a divorce, but that's not it. Far from it.

I change into a pair of comfy lounge pants and a tank top, cuddle into my sofa, put on HGTV, but all the while, I'm trying not to think about a Stranger.

I skim through his work. I know better than anyone that the type of work we produce as writers bears little reflection on who we are.

But his work is dark, heavy, heartless in a way I've never come across. And the details in the murder scene. Whatever Stranger Lowe's life has been like, he knows how to murder someone.

He scares me. I won't lie.

I reread our conversation a few times. He's funny, but there's an edge to the humor, an angle almost, like he wants something.

I can practically hear my mother hissing a warning in my ear. *Don't talk to internet strangers. He could be anyone, Mia. ANYONE. And the tattoos!*

I edit the scene I wrote earlier, which isn't as bad as I thought, and watch the clock slide past 9. Then past 10. I keep checking my phone.

Finally, when I can't stand it anymore, at 10:15, I message him.

> Mia: I finished my glass.

> Stranger: Nice.

> Mia: And now I'm waiting.

> Stranger: For?

Mia: You. You set me up to wait for you.

Stranger: I did not. The ball was in your court.

Mia: It was deliberate. You were daring me.

Stranger: Got me.

Mia: Why? What do you want with me?

Stranger: A guy can't chat with a pretty writer?

Mia: He can. But you're not just a guy.

Stranger: What am I then?

Mia: I have no idea.

Stranger: You think a lot, huh?

Mia: Don't you?

Stranger: I try not to overthink. I've got my beer. Slide over on the couch, Mia Reed. Tell your secrets to me.

> Mia: There's plenty of room. My couch is long. I don't know you, so keep to your side. What kind of beer?
>
> Stranger: Heineken. I'm a big guy. Long arms. I could sit close enough to put my arm along the back. Spread my knees out, bump them against your thigh maybe.
>
> Mia: I'd give you some side-eye if you did that.
>
> Stranger: Nah, fifteen minutes, you'd be facing me on the couch, knees up, scooting just a little closer. I can see it perfectly. That perky smile.
>
> Mia: Perky? Your narrator makes me sad.
>
> Stranger: Why?
>
> Mia: He's not very nice.
>
> Stranger: That's true.
>
> Mia: He's cold. Empty. Dead inside.

There's a pause. So long I start to think I've offended him. Some writers are prickly about their work. I didn't think he would be. But then after three minutes, he responds. Maybe he was just doing something.

Stranger: You don't like being called perky? How about prissy?

Mia: I don't think I'm prissy. I have no cats and I don't wear heels on the treadmill.

Stranger: Haha. But… I bet your wallet isn't black or brown.

Mia: It's the color of watermelon guts.

Stranger: Case and point. He's not all bad. He has to go dark places for his work. That's all. Plus of course, the choking.

Mia: Yeah… I can't get into choking. All that BDSM stuff. I don't know.

Stranger: Not like the buckets. Prim?

Mia: I'm not into buckets either. I'm maybe a little prim.

Stranger: Okay. Prim, Mia. Fifteen minutes in, you'd be facing me. Ten minutes more and I'd play with your hair.

Mia: You work fast.

> Stranger: You say you don't like them, but you write cum buckets anyway. Why not BDSM? What's different?
>
> Mia: I'm honestly stumped. I don't know. But I do know this, I think if we met, you'd scare me, Stranger Lowe.
>
> Stranger: Maybe you kinda want to be scared.

We chat for a long time, about writing, about random stuff. How he used to think writing was for losers, and I always loved it. How he barely graduated high school, joined the military, and I have my masters in Economics. How he started writing as a lark, a hobby and somehow just kept at it. How I started out in my twenties. How he's never let anyone read his work before. How he can't stand being around people. How I crave them. How he spends all day hiking in the mountains and writes at night. How I write during the day.

He asks if I'm a nervous sort of person. I never noticed before, but yes, I am. I worry and wonder and doubt every single thing I do. I tell him anything that occurs to me. Somehow, he beat away my filter, through a combination of open acceptance and humor.

The one thing I don't mention is Jeremy. I don't know why that is, but this time with Stranger feels like a dream, like an interlude, like a game, like make-believe, like I am the lead character in a book I'm writing.

And when I say it's too late, and I need to go to bed or I'll turn into a pumpkin, he types *haha*, and I wonder if he's really laughing somewhere, in a house in the middle of nowhere, surrounded by wilderness. I wish I could hear it.

The last thing I notice as I fall asleep, is that Jeremy texted me long ago and I didn't even see.

He canceled. Tomorrow I'll be alone on a Friday night. For some reason, I wonder if Stranger will be online, if he'll want to talk to me again.

And then, morbidly, I think: why?

When I wake the next morning, I refuse to check for messages from Stranger. I reached a decision while unconscious. It's not appropriate. This... whatever it is. I spent all last night flirting with a man, and even though it was online, it's not okay. If I found out Jeremy was talking to some other woman... about sex no less... I'd be furious. And so hurt.

No more.

Jeremy texted several times, and I just ignored him. Worst of all, he thinks I'm mad because he canceled.

> Jeremy: Mia, please don't be upset. The rep from Beijing is on a plane as I text. He's coming to see me.

> Jeremy: Come on, honey. This is silly. You know I don't want to cancel. I don't have a choice. You'll see me Saturday. I'll pick up sushi and come to you.

> Jeremy: Or we can go out? Anywhere you want.

> Jeremy: Mia? Please text me. This is crazy.

> Jeremy: I'm going to sleep now. I hope you're okay.

I'm a bad person. A very very bad person. He deserves so much more. He is sweet and good, honest and dependable. I'm terrible.

> Mia: No, Jer, I'm not mad. My phone was on silent and I went to bed early. I'm really sorry. I didn't see your texts.

I'm done with Stranger. Seriously. I mean it.

AND SO THE LYING BEGINS

MIA

There are no new alerts the day after our late-night chat fest.

That's good, I tell myself. I didn't want there to be any anyway.

I keep checking in on and off, but I have a very productive day. It's good. And I decide not to be pathetic, not to stay home alone just because Jer isn't available, and definitely not to chat with Stranger Lowe. So I text Erica, and we go out to dinner and then to a bar. I drink a martini, and studiously try not to think about Stranger.

When I get home, after I've taken off my makeup and gotten dressed for bed, just after I slide between the sheets, I can't put it off any longer. I finally check in on WritersWrite.com. There are other writers there who I care about.

A red dot.

I groan. Ignore it. Ignore it. Ignore it.

I don't. I can't.

He PMed three hours ago.

Click.

> Stranger: Do you write all day?

> Mia: Mostly. Yep. As much as I can.

Don't wait up. Don't wait up.

I do.

It takes him nearly fifteen minutes to answer.

> Stranger: Do you go out often?

> Mia: No. Not like when I was in school.

> Stranger: So, you're alone a lot?

> Mia: I guess. My fiancé works a lot, and weird hours. I spend most of my days alone.

> Stranger: Do you ever get lonely?

For some reason, that makes my eyes well up. Maybe it's the vodka, or listening to Erica talk about how fabulously and profoundly and insanely in love she is with Caesar, but it makes me overwhelmingly sad, imagining Stranger out there, in the middle of nowhere, all alone, and me here alone and about to marry a man I never see. What will my life be like in ten years? Will I be in a house somewhere, surrounded by darkness and sleeping children while Jer is off traveling the world?

I hadn't really realized it, but yes, I'm lonely.

And so must Stranger be for him to want to spend so much time speaking with a woman online.

> Mia: Do you?

> Stranger: Yes. Your turn.

> Mia: Yes, I'm lonely sometimes. I thought you hated people.

> Stranger: I don't like people in general. But one person, one on one, I like that a lot.

> Mia: Why move to nowhere if you didn't want to be alone?

> Stranger: My brother was injured in service. He's living with me while he recovers. But, yeah, I like to be alone. Sometimes it starts to wear though. After too long, I start to miss that connection. Want to touch someone else's skin or hear their human sounds, smell them.

> Mia: I'm sorry about your brother. It doesn't always work that way though. Sometimes I feel the most alone when I'm with people.

> Stranger: Like when? Who?

I toss my phone across the bed. I am not going to admit that sometimes, when I'm alone with Jeremy, I try to tell him about my writing and I can tell he isn't listening. I try to talk about something else, and I can see he doesn't care. Jeremy's a face-value person, he thinks discussion is mostly a waste of time, and talking is only valuable if there's a point.

Sometimes I sit next to him and have to work to come up with something to say.

I'm not going to tell any of that to this stranger.

> Mia: No one in particular. I'm drunk. Going to bed. ZzzzZzzzZzzz.

The next morning, I avoid checking in on WritersWrite.com . Stranger messaged me back after I said goodnight. Curiosity is my eternal companion today, like hot breath on the back of my neck.

My hands keep reaching for my phone to check for that friendly red circle, and I have to deliberately freeze them.

Greg is going back to the office full time now, and Annie will be alone for the first time all week, so I bring bagels, lox and cream cheese, and a couple bags of groceries, and head back out to their place in the country. It will be nice to see her alone this time.

We sit on the floor in the living room.

Hart's sleeping in one of the swings, snuffling and snorting like a small adorable beast. Hadley's awake. She blinks owlishly at me with her slate gray eyes, her tiny onesie covered in pink polka dots.

"I swear they've already gotten bigger."

A little smile tugs at the corner of Annie's lips.

I can't resist stroking Hadley's tiny soft head. Like feathers.

"They're so cute it hurts. Do you ever get tired of looking at them?"

With a grin, Annie flops onto her back and does a few thigh lifts. Up and down go her long, thin legs. "It's a trick. Nature made them cute so we don't kill them. She screams like a banshee."

"I haven't seen it." I pick up Hadley's tiny body, hold her up in front of me, my index fingers carefully behind her neck like Annie taught me. "You scream like a banshee?"

Hadley burble burps, and a stream of white oozes out of her mouth. I can't help but laugh.

Annie stretches up and blots at the drool with one of the white cloths that have become ubiquitous in this house.

She looks like crap again. It's only been a few days, but I wonder if her last shower was when I brought over dinner last time. Her hair is a tangled mess. She has no makeup on. Her clothes are wrinkled and stained.

"Are you taking showers?" I lay Hadley on my thighs. Her tiny legs curl up like a frog against my belly.

Annie looks up at the ceiling. I know that gesture. It's what she's done when she's frustrated since college. She resumes her thigh lifts. "I shower when I can, Mia. You've got no idea what it's like."

"Can I come more and help?"

She freezes, one thin leg up in the air. "No one else can feed them or make them sleep. Just me."

"What about your mom? Can she come up?"

"I thought she'd be here." She lowers her leg down, rests her hands on her still-squashy belly. "Honestly, I'm a little shocked that she isn't. I don't know what's going on."

"Have you considered hiring someone to help?"

She pulls an Elvis lip. "It's expensive, and I'm not working."

I frown. Annie and Greg are pretty well off. Expensive is obviously relative, but how much can it cost to hire a night nurse? I know people who've done it.

"Are you going back?"

She stretches into corpse pose, but doesn't say anything.

"Talk to me." I poke her with a sock-covered toe.

"I hate breastfeeding. It feels like my nipples are being peeled off."

I shudder, and lie down next to her, holding Hadley's little fists in my hands. "Then stop. No one breastfeeds twins."

"They say it's soooo healthy for the babies. The lactation consultant swears it will get better. She says formula is evil. And the boob is nature."

"Screw the boob. My mom gave me formula. I'm not evil. Neither is my brother."

"My mom keeps saying that on the phone, but It's just..." She trails off, her shoulders slumped. "If I even mention it to Greg, he gets all weird. Like I'm saying I don't love the babies or I can't hack it. And the consultant gets this pinchy face, like I've suggested letting them sleep in the dishwasher."

"That's ridiculous."

"Yeah, but..." She strokes her hand along Hart's tiny round head, the dark, wispy hairs there flattening down. "Marriage is so hard, Mia. You've got no clue."

I have to resist the urge to feel annoyed. She keeps saying that like I'm too dumb to understand, like I can't imagine, like she's advanced a few levels and left me behind.

I blow out a long breath. "You're right. That's one nice thing about Jer working so much. Can't argue with someone who isn't there."

She tilts her head side to side and up and down. Kind of a non-committal simultaneous affirmation and negation. "He won't always travel so much. And once you have kids... he just can't. It's not possible."

Oh, he will. Jer will always find a way.

"Go nap in the shower or something," I say, because I don't know what else to say. "I'll watch them."

She flashes a tired grin and hops to her feet lightning-quick. "I'll be fast."

"Go! Go!" I flap my hands at her.

She disappears down the hall, and I prop myself up on a pillow so I can study Hadley some more.

She's so tiny, I can hold her whole body as easily as I do my iPad. Her nose is smaller than the pad of my thumb.

She's patient, this baby. And after a while her eyes begin to droop. I think we will be friends, she and I. Someday, maybe I'll be her fun aunt, the one she runs away to, the one with good advice and no judgment.

I tuck her against me, snuggled in my arms and stare into her tiny, blinky sleepy eyes.

We reach an agreement.

No more talking with Stranger.

There's wisdom in those eyes. I swear at one point she almost smiles just as she drifts off.

I settle her into a bassinet beside her brother and make myself busy. I empty the dishwasher. The kitchen is surprisingly dirty. The counters are sticky, the trash full, crap litters empty surfaces. My place is cluttered with my own collections, plus wedding presents sent in advance of the coming wedding, but this is borderline filthy.

I grab disinfectant and set to work.

There's a pile of papers close enough to the trash, I can't tell if they should go in the recycling. So I look. I'm not snooping, I swear, but I can't help but see what it is.

An American Express bill for $38,712.96.

With an overdue notice. Yikes.

My hands move on their own, flipping through the pile. All bills.

I finish wiping and tidying quietly and drop down to the floor near the babies. For the life of me, I can't make sense of that bill. Annie drives a Cayenne. They have a massive house. They are members of a country club. They have plenty of money. Why in the world would they have debt like that?

In my world, people just pay bills. A couple times my dad has made noise at my mom about not paying an especially large bill early because of float or something.

I don't have much time to wonder though, because a few seconds later, the floor creaks and Annie's back. Her skin isn't pale and sallow, and her clothes are clean. Though, she has damp stains on her shirt right over her breasts, like her nipples are crying. She settles into the couch and lays down. Annie used to be so full of life. Now...

"Are you okay? Is this post-partum depression?"

She draws in a long breath, her hands flexing. "I don't know. Maybe?" Her eyes well up again and her face crumples. "I'm just so tired. I never know what I'm doing. I haven't slept, like really slept, in weeks. Only an hour here or forty minutes there. Breastfeeding hurts. The babies just scream and poop and sleep, and then they want to eat, all the time, and it hurts. I'm just... I don't know what day it is or who's running for the next election cycle. I haven't left the house in weeks. I'm failing at life right now. I miss working."

Being a mom has never sounded less desirable.

"I'm sorry, friend." I look at her and I see my whole future unfolding before me. Moving to the suburbs, two kids, working from home, diapers, sore nipples and no sleep.

On cue, Hart wakes up, wailing. Annie sets him to her breast, wincing, hissing, cursing, her whole face pinched up tight like someone's cutting out her liver with a rusty spoon. After a few minutes she quiets, and all I hear is Hart gulping and grunting. Maybe the pain got better.

She looks at me. "Tell me something fun. Tell me about Jer."

"Jer's busy with the business."

She makes a face. "If you see my dad, don't bring that up. Mom said he's furious."

That surprises me. Jer didn't mention anything. "About what?"

Her brows raise. "He lost a big client. He didn't tell you?"

I hide my surprise. "Maybe he didn't want to tell me over text? But I know some new client just flew in from China. I'm sure it will be fine."

Annie lifts a shoulder, but her lips flatten. "I don't know about that. I just know what Mom says."

I know nothing, and I'm still stuck thinking about that bill, so I ask the question at the front of my mind. "Are you going back to work?"

"I don't know, Mia. New subject." She waves a hand at me. "Tell me about your latest book."

I tell her about shifters and dirty sex, finally getting a couple laughs out of her. For a moment, she's like the old Annie.

I give her another big hug. "It will get better. My mom told me she cried on the floor of the kitchen pantry every day for a year after my brother was born. You'll find your way."

She gives a sputtery smile. "Yeah, definitely. I know. I'm fine. Don't worry."

"I'll come back on Monday, okay? I'll bring cookies."

As soon as I get to my car, I pull out my phone. I ignore three texts from Jer and go straight to WritersWrite.com. I click on that red dot like it's a lifeline.

Stranger: Sweet dreams, Mia Reed. How do you sleep? I imagine you curled up on your side. All warm and soft with your hair all over the pillow.

Oh man. Do not answer that.

So, I check Jer's multiple texts.

> Jeremy: I'd really like to go to Fort Meyers to see my parents. We won't always be able to go. Not once we have kids.

> Jeremy: Plus, your mom likes Thanksgiving the best. She won't care.

> Mia: Are Annie and Greg doing okay financially?

> Jeremy: I think so. Why?

> Mia: No reason. I just wondered. She's not doing well, Jer. You should call her. I'm going back on Monday.
>
> You know how much I love Christmas. It's my favorite holiday and Danny already said he's going to come home. Maybe your parents could come up. Annie isn't traveling down there with her babies. They should come see her. We could get everyone together, like old times.

> Jeremy: She isn't. Greg's parents are coming for Christmas. My mom and dad will be all alone. It'll be fun. We'll decorate a palm tree and eat coconut shrimp. Dad will make margaritas. Spend the day in the sun.

> **Mia:** Annie says your dad is mad at you for losing a client. I don't want to decorate a palm tree. I want a pine tree and snow. Let's go to Florida for New Years? Invite them here for Christmas?

> **Jeremy:** And have them stay in a hotel? That's not nice.
>
> Let's talk about this later. It's fair for us to see my parents for either Thanksgiving or Christmas. And we're going to your parents for Thanksgiving.

> **Mia:** It is fair. But they chose to move to Florida. It doesn't make sense to travel at Christmas. The airports are a mess and it will be stupid expensive.

> **Jeremy:** They're old. This might be one of the last years we can do it.

> **Mia:** Why is that?

> **Jeremy:** You might be pregnant or have just had a baby the Christmas after next.

Ugh!
I throw my phone onto the passenger seat and put the car in gear.
I try not to be mad. I do some deep breathing.
Tell myself a hundred rational reasons why what he said is fine.
We've talked about it.
We both want kids.

And he's right. In all likelihood, according to the schedule we've mapped out for our future, we will be married in eight months, and start trying for a baby this time next year, which means I will be pregnant or a new mom in two Christmases.

I just hate that he's right, that it's set in stone, that I have to go spend a week in Florida with his boring parents. That in two years, I'll be drenched in milk like Annie, tired and crying and sleepless with no time to write. With bloody nipples.

As soon as I get home, I open my computer and critique six of Stranger's chapters.

One after another.

I immerse myself in his dark world. A world where people kill each other at will, where no one is trustworthy, where secrets are dangerous. I stop for air a few hours later.

He's good.

Really good. I keep finding my eyes going back to that picture of him. I want to know where it was taken, when it was taken, who took it, how old is he?

I want to know if he's ever looked at my picture and wondered the same things about me.

But I'm ignoring him, so instead I check on my sales and read a few new reviews. Most are four and five stars, all full of praise for my latest book. But one makes my stomach sink.

> Anonymous: I beg of you, Mia Reed, do the world a service, stop writing, and go away. We want nothing more from you. You suck. Your characters suck. Your plots suck.

It's so mean, I'd laugh, except I can't help but worry if there's any truth there. I try so hard to bring my characters to life, to come up with exciting stories, to keep the tension high. But maybe I'm no good? I keep reading it over and over again, torturing myself.

I check in on my various social media outlets. There's nothing too unusual. A few fans have already read and are excited about my latest release, Shame.

There is one that reads:

> Anonymous: I wanna fuck your coint until you bleed.

Charming. They can't even spell the C word. I'm shaking my head. Spelling has gone by the wayside in school.

I do what I always do.

Delete.

Block.

I'm not sure if it's one creep who follows me around—that's what Annie says—or if it's multiple creeps who find me. Doesn't matter either way.

The internet brings out the worst in people. Or maybe it just brings out the worst people and lets them share their hate anonymously.

I pull up Stranger's face and type him a message fast. He has become an escape from everything I hate about my life. An escape I crave, I'm desperate for.

> Mia: Yeah, I sleep on my side. How do you sleep, Stranger?
>
> How old are you?
>
> Who took this photo? When did they take it? What are your tattoos of? What do you do when you aren't writing?

> What do you want from me? Why do you talk to me? Why do you care how I sleep? Or if I drink coffee? What are you doing right now?
>
> I'm alone. I'm sad. And yes, I'm lonely. I'm so lonely. All the time. I didn't even notice it until you pointed it out.
>
> My fiancé is never around and when he is, it's like he isn't even there. The loneliness is worse when he's around. I just got a terrible review and for some reason you're the only person I want to tell about it. You're the only person who would really care.
>
> That's not true. My friend and her husband would care, but he'd only lecture me. He'd start checking in on my social media and get bent out of shape at every weirdo and pervert.

Each word, as I reread them, is like a scratch, drawing blood straight from my soul.

My eyes well, and I delete every single letter.

Until there's nothing there but a blinking cursor, an empty screen, and me. All alone.

EVERYONE LIES

STRANGER

After our constant messaging, Mia's decided to ignore me today. Adorable.

I imagine her grappling with guilt about her fiancé, uncomfortable with our conversation, uncertain how to proceed. I add this unique response to everything else I know about her. There's something almost childish in her behavior.

She's had no experience with a man like me.

And thanks to my access to her hard drive, and her phone, I know her every lurid sex fantasy, her reading preferences, her interactions with friends and family.

She's been opening up to me each day, slowly spreading her petals wide, and I am fascinated.

She's peachy sweet. But with so much naughty potential. Like a gift for me alone.

And she collects the weirdest shit. Fills her life with things and people, and keeps them all. How? Why?

I don't want to like her, but it's hard not to. She doesn't have a mean bone in her body. She's like a bird, a bright, happy, fluttery, bubbly, colorful bird—a tropical bird like those parrots beside her bed. And she's trapped herself in a cage, surrounded by people who insist on seeing her as a sparrow. Pretends to be drab. Hides all those bright colors and thoughts away in her writing.

In no possible way has she revealed anything to me that says she deserves to die.

Still... I want that money. I want it for James. No matter what he says, his life won't be roses and chocolates after he gets his prostheses. Life isn't easy for amputees. He has no one else. All I can offer him is money, and after that distance.

I'll go to one of my storage units in another country, get a new passport, take a few jobs and live out my days quietly. Maybe in the mountains somewhere. Alone. Where I can't hurt anyone.

I enlarge her image on my phone.

If I don't do it, someone else will. They'll get the money, and she'll still be dead.

Except, a childish part of me whispers mine. I don't want anyone else killing her either.

She critiqued me last night, but so far, hasn't responded to my message saying thanks.

I tuck my phone in the ass pocket of my jeans and put on Gogo's leash.

James' nurse, Tasha, who comes every morning, is here now. They're out back. I don't disturb them. She's cute, warm with brown skin, thick curling hair, and a smile that never falters, no matter how James glowers.

Maybe there's something there.

I hope so. He seems less broody when she's around. And she genuinely seems to like him.

Nothing would solve his rage at his own newfound physical limitations quite like having a beautiful woman bounce away on his cock.

I head out with Gogo for our daily hike.

I let her off her leash as soon as we hit the treeline. Mia will respond eventually, it's just a question of when.

A woman like her was raised to be polite.

A few hours of deliberating on if and how to respond will keep her busy thinking about me.

We walk the mile to my mountain fast, and climb up from there, staying under the shade of the birch, pine and maple trees. Today, I feel like finding the waterfall, so that's what we do.

It takes a couple hours. Gogo pees on every bush, following some pattern of her own devising, circling around, following her nose, squatting, jumping, wagging her tail.

I love this place.

It's rarely disturbed. The water barrels down from six to seven feet, sending spray into the air that feeds moss and lichen that cover the rocks, and the temperature drops palpably in the area around it.

The leaf cover is thick enough that the only patches of sunlight that make it to the bottom are dime-sized or smaller.

Gogo doesn't like water, but she cozies up on her favorite stone in the shade, and I pour some water in the collapsible bowl I've started carrying for her.

It feels like it belongs to us alone, this pool.

I play out a mild fantasy of bringing Mia here. She doesn't seem like the outdoorsy type. I imagine her wrinkling her nose, chewing her lip, eying the water and the stones. Are you sure it's safe?

I tug my shirt over my head and drape it over the crotch of a birch tree so my sweat can dry. I picture Mia looking away nervously, almost twitchy with indecision. I can't help but grin. She'd hesitate, question, doubt, worry, eventually, she'd just do as I said. Jump.

She'd do it, and come up, sputtering and splashing and squealing at the cold. And then we'd fuck on the river bank.

Rhode Island isn't too far away.

The thought sobers me.

I'll see her again.

I kick off my boots and yank down my jeans.

Who the hell hired me? Her fiancé? A family member after money? Who could have a grudge against a woman like her?

Before I get in the water, I check my phone.

She PMed.

I grin.

> Mia: How old are you?

She doesn't usually ask me personal questions. It's working. I'm in her head. She's curious about me. I should ignore it just to fuck with her head, but something in her tone feels sad somehow.

> Stranger: 32. Are you okay, Mia?

> Mia: Yes. You?

> Stranger: I'm about to swim in a waterfall, so I'm... peachy. You sure you're okay? You seem off.

> Mia: Peachy, huh? I got a horrible review today.

> Stranger: I'm discovering I've got a thing for peaches. Aren't you used to bad reviews by now?

> Mia: No, actually. I almost never get bad reviews.

> Stranger: I didn't mean it that way. I just mean, aren't you used to the ups and downs of fans.

> Mia: Normally. This one just seemed especially cruel. Especially personal.

I pull up her sales page and click on her latest book, read the latest post.

Jesus. It is mean.

> Stranger: It's an internet asshole. Probably never even read your books. Let it go.

> Mia: I know. Sometimes it feels better to share it, though. And I can't talk to many people about my writing.

> Stranger: Why not?

> Mia: Not many people know I write.

> Stranger: What do you tell everyone else you do?

> Mia: Everyone thinks I work in publishing.

> Stranger: That's a pretty big lie.

> Mia: I lie a lot. It's terrible.

> Stranger: Everyone lies.

> Mia: Do you lie?

> Stranger: Everyone lies, Mia. You lie. I lie. We all lie.

> Mia: What do you lie about?

> Stranger: Stuff I need to lie about. Same things as you.

> Mia: Can I trust you?

I scratch the back of my neck. Stare up at the sky through the leaves. Think about how much James' next surgery will cost. How much Tasha costs a month. How much the new prostheses will cost. The land next to mine. The likelihood that I'll die or be arrested.

I think about Mia's face. And the open honesty of her stupid question, and it is a stupid question.

I'm either a liar or I'm not. And either way, the answer would be the same.

> Stranger: Yes.

I WANT TO RUIN YOUR PANTIES

MIA

The nights get longer and the days get shorter as September gives way to October.

Jer is working longer hours, traveling more. This will be our marriage, I realize. Me at home, bored and lonely, while he travels and works. If we have kids, will I raise them alone? Will I still talk to Stranger? In a year? In six years?

No. This is not sustainable.

He and I chat all day now, every single day. I let him in when I told him about the review, trusted him with my own insecurities, admitted to my lies. He made me feel better. A dam broke loose somewhere between us, and a whole wild waterfall gushed out.

We don't talk about sex. Not after that first crazy night.

Now, we talk about everything *else*.

We say good morning. We say goodnight.

He eats eggs. The smell makes me gag. I eat wheat toast with peanut butter. He thinks that's weird.

He likes the night. I like the day.

We eat together. Take a writing break and chat. He eats sandwiches for lunch most days, tuna or turkey with carrots and apples. He's healthy, this stranger of mine. I eat salads because I'm always dieting for a wedding I should be planning but am not. A wedding that gets closer by the day and yet somehow feels farther and farther away.

We chat about nothing. The best pizza we ever had, our favorite drinks, travel and TV shows, books and movies. How annoying passwords are and the systems we use to keep track.

He has a spreadsheet to track his passwords, and always uses names of beer for his.

He never makes mistakes. Or so he says. My dad always says everyone makes mistakes.

I use fruit and numbers and have to reset my passwords constantly because I forget them.

We are opposites. In every possible way.

He reads serious novels, ones about death and suicide and the state of the universe, I read trash and I'm proud of it. He says he's proud of nothing, but I know it's a lie. He's proud of a lot of things. He's proud of what he's accomplished. He was in the Marines. His dad died when he was twelve. His mom had trouble paying the bills, so he started stealing and dealing drugs. I can't even imagine that life. While I spent my summers in Europe, he was in foster homes, group homes, juvenile detention centers.

With Stranger, there's a lot left unsaid. I can read him, not that I'd tell him that. I can tell he feels guilty about leaving his brother behind when he joined the service.

He can read me too. Far too well. And he keeps me guessing, off-balance. Randomly disappears all day. I'm left anxious, checking constantly, desperate for the red circle, feeling frustrated, resentful, irritable. But then he comes back with a silly anecdote about a hike he took early in the morning with his dog, and all I feel is relief that he's back. That I'm not alone anymore.

I know what he's doing most of the time, when he goes for walks, when he writes, when he sleeps and eats. And he knows the same about me. I tell him about Jeremy and Annie and the babies. He knows about my mom and my dad, my brother Danny.

I convince myself it doesn't matter, whatever I feel for him, because this is the internet.

It's meaningless. Smoke. Words online.

But his words do matter.

He's opening me up, dissecting my brain, unearthing hidden parts of me I'd never even thought of. I didn't know I could connect this way with another human being. I had no idea men could talk like this. My dad only talks about golf and football. Jer only talks about work and himself. But Stranger...

He's like the best girlfriend I could ever imagine, with a little extra added layer of dominance, sex and danger.

When Jeremy sleeps over, I lie beside him in the night, listening to his quiet even breathing and I wonder what Stranger sounds like when he sleeps. Does he snore? Does he kick? Does he like to cuddle?

I can guess. The answers are probably the opposite of mine.

It makes me smile, thinking about him and imagining him somewhere thinking about me. There's so much curiosity and doubt. Maybe I've inflated this in my head, maybe it means nothing to him, maybe he just pities me.

Or maybe he's jerking off somewhere to a picture of my face on the phone of his screen like a perverted stalker. Does he get turned on reading my sex scenes?

I want to ask. But I don't dare.

He's my mysterious stranger, my dark secret, my private escape, and part of me revels in the doubt and secrecy and wonder of it all.

I reach for my phone first thing in the morning. It's still dark outside. The streetlights cast their orangy glow against my curtains. The temperature must have dropped overnight, because my room is cold.

Jer slept over last night. He's still asleep on his side of the bed, a distant, breathing lump in the covers.

As always, the first thing I do is check to see if Stranger PMed.

He did.

> Stranger: I want to hear your voice.

My belly hitches. He hasn't said anything like this before. We've both been so careful. We've never played our hands before. We've always kept it neutral. Kept it professional—at least since the cum bucket conversation.

But I've had the very same thought about him so many times I've lost count. I'm starved for clues about this man. This is another turning point.

I could back away—he'd let me.

Or I could shift closer—he's clearly ready. Am I?

> Mia: Worried that I'm secretly a man?

He doesn't answer right away. I knew he wouldn't. It makes me laugh, imagining him staring at the screen, vaguely annoyed. He tries to control the flow of our conversation. He thinks he can predict what I'll say next. I try to make sure he can't.

I go for my run in the rising dawn, in air that is fresh and crisp with fall.

When I come back, Jer is dressed in his suit, standing in the kitchen, freshly shaved. His dark hair is smoothed and gelled, his tie perfectly knotted. He's looking thinner than usual these days. Maybe he's feeling the stress of the coming wedding too.

He smiles when he sees me, and I ignore the flash of bitter guilt and irritation.

Jer has this way of smiling that makes him look bashful and sweet at the same time. He holds out a hand to me and even though I'm all sweaty and he's wearing a suit—and he's meticulous about his suits—he tugs me against him and wraps me in a big bear hug.

My heart twists.

"Sorry we couldn't run together. I slept in. Still jet-lagged from the London trip."

"It's okay." I tug away from him. "Did you find coffee?"

"I'll get it at the office. Can I see you tonight?"

I grab a bottle of water from the fridge. "Sure, I was going to take sushi out to Annie, and help with the babies. Around seven. Want to meet there?"

He presses a kiss to my neck. "You're a good friend. You two have your girl time. I'll grab something on my way home and stay at my place."

I squeeze my eyes shut and take a deep breath through the relief that he won't stay over tonight, because then I can spend my evening glued to my phone. How will this work after we marry and move in together?

I need to focus on Jer, on our lives together, on the wedding, on finding a house. But somehow, the thought has my throat tightening. Is this just cold feet? Is Stranger a symptom of some sort of quarter-aged crisis?

Is any part of it real?

I turn in Jer's arms, look up at him. I want him to kiss me, see if we have any real chemistry at all, maybe have wild sex right here in the kitchen just to prove we do.

He looks down with his kind eyes, leans in, and presses a chaste kiss to the side of my mouth. "Have a good day."

It's almost 9am when I sit down at my desk, showered and dressed for the day.

Jeremy. *You love Jeremey. You're wearing his ring. You're marrying Jeremy. Focus on Jeremy. Jeremy.*

I'm being cool. I'm not totally focused on Stranger. But I do have to check my phone, right?

He's answered. I'm not strong enough to resist.

> Stranger: I know you're not a man.

> Mia: How can you be so sure?

> Stranger: Worried I'm a woman?

> Mia: No. I know you're a man.

Stranger: How?

Mia: Just do.

Stranger: Ever wondered what I sound like?

Mia: Once or twice... Okay. Maybe a few hundred times.

Stranger: We could fix that. Very easily.

Mia: No. We really can't. It feels like too serious a step.

Stranger: Talking to me on the phone feels like a serious step? What century are you from? I didn't ask you to move in.

Mia: Ha. You're an internet stranger.

Stranger: You still think of me that way?

Mia: As a stranger? I mean... you could be a pervert or a psychopath. God knows what you're doing on your end of the internet or what plans you have.

Stranger: I am a pervert. And believe me, I have great plans for you.

> **Mia:** You're a pervert? Do you flash old ladies?

> **Stranger:** No. But I have thought about fucking you five times today already.

All the air rushes out of my lungs in one giant gust. I whimper. I've waited for him to say something like this for so long. I've wanted it. I've dreaded it. He's teased me. Starting hot and crazy, then going chaste. Right now, I could tell him to stop. I could tell him this is too much. It's not appropriate. I'm engaged. We can't go there. Or I could go there right along with him.

> **Mia:** It's not even 10

> **Stranger:** Exactly.

I'm supposed to meet with the florist later today to plan my wedding. I'm supposed to be thinking about Jeremy. I could rebuff Stranger now. Turn the flow of the conversation away. He'll let me. I should do it. End this now before it gets worse, before it's too late, before it destroys everything.

But I'm so curious.

I bite my lip.

I have no self-control. I'm pathetic. I'm putty. I have to know how he'll respond.

> **Mia:** And? What do you think about?

> **Stranger:** What we'd do if we met, where we'd go, how we'd be.

Mia: Make any decisions?

Stranger: We'd be fucking glorious.

Mia: How would it go?

Stranger: We'd meet in a public place. A restaurant or a bar. Someplace you'd feel safe, where we could settle in, have a drink. See what happens.

Mia: And then?

Stranger: Electric, Reed. We'll be electric.

Mia: What if I'm not like I am online? What if I'm shy?

Stranger: You'd still be you inside. I'd just have to work harder to find it, make you comfortable.

Mia: What if you don't like the way I look?

Stranger: Looks aren't all that important.

Mia: What if I don't like how you look.

Stranger: Looks aren't all that important.

Mia: Then what?

> Stranger: …

> Mia: …?

> Stranger: I sometimes hold back with you.

> Mia: Why hold back? I'm a grown woman.

> Stranger: I don't want to shock you.

> Mia: Shock me. Please. Make my boots shake.

> Stranger: Fine. Fuck it. I want you in my bed, under me, I want to feel you on my skin, smell you, taste you. I want to ruin your panties, suck on your tongue, see how wet I can make you. I want to fuck you, fill you up, make you scream.

I blow out air like a balloon slowly deflating.

Stranger doesn't do things in halves. He's relentless when he wants to be.

I've been on this planet for twenty-seven years. No one has ever said anything like that to me in my life.

I've written dirtier things, but that comes from my head. Crazy people online have said weird stuff, but I don't know them. This is him. My bizarre fixation, my dangerous desire.

I'm shaking.

I'm scared.

I'm really turned on. I have this sickeningly clear image of myself, licking our combined fluids off his fingers.

> Mia: You just did ruin my panties.
>
> Stranger: Good. Then why are you still wearing them?
>
> Mia: What am I supposed to do.
>
> Stranger: Duh. Take them off.
>
> Mia: Uhhhh…
>
> Stranger: Don't think. Just do it.

He dominates me this way. I see it happening. Curiously, I like it. I don't know what that says about me, but I do. I like the slither of fear that rides up my spine, I like that I'm so wet between my thighs I'm dripping. I like the danger of all this. He could be anyone. He could be a criminal. He could be a monster. He could be my dreams come true. He could be anything.

My eyes water with some unnamed emotion. Relief? Fear? Sadness? Like I've been looking for something my whole life and here it is.

Take them off.

My lips shake and a fat tear slides down my cheek. My nipples are so hard they hurt. And I wasn't exaggerating about my panties. I reach under my dress and tug them down, let them slide down to the floor.

What am I doing? I have no idea. I'm doing what I want.

> Mia: Done.
>
> Stranger: Give me your number.

Mia: I don't know....

Stranger: You want to hear my voice.

Mia: You probably sound like an old woman.

Stranger: I don't.

Mia: Maybe you have a lisp.

Stranger: You're curious.

Mia: I am. You really want to talk for the first time right now?

Stranger: Why not?

Mia: I always imagined it at night, pouring a drink together. Sitting down. Talking. Like how you described it, only without the bar.

Stranger: We'll do that next.

Mia: I'm engaged.

Stranger: I know. I can back off if you want. Am I making you nervous?

Mia: A little. But I don't want you to back off.

Stranger: So, you're saying you want to talk?

Mia: Kindamaybesorta.

Stranger: Absolutelydefinitelyyes. Number, Mia. Now. Do it. Quit overthinking things.

I do it.

I just type it in really fast.

Ten little numbers. I don't let myself think. I just ruin my relationship with the man I'm supposed to marry.

This is it, right here.

Trust corroded.

TRUST CORRODED

MIA

I grab my cell.

I want to be in bed when I hear his voice the first time, under the covers, cozy and warm.

My stomach keeps dipping and fluttering.

And I'm still shamefully wet. It's like this ravenous beast took hold of me. I'm pulsing and throbbing and so hot and empty. And it's so much easier to focus on my body than to think about what I'm really doing and what it means.

What am I doing?

Not overthinking this.

I crawl onto the bed on wobbly knees, with shaky hands, my fingers sinking into the hot pink roses on my blue bedspread. I've never been so turned on. Not once in my whole life.

Stranger keeps on teaching me new things about myself.

I let the image of him play in my mind. A stranger with eyes that cut right through me. This mysterious man who sees me more clearly than anyone ever has, even though he's never even met me.

I can see it perfectly. A darkened room, a warm bed. I picture him lying on his back. I'd straddle his thighs. He'd come inside me, hard with a grunt. I can practically see his eyes clenching, his mouth tightening. But I wouldn't have come. Not yet. He'd withhold it on purpose, toy with me, keep me on the edge, make me so stupid with desire I'd do anything for him.

Our eyes would lock. His dark and unreadable. I see it, like a dream so real I can feel his breath tickling over my breasts. He would slide two fingers inside me, rub them over my lips, smearing them around my face, defiling me, violating me.

He likes it like that. I know he does.

And apparently so do I.

In my mind, his eyes flare. The taste of him, of me, of us fills my mouth.

My phone rings.

Oh god. It's him. Can I do this?

This is another one of those turning points. I could ignore him. I don't have to answer.

I could block him.

It's a number from upstate New York. Oh no, he's not even that far away. How did we not talk about that already?

I roll onto my back and pick up the phone.

"Stranger?" My voice comes out breathy and pathetic. I'm so nervous my hands are shaking.

"Mia."

His voice vibrates through my ears, so palpable my neck arches. I've wondered about it, worried about it. What if it's falsetto? What if he stutters? What if he has some horrid accent? What if he's one of those people who ends every sentence with a question mark?

I should probably say something smart or funny.

I know so much about this man—but so much is still unknown. And that has my throat tightening. My eyes well up. I cover them with my hands.

"Hey."

Who am I?

I am a woman who talks to strangers online when by all laws of humanity, she should be planning her wedding to another man. I am a woman with sex fantasies. A woman who isn't sure about what she wants from her future anymore. A woman who isn't sure she knows who she even wants to be.

All my life, I've known what my future looked like. The husband, the house, the kids. But somehow I ended up writing sexy books. Somehow I ended up talking to this weird internet Stranger. And somehow, he's all I think about, all I care about.

Why?

When did I become this person? When did Jer become the other man?

"Did you get in bed?" His voice is not falsetto. It's rich and deep and just a little gritty. And he doesn't have an accent, a lisp, or a stutter. He just sounds sexier than hell.

I let out a frustrated laugh. "How did you know?"

He laughs, and the sound is beautiful. A low chuffing, like a cross between a throaty groan and a breathy sigh. I picture him smiling.

Ten minutes ago, all I wanted was to hear his voice, now I want to see him smile. I want to know the shape of each and every tooth. "Just a guess. I picture you with flowers."

He knows me so well. I'm constantly surprised in moments like these.

"My bedspread has pink flowers. Where are you?"

"In my kitchen. Sitting at a barstool. Overlooking the hills in my picture. Tell me about your panties."

"Absolutely not." I pinch the bridge of my nose. "I refuse to have our first conversation be like that."

"What do you want to talk about?"

"I need to get used to your voice. I'm nervous."

"Cute."

"Just talk."

"No, Mia. I don't just talk. You'll have to ask me a question."

"You're kind of a jerk."

"Surprised?"

"No." I chew on my lip. "Tell me about the hill."

"My mountain? It's in my picture. You've seen it."

"Yes."

I tug down the covers and crawl under them, rest my head on a pillow.

"It's in my backyard. That's where we hike."

"Why?"

"Gogo likes it."

I smile.

"And you? Do you like it?"

There's a pause, like maybe he's thinking. I'm not sure. And then he starts talking. "Yeah. My dad was a hiker. Used to take us with him. My brother and me. Whole summer sometimes. Just the three of us. Hiking reminds me of him. He's dead now. Been dead a long time."

I close my eyes, and try to imagine his face, try to picture what he's doing, and I can't. He comes up almost blank. It doesn't really matter. He's real, this man. And it's surreal to hear him talk.

"I'm sorry." I feel stupid saying it, but it's what people say.

"He took us all over the place."

"Does James hike with you?"

"He used to." Another long pause. "He can't hike anymore."

Oh. I squeeze the bedspread, wondering if it happened while he was in the Marines. "How badly was he injured?"

There's a noise in the background, like he's tapping his foot, or a hand or something. "His unit took an RPG to a rear wheel of their transport truck. Fired from an apartment complex. He lost both legs."

My heart clenches. That's why he lives with him. Stranger takes care of him. "I'm sorry, Stranger."

He makes a noise that both acknowledges and rejects my words. "You don't have to say that Mia. You didn't hurt him."

"I know."

"New subject," he says.

"Send me a picture of you," I blurt.

"Right now?"

"Yes, right now. One where I can see your eyes. One where you're smiling."

"I don't smile."

"Bad teeth?"

"No."

"Irritable bowels?"

He laughs, I think more from surprise than anything else.

"You know, you can't laugh without smiling. So you just smiled."

"Alright. I'll send a picture. Take one of yourself. Right now. I want to see you, just as you are."

I lift my phone, switch it to the camera screen, spend a few seconds slithering on the bed to get a flattering angle. The light is bad. I've looked better, but my hair is all spread out over a flowery pillow and I look like a woman in desperate need of a few orgasms. I shrug, make my mirror face.

Click.

Before I can think about it, I send it to him.

His comes back to me a second later. He's kind of frowning at the camera, but I can see his eyes. Finally. They're hazel, slightly angled up at the corner. He looks a little amused, his kitchen behind him. A stainless-steel range, a wood table in the distance, spartan, no-nonsense. It makes me sad for some reason.

"You have good eyes," I say. They are a rich amber, green and gold swirling together. Thick brows. A Roman nose. And those cheekbones.

Oh no.

He just got way hotter.

That dimple. That perfect dimple. And in the edge of the photo is just the tiniest flash of a biceps at the bottom of a simple white cotton tee. A very, very nice biceps, covered in bold colorful swirling tattoos.

I swallow. "Why can't you be ugly? Or scrawny. It would make it so much easier."

He's quiet for a minute. I picture him staring at my picture.

"You're pretty."

I'm used to men telling me I'm pretty, but for some reason, the simplicity of his tone makes me feel like he doesn't just mean my face. He means me, the me he's gotten to know in these months of frenetic messaging.

"Tell me more about those hills," I say.

And he does.

He tells me about a trail he takes, the flowers that come out in the spring, and the deer, foxes, blue jays he sees, the wineries he passes. I ask questions, little ones, enough so he doesn't start to worry that we lost our connection, enough to let him know I'm there, and I'm listening. He talks about Gogo and how she has her favorite trails.

He's chattier than I imagined. I'm glad he can't see me, because I'd look ridiculous just smiling, my face half buried into my pillow, hanging on his every gravelly-voiced word.

Stranger tells me about this wild encounter he once had, how he turned on a trail and stumbled into an old couple—with white hair—he says that part like it's the most important part, having wild sex against a tree.

"What did you do?"

"I left them to it. Backed right up. What was I supposed to do, clap? Watch? What would you have done?"

I spend the whole time laughing or smiling, and so happy. He's real. I'm not sure I've been so happy in my whole life except as a child, during summer evenings at the boardwalk, on roller-coasters under a sunny sky.

And finally, after a while, he goes quiet. "Tell me about your fiancé."

The question comes out of nowhere or maybe everywhere. If Stranger feels even half of what I do—he must be desperate to know about Jeremy.

I groan. "Can we talk about something else?"

"He's off limits?"

"No. It's just... I feel guilty."

"About talking to me?"

About dropping my panties for you, about thinking about you in my every waking second and half my sleeping ones. "About all of this."

I'm so afraid he'll downplay it. Say what? We're just friends.

But he doesn't. "I get that. This is... unusual."

I hold my breath, wait for him to elaborate, but he doesn't, so I ask, "for you? I've never done this before."

"Neither have I."

"You don't meet women online all the time?"

"No. And this is months of buildup. If this is too much, if it's too awkward, we can stop."

I pluck at the covers.

"Do you want to stop?" he asks.

I don't know. "I don't think so. I'm just confused. I don't know what I want. We're supposed to get married in February. A white wedding. But instead of planning it, I spend all my time talking to you."

"Should I apologize for that?"

"No."

"Then what do you want me to do?"

"I don't know. It's just... He runs a business. He works constantly. He's tired and overworked," I say lamely. I don't want to think about Jer, with his gentle hooded eyes, his slender frame, his nervous habit of chewing on his thumbnail. "He's a good man. He's kind."

Stranger doesn't say anything. The silence builds.

"Are you kind, Stranger?"

"I can be. But no. In general, I'm not a kind man."

"That scares me. You scare me. You don't just make up your stories during walks in the woods."

"No."

"Where do you get them?"

"I don't want to lie to you. Tell me something nice. Tell me about your family."

I do. Maybe it's willful ignorance, but I let him keep his secrets, and I blabber. Just talk. I don't even know how long. At some point my phone's battery gets down to a thin red bar, and I'm embarrassed. I just blabbed his ear off. He's a good listener. "Can I tell you a secret, Stranger?"

"You can say anything. I'll listen."

My eyes burn. My throat tightens. "I don't know if I want to marry my fiancé."

There's a long pause. The words are there, like great big, looming smears in the air. I want to take them back. Sweep them away.

"Because of me?"

"No. Sort of. Not because I want you, but because I always had this little nugget of doubt. And it's like I can see now how it could be if I were with a different man. A man who talked to me. Who listened like I had something worth saying. Not you, but maybe someone like you."

"But not me?"

My face crumples. "I don't know. I feel like I don't know anything anymore." My voice rises. "I didn't even know I liked cum buckets. I just thought I wrote that weird stuff, and then you sometimes say things offhand and it's like… it strikes a chord. It resonates, and I realize I've been wanting something my whole life and I don't have it. It's like there's been this hole, and you're filling it up. But I don't even know you."

I said it. The silent fear that's been building, that I've been alone my whole life, just found the perfect person who could complete me, and I'm going to lose him. That he isn't real, doesn't feel the same way, is just some painful, hateful dream.

The silence hurts.

My heart thunders, and my throat tightens.

I imagine him replaying my words, analyzing them, picking them apart. He has a talent for that.

There's a soft wet click, like he just opened his mouth. "I'm just a man, Mia."

But can I trust you? Can I trust you not to break my heart? What do you want from me? What's in it for you? What will happen when this fizzles out, when you're gone and I'm alone again? It wasn't so bad before, I didn't see that I was alone, but now I know, and how will I handle that? The questions build, inflating and filling the room around me with unspoken menace, making the silence almost smother me.

"Are you married?" I finally ask.

"If I were, I wouldn't be talking to you."

I flinch.

He draws in the kind of breath people do when they're working up to saying something big. "I know this is weird for you. I just like talking to you. I think about you a lot."

I scoff, all tear-clogged and wet. "About fucking me. It's not the same thing at all."

"Not just that. I find myself thinking about you at random times. Walking through the woods, I see something and I wonder what you'd say. I wonder what it would be like if you were with me. Sometimes it's sexual. Other times it's not."

"Like... what?" I know where this is going. I'm not dumb. I can't pretend I don't know, but it's just... I want it to go there, need something more. Even knowing this is wrong, I crave it.

"I'm curious about you."

I wait. I don't even breathe, just squeeze my eyes shut and fear-hope what's about to come out of his mouth, in his deep, sexy, gritty, velvety, powerful voice.

"How you smell. How you move. How your skin feels. How your tongue tastes."

I make that whimper. It's completely involuntary. In the back of my throat.

His words linger on my skin like an incantation. He has magic, this man. And he's working it on me, enthralling me. "I imagine just being with you," he says. "Interacting. Do you ever think about me?"

"Far too often."

"What do you think about?"

"I want to smell your neck." I wince after saying it. His answer was so much better.

He laughs. "My neck?"

"Yeah. Like, right behind your ear. I want to touch it with my nose, breathe you in."

He's quiet.

I scrunch up my face and force myself to press on. "I kinda maybe just a little bit, have thought about sitting on your lap, feeling the heat of your body, touching your hands, feeling you breathe. Just, you know, to know you're real."

"I'm real. What do you think we'd do if we met?"

It's my turn to awkward-laugh. "A lot of things. That's why we can't ever meet."

"Never?" His voice is so incredulous that I can't help but laugh again.

"I'm engaged. And this is... insane."

"I think," he says in his slow and measured voice. "It would be sad if I never got to look you in the eyes."

I laugh in spite of myself. "Are you just telling me what I want to hear?"

"No."

"Yes. I don't trust you, Stranger Lowe."

"That's because you're smart."

"Why are you doing this?"

"I want you."

I swear my heart skips a few beats. Maybe a hundred. I don't know. "Why?"

There's a long pause. So long I start to worry that I've made him uncomfortable, stretched this out to be more than it is.

"I don't know, Mia. This means something to me. This... whatever it is. It feels important somehow. Like we're building toward something. Something real."

My throat is tight. It's been months of this strange dance, where we shift around the meaning of things, ignore what's right in front of us, pretend this is okay, what we're doing. That it doesn't matter. I'm terrified that he's an illusion, a catfish from the bottom of the swamp, that he's destroying my life for fun. For so long, I've been so afraid that he's nothing but a liar, a con man who says whatever I need to hear. Maybe he is.

"I don't know what to think. I'm engaged. To a good man. And this is..." I close my eyes, accept it, own it, acknowledge it, stare my own darkness in the face. "This is emotional infidelity, what I'm doing. It's wrong."

He lets out a long, protracted sigh and I stare at his face on my phone. I try to imagine his brows furrowed, his sexy perfect lips tight with frustration. "Look, Mia. I'm the kind of guy who goes after what he wants. I don't back off. But I will. If you want me to, I'll go away, leave you alone."

His voice echoes in my ear. I burrow under the covers. Goosebumps rise over my skin. "You never do what I expect."

"Do you want me to go away?"

"No."

"My neck smells like soap."

My lips stretch into a wide grin.

"We will meet, Mia. You'll like me."

"Even though you're a jerk."

"I wouldn't be a jerk to you."

My eyes well up all over again. And now I'm back on the roller-coaster, the big one, the upside-down kind, where you lose your stomach, and for a second you think you might die, but then the world turns over again and you're so insanely joyous to be alive. It's a high, talking to him like this. I'm off kilter. The world is shifting. And I want it to keep right on shifting. I want it all to crumble.

"I should go," I say. "My phone is dying."

"Let's talk again soon, pretty Mia. And next time, you're going to tell me about your panties."

ONE-EIGHT-HUNDRED-HIT-4-YOU

STRANGER

James's wheels go silent when they hit the carpet in the living room. I'm at my desk. My back is to him, so I can't read his expression. But even his wheels sound dour and disapproving.

I don't turn to face him, just stare out at my mountain in the distance.

He'll make his point when he's ready.

Gogo loafs over to him, and from the sounds of scuffling and breathing, I can tell she's dropped her head in his lap, and he's petting her. She's becoming as much his dog as mine. Which is a good thing. It won't hurt her as much when I leave her with him.

I can't take her with me.

He'll take good care of her.

"Ready to talk to me?" he asks after a few more moments pass.

No.

The sky is swollen and gray. I took Gogo out this morning because the weather called for afternoon rains.

"About what?"

James gives me a minute, because that's what he does now. He waits, patient on the outside, roiling on the inside, like a cork plugged into a shaking bottle, fit to explode. He keeps it all contained. He thinks I can't see how it eats at him, the inability to stand up, walk away on his own, throw his weight around like he used to.

I can imagine the stifling, claustrophobic frustration of it. It will be easier when he's mobile, when he can stand.

He exhales a steady stream of air. It hisses through his nostrils. "You owe me an answer, Stranger."

"Do I?" Now, I turn. He hasn't bugged me about Mia in months. Hasn't even mentioned my career and how it pays the bills. "Why?"

He doesn't look at me, glares at the floor with his hands flexed on the arms of his chair. "It's just one more month, Stranger. I'll have the prostheses, I can get a job. I won't nee—"

His jaw clenches tight as he breaks off. He won't need me. I know that. He doesn't need me now. Just the money and the house.

I lean forward so my elbows are on my knees, drop my chin into my hand.

"I won't always be so dependent." His voice rises slightly, and he glares at me.

"Never said you would be. You barely are now."

"You don't have to do this..." He points at my computer as if it's to blame. "You take these jobs because you want to make sure I'm okay, but I already am."

I look around, thinking about that. These jobs. Like I'm a handyman taking odd jobs to make ends meet. Not a killer. Ending people's lives.

In the last few months, this house has become more his home than mine. A stack of books covers a side table. Friends of his from around the world have sent cards and photos. He's been tacking them up on a cork board over the sofa. Tasha brought him a fruit bowl. It sits on the kitchen counter. He ordered a rug for the living room online. He said Gogo would get cold this winter.

They'll be fine without me. Once James gets his prostheses and can drive, he won't even need me to get groceries.

"It's not about you, James."

A sputter leaves his lungs. He's practically vibrating with his rage. I get it.

If it were me, and I went from being big and fast, normally the tallest guy in the room, to spending my life on my ass, stuck in a chair, forced to accept help for mundane shit, looking at a future walking on titanium pegs, I'd be mad as hell.

I am mad as hell for him.

If I could fix it, go back, I would. But I can't. So I did the one thing I could do. Bought the house, hired the architects, got it ready for a guy in a chair. Found the nurse. Found a housekeeper who'd keep her mouth shut about the locked basement when she comes once a week to clean up after us. I stayed here, fucking helped him however I could.

Now, I just sit here and feel useless and guilty.

He joined up because of me. It's my fault. I left him in a group home. He followed in *my* footsteps and now look at him.

It should have been me in the chair. He'd have handled this better than I am. He'd have helped me with a joke and a grin.

Because my throat is suddenly thick and I have no idea what else to say to make this minute better. "What do you want to know about Mia?"

"Are you going to kill her?"

I rub the back of my neck. "Undecided."

He makes a noise in his throat that tells me he thinks I'm lying. "Tell me about her."

I type Heineken into the password bar. James' favorite beer. I could go with a more complex password, but there are layers of protection—and I'll destroy this laptop when this is done.

Her face fills the screen.

He moves closer, and I shift my chair so he can sit beside me at the desk. "She really is pretty."

I don't comment, but he stares at me for a long moment, before his posture relaxes.

I pull up a picture of Jeremy's face from his social media. "This is the fiancé, Jeremy Dixon. He travels a lot."

James leans forward and studies Dixon's face. The long nose, the light blue eyes, the slim jaw, long narrow nose. "You think it's him?"

"Not really."

"What do you know about him?"

"Not a whole lot. Old money, took over his dad's business. Mia thinks it's going well, but he's lost a few massive clients in the last months. The business isn't doing as well as she thinks."

"So he needs money then?"

"Maybe. He's got a penthouse and a new Mercedes SUV. Works a lot supposedly."

"But if the business is failing..." He leaves the question unfinished.

I shift. "Maybe. It's just... Maybe he needs Mia's money. That doesn't mean he needs or even wants her dead."

James is quiet for a while, clicking through the photos on Dixon's social media account.

Since that day by the waterfall when she asked me if she could trust me, I've been chewing on the mystery in my hands. Who wants Mia dead? Who has the motive, the money and the means of finding me?

I have sifted through the internet, called Jeremy's office and Mia's father's, pretending to be a prospective client. I cold-called Annie and Greg and Jeremy's parents and a few of their friends, just to hear their voices. And there's a lot of information to be found online.

"The firm manages endowments and trusts. They've got clients in China, South Africa, Luxembourg, London, France, the Caribbean, across the U.S."

James glances back at me. "You think if it's him, that's how he found you?"

"Maybe. He must brownnose with government people on occasion but no one at a yuppy cocktail party mentions they know a contract killer. That doesn't happen. Not even in Bond movies."

"So how else do people find you?"

I shake my knee. "That's been bothering me from the beginning."

"You mean you don't advertise?" James laughs. A real laugh. I'm not sure when I last saw him laugh. We had little contact in the years after the group home. We'd meet up for dinner or lunch. Catch a ballgame when we were both on leave. Have conversations that consisted mostly of silence, and carry on our way. Silent ships with an ocean of unsaid crap between us, passing each other by once or twice a year.

His cheeks line with laughter, his head falling back a little. "Assassin for hire. Special summer discount, two for the price of one."

I raise my brows.

His laughter carries around the house.

Gogo wags her tail. "You could have a jingle one-eight-hundred-hit-4-you."

He actually sang that, and I have to work not to laugh. "You done?"

"Not really. I can see the ad perfectly." He holds his hands up, like he's framing the camera shot. "A lone woman, crying into her pillow. Her husband bangs on the door, screaming. She's terrified. A deep male voice-over." He pitches his voice low. "Are you in trouble? Do you need help? Is there someone in your life you need taken care of? The assassins of Hit For You Enterprises can help. Call today. Don't miss this once in a lifetime opportunity. You aren't alone. You have… the Hitman on your side. She reaches for the phone, visibly relieved. We close on an optimistic piano riff. Saving lives, one body at a time."

I do laugh. A little. Mostly just because it's nice to see him happy. "You done now?"

"Fine."

There are plenty of assholes who do advertise in certain forums. "It's more like five K a pop for some ex-con to knife someone down."

His face sobers. "So, who can find you?"

"No one outside government people for the most part. Someone who'd been involved in black ops with me, someone on a committee, maybe CIA. Most of my jobs come from governments. With government budgets."

James rubs his hands together. "So… Okay, theoretically, Dixon—or his dad, the original owner—could have gotten tipsy with someone who knows something they shouldn't. Your name is dropped. Dixon remembers."

"Jesus, I hope not."

No one namedrops assassins, complete with email addresses. I thread my fingers behind my back and cradle my head in my palms. "I don't buy it. I don't even know who hires me, usually. And they don't know anything about me."

"An email address is all they'd need, though, right? Maybe someone listening in on a conversation between two senators, who knows. But, it's possible. Right?"

I stare out at the mountain, the leaves in browns and oranges, play out the scenario a few times. It's highly doubtful. "I guess."

James nods. "Okay, who else?"

I pull up Annie, Dixon's sister, so James can see her.

"They look alike," he says. It's true. The same narrow face, pale blue eyes, dark brown hair.

"She was a reporter until a few months ago. She was put on bedrest early in her pregnancy. The babies are a few months old. She hasn't gone back yet."

"She and Mia get along?"

I nod. "Best friends since college. Mia loves her. She's the twins' godmother."

I pull up Annie's husband's face now. Greg. "This is Annie's husband. Of all of her friends and family she's mentioned, he's the only one smart enough to mention her physical safety and the potential risks inherent to her work."

James sends me a surprised glance. "You like him?"

I think about what Mia's told me about Greg.

"I didn't say that. But I respect what he said to her even though it pissed her off. Also, I can't imagine someone who wanted her dead encouraging her to look out for her own self-defense."

James studies the light brown hair, the big white teeth, the self-satisfied grin. "Unless he was asking so he could isolate holes in said self-defense."

"That would be like looking for holes in the sky. She has zero self-defense beyond a flimsy lock on her door. She just assumes everything will be okay because it always has been."

James rests his elbows on his knees. "So, you don't think it's him?"

"It could be any of them. I just think... I don't know. I want more information. Whoever took out the hit has money to blow. Makes me think it's not about the money. It's more personal than that."

I put up Mia's father's face next. "Keith Whitten. Her dad. Private wealth manager. Clients include a general, a governor, some low-level celebrities, a few sport's players, and a lot of lawyers, doctors and miscellaneous business persons."

James studies the guy's face. He looks exactly like what you'd expect a rich east coast guy to look like. White hair, dark suit, cautious smile, calculating eyes. He looks like old money.

"So he has maybe an even better chance of some kind of late night, cigar and scotch talk with someone who knew of you."

I lift my shoulders. "I guess. But why would he kill his own daughter? He's a signatory on her trust. He wouldn't benefit in any way I can see."

"Unless the money's drying up?"

"Maybe. It's weird to assume someone with money problems has that much cash lying around, though."

James frowns. "Takes money to make money."

I'm unconvinced.

Gogo whines and James resumes her head-scratches.

Next comes Mia's mom. Coiffed honey-gold hair, enormous gold and diamond jewelry. I got this picture from the website of the tennis group at their country club. "She's a lady who lunches. She and Mia talk every single day. They're close. She's never worked. Isn't on social media, and Mia says she doesn't even really understand how to text. Apparently, she signs them all love, Mom."

James smiles. "Not the mom then. Who else?"

I bring up Mia's sales page and show him the bad review. "This could be nothing, but there's an ugly feel to it. A few similar posts on her social media, and a few that smack more of men just harassing her because she's pretty, but she deletes those instantly."

James gets distracted by the cover and the blurb of Mia's latest release, Shame. The couple on the cover are partly naked and full on kissing. The blurb mentions anal play.

His brows go up way high. "She doesn't mess around does she?"

I send him a look. "No."

He grins, looking happier than he has since before the accident, and I find my own face trying to smile in response.

"Who's left?" he asks.

"Jeremy's mom and dad, I guess. They live in Florida though."

James flips through the screen again, rereading the information I've gathered on each of them. It's all there in the doc. The photos, the information I've found to date.

There's a lot to be found online, but I need more. I want financial details on them. I want to know who's loaded and who's struggling.

"What about her brother?"

I put Danny Whitten's face up. "He's running an acting agency. His family doesn't know that. They think he's a lawyer. But aside from that, he and Mia get along. He's got a girl named Penny. Decorator or something, zen shit. He's in LA."

James rocks his chair back and forth. "So what do we do next?"

"We?"

He looks at me, his eyes, so unsettlingly like mine, serious. All humor evaporated. "Yeah, we. We're going to save this girl, Stranger. Together."

I've never saved anyone before. Even in the army, I was black ops. Silent strikes in the night. Me and a small team. I take lives. I don't save them. "You want to be my Robin?"

He spreads his hands wide. "I mean, I was thinking more like Watson, but I'll take Robin, long as that's what this is? Saving her."

Even if I hadn't already decided a long time ago that Mia was safe from me, I think I'd agree just to see him so happy. "Yeah."

"So what happens next?" He looks at me expectantly.

"I'm not a detective."

James sucks his lips between his teeth. "We need information. Let's go see this fool Dixon. I want to read his mail, know what kind of bills he's got. Same with his sister and her husband. The dad too."

Because I want to, I text Mia.

> Stranger: What are you doing right now?

"That's what cops do on TV." James rocks his chair back and forth.

That makes about as much sense as anything else, so for now, I'm happy to let him find whatever happiness he can from playing detective.

My phone vibrates.

> Mia: Writing. You?

> Stranger: Thinking about you.

> Mia: That's sweet.

> Stranger: I think about you a lot, Reed. I want to see you.

Mia: Me too.

Stranger: Tonight.

Mia: No.

Stranger: When?

Mia: Soon. Maybe. I don't know. We'll figure something out.

"And," James says, "tell Ender you need a deposit."

I look up at him distractedly.

"Take the job, Stranger."

MY OVARIES ARE BLUE BLUE BLUE

MIA

Everything changes.

We can't go back. Everything is charged now with this fatal layer of sexuality, vulnerability, promise. Hope. Doubt.

Plus, now I know the tone of his voice. The way he pauses a split second before he answers, how cautiously he weighs his responses, the deep timbre that makes my insides melt.

I know all that, but mostly I constantly wonder at his motives.

Why does he want to talk to me so much? A man like him, he could be with any woman. He doesn't need to talk to me. I'm predictable, inexperienced, *boring*.

I'm pretty enough, but I'm nothing unusual. And he can't even see me. What is so special about me?

It's a constant dance of *does he like me? Doesn't he? Do I like him? Do I not? Is this real? Is it not?*

We are a mystery I'm both desperate and terrified to solve.

We've been getting to know each other slowly, but now it's an explosion. We text for hours on end. About everything, but about sex too. Constantly.

Late one night while Jer lazes on the couch beside me, I huddle under a throw blanket. A movie I couldn't tell you a thing about drones away in the background. I stare at my phone.

> Stranger: Are you wearing panties right now?
>
> Mia: Always.
>
> Stranger: Not always. What color are they?
>
> Mia: Are you imagining them?
>
> Stranger: I'm looking at your picture. Yes. I want to imagine you in nothing but your panties.
>
> Mia: They're white and lacy.
>
> Stranger: Ugh, I wish you were here.
>
> Mia: Why?
>
> Stranger: Are you asking what I want to do to you, Mia?

Mia: Ummmm... I hate you. Fine. Yes.

Stranger: I would back you up against a wall, slide my hands around your throat, watch your eyes go from fear to trust, pry open your mouth with my thumb, taste your mouth.

Mia: I don't think you'd have to pry. I'd open for you willingly. I want your tongue in my mouth.

Stranger: See. That's what I mean. Perfect.

Mia: And then what?

Stranger: I'd do whatever I wanted with you.

Mia: Like what.

Stranger: Tell you to get on your knees.

Mia: Eh, maybe.

Stranger: Definitely.

Mia: Then what?

Stranger: I'll push you to the edge of what you think you can take, and then demand a little more. You'll love it.

Mia: What if I said no?

Stranger: You wouldn't.

Mia: What if I did?

Stranger: I'd ask you what you wanted, and we'd do that instead.

Mia: I almost believe it.

Stranger: Is he there?

Mia: Yes. He's watching TV.

Stranger: Take your panties off.

Mia: Now?

Stranger: Yes. I bet he doesn't even notice.

Mia: …

Stranger: Do it.

Mia: Done.

Stranger: You'd kneel and you'd love it.

So confident.
How could I not wonder?

And he's right. For him, I would kneel, I would choke, I would drool, I would beg. I think I'd do anything he asked—at least if our chemistry in the flesh is half as electric, as vibrant, as potent as it feels now.

This is the game we play. He proposes a sexual topic of conversation, I skirt it, dance around it, but never quite give in. I pull away.

We do this constantly.

My work suffers. I ignore Jeremy, neglect Annie, avoid my family.

I respond begrudgingly to texts from friends, arrange for a double date with Erica and Caesar the day after Thanksgiving. Erica suggests driving to the coast to stay at a B&B by the sea.

I suggest the Finger Lakes.

She finds us a hotel there, a fancy resort with fireplaces in every room.

I don't mention, though, that the Finger Lakes is close to where Stranger lives. I'm forcing our lives to bring us closer to one another, making it possible I might see him sooner than I'd ever imagined.

He's a sickness in my blood. The sickness is spreading. He's in my brain now, stretching his tentacles toward my heart.

Thanksgiving approaches rapidly.

I become paranoid about my phone.

I actually googled 'how to hide text messages?' and followed recommendations from cheaterstricks.com. Yes, I actually visited a website by that name, my face burning, my stomach rebelling, loathing myself as I did it. The advice was to use a friend's name, turn off notifications, disable the preview settings, delete all convos instantly, and of course, keep your phone on you at all times.

All of which made me feel like the moral equivalent of a slug.

I refuse to delete our conversations. I need a record of Stranger, proof that he's real. I spend lazy mornings rereading our discussions, analyzing them, laughing at them.

He sent me a pic of his tattoos, well, really of his whole body, in the mirror, almost naked.

Tattoos cover his shoulders, arms, chest and part of his stomach. They're beautiful and swirling and vibrantly colored, patterns and letters, a kaleidoscope of color. I want to touch them. I want to lick them.

And he has abs. Deep thick abdominal ridges. Thick biceps. Enormous shoulders. He's glorious.

I should delete the picture of him from my phone, but I don't. I email it to myself, save it to my notes and back it up on my laptop. I love that photo.

It's a wild risk—all of it. A social one. I will lose Annie's friendship if I break Jer's heart. An emotional one. I will lose Jer, who's been my anchor for so many years, I don't even know what I'd do without him. A financial one. I would lose the safety and comfort of his income. A filial one. My parents would disown me. And that carries its own fear, because they control the trust my grandparents set up in my name.

They'd be embarrassed in front of all their friends.

I could lose everything.

And him? Stranger has nothing on the line.

I try with Jeremy. Try spending time with him, but he's always busy. I try talking to him on the phone, but he just asks in his exasperated tone what it is I need, and the sad answer is... nothing. I need nothing from Jeremy. Stranger gives me everything I need.

It never stops. October slides into November. Every day, he's there in my phone. And because we're locked in this game of mutual attraction, it's a daily barrage. He starts sending me photos of what he's doing all day. And I send them back. My lunch—I send him photos of my salads. I don't even know why I do this. But it's fun. We talk about it. It feels like being together.

His lunch. Egg salad sandwich covered in pepper.

> Mia: Barf.

> Stranger: Says the woman eating canned tuna with frozen corn.

> Mia: It's good. And has very few calories.

> Stranger: Doubtful.

We do this all day, share inconsequential and meaningless events with each other.

> Stranger: Would you ever get a tattoo?

> Mia: I don't know. I kinda always wanted to…

> Stranger: Really?

> Mia: Yeah, but I'm too chicken.

> Stranger: What would you get?

> Mia: A quote.

> Stranger: Of course.

Mia: Why 'of course?'

Stranger: It's just what I expected you'd say. What quote?

Mia: Hmm... An Anais Nin one?

Stranger: Interesting. Which one?

Mia: 'What a mystery...'

Stranger: The lovesickness one?

Mia: Yes. I shouldn't be surprised that you know it.

Stranger: Why that one?

Mia: It's the quote that made me want to write. It's the feeling I always want to capture.

Stranger: You should get it then.

Mia: I can't.

Stranger: Why?

Mia: I just... my mom would hate it. My fiancé would hate it.

There's a long pause. He doesn't like it when I bring up Jeremy or my future with him.

> Stranger: It's your body.

> Mia: It's too late anyway. What would be the point now?

> Stranger: Sometimes you talk like your life is over. Where would you get it?

> Mia: My shoulder blade. In another language. Arabic maybe.

> Stranger: Why Arabic?

> Mia: Because it's pretty. And I don't really want everyone I meet to know what I have written on my back.

> Stranger: That would be pretty. Small black Arabic font. Tidy little lines on your smooth skin.

See, best girlfriend ever, only he has a cock, and he never lets me forget about it.

Now instead of watching an hour or two of TV at night, I sit in my bed and text with him. Increasingly descriptive, graphic and personal conversation.

Highly sexual. Highly explicit.

The week before Thanksgiving Jer is working late again, and I'm in bed, my face buried in my phone, telling him about the exercise videos I do.

> Mia: It's a lot of jumping. Fake punching. Dance moves.
>
> Stranger: I need to see this.
>
> Mia: Umm... No.
>
> Stranger: Oh, yeah! I'll sit on the couch right behind you, drink a beer and stare at your ass.
>
> Mia: You would make so much fun of me.
>
> Stranger: All the fun.

I can see it so perfectly. It feels so homey it makes my heart twist. That's what we'd be like as a couple. He'd be there, enjoying these stupid moments, teasing me, making me laugh, liking me, just being together. I have never had that before with a man.

> Stranger: And then I would fuck you.

That surprises a laugh out of me.

> Mia: Hmmm... I don't know, I get really sweaty. It's hard dancing like that.
>
> Stranger: I don't mind a little sweat. I'd stroke my dick, memorize the shape of your ass in your leggings, your tits bouncing for me.
>
> Mia: That would sort of ruin the point.

> Stranger: Oh?

> Mia: I mean, I'd probably just want to come over and help you out rather than keep up with the video.

> Stranger: What would you do?

He does this to me, Stranger. He forces me to say things, engage with him in these sorts of dialogues that leave me clueless as to how to proceed. I want to keep going, I want to play with him. I spend so much of my time frustrated and aroused, but my polite mannerly self wars with the horny little sex freak he's turning me into.

I clamp my lips together. He's waiting. He knows what he's doing. He plays me so well.

> Mia: Depends on my mood.

> Stranger: ???

Why can't he ever show me what to do? There's still so much I don't know about this man. He says he rarely smiles, even though I know he does with me sometimes. I wonder what I would do. Play out a few scenarios. Imagine straddling him, consider kneeling before him, maybe dancing closer and staying just beyond his reach?

> Mia: I don't know. Would I be comfortable with you? Would I be scared of you?

> Stranger: You'd get used to me.

Mia: Hmmm. I'm a pushover. I'd probably just glare down at you?

Stranger: That's all you got, Reed?

Mia: I can mean glare.

Stranger: Wouldn't phase me. I'd just sip my beer. Stare at your tits, keep stroking my dick.

Mia: I'm not patient. I'd get even more annoyed.

Stranger: Brat.

Mia: Definitely. I'd push at your thighs, shove at your beer, drop down between your legs. You can't ignore me.

Stranger: I'd tuck your hair behind your ear, pull you closer.

Mia: To make me suck your cock again?

Stranger: No.

Mia: Then what?

Stranger: To kiss your lips.

> Mia: Sigh.

> Stranger: Are you touching yourself?

I pause again. I wasn't. Not before. But I want to. My whole body is laser focused, a hundred percent on him. I go ahead, slide my hand down my pants. Try to get used to texting with only one thumb.

> Mia: Yes.

> Stranger: Are you wet?

> Mia: You know when you slide your hand down a woman's body, over the rise of her pelvic bone?

> Stranger: Yes.

> Mia: Down over the folds, where the skin is soft and warm, to the bottom, and sometimes you have to open her up?

> Stranger: Sure. Spread her open, get a finger inside, find out just how wet she is.

> Mia: Right. It's… dry on the outside, but then you find this one spot and it's all slippery and warm, and it opens up from there.

> Stranger: I know that feeling. It's the best feeling.

> Mia: That's not me right now.
>
> Stranger: ???
>
> Mia: There's no dry on the outside. I'm a mess. All the way through my panties.
>
> Stranger: ... Nicely done, Reed.
>
> Mia: I'm serious, Stranger.
>
> Stranger: I like that. I want to lay you back, spread your legs wide, lick your clit, fuck you with my tongue till your thighs shake.

I'm not even thinking anymore, I'm just doing whatever occurs to me, one handed and it's the longest, strangest foreplay I've ever had, but I have never been so turned on in my life. It makes sense in a way, we're writers. We think in words. This is an extension of that. I should feel guilty, but right now I'm not letting myself feel anything at all except how badly I want him.

I reread his words, touching myself.

> Mia: Pathetic whimper.
>
> Stranger: I'd make you lick my fingers, fill your mouth with the taste of your cunt.
>
> Mia: Hmmm... I don't know.
>
> Stranger: Keep touching yourself.

Mia: Trust me, I am.

Stranger: I like the idea of wrapping a hand—I've got big hands—around your neck, pulling you into my lap, a little rough, manhandle you, make you work for it.

Mia: Do it. I won't break. I can handle an awkward clamber into your lap.

Stranger: I like that. Awkward clamber. Get the angle right, my palms on your ass, line it up and slam you down. Fill you with my cock.

Mia: It would glide right in. I'm that wet.

Stranger: And I'm that hard. But I don't really like the girl on top. Not for long.

Mia: I hate being on top.

Stranger: You would. I'd toss you on your back, force your legs open wider, hold you down, kiss you gently and fuck you hard.

Mia: I love kisses!

Stranger: I'd give them all to you, stroke your face with my thumb, hold you still, all mine. Where would you want me to cum?

I blink at the phone.

Mia: Hmmm… what are my choices?

Stranger: Pussy? Ass? Mouth? Tits? Other?

Mia: Too hard to choose. Maybe not ass?

Stranger: 'Maybe' with a question mark. I like it. We'd be good together.

Mia: I think we would be.

Stranger: We understand each other.

Mia: Sexually yes.

Stranger: Definitely. How wet are you now?

Mia: It's disgusting. I may have to change the sheets.

Stranger: Killing me.

Mia: Are you touching yourself? Right now?

Stranger: I'm so hard it hurts.

Mia: I wish I could see.

Stranger: I could show you. We could face-time right now?

> Mia: No! Seriously. I'm not ready for that.
>
> Stranger: You could take it.
>
> Mia: Could is different than want to.
>
> Stranger: Fair enough. But Mia?
>
> Mia: Yeah?
>
> Stranger: We just officially sexted.
>
> Mia: Ohmygod! We did.

He's right. I didn't even really notice. I was just having so much fun with him, acting out the scenario, playing along, laughing, so turned on.

> Stranger: Yeah.
>
> Mia: I feel so awkward now.
>
> Stranger: Don't.
>
> Mia: I should go to bed.
>
> Stranger: Wait.
>
> Mia: I'm here.

> Stranger: Are you freaking out?
>
> Mia: No, I don't know. Maybe? I'm confused. And frustrated. Guilty.
>
> Stranger: I can understand that.
>
> Mia: I… want to go.
>
> Stranger: Right now? Go where?
>
> Mia: To sleep. I need to have an orgasm. I think my ovaries are blue blue blue
>
> Stranger: Do it. Think of me. We'll talk in the morning.
>
> Mia: Good night, Stranger.
>
> Night: Night, Sexty Mia.

I drop the phone on to my bedside table. It takes less than two minutes for me to have a truly impressive orgasm.

I fall asleep moments later.

When I wake in the morning, I convince myself that it was a one-time thing. That it won't happen again. That I'll talk to Stranger, break it off, end it.

But there's a text from him.

> Stranger: Stop beating yourself up.

I'm lying to myself.

I'm lying to everyone except this one person I've never even met.

A liar, that's what I am. And according to Stranger everyone lies. Does he lie to me? About what.

This is all a mess and it's getting messier.

I hate myself.

I have to talk to Jeremy. But when I call him first thing, he says that he just booked a two-week trip to Hong Kong. He's on his way to the airport now. When he comes back it will be Thanksgiving. I can't tell him over the phone. I can't tell him on a holiday. There's no time.

So, I don't tell him.

Instead, every single night for a week, I find myself in bed, texting—usually one-handed—or speaking with a strange man I've never met, but who feels more real than anyone I've ever known.

A BIG PINK DILDO

STRANGER

The wind off the Atlantic is fierce and salt-thick as I look at my phone. Mia just texted me a picture of her new body wash.

Juniper raspberry fizz.

I laugh.

> Stranger: That sounds like a cocktail.

> Mia: You can lick it off me later.

> Stranger: Deal.

> Mia: Smooch.

I tuck my phone into the pocket of my fleece. She does this a lot, sends me pictures of her shoes, flowers, new shit she's bought, her leafy healthy salads, funny reviews, things fans say, her friend's babies.

Stuff I'd normally find too boring to bother acknowledging.

But I don't. I encourage it. She's following my lead. I started this. Forced her to know the mundanity of my life so she'd start to care about me.

It's backfired.

She's turned me into her girlfriend.

Only, I'm not just a girlfriend, because 80% of the time, we are talking about sex. So even when I want to be free of her, her pussy is there in my mind, a magnificent mystery pussy, all wrapped up in this alluring secretive package. A woman who is prim on the outside, and wet hot and filthy on the inside, I just know it. Only I can't open this package. She's just there, tempting me, taunting me. Haunting me.

It's like the moment before a violent explosion. Something will have to give. Soon. We want to fuck each other badly, but we can't have each other. Not yet.

So instead, we talk about it. All the time.

It's fucking frustrating. I could just drive down there tomorrow if she'd let me.

But she won't.

Cold wind slaps at me as I pull open the door of a seedy casino at the ass end of Atlantic City.

The cold doesn't bother me. An ice bath wouldn't bother me. I'm always half hard and entirely frustrated these days. Jerking off and cold showers do nothing.

Fuck this.

I want to know how her ass cheeks would feel in my palms, and how her tongue tastes. I want to know how her pussy feels. I want to see the look in her eyes when I push inside her for the first time, hear the sounds she makes when she comes, feel her wiggle when I stick a finger in her ass. I want to hold her in my arms while she sleeps. I want to read with her and write with her and eat with her, shower and hike with her, watch her face change as she laughs.

Mostly, I just want to fuck her. Hard. Several times. Get this obsession with her out of my system.

Sometimes we put on documentaries, or set the TV to the same channel and watch at the same time, a simulation of a real relationship. It's fun but it's also stupid. All this time, so small a distance between us. I want more than text messages and a few phone calls. I want to sit on a couch with her head in my lap, watch a movie together in the flesh, a thought that bothers me because that too would be stupid. It would only hurt her once I'm gone.

More than anything, I want to know who wants to kill her. And why.

I ask her about her family, about her friends, about possible enemies, about her fiancé. But according to her, everyone is lovely and she is the worst human to walk the planet just for talking to me.

There is someone worse in her world, make that two someones.

Two killers. But only one of us actually wants her dead.

Which is why I'm here, staring across the bar at the man who she still pretends she wants to marry. Jeremy Dixon. Mia thinks he's in China. But he isn't.

He's here, in Atlantic City, where he comes two to three times a month. I know this because James and I have been playing at Sherlock and Watson, spying on him and everyone else in Mia's life.

No one could possibly think this casino is anything but a dump. And yet there he is, her baller of a fiancé, sitting at a blackjack table, his hair a mess, gambling away a thousand dollars an hour on a table that appears not to have been cleaned since Michael Jackson was the most famous person in the world.

And by his side? A woman I am certain is a prostitute. He shakes his head at her ruefully, scrubs his hands through his hair, and tosses a few more coins across the table as negligently as if they were useless. Another two hundred dollars down the shitter.

As far as gambling addictions go, his is mild. I've seen people toss a hundred grand around like it's air, but he can't afford that. Not anymore.

Jer, as she so sweetly calls him, is broke and gambling away his last dimes.

Mia, with her trust fund and paid-in-full townhouse, must look like easy money to him.

I shake my head. *He's a good man. Kind.* That's what she always says. He doesn't deserve this.

He sure as fuck doesn't deserve her. Not that I do, but still. I justify the destruction of her relationship with him by telling myself, she'll be better off alone than with him.

Dixon may or may not be Ender9551. But he could be.

Either way he's cheating on her.

James and I have been doing this for a while now. I've followed Jeremy to three separate casinos. There's always a woman. He always gets steadily drunker until his eyes are out of focus. He always loses. Eventually the woman will drag his sloppy ass out of here, and he'll stagger to the elevator.

We've watched the others too, looking for a clue. All we find are lies. This family is full of them.

James spent two whole days at the mom's country club, all decked out in golf clothes, a polo shirt, his hair styled, khaki shorts on. No one pesters a guy in a wheelchair, it's great cover. I wish I'd thought of it years ago.

He saw Mia's mom, took a picture of her kissing a man twenty years younger.

I went to see Annie and Greg personally, dressed up in a UPS uniform I bought online. Visited his law office, their house. She looked like what she is, tired and exhausted, though she did manage a quick smile for me when she noticed the package I tried to get her to sign for was for a different address.

Sorry, she said.

Greg... he looked like the kind of guy capable of killing someone, but he seemed like the type who'd do it on his own. There was something about the even, steady look in his eyes. I don't think he'd hire out his dirty work.

Jeremy though, he does seem like the type to hire a hit.

I watch him gamble for another hour. When he's so drunk that he spills his drink, I leave the bar, head through the lobby and up to the shitty hotel room I'll be staying in tonight.

I want to hear her voice.

It's 9:14pm.

She'll be at her desk like a good worker bee, typing away, probably writing about cum buckets and true love.

I tap my thumb on the name, but at that exact moment, my own phone buzzes. She's calling me.

"Hey," I say.

"Stranger?" Her voice is breathless. Maybe she's not at her desk.

"Yeah."

"What are you doing right now?"

I take the stairs up three at a time toward the fourth floor. "Nothing fun."

"Sit down."

"I'm fine."

"It's big news." She's smiling. I can hear it in her voice. I've never known anyone who could smile with just their voice.

I find my face stretching in automatic response. "I'm good."

"I really think you should take a seat," she chirps out, and I picture her bouncing on her tiptoes.

"Hit me with it."

"Okay, get ready. I'm so excited." She blows out a long stream of air. "I've wanted this forever. Ready?"

"Yes." I stick my key card in the slot.

"Okay, okay. Okay." She takes a deep breath. "Are you ready?"

"Mia."

"Okay. I was just selected to be featured by Wet Panty."

I pause, one foot in the door. "I understand no part of that sentence."

She laughs. "It's a blog. A big deal blog. I submitted months ago."

"A blog called Wet Panty?"

"Their real name is Wet Panty Readers, but everyone just calls them Wet Panty."

"Everyone." I picture the President of the United States talking about Wet Panty over cocktails with various heads of state. Oprah on her talk show. "The Queen of England." I make my voice sound old, breathy and high, mimic a fancy British accent. *"Whet pehnti."*

"Yes!" she says, laughing. "Everyone. They're a big deal. Don't mock me. This is huge, Stranger! Be happy for me."

"I am happy for you." I close the door softly, so she won't hear and ask questions I don't want to have to lie to answer. "When will this happen?"

"April."

"That's good. So an interview?"

"An interview, and they're even going to do an excerpt from my latest book."

"We should celebrate."

She laughs. I like her laugh. It makes me forget everything else, forget that when James is walking, when she's safe, I'll be long gone. "How?"

I think for a minute. "Tell me what you're wearing."

"It's not sexy. At all."

That makes me smile. "What is it?"

"Leggings and a big chunky sweater."

That doesn't seem bad. I picture sliding my palm down the bare, smooth skin of her abdomen under the sweater. "And your panties?"

"You've got a thing for panties."

"I've got a thing for your panties." Let them be the dayglow ones.

"They're enormous."

"Why?"

"Why not?"

That's a decent question. I can hardly mention I've seen her panty drawer. "Big panties can be hot actually. What color?"

"Black."

Not neon then. That's okay. I like that image. Dark panties against her pale skin. "Take the sweater off."

There's a pause. This is what she does. She has to pause, think, analyze, get herself all charged up, process the guilt, outweigh it with the excitement I offer. I imagine it's exactly how she'd be if we were standing at the top of the waterfall I hike to, and I told her to jump in. She'd peer over the edge, think about it, acknowledge the fear, bite her lip, ask some questions... and eventually, after great deliberation, jump.

"I took my bra off a long time ago."

"So?" I ask.

"So... I'll be tits out."

"Perfect. Take off your pants too."

A long, dramatic inhale. Just like I expected. And then a pause with rustling in the background. "Done."

My phone pings. James texted.

"Hang on, Mia."

> James: Check it. Greg curbsided a guy in college, sophomore year. The guy lost a bunch of teeth. Greg's parents paid for a new set, and it was wiped off his record. The judge gave him some community service. A guy like that…

> Stranger: Where are you getting this?

> James: Old facebook posts. AND get this… Penny, the girlfriend of the brother, the zen decorator—her dad killed her mom in a drunken rage and then killed himself.

I frown, unsure what to make of any of that. It's a lot to process.

"Stranger? You okay?"

I clear my throat. A guy who'd curbside someone is a guy capable of extreme and inventive violence, but still strikes me as the kind of guy who'd save himself the money and kill Mia himself. "Your big black panties. Take them off too."

I'm not sure I think anything at all of the revelation about Penny's dad, except she had shit for a childhood. Where the hell did she go after her parents were dead?

A foster home probably. Hopefully better than the ones I knew.

Mia hums softly. "Are you fully clothed?"

"Yes. That's how it has to be. Get naked for me, Mia. No panties."

She whimpers. "Okay."

I grin. "Now walk to your fridge."

I walk to the minifridge and open it, stare at the array of bottles. "What do you see?"

"Food mostly. It's cold, Stranger."

I imagine hard nipples and sigh. Someday I will fuck her in her fridge, with her face all pressed up against the cheese drawer, her head knocking against a milk jug. I will palm her tits as they bounce in the cold. "Pick out something celebratory. We're going to have a drink together."

I pull out a beer, remove the cap, and listen as she opens a bottle of wine, pours a glass.

"This is silly," she says. "I'm just hanging out naked in my apartment."

"Then go into your bedroom. Take the wine."

She swallows so thickly, I can feel it.

"How many vibrators do you have?"

Silence.

"I hear crickets, Mia. Answer the question."

"Two," she says, a little squeaky.

"Take a picture. Text it to me."

"No."

I raise my brows. Mia rarely says no. She's a yes person. A giver. In fact, she has a dangerous compulsion against saying no. If the wrong person got a hold of her, they could take serious advantage of her.

Like me.

Or that fuck, Dixon.

"Why not?"

"Please, Stranger. One of them isn't embarrassing. It's just a little thing that buzzes. But the other one…"

This will be good. I grin. "Do it."

"Don't judge me?"

"Never."

"Promise?"

"Yes."

Another one of her long, slow inhales. "Fine."

See? For me, she always jumps, eventually. I sip my beer and wait.

"Why do you like embarrassing me so much?"

"It's funny. And you like it. If you didn't, you'd ignore me."

"I want something in return."

This is new. Mia, the negotiator. "What?"

"I don't know."

I shrug. "Think about it. Let me know. Send me the picture."

"I just did."

My phone blips a second later, I glance down at the screen. I smile. "Perfect."

"I didn't buy it!" she says, high-pitched.

It's hot pink, and though it's hard to tell from the photo—it's not like she laid a ruler down beside it—it appears to be enormous, with thick veins, a broad mushroom tip, and a hefty ballsack at the base.

I laugh. "Have you used it?"

She's silent.

"That's a yes." I take a long sip. "Use it now."

"Right now?"

"Are you wet?"

"For you?"

"Yes, for me."

"Always."

Like that, my dick is hard, straining in my pants. "I want to see."

"Hang on."

She does something, muffled noises in the background. I sip my beer and wonder. I doubt she'd send me a photo of her pussy. I haven't asked. I've thought about it so much it's pathetic. Wondered at the shape of the outer lips, the inner lips, the color. I know she waxes. She's told me that. And she's told me she's a real blond, though not so much down there.

This is like the fucking longest striptease in the history of blue balls. I've never had to work so hard for a chick or a hit in my life.

My phone blips again.

And I suck in a long breath. She sent me a picture of her fingers. Index and middle, glistening in low light, covered in pussy.

That's unexpected. My dick is jealous. "Not bad, Reed."

"You were hoping I'd send you a picture of down there."

"No. I knew you wouldn't."

"Are you disappointed that it wasn't something else?" Her voice sounds small.

"Not at all. If you were here, I'd lick your fingers, back you up onto that bed of yours, and fill your cunt with my rampant, swollen, angry, frustrated dick and make you gag on that big pink dildo while you did it."

She whimpers, all breathy and sweet.

"Now shove that thing in there and pretend it's me." I drop down onto the crappy queen-sized bed, take pity on my poor dick and unbutton my way-too-tight-in-the-crotch jeans.

She lets out a soft lady-grunt, and I picture her brows lowered, all intense focus while she tries to work that ridiculous thing into her pussy. I wrap my hand around my cock and wince. It's painfully hard.

This would be a shitty celebration though if all we did was jerk off. "Who'd you call first when you found out about Wet Panty?"

"You." Her voice is all breathy. "I've wanted this since I started writing. No one else would understand what it means to me."

"I'm happy for you, Mia." I wish I could be there with her, actually hold her body, feel the warmth of her skin, breathe her in.

"And honored you thought of me first." I'm not sure anyone else has ever done that, wanted to share their accomplishments with me. Is this how couples work? Is this what Mia would be like if we were truly together? Wanting nothing more of me than to share the good times and the bad?

"I wish you were here," she whispers. She's never actually said those words before.

"Me too." But it makes me instantly uncomfortable. I'm not that guy. I don't stay. I ruin things. I kill people. Leave them. I abandon them and break them. I fuck everything up. All I need from Mia is to know she's safe. "Now get in your bed."

"Already am."

"What is your favorite book you've written?"

She thinks for a minute. "Maybe my third one."

"What's the name?"

She tells me, and I pull it up online and download it.

"What's your favorite sex scene in the book?"

"The one where he bends her over the dining table."

That makes me smile. Mia likes it from behind. "Open your kindle to that page. Tell me what percentage to go to."

"You just bought it?"

"Yes."

There's a long pause. "That's... really sweet of you. Thank you, Stranger."

"Percentage?"

"Forty-four."

I scroll through until I get there. "Start reading. I'll do the guy's dialogue. You do the rest."

"Oh my god. This will be so embarrassing."

"It will be fun. When we're done, you'll use that other little vibrator of yours, give yourself an orgasm, and I'll listen to you come."

She's breathing fast now. "And you, what will you do?"

"I'll jerk off listening to you, I'll pretend it's my dick inside you, fucking you."

She starts to read, a little shaky at first, but pretty soon she's laughing, and then she stops laughing, and I know she's really turned on.

By the time we're done, I know something new. Mia yelps when she comes, a crescendo of panting, rising *ah, ah, ahhh, aaaahhh, AAAAHHHH!*

"Stranger?" she whispers, later.

"Yeah." I lay back on the pillow, close my eyes and pretend we're together, that I can feel her breath on my neck, her head getting heavier as she drifts to sleep.

"I know what I want from you."

"What's that?"

"I want a dick pic."

I'm almost too tired to laugh, but not quite.

"I do!" she says softly, fading away from me. "I want to see it."

Her breathing slows, going even and steady.

"Mia?" I say, but there's no response. She fell asleep on me.

I lie like that for a long time, listening to her sleep. For a while, just for fun, I let myself imagine a world in which I'm a different man. The kind of man who gets to keep people.

I'd keep her. We'd sleep together like this. Maybe buy the land near the farmhouse, build a second house there near James. Write together. Laugh together. Share nights like tonight, celebrate our wins together.

But just as I close my eyes, I remember something. I destroy everything I touch.

I don't want to destroy Mia.

So at some point, after we find Ender, I'll go ahead and tell her the truth, leave her life for good.

Hopefully it will come soon, maybe before Thanksgiving. This whole thing is starting to hurt me some place I thought was past feeling.

A DICK PIC

MIA

Thanksgiving Dinner is at my parent's house. They live about thirty minutes away in Newport, in a house overlooking the river.

Jer picks me up.

Alone.

Which makes me sad because usually Annie and Greg come with us. This year, because of the babies, they can't come, so we're staying the night.

My brother flew in yesterday with his new girlfriend, Penny.

It will feel so quiet and lonely without Annie.

> Mia: I miss you. You sure I can't convince you to come? Or let me drop off food tomorrow? Anything?

> Annie: No. Seriously. NO! Please. Greg is home for the next few days. I just want to let him suffer the misery of babies. I plan to sleep the entire time. Distract me. How is work?

> Mia: WET PANTY ACCEPTED ME!!!!

> Annie: I knew it! When? WHEN?

> Mia: Not for a while. Spring. But I'm so excited. So excited! It's working, Annie. My writing!

> Annie: I'm proud of you, friend. I'm living through you now. The highlight of my month was the UPS guy who came two weeks ago. He was really dumb, stared at me like he didn't speak English, brought the wrong package, but holy hell, he was hot, like something out of one of your books. So, I'll just quietly live through you. Keep up what you're doing. So much love.

> Mia: You'll be back at work soon. This is just a temporary thing.

> Annie: No, Mia, this is my life now. Shit and screaming. I'm adapting. It will get better.

I want to ask her if this is normal. Most people like their kids, right? I mean, shouldn't she feel excited about the twins and the future and what they'll do next?

I don't know. I just wish she weren't so unhappy.

When we arrive, Mom banishes everyone from the kitchen but me. I barely have time to wash my hands and tie on an apron before she shoves a butcher's knife in my hand and sets me to work. On onions, of course. Mom's nothing if not canny and she hates how they make her eyes tear up and ruin her mascara.

By the time I'm done with the four that needed chopping, I'm full on crying, tears pouring down my face. "These onions must have been genetically modified."

She rolls her eyes. "For goodness sake, it can't be as bad as all that."

"Then why didn't you do it?" I wipe my eyes for the fifteenth time with tissues. "I'm going to have to go redo my makeup."

"Wait until Danny's girlfriend comes down. I'll put her to work on the Brussels sprouts. She's been up there forever."

I recognize that tone. Here we go.

"Is she nice?" I turn on the burner and lay down a few thick slabs of bacon.

"Her real name is Penelope. Did you know that? But she chooses to go by Penny."

She says it like it's a bad thing. Like the name Penny means something sordid.

"What's wrong with the name Penny?"

She raises a brow and blows her honey-gold bangs out of her eyes. She shakes her head tightly and uses her foot to close the under-range oven door where she's just basted the turkey, her earrings sparkling in the dimmed pendant lights in the kitchen.

"Wait until you see her breasts."

I wish I could record this conversation for Stranger to hear. He'd love it.

"What's wrong with her breasts?"

Mom holds her hands in front of her chest like she's cupping a pair of melons. "Humongous."

"Mom! She can't help that."

She makes a face. "They're fake."

From the sofas on the other side of the island, Jer chants at the TV, and Danny and Dad join in. "No. No. NO! NO!"

"Like that's a sin, Mom," I say. "Lots of women ha—"

On the screen, the football slips through the player's fingertips, hits green turf and bounces out of bounds.

My dad surges to his feet. "Did you see that? How could he drop that pass? He gets paid millions of dollars. To catch a goddamned football. How the hell did he drop it?"

Jer rests his long fingers on one hip. "Bastard even held out for more money on his contract this year."

"Why are they even playing him? Desanto is way better," Danny says.

"You've got to be joking. He couldn't catch his own balls with both hands." Dad drops back into the sofa.

Jer sips his beer, still shaking his head at the TV irritably. He laughs at whatever Danny said, too quietly for me to hear. He fits in with them. He's comfortable with them. He likes them. They like him.

Jer is family.

I try to imagine it with Stranger, picture the tattoos on his arms. The full sleeves of flowers, a dragon, scales, a swirling assortment of images that mattered to him at various points in his life. Vibrant and bold, blues and greens and reds. I picture his unshaved jaw, his too-long for fashion hair.

He would stick out.

Does he even watch football? I doubt it. Oddly, it's something we haven't discussed before. My fingers ache to text him and ask.

If he were here, he'd have sweet-talked Mom into letting him stay in the kitchen with us. I bet he'd have her laughing, telling all her secrets, giving him early bites of food. He's charming when he wants to be.

Jer, on the other hand, may as well have been born to my parents, in his pressed chinos and his brown loafers. He's a handsome man with his ascetic face, his easy grin, his carefully groomed hair. When I look at him, I feel comfortable.

Mom purses her lips. "Who chooses to be called Penny?"

I turn off the stove and use tongs to move the bacon to a plate covered in paper towel. "Her mother probably."

"It's rude though, isn't it? Spending so long getting ready? She didn't even offer to help us cook."

I blot at the bacon with a paper towel.

"Worried about losing him, Mom?" I shred the bacon, and dump it in beside the peppers, onions, celery and toasted sourdough.

She makes a face and pulls the oysters from the fridge. "She's from California."

Yep. There's the problem. She's scared Danny will fall in love, stay on the sunshine coast and we'll never see him again. She's probably right.

She mixes in the oysters.

I pat her back. "It'll be okay, Mom. I promise. We can facetime."

"Facetime," she grouses. "Why can't he marry a nice local girl. Someone whose parents we know."

"Someone close by?"

"Yes. Not someone who lives across the country. Facetime. Pah. And her *mother*. Don't even get me started. Every time I ask about her family, she gets all pinchy-faced. She's lying about something. Trust me."

She keeps talking, but I'm barely listening.

I keep thinking about Stranger.

I'm always thinking about Stranger.

I want to facetime with him. We've talked about it. But I'm nervous, what if we do and we suddenly realize there's nothing there, that it's all an illusion.

As if on cue, my phone buzzes from the counter in front of me. I turn it over while Mom stirs eggs and turkey drippings into the stuffing.

It's him. It's always him now.

> Stranger: Thankful, baby?

> Mia: Baby? I'm always feeling thankful. Happy Thanksgiving, Stranger.

> Stranger: I dunno. It came out. No good?

I think for a long moment. No one has ever called me baby before. But, no. I don't think Stranger thinks I'm inept or childish. I think it's his way of letting me know he cares.

> Mia: Baby is fine. I kinda like it.

> Stranger: I kinda like you.

> Mia: Sigh.

> Stranger: What are you doing at this precise moment in time?

> Mia: Making stuffing with my mom. You?

> Stranger: So... you're saying it would be weird if I sent you that dick pic?
>
> Mia: Not at all! SEND IT!
>
> Stranger: How do you make your stuffing?
>
> Mia: Like every good New Englander. Bacon, oysters, sourdough and peppers. You? QUIT TEASING ME, I WANT MY PIC.
>
> Stranger: James and I are grilling a turkey. Our dad made it with fruit. James wanted to recreate it. Apples, cranberries and shit.

I freeze for a minute, reading his message. I want to ask so badly about his mom. He rarely mentions her, but somehow I know something bad happened. Things he hasn't said, more than anything. He just... he seems so happy right now. I don't want to ruin that.

> Mia: That sounds good, but weird. It's sweet? Wait... Are you grilling OUTSIDE?
>
> Stranger: Sweet but salty too. It's good. You'd like it. Yes, outside. Drinking beer.
>
> Mia: It's like... 33 degrees out, down here. It must be freezing up there. DICK PIC ME. NOW!!!

> Stranger: We've got coats on. Built a big fire in the pit. Gogo has a dog sweater and boots on. She thinks she looks so cool. It's nice. One thing is missing though…

> Mia: Football?

> Stranger: You.

> Mia: Sigh.

> Stranger: I wish you were here. I miss you.

"What in the world are you smirking at, Mia?" Mom's voice cuts through me.

I jerk so hard, I nearly drop my phone.

Jeremy looks up from his seat in the living room. His eyes glide over mine, his jaw tightens. He's noticed that I've been more absent lately—I can see it in his eyes.

"Sorry, Mom. It's the wedding website I told you about. Someone likes my bouquet selections."

"For heaven's sake, it's Thanksgiving, Mia. Focus on your family, not internet wackos. Jeremy!" she calls. "You need to do something. She's practically having an affair with the internet."

My cheeks heat.

"She's doing a good job planning the wedding." He smiles, but it doesn't reach his eyes as he turns back to the TV.

Mom shoves the stuffing into the oven. Dad did a lot of the prep work earlier. He loves to cook, but Thanksgiving Day, Mom doesn't like anyone in the kitchen but me. She's happy here, slicing away, rolling her eyes and pretending to hate football.

While she's distracted, I turn back to my phone.

> Mia: Me too. That sounds like fun. Cold, but fun.

> Stranger: I'd keep you warm. We could snuggle by the fire.

My belly does a little happy dance. It's so easy to imagine. Being there, with them, instead of here. Cold outside, but warm by the fire, against his big warm body,

I put the phone down in the shadows behind the fruit bowl where no one will see it.

Penny comes down.

She's beautiful. With thick dark hair, puffy lips and wide green eyes. Her breasts are large, but they're not porn-star large like Mom let on.

She offers to help, but my mom shoos her off into the living room and then frowns that she isn't in the kitchen helping us.

Poor Penny. She will never be able to do the right thing by Mom.

When the food is all prepped or in the oven, the amaretto carrots and the mashed potatoes, the butternut squash, the creamed corn and the sweet potatoes, I sit on the edge of my dad's chair.

The game goes on forever.

Penny knows the teams, the names, the rules. She sits beside Danny and holds his hand. It makes me smile. They seem like a unit.

Mom brings out a tray of cheese and meats, nuts and fig spreads. Dad opens a couple bottles of red wine for dinner and gets them decanting on the table.

I keep thinking about Stranger.

Jer rests his hand on my thigh. He smiles, but again, it doesn't reach his eyes.

I wonder for the millionth time what he thinks. If he senses me pulling away.

I lose the battle, I can't resist the pull of Stranger.

"Gotta go to the bathroom," I say.

I check my phone. And laugh. Then I stop laughing, because everything gets all hot and throbby.

It's a dick pic.

It's perfect. Just exactly what you'd expect. Long and thick, some veins, those abs, the tats. A big round head that makes my mouth water. I want it… everywhere.

The message:

> Stranger: You're welcome to come up anytime. I mean that. Also, you have no idea how hard it is to get a fucking boner when your hand is this cold.

I blow out a long, shuddery breath.

That's Stranger's insane magic.

Sex… and unexpected sweetness with a little humor and odd curious factoid. I immediately have a million questions about penises and cold and bloodflow, and what he had to do to overcome it all.

And then, I just want to see him.

We've discussed meeting. It's like a game we play. We envision crazy scenarios, play them out. Imagine it together, like a joint game of make believe, what would happen if we met in a bar, a restaurant, a hotel, at his house, at mine. But we never quite so expressly laid it out there.

I glance at the living room. No one is paying any attention to me.

Mia: Be there in ten with pie and wine. (I LIKE THE PIC. A LOT.)

Stranger: Fuck pie. Front door is open. Bring whipped cream. Leave your panties behind.

Mia: Panties go where I go. I hate whipped cream.

Stranger: Not with me. I will wreck your panties. Bring the whipped cream for me. I'll lick it off your missing panties.

Mia: Are you drunk, Stranger?

Stranger: Very. Come.

Mia: Come to you? Or just plain come?

Stranger: Either. Both. Buckets. I don't care. I just want you. Are you still insisting we kindamaybesorta won't ever meet?

Mia: A little bit.

Stranger: You'll give in eventually. You know it. I know it. You're in Providence, right?

Mia: Usually. Tonight, I'm at my parents. Newport.

> Stranger: That's not even a three-hour drive. We could meet tomorrow half way between in a cozy sea-side fishing town. Nice warm B&B overlooking the Atlantic, cuddle under the covers and watch the gray waves.

> Mia: We'll figure something out. Definitely not tomorrow.

> Stranger: I want to see you, Mia. Keep your panties on if it helps. At least at first.

> Mia: I want to see you too. With or without panties.

> Stranger: Both. Soon.

> Mia: Soon.

> Stranger: No panties.

> Mia: Panties.

> Stranger: Half panties.

> Mia: Deal. Half panties. Whatever those are.

> Stranger: Half panties. Half the time. Deal. No take backs.

"Mia? What are you doing?"

It's my mom again. So close, I jump.

She moves in, leaning over so our shoulder touch, peering down at my phone.

I black out the screen.

"You're texting someone. That's not a website, Mia."

Nothing comes out of my mouth. My brain can't produce a single word.

"Are you cheating on Jeremy?" she hisses.

"What?" I step back. "No. Of course not."

Her mouth hardens. "You're lying."

"I am not."

"You are. You always say *what!* all innocent, with big wide eyes, right before you lie."

At least she's whisper-shouting rather than actually shouting. I'll give her that much.

"I'm not cheating on him, Mom. Jeez. I'm just texting with a friend."

Her eyes narrow. "A *male* friend?"

"Yes."

"Someone you met online?"

"Yes."

"An internet stranger man?"

"Mom. Back off. I mean it."

She doesn't back off. Her lips tighten like they always do when she gets mad, the diamonds in her earrings glittering like shards of ice. "You are *engaged*. To a very nice boy. And beyond that, the internet is full of freaks. He could be a three-hundred-pound child-molester. *With no teeth!*"

"You make it sound like having no teeth is worse than being a child molester."

"I didn't raise you to be stupid. Or callous. Have you forgotten about Jeremy? Don't you dare break that man's heart. We just put down a deposit on a band for crying out loud."

"What! Mom, it's just a friend. Please, stop."

Her eyes narrow to slits. "You said 'what!'"

I sigh. Put my phone away. "It's nothing, Mom. Please. Let's just enjoy the holiday."

The oven beeps. *Thank you, oven.*

In icy silence, we set about preparing the last of the food items. Biscuits, gravy.

She begrudgingly lets Penny help add the garnishes to the turkey, and we all carry the food to the table where we say what we're thankful for before eating.

Jeremy says me.

I say him, but inside I'm thinking *Stranger, Stranger, Stranger.*

Mom shoots me a glare like death.

She asks Penny what she's thankful for.

"Danny," says Penny instantly. "So, so thankful for him. It's like I got a family when I met him."

Mom narrows her eyes. "What about your own family?"

Penny's eyes flit from her plate to Mom's. "I love my family. I just meant another one. Family is important to me."

Mom's eyes narrow to slits. "Danny, how's work?"

Danny sighs into his wine. "Let's talk about anything but my work."

Mom shakes her hair behind her shoulders. "Why will neither of my children ever tell me about their jobs. Fine, Jeremy, how are your parents? Keith misses golfing with your dad."

Jer starts blabbering about our Christmas trip to Fort Meyer. In detail. I still haven't agreed to go.

I take a deep breath, think about my dick pic.

And we all tuck in.

After dinner, everyone who didn't cook cleans.

Mom goes to bed early, casting me a lingering, suspicious glance.

Penny and I drink a little too much wine.

She admits she's head over heels for my brother, which makes me happy. She says she thinks Jeremy is cute. He is.

Cute.

Sweet.

Nice.

Safe.

I go upstairs, fall into my childhood bed, with its white and pink striped coverlet, flowery wallpapered walls, the sounds of clanking dishes below where the guys are scrubbing a pile of dishes the size of the Empire State building, and I'm alone, staring at my phone.

That's all I do now.

Stare at my phone and wonder.

> Stranger: Facetime?
>
> Mia: Right now?
>
> Stranger: Why not? Is he there? I just want to see your face.
>
> Mia: Not at the moment.
>
> Stranger: We can be quick. I just want to see you. It's Thanksgiving. I'm thankful for you.

I stare at my phone.

I should have at least half an hour before Jer comes up to bed.

What am I doing?

I think this every day, all day.

Stranger came into my life at the exact moment it felt like doors were slamming down around my entire life. Talking with him is like gulping down great big breaths of fresh sunshiny air after a lifetime indoors.

> Mia: Okay. If I hang up real fast, you'll know why.

I consider locking the door, but I think that would be more suspicious. Instead I go into the bathroom, lock that door. Sit in the bathtub and pull closed the hot pink shower curtain.

The phone sings, I answer, and there he is.

Stranger and I are facetiming.

His face fills the screen, dark hair, light eyes, almost-bearded chin. He's in his house, sitting on a couch, his dark brows all furrowed.

"Quit glowering at me," I say.

"Are you in the shower?"

"Yes."

His brows lower for a single second, and I imagine him thinking that's a strange choice, then figuring out why, and his mouth tightens a little. "I feel bad. I shouldn't have pushed."

"It's okay. I wanted to do this too." I stare at my face in the little icon at the top of the screen. I should have taken a minute to check my makeup. My hair's a mess, my nose is just slightly red and my mascara has left black smudges under my eyes.

I move the angle a little and fix my hair.

"Stop," he says.

"Stop what?"

"Worrying about what I'm thinking as I look at you. I like how you look. Relax."

I suck in my lips. "I'm totally relaxed, squatting in my childhood bathtub, talking to you." Big sigh. "My mom accused me of cheating on Jer."

"With me?"

"She called you a wacko and an internet freak. Said you probably weigh three hundred pounds and molest children. And have no teeth."

"Two-ten. I molest no one. Maybe you. I have all my teeth." He grins, flashing his pearly whites. "You okay?"

"Yeah."

"I wouldn't know, but it seems to be a running joke in our society that Thanksgiving dinners make everyone unhappy. You're not alone."

More than ever, I'm curious to know more about his mom, but I don't ask. "Mom hates my brother's girlfriend."

"Why?"

"Her name is Penny and she has big boobs."

"And your mom has a distinct preference for quarters and flat-chests?"

"Something like that."

"What would she say about me?"

I wrinkle my nose, narrow my eyes and lean toward the screen. "*Tattoos*—all over his *arms*, his neck, his fingers, in *color*, and god only *knows* where else! And *beard* scruff! Never *seen* such a *thing* in my *life*."

He smiles and does his breathy, sexy laugh thing, those dimples dancing in his cheeks. I've been afraid of this. That the reality would dissipate, pale, weaken all of it somehow.

It doesn't.

This man... I think he could have a wart, and I would swoon.

This keeps getting harder and harder.

"How's your brother?" I ask.

"He couldn't hang." He turns the screen around, and as he gets the screen angled the right way, I see more of his house. A fire in a stone fireplace, a mossy carpet laid over wood floors, a cathedral ceiling, an espresso dark leather sectional.

And a man, laying on it facedown, his arm dangling down to touch the carpet below, a blanket over his torso. And no legs. There's nothing there beyond a few inches of thigh below his groin. Stranger turns the camera away fast, too fast, almost like he didn't mean for me to see.

"What does that mean, 'couldn't hang?' He passed out?"

"Yup." The screen narrows in on his brothers face. He's handsome, though his hair is tidier and his face is more clean-shaven, sweeter maybe, than Stranger's, so he seems less threatening. He, too, has tattoos on his arms.

The screen turns again, and Stranger is back. With his dark, hooded eyes. A little farther away though. A tight navy Henley clings to some very nice pecs. "Drank his ass under the table."

"Onto the leather sectional you mean."

"Or that."

"How's Gogo?"

"Took herself off to bed hours ago. She can't hang either. Talk to me, Mia."

"I don't just talk," I mimic his words.

"Tell me about those half panties."

"Do you have a panty fetish?"

"Only for yours. Fuck Mia, the things I would do to your panties."

Full body hot flash, I swear. "I'm wearing a thong."

"Color?"

"White."

He makes a face like that's disappointing somehow.

"What's wrong with white?"

"Nothing. Lacy? Silky?"

"Lacy."

"Show me."

"You seriously want me to show you my underpants right now?"

The dimple flashes in one cheek. "I showed you mine."

That he did.

I chew on my lip, narrow my eyes. Don't overthink it. "Okay."

I stand, step out of the tub and move to the mirror. Why not? I might as well own this. Accept it. Quit fucking around. I'm engaging in an emotional affair with a man I've never met.

I angle the screen so he can see me in the mirror. His eyes move and I know he's probably checking out my body. He's got to be curious.

I'm wearing a black dress. He can see some things, but not everything. "Hang on, Stranger."

I put the phone down, ruffle up my hair, fix the mascara bleed under my eyes, and whip my dress over my head.

White thong. White bra. My breasts aren't big, but they look okay. It's the end of the day and I just ate like a hog, but I'm not fat. I suck in a little.

Who am I? Who am I? Who am I?

I am a woman who shows her body to Stranger. Over the phone.

I hold the phone up so he can see me.

Twist at the waist so he can see my butt too. Go big right?

He doesn't say anything for a long moment. My skin rises with goosebumps. I instantly regret it.

I turn the screen around so he can only see my face.

There's a new gleam in his eyes, something that almost smacks of possession.

"When are you going to give in and agree to meet me?"

I chew on my lip. I want him to say something about my body. Something nice. Something good. So I don't feel stupid.

"I don't know."

"Figure it out. You just showed me your body because you wanted me to know exactly how you looked. So there wouldn't be any surprises. Whether you know it or not, you're getting ready. And if you think for one second I'm going away now, after seeing you like that, you're wrong."

"Soon, maybe. We'll figure it out."

"Start thinking more seriously about this Mia. I asked for a glimpse of some panty, you stripped down. You just escalated this exponentially." There's a menacing growl to his voice now. He's issuing orders, commanding, making demands.

I like it.

"Really?"

His teeth flash in a wide grin. "Really."

"How much? Like if it were a scale. One through ten."

"A scale? You took this from a five to an eight."

I gape at him. "We were at a *five*? All those raunchy texts? The dildo? The dick pic? That was only a *five!*"

His lips curl. "Yes. A five."

"What was one?"

"When you admitted you liked cum buckets via chat."

"That was an accident. And a two?"

"When you gave me your number and took off your panties." That word, from his lips, takes on a totally new meaning. He says it like a caress, like he's dragging his nails down my spine.

"I feel like that should have been more like a three or a four."

His lips stretch into a half smile. "It was a two."

"Three?"

"The dildo."

"Four?"

"When we fell asleep on the phone together. That was an emotional one."

"Five?"

"Just now, when you agreed to facetime."

I laugh at the screen. "You have this all planned out?"

His face wrinkles up and his eyes close in a laugh. "Not really. I just like messing with you."

Dimples and warmth. Stranger is breathtaking when he laughs. He makes me feel like I'm the only woman in the world. I'm dead. Just dead and gone.

"What comes next?"

"Meeting."

I purse my lips. "What's a nine?"

"When I fuck you." My stomach tightens. I can see it in the mirror. It's a physical response, almost like I've been kicked.

"And a ten."

He swallows, looking at me with eyes that look conflicted, doubtful for the first time. He shakes his head. "I don't know, Mia. I'm just fucking around."

I stare back for a long time. "You said you never smile."

"And?"

"You've been smiling this whole conversation. Until just now."

He drags his hand over his mouth like maybe I struck a nerve. "Go to sleep, beautiful Mia."

THAT HOT GUY WITH THE EVERYWHERE TATS

MIA

Jer comes into the room about five minutes later. When he sees me standing in the bathroom wearing nothing but my bra and panties, his eyes widen briefly. "Really? You want to do it? Now? Here?"

He shuts the door fast, looking around like a kid caught trespassing.

I'm brushing my teeth and pause to spit in the sink, a big sudsy pile of white glop that lingers over the drain cover. I don't answer, just keep brushing.

"We've never done it here. What if they hear us?"

I cup water in my palm, rinse out my mouth, spit. "You're probably right."

He touches my hip, and I resist the urge to pull away. He pushes me toward the bedroom. "I'll be right in."

My phone is still on the bathroom sink.

I cannot leave it there.

The text chain.

The evidence of the facetime.

The dick pic!

All it would take is Stranger texting at the wrong moment. Or Jer suddenly getting curious.

"I still need to wash my face." I slide around his body, back toward the sink.

He doesn't say anything. Just sets about his own nighttime routine. Is this what happens to everyone when they've been together long enough? Would this happen with Stranger if we were together for five years? Does it always become predictable and staid? Or are some people just more suited to one another?

"Jer?"

"Hmmm?" He's flossing his teeth, rotating his jaw and baring his teeth at the mirror like an aggressive orangutan. It would be funny if he weren't so earnest.

"Jer? Do you ever wonder if we're right for each other?"

His gaze snaps to mine in the mirror. He stiffens, lowering his hands, the seagreen floss stretched tight between them, tethered between his thumbs.

"I know we are." He turns toward me, the floss going slack as he unwinds it from his fingers, cocking his hip like he does when he's annoyed. "Life isn't like one of your books. You do know romance novels aren't real, right?"

That takes me aback. "What do romance novels have to do with anything?"

"You read that shit, you write that shit, and it sets up false expectations."

My mouth drops. "Shit?"

He sucks in a long breath. "That's not what I meant."

"I think it's exactly what you meant."

I trace my tongue over my teeth, trying to decide if I'm even mad that he called my work shit. I'm not. I don't care what he thinks about my work. And that in itself bothers me more than anything.

"I just meant, no man is like the characters you write, you know that, don't you?"

I actually feel my own nostrils flaring, and draw in a breath to keep from raising my voice. "I do."

"I can't compete with a six-and-a-half foot alien with a cock like a foot-long who was written by a woman." He drops the floss in the trash and unbuttons his dockers.

"Who said you should?"

"You live in a dream world of fake cocks and wild tantric sex under the stars. This is reality. We've been together for a long time. You know me. We want the same things out of life. We get along, our families get along." His jaw takes on that stubborn edge it gets when he's annoyed. "What do you want from me?"

"Nothing." I say and brace myself, but he doesn't even blink. I rest my hand on the counter, tracing a vein in the marble. "What do you want from me, Jer?"

"For you to be exactly as you are. It feels like you're constantly expecting me to be something I'm not. I don't want you to change."

"You do want me to change, Jeremy. You want me to stop writing."

"I never said that."

"You called it shit. You don't want me to tell anyone what I do."

"I was angry. I'm sorry." He stalks past me into the room, pulling his shirt over his head. I stare at the clean lines of his lean back.

"But you are ashamed of what I write."

He doesn't look at me as he sits down on the bed. "Let's just..." He slices an angry hand through the air. "Let's just finish this conversation in the morning."

I slide my phone from the counter as casually as I can and follow him into the bedroom.

I barely sleep that night. I replay a thousand conversations with Stranger, and I realize something. We've discussed a hundred things, a thousand. Sex is there—it's always there—but it's not all there is.

Stranger and I talk about things. A lot of things. The world, philosophy, economy, art, literature, politics, travel. We talk about crackers, juice, our childhoods. We talk about the weather. We talk about anything. We talk about everything. And it's fun. He can make me laugh describing his lunch.

And, yes, we do talk about sex. The wild, crazy, panty-wetting kind. The kind of sex I want to have. The kind I crave.

But maybe Jeremy is right, maybe I need to find out if sex is all this is. Maybe it's just an illusion.

It's 3:11am when I finally give in to the impulse, and text Stranger.

> Mia: I'll be in the Finger Lakes with friends, at a winery called Cayuga for a tasting at 7 tonight, spending the night at Cayuga Hotel and Spa. Maybe... I don't know. It's not far from you?

I fall asleep after that. In the morning, there are two pictures and a message waiting for me. One is a picture of Stranger, a selfie of him sipping from a mug of steaming coffee, standing outside surrounded by snow, the mountain glowing in rising sunlight behind him, with its barren trees. He's got on a fleece—the same one from his profile picture—and he's rugged and unshaved, his eyes all crinkly and warm, like he's smiling just for me. The other is a picture of Gogo in her sweater and booties, looking ridiculously proud of herself in the snow. And the third is a text.

> Stranger: Cayuga is twenty minutes from my house. It snowed last night but there's ice under the fresh stuff. Drive carefully.

My stomach does a big lazy slow circle somewhere between turned on and terrified. Like that rollercoaster I'm on just went over a massive rise and I'm plummeting a straight path down.

I need to tell Jeremy. I need to talk to him. This isn't just fun anymore.

He is already awake. The bed is empty.

I stagger down the steps, slightly hungover, but mostly tired from the sleepless night.

Mom sends me a dark glare.

Penny and Danny announce they want to come with us to the winery.

Jer clears his throat. "I already checked with everyone. They're glad for more company. You know Erica."

A chill runs down my spine.

Our friends. They are truly ours. Neither his nor mine alone. What I'm doing could destroy so many relationships. If Jer and I break up, he will get Annie. My heart twists at the thought. She'll never speak to me again. I will probably get to keep Erica and Caesar though. Erica is bawdy. Jer doesn't really like her.

Danny and Penny are my family though. I'd get them.

I smile at Penny.

She smiles at me.

I part my lips. I need to ask Jeremy to go out for coffee or something. I need time with him.

Time alone.

As if fate hears me though, Dad immediately drapes an arm around Jeremy's shoulders, slapping his back. "Want to go shoot some balls at the new indoor range?"

Jer's eyes slide, blue and cool, over my face. "Hell yeah. Can I try out your new driver?"

My lower lip starts to wobble. I don't even know why, so I turn away from everyone, get really busy refilling my coffee mug.

I hear Dad's voice behind me. "Anyone else want to come? Mia? Danny? Penny?"

"No thanks." My voice is only half clogged.

Jer comes up and presses a perfunctory kiss to my shoulder.

There won't be time to talk to him now. And what will I say? Everyone loves you. We're clearly perfect, but I want to meet up with this tattooed writer guy just to make sure that there isn't some other way I'm supposed to live my life. Is that cool?

It would gut him.

My vision blurs with thick, hot tears. One spills over. I'm losing control.

I wipe my nose and eyes, trying to be cool, but I'm standing in the corner. Someone will notice. Soon, someone is going to wonder why I'm facing the corner. I can't help it though, it's like something is broiling inside me, something new and terrifying, and if I tell anyone about it, everything will explode. All of it. At once.

I clench my teeth.

Dad and Jer grab their coats and leave, and I'm still in the corner, blinking at the cupboard, willing the tears to leave me alone.

"What's wrong with Mia?" Danny asks.

I don't say anything.

"Seriously, Mia? Are you *crying?*"

He says crying like it's something mysterious and horrible, like he's terrified it might be true and then he'll have to comfort me.

"No," I say.

"You *are?* What's wrong?"

It doesn't really matter how old I get, there's something about my baby brother being concerned about me. My stupid nose is running, I keep my back to everyone. "I'm fine, Danny. Really."

Mom comes up. I know it's her. I can just tell. She's in my space. She touches my shoulder. "Mia, honey?"

"I'm fine." I wipe my nose on my wrist.

"You aren't fine." She pauses a moment, and whatever she's working up to say, I don't want to hear it.

"I just need to be alone, Mom. I'm going out."

She stares after me as I run upstairs, I can feel the weight of her eyes on the small of my back.

I take the fastest shower I can. I know exactly what I'm going to do today.

Twenty minutes later, Penny finds me in the mudroom as I sneak my way into the garage to borrow Mom's car and go into town.

"Mia?" she says, her dark brows wrinkled. "Are you okay?"

I swallow. I have a hard time when people worry about me. I always have this need to reassure them that I'm the last person in the world anyone needs to ever worry about. I've got my life in order. I'm smug. I'm happy. I'm perfect. So I plaster a big smile on my face. "Yeah. I'm great!"

She pulls her coat off a peg on the wall. "Good. Then I'm coming with you."

"You don't even know where I'm going."

"I don't care."

I open my mouth to argue, but she just yanks her zipper up.

"Whatever you're doing, I don't care. I'm coming. I'm a good listener. And no offense, but I'm not spending the whole day cooped up here with your mom. Besides, she asked me to make sure you're okay."

I can't help but laugh. Good old Mom. I jerk my head at the door to the garage. "Alright then."

We get in the car at the same time. The doors thudding heavily. Mom's car smells the same as it always did. Leather and a faint whiff of the same Chanel perfume she's worn since I was a kid.

"So..." Penny clears her throat pointedly. "Are you going to tell me where we're going?"

I turn on the car, and flip it in reverse. "Do you have any tattoos?"

"Yes."

"Really?"

She hums in agreement. "Four. Your brother has two."

Really? "I didn't know that."

Penny makes a face. "There's probably a lot you don't know about Danny. I think he sometimes feels... uncomfortable telling you all things."

"Because Mom's so judgy?"

"I think it's more... he doesn't want to disappoint, and he always says how perfect you are."

I laugh. If only they all knew I write books with spankings and anal, and made plans to meet with an internet Stranger.

"He just wants you all to be proud of him."

"I'll always be proud of Danny. No matter what." I back into the driveway and hit the remote to close the garage behind us. "And I'm glad you're here."

She glances at me, tucking her dark hair behind her ears. "Why's that?"

"Because you love him. But also... I'm going to get a tattoo and I have no idea how bad it's going to hurt."

The drive to Cayuga that afternoon is uneventful. I sit in the front and help Jeremy navigate his massive Mercedes SUV over the roads. All the while I try not to itch or worry about the tattoo tingle-burning away on my back. I want to look at it, touch it, remember the sharp sting as the artist inked it into my skin. I want to talk about it. But I don't. It's my secret. Well, Penny knows, but she promised not to tell anyone.

Penny got one too. A tiny symbol she said was Zibu for hope, a swoop with three dots on the inside of her wrist.

It took some work for us to find a tattoo parlor with an artist who spoke Arabic well enough to do the translation, but we found one. It hurt. Badly. But I'm so glad I did it.

On the way home, she touched the bandage. "Can I tell you a secret Mia?"

I turned in the car, remembering Stranger's simple words and how they'd cut me to the core. *You can say anything. I'll listen.* "Anything."

She swallowed thickly, and I think I already knew something big was coming.

She chewed on her lips, her eyes getting big. "I don't have a family. Not anymore. I lied. I'm so sorry. I'm an orphan."

The car was quiet, a 90s music station playing something angsty. "Don't apologize."

She shook her head tightly, but somehow it felt more like a nod. "Danny's my family now. I just... I don't ever talk about it. The truth." Her voice drops to a whisper. "It's bad. My dad..."

I touch her wrist. "Penny, don't tell me anything you aren't ready to tell. Your secrets are yours. I get it."

Now, every time I meet her eyes on the drive to Cayuga, I want to hug her. I like this woman. Mom will too someday, I just know it.

Every time I lean back against the seat, I'm reminded of my tattoo and I feel giddy all over again. I feel wild. I feel alive. I feel excited. I can barely sit still.

Jer turns onto a tiny one-lane road toward the lake. The car pitches and bucks over potholes and snow piles, but it handles well. He bought this car right after we got engaged because *it will be great for kids.*

At the time, I thought that was sweet and thoughtful.

Now?

I glance at my phone. Three messages from Stranger.

My stomach heaves.

I want to see him, but also, I'm terrified.

And because I don't know what to do, I do nothing. I don't even read them. I just curl my fingers into fists and focus on the hotel as it comes into view.

It's beautiful. A perfect winter New England hotel nestled between snow-covered trees. White wood with brick chimneys, dormer windows and black shutters.

The lobby is just as nice. Gleaming wood floors draped with woven rugs, cozy tufted furniture, massive windows overlooking the frozen water, interrupted occasionally by birch and maple, naked with winter and crusted with frost.

Caesar and Erica already checked in, but they're waiting for us in the lobby, curled up on a sofa by the fire. They're reading together.

It hits me hard.

I want that.

Exactly that.

I want to read with someone. Read and cuddle together. Pass our time, together, happily occupied in our literary worlds, but still connected.

Jer never reads.

Stranger reads. He reads all the time. I bet he'd love for me to put my head in his lap and read with him.

Jer and I check in and take our bags to a room that overlooks the frozen lake.

I finally relent and text Stranger. This is new, feeling guilty about not responding to him, like I owe him something, like I just know he's worrying somewhere and it's cruel not to respond. How did we get here? Why? It doesn't matter. I know him well enough to know that he is worrying.

> Mia: Roads were great. Plowed and salted. We just got in. Not sure about timing. I'll let you know if anything comes up.

> Stranger: Ok.

I put my phone on silent and shower. I can't tell for sure, but I think that *Ok* was one of disappointment. Jesus, I'm in too deep, sinking so fast the shore is a distant memory and I'm not sure I even want to go back there again.

When I get out of the shower, I turn to study my back in the mirror. The tattoo is a little red at the edges, but it's beautiful. I smile at the elegant squiggly letters. If I showed Stranger, would he smile? Laugh? I imagine him stroking a calloused finger over them and my nipples harden, goosebumps breaking out over my skin. I have to show someone. It's a secret I can't keep to myself.

There's only one person I want to see it. I don't even care if I sink all the way to the bottom of this new sea. I like this sea.

I snap a photo of my naked back, including the curve of my ass, and my make-up-free face in profile, my hair wet and dripping down my spine, the letters clear across my shoulder blade.

I send it to Stranger.

I linger over my makeup, mostly to avoid having to focus on Jeremy, who's been especially hang dog all day, and dress in a black sweater dress and knee-high boots.

We've barely spoken.

He watches me from the bed, fully dressed, his eyes narrowed, head cocked like he's trying to understand what's suddenly so different about me. "You look nice."

"Thanks."

He rises from the bed and takes my hand. "I shouldn't have said that about your writing. I didn't mean it."

"I got a tattoo." I turn to the window, stare out at the frozen lake.

There's a long pause.

"Where?"

I tug down the back of my dress, move my hair out of the way.

Another pause. "What will you do at our wedding?"

He didn't even ask what it says. I could be deliberately obtuse and ask what he means, but I know what he means. My dress is strapless. He's worried about it showing, about our friends and family seeing it.

I look back at him, study his pale blue eyes, and I realize something. He doesn't really care about me. If he cared, his first question would have been *why, Mia? Why did you get a tattoo out of the blue? Is everything ok?*

"You've never bothered to read my writing. So how would you know if it's shit or not?"

He's silent.

"Maybe it's awful."

"I'll read it now if you let me."

I shrug. "Fine. I'll pull up a book on my tablet. Open it to a scene. You can read it on the way to the winery."

"That's not really what I—"

"You can read it in the car." For some reason my face starts to crumple and my throat tightens, so I turn my back to him. "Read it in public. And then tell me you aren't ashamed of me. Erica and Caesar have read it."

Erica is in the lobby when I get there, her red hair pulled up into a sleek bun. She's wearing a skin-tight green dress that makes her look like a Barbie, full-blown and gorgeous.

I drop my head on her shoulder.

Jer loiters awkwardly at the bottom of the stairs.

"Jer just agreed to read a scene of mine," I whisper.

She grins. Erica has this way of smiling with her whole body, it's a squeal-slash-shoulder-motion combined with an ass wiggle. It's infectious. She's like a never-bursting bubble of energy.

Her shoulder bumps against my cheekbone as she wriggles. "Which one are you going to give him?"

"I don't know. What do you think?"

She laughs, deep in her throat. I love her. I wish I saw more of her. She and Caesar live in Albany, a lot closer to Stranger actually, than to me down in Providence. She reads everything I write. "Yes! The one where Creed gets pissed and spanks her."

Jer's eyes get wider than I've ever seen.

Danny and Penny come down the stairs too, and he frowns. "Spanks?"

Penny looks like she's trying desperately not to laugh.

"Okay," I say. Penny told me her secrets. I'm going to be spilling secrets today. Might as well start practicing now. "I write romance novels. I don't do accounting. That's why I don't talk about work, ever. I've been lying for years."

Danny stares at me for a minute, scrubs a hand through his hair. "Cool."

"Spanking romances?" asks Penny.

I can hear Stranger in my head. *Do it,* he'd say. *Own it. Don't be ashamed of what you write or who you are.* "Sometimes. They're erotic shifter romance novels. And people like them."

"What's your pen name? I might have read them. I love shifter romances," Penny says without missing a beat, and I swear to god, I can't wait to call her my sister.

"Mia Reed."

Danny wipes his hand over his mouth and stares at Penny. "You read erotic books with spankings?"

"Heck yeah." She pulls on her coat. "And I'll be reading a Mia Reed original first thing tomorrow.

Danny looks confused, like maybe he finds it a little hot that Penny reads books about spankings, but then somehow his sister is involved so that makes it kind of awful. "If writing them makes you happy, I'm happy for you."

That was easier than I expected. "Don't tell Mom."

A look of total understanding crosses his face. "I won't."

Caesar comes out of the bar with a couple glasses of champagne and passes them around. He's the kind of guy who always looks like he's biding his time before he tells you something outrageous, like he's got some awesome story in his back pocket.

He hands a glass to Jeremy.

Erica does a shimmy. Seriously. But she can pull that off. "Jer is going to read one of Mia's sex scenes on the way."

Caesar nods like that makes sense. "Make it that scene you read aloud to me a few weeks ago, babe. Which was it?"

"Oh! The thumb in the bum scene!" Erica laughs again. "Oh my god." She fans her face.

Jer's whole face shuts down. Danny drags his hand over his mouth again.

Penny's eyes gleam. "I want to read that."

"I don't," Danny mutters.

My cheeks heat.

"Thumb in the bum. Done," I say, brazening through the awkward, *owning it,* and flip through the book to a scene where Creed bends Rielle over a table and fucks her from behind. It's... dirty.

I would spare my brother the details, but Erica has no such tact. She regales Penny with the whole sordid story as we climb into the car that will take us to Cayuga.

Danny looks... uncomfortable.

Caesar just laughs.

Jer blanches when I hand him my tablet. "Is this a test?"

"No." But it is. For both of us.

He reads in silence.

I peek over his shoulder, surprised that he's actually reading it. I beat back the simmering layer of humiliation and shame that I write books with thumbs in bums and spankings.

There's something to be said for just laying it all out there. I studiously avoid meeting his gaze on the way there.

Cayuga Winery, when we get there, looks like a colonial schoolhouse had sex with a warehouse full of glass and they made a baby together. We get there after dark and it's lit from within, glowing, the old shingled schoolhouse parts already strung with Christmas wreaths, and the modern glass parts gleaming.

"Welcome to the holiday season," Erica shouts like a showman as she hops down from the car.

"Snow and Christmas lights." Penny's eyes gleam. "You don't get this in LA. This is perfect!"

Jer hands back my tablet, and turns up the collars of his wool coat.

"Well?" I say when I've climbed out, my heels sinking in the snow on the winery's front drive.

"I'm not sure it's safe for you to be writing like that."

"Like what?"

"You could attract the wrong sort of attention. People might get ideas."

"Like you? Did you get any ideas?"

He makes a face like he's just swallowed something gross. "Are there men on that writing website? Do they read scenes like that?"

"Sometimes." I tug him toward the winery. "Did you get a little hard?"

"Mia? Jesus. No. We were in a packed car!" He follows me, his expression grim.

"Not even half way? Maybe a quarter of a boner?"

Stranger would have laughed at that.

Jer scoffs. Actually scoffs. A little huff of air that chills me to the core. "No."

He reaches over my head to hold open the door for me, and gestures me in as an extra long, cold gust of air sends my hair swirling around me. "Are you into that?"

"Spankings, doggy and fingers in bums?" I tilt my head.

"Yeah."

"Absolutely."

He doesn't respond.

I'm not even mad. He was right. That was a test. And we just failed. As a couple, we failed.

Jer and I don't fit together. Not even a little. I need to tell him. I need to woman-up and tell him the truth. It's not even about Stranger anymore. It's about Jer and me and us together.

I will tell him. As soon as we get home, I'll tell him the truth, give him back the ring, focus on my career for a while, figure out my life.

I've been fixating on Stranger, but it's not about him. I need to get control of my life.

I pull out my phone and text Stranger.

> Mia: Maybe I can fake getting sick or something?

> Stranger: I like your tattoo. You overestimate my self-control.

Huh?

I cock my head, but can't respond because Jer is staring at me.

Everyone else is already at our table. I take a seat beside Penny, at a long table by a fireplace. Our tasting is already laid out for us.

Caesar and Erica flirt/bicker about food, but they order a variety of samplings for us to have with the wine: breads, cheeses, cured meats, nuts, dates, spreads.

Everyone is talking a million miles a minute, which is handy. It means I can stay quiet.

My purse hangs over the back of my chair, and I can practically feel my phone inside it, pulsing away like a second heart. I long to check it. I want to tell him I'll meet him tonight.

But I'm a coward. What if we meet and the luster is lost?

I sample the first wine.

Jeremy's across the table from me laughing at something Erica said. Maybe if I break it gently, if it's not about another man, he won't hate me, and Annie and I can stay friends.

The wines here are typically minerally and just slightly sweet, because of the cold weather. This one is tart and delicious.

I'm somewhere between my fourth and fifth tasting, which means I've probably had a solid glass and a half. Enough to be warm and happy. I take a sip of a red and roll it around my tongue. Pretend like I'm analyzing the taste. But really I'm just wondering what Stranger meant by the self-control comment.

Penny elbows me in the side and whispers, "That guy over there is staring at you."

Mouth still full of wine, I glance at her and raise my brows.

She jerks her chin toward the stairs leading to the barrel room. "That hot guy with everywhere tats. Next to the guy in the wheelchair."

I follow the line of her gaze, see a tall man.

Brown leather ankle boots.

Dark jeans.

A tight, white Henley rolled up to his elbows, revealing swirling colorful sleeves of beautiful tattoos I know so well by now.

I nearly spit my wine across the table.

It's sheer force of will that has me swallowing.

I know that face.

And he *is* staring at me.

HE'S A STRANGER TO ME

MIA

"Do you know him?" Penny whispers in my ear, and I could kiss her right there. For her tact, for her quiet voice, for the fact that she doesn't draw any attention to me.

I swallow my wine and set the glass down carefully with hands that are suddenly shaky.

I drag my eyes away from him, but it's like the image of him is burned on the back of my eyelids. Every time I blink I see him.

He wasn't lying. He is tall.

And the pictures were accurate. He is hot and looks just a little mean.

And those pecs, and his arms, the tattoos. His shoulders.

Even his thighs are beautiful in jeans just a little snug. Not emo tight, just like his thighs are so developed, they fill them up where other men wouldn't.

His eyes, I can only describe them as tight, intense. After a long moment, he inclines his head briefly and says something to the man beside him in the wheelchair, a man with the same dark hair, thick brows, strong thick chest.

James.

My heart tightens in my chest at seeing his missing legs in person and the way they look at each other. There's a deep connection there.

I want to do what feels natural to me. Cross the room, introduce myself, thank him for his presence in the life of a lonely man who loves him. But I can't.

"Mia?"

"He's a stranger to me," I whisper.

"Hell of a stranger. He certainly seems to know you." She bites her lip pointedly. "If we were single..."

My stomach is doing a constant slow roll. I'm almost nauseated with it. My chest feels tight, my cheeks blaze hot, my nipples pebble hard. I can barely focus and I can't stop my gaze from moving constantly, relentlessly toward him.

Penny bumps me with her shoulder. "I would be dragging your ass straight over there to find out what that look meant."

He turns to pick up a glass of wine from the top of the bar, and catches me staring at him. His mouth stretches into the half-smile I remember from facetime.

And like that, the tears that seem to always be half a step away from spilling start burning the backs of my eyes.

I look away, blinking fast, trying to pay attention to the convo, but it's like my eyes are attached to invisible tethers, and he keeps yanking on them, because I can't stop looking back at him.

His brows draw together.

And James, in his chair, keeps casting stray looks my way.

I sit there as long as I can, barely managing to follow the elaborate story Erica and Caesar are telling about a trip they just took, and how they crashed their car in a ditch and had to walk in the rain. I finish my wine, gradually forcing my heartrate to slow.

Finally, when my cheeks aren't burning, I jerk my head at the hallway that leads to the bathrooms.

Stranger's brows lift.

I jerk my head at the hallway again.

"I need to go the bathroom," I mutter to no one in particular, rising from my seat.

Jeremy nods vaguely, still focused on Caesar, and I walk toward the bathroom.

As I walk, Stranger stares at me intently, eyes narrowed, body tight.

I stare back, nervous, terrified, excited.

I stand in the hallway, shaking, my heart thundering like mad.

I don't even have time to plan what to say, because then he's there, blocking out the whole world with his gigantic shoulders. The light is behind him and it's just the two of us now, standing in the dark.

Silence drags between us awkwardly.

He's so big.

So huge.

And he's staring at me like he's equally uncertain.

"What are you doing here?" I say. It just bursts out.

He makes a face. "You told me to come here."

One of the bathroom doors opens, and we both freeze when a man walks out of one of those unisex, single stalls.

"I didn't tell you to come here." I yank the handle open and stalk inside.

Stranger follows. And the room isn't big, but man alive, he is. He fills it up with shoulders and tallness and... man.

"What were you thinking?" I say.

He studies me. "You told me a location and a time that you would be there, twenty minutes from my home. I thought you wanted me to come."

"I'm here with my fiancé."

His jaw clenches tight, the little muscles in the corner of his mouth dancing, making my knees wobble. "Want me to go?"

I study the rounded black tips of my boots. I don't want him to go. I want to stare at him, at his hard, bristled jaw, his black hair, his hazel eyes. I want to touch his chest and smell his neck and feel the warmth of his skin.

I curl my hands into fists. "That would probably be for the best."

I tap my toe on the floor.

A brown boot steps up, toe-to-toe with my shoe. It's big, and scarred, and it creaks a little. A broad warm hand settles on my waist, his thumb grazing my hip bone. I draw in a breath of air that smells soapy and manly and so delicious my eyelids get heavy.

That hot thumb traces down, from my hipbone along the ticklish skin of abdomen, like a brand.

All the anxiety and fear and frustration fades away, and I'm left burning and wet and stupid.

My lips part, and I look up at his face. He's close now. So close I'm spinning, dizzy with the very real, very solid, very intimidating presence of him.

I think if I don't touch him, hold on to him, I might fall over.

He's moving so slowly, too slowly, like he's afraid I might scream at any moment, as he touches my chin, his long, calloused fingers sliding along the back of my neck.

My hands shake, my knees shake, and so does my heart, as I touch a hand to his shirt, spread five fingers over the soft material stretched over hard muscles.

The Henley bunches at his elbow, his Adam's apple bobs sharply. His breath and mine come faster and faster.

He lowers his face, I rise up on my toes, so we're hovering, only centimeters apart. His breath drifts over my cheeks.

"Hello, Mia," he whispers against my lips. "That's what I wanted to say to you. I even planned it out. I was going to whisper in your ear and say 'hello, Mia.'"

I've never done heroin or ecstasy, but this is what I imagine it feels like. Some evil spirit just injected me with pure lust and it hits me low, ripples through my blood, stealing under my skin like a fever and I'm... lost.

I'm not me anymore. Kind, decent, wants-to-be-good, Mia. All I am is a primitive woman who wants this one man.

"That was your line?" A bead of moisture slides out of the corner of my eye. I don't even know why. It's just... too much. After all this time.

"Yes. What was yours?" He thumbs the tear.

"I didn't have one. I was going to let you lead."

His eyes flare at that, his grip tightens on my waist and he leans down so his lips graze my ear, all bristle and sex. "Then hello, Mia."

I whimper, that pathetic dumb breathless whimper he drew from me at our first crazy PM about buckets. "Stranger."

I lean right into him, close the distance between us, desperate for the first touch of his lips on mine. Me. It's my choice.

His lips are soft, but not too soft. Smooth and firm.

I open to him. His grip on my neck tightens as he tilts my face back, gets the angle right, slants his head and strokes his tongue deeper.

He tastes like wine, and so do I. Jammy and bright. Like sex and rich tannins and man.

My hands slide up his chest.

This is so wrong—his tongue strokes over mine—but it feels so right.

I press against him with my hips, seeking out the long, hard bulge in his pants.

It's like it snaps, the whole dam of pent-up need that he's been building inside me since his very first message.

He groans impatiently, changes the angle, tugs me closer.

A massive hand slides down my back to palm my ass in a grip so possessive it demands reaction.

My hands clutch at any part of him they can get.

I get my hands up his shirt, moving restlessly over scorching hot skin, over the hard, bunching muscles of his stomach, the thick rise of his pecs.

He grunts, I sigh. He pushes my hips, I pull his. He backs me up against the door, I writhe against it, and when he growls low and deep in his throat, I'm amazed I don't orgasm on the spot.

He works my dress up and his rough palms graze over the bare skin of my ass. His lips coast down my neck, I roll my head against the door behind me, hooking a leg around his waist, drawing him in closer to where I need him. My whole body is desperate, annoyed, frustrated, determined to have him.

I want him inside me, filling me, driving inside me with a cock that practically feels like a religious destination after all this time. How many nights have I laid awake and imagined, wondered. I want him everywhere.

I buck against him. He jams his hard thigh between my legs, and I swear on whatever there is in the world that is holy, I hump his goddamned leg. I'm that far gone.

"I told you it would be like this."

His words tug me out of the moment. *Like this?* I blink up at the ceiling. Of a bathroom. A public bathroom at a winery. A winery I came to with my fiancé. Cheating. Whatever Jer won't be tomorrow, right now he *is* technically my fiancé.

Ugh. This isn't what I wanted. "Kissing next to a toilet?"

His teeth scrape my earlobe, his stubble scratches my neck.

I shove at him, ignoring the wet heat pooling between my legs.

He straightens, his gaze roves over my face, and that hot, hard thigh leaves me. "What's wrong?"

I pull away.

"Wait, Mia. I still don't know your body language well enough to read you." His brows draw together. "Talk to me. What's wrong."

"Everything. My fiancé is thirty feet away."

"Don't call him that." His mouth hardens. "You don't belong with him."

That echoes around the still room, off the hard surfaces. The faucet leaks a steady *dripdripdripdrip* in time with my heart.

We stare at one another.

"And what? I belong with you?" Maybe it's panic, but I want to run now, fast, away from him, from Jer, from Cayuga. Someplace far away where no one needs or wants anything from me at all.

"Maybe." His deep voice drags around my ears and gives me chills.

"I don't even know you." I turn away. Reach for the door.

And then he's there, surrounding me from behind, holding me still. My face presses into the dark black wood of the bathroom door.

"You don't know me?" He hisses, his breath touching against the back of my neck. His lips, and the bristle surrounding them graze against my ears.

"You know me, Mia. We've been inside each other's brains for months. All this time, getting to know one another. I know your schedule, I know your dreams, I know your likes and your dislikes. I know what you're doing every fucking minute of the day. There is no one in the world I know better. And you know the same for me. We may be touching for the first time, we may still need to learn each other's bodies, faces and expressions, but don't you dare fucking pretend you don't know who I am or that I don't know you."

He slides a hand down my dress, all the way down to the hem, strokes his fingers up over my bare skin, higher and higher until he touches the top of my panties.

I don't know if I want to move away. I know I should, but I also know he's got me trapped in his spell. My neck arches, my core spasms, my nipples burn. I can't even think. I just sag against the door, panting, as his fingers slide up to the bare skin of my stomach, and down under the top of my panties, lower over the smooth rise of my pubic mound, and down between the slit at the entrance of my core.

He touches me like he has every right in the world to do so.

My mouth hangs open. I grind my ass backward, against the hard bulge that he settles right between the crack of my ass. Holy mother of god, I want this man inside me like I've never wanted anything in my entire life.

His fingers slide inside me. One at first, then I think it's two, but I'm not even sure. I just know I feel instant relief with his long fingers filling me for the first time.

The hard heel of his palm presses into my clit, his teeth drag over the skin behind my ears, shoving and pressing until I'm clawing at the door, riding closer and closer toward a high I'm not sure I can ever come back from.

It builds so fast, with such strong momentum I can't stop the long keen that comes from my mouth. It's like the orgasm that never ends, it just keeps spiraling and piling on top of itself, my body clenching around his fingers. I'm dimly aware of his voice in my ear, calling me a good girl, praising me for coming all over his fingers, telling me I'm perfect, telling me I'm going to do that again soon, only with his cock inside me, all the while massaging my clit and pumping his fingers inside me.

It triggers another one, a bigger one, that leaves me drained. I sag against the doorway, vaguely aware of two things.

His cock is still wedged against my ass, rock hard.

And ... I'm drooling.

I blink, dazed as a long line of saliva drifts, glistening in the low light to the floor.

I'm a mess.

When his fingers leave me, I blow out a long breath.

In this moment, all I want is to turn around, wrap my arms around his waist and fall asleep on his chest, shut out the rest of the world, tell him to take me somewhere else, somewhere we can be alone, find out what the hell this is.

The connection, the chemistry between us is even stronger in person.

I wipe the drool from my mouth. "That was intense."

He turns me around so I'm facing him, a massive smile spreading across his face. *"Was?* We're not even close to finished."

"We are. I can't stay here." I blow out a long breath.

His smile fades.

"Everyone is going to be wondering where I am." I open the door behind me and take a step out.

"Fuck them. This matters, Mia. Quit pretending it doesn't."

"I never said it doesn't matter. I just... I need time. I have to end it with Jer."

15 HALF GROSS, HALF HOT

MIA

I stagger halfway down the hall before I remember my face is probably a mess. I need a mirror. When I toss open the door, Stranger is still in the bathroom, leaning against the sink, his arms braced wide, his rainbowed forearms rippling, like he's just been staring at the mirror himself.

A thick brow raises.

"I need the mirror." I cross the small room, and elbow him out of the way.

He backs up. Barely. Stays right there behind me, looming around me, watching me intently, so my hips press against the sink and my ass presses against him.

"What were you doing?" I meet his gaze in the mirror.

"Summoning the Candyman."

I shudder. "Stop. You'll give me nightmares. My brother convinced me to do that when we were kids once. I couldn't look in the mirror in the dark for weeks."

He puts a hand on my waist, and my belly does a little flipflop.

The hard bulge of his cock settles against me again. "I was trying to decide if I should just jerk off real fast or wait until my dick calms down on its own."

I try—and fail—to resist the urge to arch against him like a cat. "Can't help you. Not enough time."

He snorts.

"There isn't. They'll all think I've been in here sick or something."

My face is a mess of smeared lipstick and mascara bleed. My hair is a disaster. My cheeks are bright red. I look like a woman who just had the orgasm of her life.

His eyes gleam as I dab at the skin below my eyes, clearing away the mess.

I can practically feel him making fun of me. "Go ahead, say it. Whatever it is you're thinking."

"I like messing you up."

I rake my fingers through my hair, settling it back into place, and raise my brows in silent question.

"You're... prissy. I was right."

My mouth drops. After what we just did... that hurts a little. "Prissy?"

"Oh, come on." The broad pads of his thumbs touch down just above the rise of my ass, his fingers looping all the way around my waist to rest on my sensitive lower belly. His chin touches down on the top of my head. "Look at yourself."

I do. Pearl earrings, modest dark dress. I smooth my hair.

His lips quirk. "You're prissy. On the outside, you're prissy."

My lower lip pushes out.

"But on the inside…" His lips spread and those beautiful white teeth flash, and the hard bulge at the front of his jeans presses against the small of my back. "You just let an internet pervert finger you in a public bathroom. It's a fun contrast."

His hand slides up and cups my breast, his thumb gliding over my nipple. His eyes flare for a second, and then he tugs on the neckline of my dress, revealing my bra.

"Turquoise," he says smiling, and returning his palms to cup my breasts.

My nostrils flare, my nipples are hard beads against the front of my thin dress. I want nothing more than for him to ruck my dress up around my waist, open his pants and fuck me hard, like a savage, like an animal, like a man laying claim to a woman.

I bite my lip.

He sinks his teeth into my ear.

He's killing me.

"I wish we could. But we can't. This *priss* needs to go back to her fiancé."

"I wish you'd stop calling him that." His grip on me tightens. Just for a second. And he backs off with an irritable frown. "We're not done."

"For now we are."

He laughs lightly but somehow, I get the impression I just baited a beast. I turn to go, but–

"Wait."

I hesitate, and he grabs the neck of my dress again, but this time at the back, and it takes me a moment to figure out what he wants.

His fingers lift the edge of the bandage. He stares at my new tattoo for a long minute. "It's perfect. Go, prissy Mia."

I flip the switch on my way out, leaving him laughing in the dark.

Penny makes a face when she sees me, her dark brows raising high, her mouth forming an O.

I realize abruptly that I'm grinning like an idiot. Maybe it's just the post-orgasmic high, but I feel happy, exhilarated, alive. More alive than I've ever felt in my whole life. The guilt follows instantly on its heels.

I wipe the smile off my face, and shake my head tightly at Penny.

Jer glances up as I take my seat. "Feeling okay?"

Everyone stares at me. It's uncomfortably clear that everyone thinks I'm having some sort of abdominal crisis, which, while embarrassing, is less horrible than the truth.

I put my napkin back in my lap. "I feel fantastic. Thanks."

"You look feverish. Were you just ill?"

"No. I wasn't ill. I am fine."

Conversation resumes. Jeremy tells everyone we may go to Anguilla for our honeymoon—which is news to me—and Danny mentions he and Penny are going to Thailand in a month.

I reach for my wine glass.

"Are you sure that's a good idea?" Jeremy says.

Normally, that would annoy me, but I can barely focus. My body keeps having sexy flashbacks, as intense as if I've been punched in the gut. My abdomen keeps tightening as though Stranger's fingers are still inside me, and I know my color must be high. My skin keeps tingling.

Stranger ambles out of the bathroom a few minutes later and I can't help but wonder if he ended up jerking off after all. I picture those tattooed forearms, a rainbow of beautiful inky patterns and images, rippling as he strokes up and d—

"He followed you," Penny murmurs in my ear while everyone else is distracted. "Did you talk to him?"

"Who?" My moral compass gives an inward cringe. Lying is becoming frighteningly natural to me.

"The tattooed guy. I wondered if you saw him."

I shake my head, dreading the day I tell Penny the truth. She was honest with me. But I can't tell her now, right here, like this. Not until I tell Jeremy. Which I *will do tomorrow, as soon as we get home.*

I try not to look at Stranger, but my heart clenches in my chest, thumpthumping away and I swear it sounds like it's saying Stranger-StrangerStranger.

We finish our tasting, and Erica orders a couple bottles of wine and more finger foods.

At the bar, Stranger raises his phone to me, a dimple flickering in one cheek.

I try not to be obvious, but I reach for my phone in my purse, check it.

> **Stranger: I didn't jerk off.**

Instantly my cheeks go hot as I imagine him, half hard in those tight jeans, uncomfortable, wanting me. My whole body melts and softens. Jer is deep in conversation telling Caesar about my dad's golf clubs. Stranger leans negligently at the bar, studying me with appraising, proprietary eyes. He looks at me like he's seeing beneath my clothes, beneath my skin, straight to the very heart of me.

James is staring at me too. I send him a rueful smile.

He waves covertly back from his chair, and I ache to go meet him, introduce myself, but I can't.

No one at the table is paying much attention to me, so I text back.

Mia: Good. Save it for me.

Stranger: Yeah…I feel like I'm going to have to just beat one out real quick though, the first time we're together.

Mia: All this build up is tough.

Stranger: So tough.

Mia: Poor Stranger.

Stranger: Poor me, indeed. It's bad.

Mia: Horrendous.

Stranger: Appalling

Mia: Odious

Stranger: So hard!

Mia: Lol.

Stranger: Seriously. Can I?

Mia: Get it out of your system?

Stranger: Yeah. This is brutal.

Mia: So that's the plan? Hello, Mia. Get on your knees, lemme beat off on your face?

At the bar, he laughs, his eyes meeting mine and glittering. He's handsome all the time, but somehow when he laughs, he transforms, he melts me.

> Stranger: Tits?

I make a frowny face, earning another laugh.

> Mia: I'm grumbling.

> Stranger: All over you then. Soak you with it. Watch it drip between your thighs.

> Mia: That's like… half gross.

> Stranger: But half hot.

"Mia? What time should I book our flights for Christmas?"

"Mmmm hmmm," I say distractedly, still focused on Stranger and all his dirty talk, before Jer's voice pulls me back to the present and I look up at his face, blinking. "What?"

There's more of that ever-present guilt inside me, churning away in my belly—Jer looks so earnest sitting there, his eyes narrowed slightly, his lips pursed. But beside the guilt, is true hope. For the first time since I met Stranger online, there is legitimate hope that what we have might be real.

I glance across the bar, and there his is, a knowing smile on his face, his phone held loosely between those great big hands, his beautiful thumbs poised over the screen.

He is real. I know he is. He's looking at me.

He is who he seems to be. And he likes me.

That knowledge burns bright within me.

Jer leans across the table. "Maybe you've had a bit too much to drink?"

I draw in a long, slow breath. "I'm okay. Thanks. Just a little warm."

He crosses his arms.

The table next to ours empties, the group putting on their coats and heading for the door.

"We agreed," I say. "That we were staying."

Stranger winks. Maybe that sounds cheesy, but on him, it's not cheesy at all.

I catch my lower lip between my teeth, and smile.

His beautiful mouth stretches, dimples flashing.

He pushes away from the bar, says something to James.

Jer says something about Florida, but I can't focus.

Stranger and his brother cross the floor of the tasting room.

There's music on, something bluesy, but I can't even hear it. Because all I hear is my own breathing.

What is he doing? He can't come here.

He's so tall. My head cranes back, he towers over my chair.

Only a little while ago I kissed those lips, touched those hard muscles.

Stranger moves a chair away from the empty table beside ours, clearing a space for James, and takes a seat of his own, filling up space with his big body, with his very presence.

It kills me, but I pretend I don't know either of them.

Erica has no such compulsion.

Her red head turns, her mouth drops. She's been sitting with her back to the bar, so she hasn't seen Stranger or his brother yet. But she's looking now. And she's a little bit tipsy. She looks back and forth between them. "Hello... is this a rugged and hot convention?"

Caesar laughs and wraps his arm around her.

"I'm serious." She giggles into his neck. "Look!"

"I see them," he says.

I don't know if she saw James' wheelchair, but a look crosses his face. I can't quite describe it. His face hardens.

She leans forward, hand outstretched. "I'm Erica, and you should join us."

Stranger rubs a hand over his mouth, hiding a smile.

Caesar kisses Erica's temple. "We aren't swingers, I promise. She's just friendly. Come join us. Always fun to meet new people."

I hold my breath. He has to say no. *He HAS to.*

"We'd love to. He scoots his chair closer to mine, his boot touching my shoe. And I swallow. He's so big. I've never felt so small in my life as I do now.

Jeremy looks annoyed.

Penny's eyes narrow.

Danny half rises in his seat, extending his hand across the table toward Stranger. "I'm Danny." He tilts his hand my way. "My sister, Mia. And this is her fiancé, Jeremy."

Stranger's eyes go warm as he shakes Danny's hand. They do that crinkle thing that is oh so charming as he shakes hands all around the table. Even Jeremy. I hold my breath, watching as Stranger's long-fingered hand closes around Jer's slender one.

He saves me for last, hand extended toward me.

I slide my fingers along the rough calluses of his palm, and shiver.

His mouth quirks. "Stranger."

"That's your real name?" Penny asks.

James shakes hands all around. I smile warmly at him.

Stranger rests his elbows on the table, leaning in. "Been called Stranger for so long, it may as well be."

That perks my interest. I thought it was his real name. I raise a brow.

He raises one back, all sly and dimply.

"It's true." James picks up his wine, his eyes landing on mine, warm and so much like Stranger's I can't help but love him, just a little. His hands are like Stranger's too. They dwarf the glass. "He's been Stranger since we were kids. Even our dad called him that."

"What's his real name then?" I ask.

James tilts and shakes his head ruefully, biting down on his lower lip, and I swear I hear both Penny and Erica sigh. James is a lady-killer. "Not my secret to share."

Stranger's boot bumps mine under the table.

This isn't how I imagined things. It's not how I imagined it at all, the first time we'd be together.

I want to climb into his lap, wrap my arms around him, press my nose to his neck, breathe him in. I don't like that this is sordid or clandestine. I want to go somewhere and sit beside him, be a couple in the eyes of the world. Make him tell me his name and what he wants with me and all his secrets.

Tomorrow, as soon as we get home from this trip, I'm going to tell Jeremy the truth.

But for now, all I can do is try to follow the conversation.

"You all go to any of the casinos?" James asks.

"No," says Caesar. "Just the one winery. Not enough time. You?"

"Earlier today. Never done it before," Stranger says. "Played some cards, lost some money."

Danny tops off various glasses around the table. "Which one?"

James lifts his chin. "You know Gray Rock?"

"Yeah. I've heard they have good restaurants." Danny leans in toward Penny. "We should go there sometime. Maybe at Christmas?" He meets my eye. "We'll be coming back."

Jer rests his elbows on the table, leaning in. "It's good. I don't like the dealers there, though."

That's surprising. I don't think of Jer as doing much gambling or visiting casinos to have an opinion on the dealers of one specific one.

The conversation swirls around me, but I barely touch my wine.

I do my best, smiling when other people do, laughing when they laugh.

It's only when Erica announces an hour later that we should go back to the hotel and play poker, that I become aware of the conversation again.

Jeremy suggests Texas Hold 'Em.

Stranger's eyes take on a weird gleam. "Where are you staying?"

"Inn at the Finger Lakes," Jer says back.

Stranger and Jer both make twin faces of surprise.

"So are we." James drums his fingers on the edge of his chair.

"That's handy," I say.

Stranger shrugs, and I pull on my scarf against a chill.

"You should play too," says Caesar.

Stranger feigns doubt.

James says, "Oh come on, it'll be fun."

Stranger's hazel eyes land on mine, a lazy half grin on his face. "Alright."

A prickle of fear has me swallowing thickly.

He did this. He planted the seed of casinos, got us talking about poker, guiding the conversation all along, and one by one everyone slowly bent to his will.

Is that what he's done with me?

Something prickles along my spine seeing him in action. He wanted this. From the beginning, he planned it all, coming to the table, introducing himself, steering the convo.

Jeremy seems to like the plan of going with these people he's never met back to our hotel to play poker.

So, an hour later, I find myself sitting around a little cocktail nook back at the hotel, watching Erica deal out hands of cards like a pro.

Jeremy is on my left, and Stranger is on my right.

JACKS DON'T ALWAYS BEAT THREES

STRANGER

Mia is conflicted. It's written in the way she sinks her teeth into her lower lip, furrows her eyebrows, glances between me and Jeremy as if together we hold a volatile explosive.

Looking at her now, her long thin neck, straight shoulders, rigid posture, it's almost impossible to reconcile her with the wild woman who rode my fingers a few minutes ago, the woman who wears turquoise bras and writes filthy sex all day.

So much of our time has been spent online, texting or on the phone, I have spent too little time studying her expressions in person, but I can already read her.

Everyone else in the room seems to be either too drunk or too distracted to notice.

The brown-haired woman, Penny—Mia's mom was right about her tits—seems to be the only one aware of Mia's emotional state. She keeps glancing between the two of us. I study her from my peripheral vision.

This is a woman whose father killed her mother and took his own life when she was barely even nine years old. A history of violence, a lousy childhood. She lies to hide that. Who can blame her? Not me. I don't mention my mother. Nor does James. Not that there's anything to mention.

The red-head, Erica, and her man are busy regaling us with stories, a two-person standup routine.

I've got no complaints. Thanks to them, James and I were invited to come back to the hotel lounge with them, and spend more time with this curious woman I've spent the last several months mentally dissecting. And as a bonus, I get to annoy this phony Dixon fucker a bit more. Beyond all that, they run solid distraction for me.

Every single extra set of stimuli in the room is a point in my favor.

Dixon is trying to focus on the game, but the alcohol, the laughter, it all stirs together to keep his attention divided. Danny keeps messing with the fire, Penny with her hair, Caesar with Erica's hair.

I think Dixon is trying to count the cards, but I doubt he's capable of it. At least not in this frame of mind, maybe not at all, judging by his debt.

He's down by only a hundred dollars so far. I'll make sure it gets higher.

James tops off everyone's glasses again. He's a good Robin. And he's surprisingly good with financials. He tracked the transfer from my account to an offshore holding company, called Broxman, Telker and Shone, based in the Caymans.

Someone owns it. And whoever owns it, is Ender. We hit a dead end there though, it's anonymously registered. Another dead end. I could call Lex, but I hate to bug her, and if I'm honest, a selfish, territorial, swamp-dweller part of me wants to be the one to save Mia on my own, and kill whatever fuck is after her.

Dixon drops his arm around Mia. My teeth clench. I hate that he touches her, that he has the right to, and I don't.

"So, Jeremy," I say. "You travel a lot?"

He tosses a card across the table, draws a new one, and his eyes gleam, before he replaces it with an irritable little frown. This is one of his tells. It's why he's a shitty gambler. He's as transparent as a freshly-cleaned window.

"A good bit." He sips his whiskey. With every sip, his good old boy façade slips, and in its wake come the jitters. I'd say it's crazy Mia hasn't noticed, but people see what they expect to see, what they're accustomed to seeing. And Mia expects him to be a good man.

He's not a good man. But he doesn't seem like a killer either.

He glances warily at me. "Just got back from China."

Lie. But he's in good company. I glance around the room. Mia's lying to everyone. I'm lying to Mia. Jer is lying to Mia. Danny is lying to Mia about his job. Penny about her family. We are a pack of liars. I wonder what Erica and Caesar lie about.

On the table is a three of hearts and a jack of spades.

I have a three of clubs, a ten of diamonds, and a six of spades.

Mia slides from under his arm, tucks her feet under her, smoothing her dress over her thighs. I still haven't seen what color her panties are. Maybe they're turquoise like the bra... or maybe not.

I set down the six and draw a new card.

Whatever the color, it's riding right over her warm slippery pussy. My fingers remember the feel of her, the clingy fluttery grip of her pulsing with orgasm.

I turn over the card. A three of diamonds.

Dixon turns over his hand and lays them out on the table with a smug flourish of his fingers and finishes his whiskey.

"Nice hand." I pause, make a show of admiring. "A pair of jacks is tough to beat."

I meet Mia's gaze. She cradles a glass of red wine.

I flip over my three.

Jeremy exhales a relieved sigh. "Jacks beat threes."

Erica and Caesar chatter away, and Penny laughs.

Danny leans forward.

I turn over the ten next. I'm in no rush. Jacks don't always beat threes.

A hotel server takes orders. Mia asks if I want more wine, but I shake my head no, turn over my last card.

"Three threes."

Caesar's voice trails off.

Dixon's nostrils flare. "You won."

I nod, and he slides the stack of bills across the table.

"My wallet's empty." He stands rigidly, but musters up a wry smile. "I guess that means it's time for bed."

He glances at Mia.

She looks around the room at Penny and Danny on the sofa opposite, and Caesar sitting on the carpet, leaning against Erica's legs, at James in his chair. "I'm having fun," she says.

His fingers twitch.

She tucks her hair behind her ears. "I think I'll stay up a little longer."

"Okay then. Please be quiet when you come in." He turns away, to walk rigidly down the hall.

Everyone starts talking all at once, covering the awkwardness of the moment. Erica stretches lazily, Danny asks if I golf, I ask him about his job just to see what he'll do. He lies badly, looking guilty. No poker face.

When the conversation allows it, I ask Penny about her family too. She lies well, sending a look toward Mia that makes me wonder if she told her the truth.

I lean back and bide my time.

They'll go to bed soon. Eventually.

Then Mia will be mine.

YOUR THONG IS NEON PINK

MIA

I'm going to hell. I deserve it.

Worse. In this moment, I want to be there.

Stranger's eyes linger on mine so full of promise and darkness that I want to do all the bad things. This man brings out the worst of me, or maybe the best, I don't know or even care. I look at him and I want it all. The good, the bad, and the blazing intensity I know we'll find together.

Jeremy left an hour ago. James wheeled himself down the hallway shortly thereafter. Danny and Penny left a few minutes ago, and guessing by the drunk horny look on Erica's face, she's about to drag Caesar away.

Which will leave me alone with *him*.

Somewhere between Jeremy's departure and this moment, I decided I didn't care about telling Jeremy before I sleep with Stranger.

He walked away from me without a second glance. He doesn't even see me. He cared more about his empty wallet, the loss of fewer than a thousand dollars, than about the man who's been eye-fucking me right in front of him. Blatantly. Everyone noticed. Even Danny pulled me aside at one point and asked if I was okay. *Everyone* saw how Stranger looks at me. Everyone except Jer.

Half an hour after Jer went to bed, the lobby bar closed up and we moved to a small library off the hallway that leads to our rooms. There's a low fire burning, almost down to embers. This is the oldest part of the hotel, I think. The original farmhouse. This nook is cozy, with a stone hearth, thick with crumbling mortar and old stones, creaking floorboards and a low, beamed ceiling.

Stranger stands up, setting his glass down on the coffee table and tosses another log on the fire. Sparks dance up the chimney, hissing and crackling.

I'm sitting on the floor with my legs crossed, leaning against a chair, and as I stare up at him, I can tell that he's thinking dirty *dirty* thoughts.

I don't bother to hide my own. I know him well by now. He likes that I want him. If we were texting, I'd bet he'd tell me to flash him my panties.

Erica stands and tugs on Caesar's hand. "Bedtime, lover."

He takes her hand. They mutter absent goodbyes but are already so focused on one another, they don't notice the way Stranger drops back into his seat, spreads his legs wide and sends me a look of such stark, unconcealed lust, my heart kicks a beat and the air rushes from my lungs.

Erica and Caesar meander off, and all the while Stranger and I stare each other down.

There are three rooms on this hall. One is Penny and Danny's, one is Caesar and Erica's, and one is mine and Jer's. Anyone could come here at any time.

Stranger's dimple glimmers in the firelight as he reads my thoughts. *The likelihood is low.*

I pull a face. *In public?*

Stranger shrugs, and I can practically hear him. *The way the floorboards creak and groan, we'd hear them long before they got here.*

I let my gaze settle on his neck, imagine sinking my teeth into the firm flesh.

His gaze lingers on my lips, and I pout for him.

I stroke my fingers down my thighs, he taps the arms of his chair. They were inside me only hours ago, thick and insistent.

His gaze drops to my tits. My nipples chafe against my bra.

I study his groin, see the bulge.

His lips stretch into a full-smile, and he tilts his chin toward my legs.

I bite my lower lip and slowly part my thighs so he can see between them. A lot of bare winter-pale skin and hot pink panties.

His smile flickers, his brows lower for a minute almost as if he's in pain, and he shifts in his seat, tugging at the front of his pants.

We haven't even said a thing. Don't need to.

We've already mindfucked so many times, his body is like icing on a cake, hot, hard, muscled, dangerous, strange icing. I want it so bad.

"Come here." His voice is so rough and raw and silky I swear I can feel the soundwaves moving over my skin.

I make him wait, savoring the power of the moment. This big hard man wants me so badly his fingers twitch.

Finally, I set my wine aside and do something I've never done for anyone.

My eyes locked on him, I crawl. Not far. Maybe seven or eight feet, but the glory of the moment is mine as he watches my body make slow, sinuous cat-like process across the rough weave carpet. I might be crawling, but there's no doubt, I hold the cards now.

I hover before him, waiting, holding my breath. "We're doing this?"

He nods.

I lick my lips. "Right here?"

"Right here." He keeps his voice low, but still it sends ripples over my skin. It's hard to believe we're actually together.

"Right now?"

His lips quirk. "Right now."

"What if someone walks in?"

"They won't."

I look around the little area. "We can't have sex thirty feet from Jeremy."

He laughs, transforming his whole face in the warm light of the flickering flames. And then the laughter is gone, I'm yanked forward and he takes my mouth in a kiss so intense it's blinding. His breath, his tongue, his lips, they rob me of air. And then it's over.

"It will be fine," he breathes against my lips.

The muscles of his arms ripple under the Henley tee, the bottom of his tattoos peeking free, swirling green and bold blue. "Trust me."

Such a simple statement, but so loaded. Trust him that no one will find us? Or trust him with *me*?

A log cracks in the fire.

I don't know if I trust him. But I'm willing to do this anyway, and that right there scares me. I'm not myself with this man. Or maybe I'm more myself. I take risks. I revel in the risks.

Trust matters, yes. But the excitement, the life that pulses through my veins matters too, and my whole life I've been ignoring it, doing the safe thing, the right thing, the easy thing.

Not now, not here, not tonight. We can deal with the trust issue in the morning. Now, in the night, we'll tackle the desire.

I snake my hands up his thighs, along hard muscles, up to the belt at the top of his jeans.

"I've thought about this a thousand times."

The belt chinks as I open it. His hazel eyes go black.

The zipper whirs. He shifts his hips, helping me tug his pants down below his knees, and there it is. Stranger's cock, in the flesh. The dick pic didn't lie.

I lean down and lave my tongue along the silky smooth skin, up the veined length, to the broad top.

"Fuuuuuuck," he hisses, long and low, his head dropping back.

I smile because I like that he's on the edge of control. I want to make him lose it.

He sees that in my eyes and laughs, pulling me back in for a rough, fast kiss, even harder than before. He was toying with me then, this time he is genuinely amped up, his tongue drives in deep, forcing me to take it. His hands clench, demanding, commanding.

I flatten my hands against his chest and wrench my mouth from his, lowering down to accept the wide, fat head of his cock, my eyes rolling back at the first vivid touch of him, the slick slide across the back of my tongue.

In that moment, there is nothing I want more. His grip on my neck tightens, and I realize something. I'm different with him than I am with anyone else, for anyone else.

For him, I'll open wide, I'll take him deep.

He leans back in his chair, guiding my head, helping me please him, and I live for his quiet moans. I'm hungry for them. I stare up with eyes wide, studying his face, so familiar and yet so new, as his eyes drift shut, his lips slide into a smile, his hips thrust.

He is not a passive recipient of my attention. He is active, he controls and dictates, he shows me exactly what he wants and we work together. And even though it's the first time, it feels like it's the hundredth or the thousandth time. We know each other so well.

Between my thighs, I spasm for him, desperate for the moment he will slide inside. But first, I want his pleasure. I wonder if this is what he felt when he slid his fingers inside me and felt my orgasm, tasted me on his own fingers. I feel powerful because it is me who is making his muscles quiver, it is *me* who has weakened this big strong man so much that he whimpers, it is me who has made his mouth go slack.

I find myself slobbering and feeling almost proud as he slides a little deeper into my throat. And when he grits out, "I'm going to cum," normally I'd pull away, but I don't. Not for him. For him I work that much harder, smiling and moaning like a porn star, savoring the noises and expressions he makes, the way his eyes lose focus and his nose wrinkles, the way his hips buck and the tip swells in the back of my throat, as he fills my mouth with bitter hot salt.

He pants and grunts and whispers hoarse words of praise to me, things that would have made me laugh if Jer even tried to say them, things that would sound stupid from anyone else, but from him, they just melt me. The best of which is, "holy fuck, you're killing me."

He drops his head back against the chair and slides his fingers through my hair with a raw laugh, tugging me closer. As I swallow the last of him down, my cheeks hollow out and I take him into the back of my throat. I have to work not to gag. My eyes water, but for him, I choke by the impulse to gag, and just open wider for him.

The look in his eyes is incendiary.

I am on fire for him.

This man and me.

We are perfect together.

I'm wet and hot and pulsing, and so frustrated I could scream. I want him inside me. I want his hands on me. I want him. That's all. Just him.

Any way I can have him.

"Told you it would be like this…" His grip tightens and I arch into his hands, letting his thickness slide from my mouth with a pop.

"We aren't done." I glare up at him.

"No." His thumb trails along my lower lip. "We aren't anywhere close to done."

His lips close down on mine, his hand slides down my spine, between the cheeks of my ass, hooking down between my thighs, and he scoops me up like I weigh nothing. I scrabble to gain purchase with my feet, but my effort is pointless. I am in his lap, my legs around his waist before I can even get my bearings.

My dress rucks up. His hands palm my ass, fingers spreading wide, as he lets out a satisfying sigh. His cock, still hard, sits against my panties.

"Your thong is neon pink."

I nod, unsure what to say or why he seems to like that fact so much.

He guides my face to his, so my forehead rests against him. We stay like that for a long time, I don't even know how long. There's so much unsaid. Something in his eyes tells me he wants to talk, say something, tell me something that will change all of this, let it all out. But whatever it is, I'm not ready.

"Don't, Stranger." I blink fast. "Please, don't."

He pulls away from me, reaching for his pants, I rise up on my knees to help him as he tugs up his jeans.

With a curse, he grips my ass, and rises fluidly, taking me with him.

I wrap my legs around his waist and hold on tight as he walks us out of the room.

The guilt is there, simmering somewhere under the surface, or maybe it's more shame. My allegiance shifted somewhere along the line. I don't see Jeremy as my partner in life. He doesn't see me the way Stranger does. Jeremy looks through me, sees the life I offer rather than the human I am.

I didn't know that was a problem until Stranger came into my life and showed me what it meant to be seen, truly seen and heard by another person. Someone who cares, deeply, about my unique needs and desires.

Stranger is right.

I do belong to someone, and it isn't Jeremy.

Maybe it's Stranger.

I owe it to myself to find out.

Morning will be here soon. My eyes shut. My head rests on Stranger's chest in the pre-dawn dark. Through the windows, it's still in the way of winter, almost eerily silent, as only places can be when they're full of people and all of them are sound asleep.

Except us.

I lay half on top of him. He has chest hair just as he said. And as he said, it's not a lot, but enough to tickle my nose as I rub it across the shadowed hollow between his pecs.

In the scarce light, he's practically a statue, too perfect to be real. Muscle ridges and smooth skin, but his body is warm. So warm, I don't need or even want covers.

I've had sex before. I mean, physically, I've done it. I know how it works, but I have never truly had sex before. Not like this.

Stranger just ruined me for anything and anyone else. I didn't know it could be like this, not really. I've been writing about love and romance like this for as long as I can remember and somewhere inside, I've always felt like I've been playing at make-believe. But it's real.

I feel like I just worked out, took a long, steamy shower, had a massage, did some yoga, slept ten hours, won the lottery, ate some chocolate, took drugs or found Jesus or, I don't even know, had about eighteen thousand orgasms.

I'm sore in all the right places, energized, and sleepy, and comfortable and so happy I want to sing or dance or run or laugh for sheer joy. I've never in my whole life had sex where I connected with the person, mind and body. It's as if I've been searching for something my entire life and I just found it. It's Stranger.

We moved together like our brains had melded, synced and worked in tandem. He used his tongue and his hands, and his beautiful cock on me, and my body took over, writhing and bucking, and when he slid inside me finally, filling me so full it almost hurt, he touched my cheek with his rough fingertips and I swear, something deep inside of me changed irrevocably.

My eyes burned and a tear spilled over and even though I felt girly and stupid, I couldn't help it. He turned me into putty.

He smiled and kissed my tear, nudging a little deeper inside. "Hello, Mia."

See? He gets me. It made my face crumple with a cry-laugh. "Hi, Stranger."

After all this time, all the texts and PMs, phone calls and doubt, having him there, in the flesh, on top of me, all around me, inside me was a revelation. And from the look in his eyes, all warm and practically adoring, he felt it too.

Absurd as it is, ridiculous as it was, my heart just split right open. And it only got better. He stoked up a rhythm that left us both sweating and panting and gasping—and yes, convulsing—until finally, he pulled out and finished on my belly, his eyes locked on mine as his face twisted and contorted.

In the darkness, his lips curved. He shifted his weight over to the side of me and trailed a finger through the cum pooling on my belly. "Not a bucket-full."

That made me smile. "No."

"What would one of your characters do with it?"

"Hmmm... My current male character would probably scoop it up on his finger and feed it to the female main character. I don't know. She'd probably secretly want that too."

"And you?"

I could see where this was going. "I'd probably ask for a warm wet washcloth."

"You don't want to lick it off my fingers."

I plucked at the bed covers. "Not really."

"Why not?"

"It's fine in theory. It's hot in theory, but it doesn't really taste that great."

"Is it about the flavor though? Or about the fact that you'd be doing something that would please me."

His eyes met mine and I'd be lying if I didn't say that my pussy clenched at the deep timbre of his voice as he said those words, and trailed a blunt finger through the splatter, gathering it onto his finger.

"Would it please you?"

"Yes."

That voice. It does things to me. "Why?"

His paused and brought his fingers up to hover over my lips so close I could feel the heat. "It's in my head now. You put it there, or we did together. Maybe a small part likes the idea of you doing something for no other reason than because I asked, wanting to know a part of me will stay with you. Maybe even know that you don't really like the taste, but you want me so bad you'll take my cum anyway."

I licked my lips. "You still haven't actually asked."

"Open your mouth, Mia."

I did.

"And lick my cum off my fingers."

Yes. If you're wondering. I did it.

I even stuck out my tongue like a woman in a porn movie, feeling a little stupid and a little embarrassed, but the look in his eyes... man alive, it made my whole body sing and beg for an encore performance, and by that point, I was so totally his, I'd have done just about anything he asked.

"Dirty, Mia."

He trailed his fingers down my tongue, and I lapped at them, savored the salt and the bitter.

I made love to his fingers like I was dying and they would save me.

He groaned like it hurt.

The memory burns through me. I still feel a little embarrassed, but if I mentioned it, he'd only laugh.

His smell wafts around me—woodsy, manly, homey soap. I don't want to leave him ever.

"I need to go," I say.

His hand tightens, squeezing my ass and pulling me closer, but he doesn't argue.

"Mia..." he says, his voice trailing off in the silent dark.

"Yeah?"

His fingers bite into my skin. "I just wanted to say, be careful, okay."

"Of what?"

"You won't like me mentioning it, but those comments on your website and your social media accounts bug me."

I pull back with a sigh. What is it with men? "It's just some idiot enjoying being anonymous."

"You don't know that, though. What if it's someone you already know."

"What if it is? Should I stop writing? Hide out? Let them win?"

He's quiet, and I can't follow his line of thought.

"It's not someone I know. No one I know would do that."

His mouth tightens. "It's just... You're way too trusting."

Now, I pull back. "Are you trying to tell me something, Stranger?"

His jaw clenches.

"What about you? Am I too trusting with you?" I try to see him through the dark. "There's a lot I don't know about you. A lot I won't ask. I've been respectful, let you keep your secrets, even though I tell you everything, anything you ask. So, tell me now, who shouldn't I trust? Jeremy? Myself? Random internet people? You?"

His grip on my ass tightens, and he flips us over, so I'm on my back beneath him, the hard ridge of his cock lying against my belly. "You can trust me Mia."

"Even though you don't trust me?"

"Who says I don't trust you?"

"You have a lot of secrets."

He gets a grip on my leg, his fingers sliding along the soft skin behind my knee, and he pulls me open wide, presses against my entrance, slides inside where I'm sore and tender from earlier.

His hisses. "Everyone has secrets. Sometimes it's better that way."

I bear down, squeezing him tight, wrapping my legs around his waist. "I don't have secrets."

He gets a grip on my hair, pulls my face up to meet his shadowed eyes. "You lie to your whole family."

"I mean from you. I have no secrets from yo—"

He silences me with his mouth. When I try to rock my hips to get him deeper, he withdraws so only the head of his cock is inside me. Over and over again he tortures me. Gentle touches that leave if I push against him. Only when I sag, limp and exhausted on the bed, does he touch a hard thumb to the throbbing bundle of nerves, making tight circles.

It's fast after that, the orgasm rolling over me, leaving me practically lifeless on the bed. He grits his teeth through the whole thing, pulling out at the end to spurt over the bare skin of my lower belly.

"My secrets don't matter, Mia."

A chill settles over me, when I remember the look on his face earlier, how carefully planned his every move was last night. How bad could his secrets be? Is it about his mom? The military? His job?

Part of me doesn't want to know.

I can just barely make out his features in the thin moonlight, slipping silver through the windows. And oddly, the darkness feels more comfortable to me than the light of the winery felt last night.

We've spent most of our relationship apart. I feel less exposed to him when he can't stare me down with those unsettling hazel eyes.

His big, rough hands slide down to my waist and he lets out a sleepy murmur that has my heart clenching in my chest.

"End it with him, Mia."

"I will."

"When?"

"Today."

"Good. I don't want you anywhere near him ever again."

The possessive tone in his voice makes my toes curl.

He's quiet for a long moment.

The hotel around us is silent. It's like we are alone here, like time could stretch on endlessly, and we'd be here, in bed, warm and naked, under the moonlight, surrounded by ice and snow.

He rolls toward me, so he's on his side, his arms looped loosely around my hips, his skin hot on mine. "How will you do it?"

"I don't know that I'll tell him about you. I think that would be crueler. I think I'll just say that I don't think we're a good fit. We aren't. He must see that on some level."

"Where though? Where will you do it?"

I play through the day. We'll drive back with Danny and Penny, drop them at Mom and Dad's, then go on to my place. I imagine telling him in the car and cringe.

"I think I'll wait until we get to my house. Then before he can get out to carry my bag inside, I'll tell him."

"Thanks for the ride. Here's your ring. Bye." His words are sarcastic, but his tone isn't. It's gentle. Almost musing.

That's something I know about Stranger. He teases me, but there's appreciation behind it. Like when he texted that he'd laugh as I danced, it would have been gentle laughter, not caustic.

My heart clenches freshly. "Basically. Only hopefully I can word it more kindly."

"Do it in a public place. Don't let him come up with you."

I can't resist tracing my hand along the swirls of his tattoos. "You're worried he'll get angry? And what? Hurt me?"

His shrug makes the mattress shift and the sheets whisper. "It happens."

"Not Jer. He doesn't have a violent bone in his body. He doesn't even kill bugs. I kill bugs for him."

He makes a noise in his throat. "Can I come down tonight after he's gone?"

I hesitate.

"I want to see you again."

The desire to see him again burns so hot in my chest, it blazes through my veins, and my mouth lowers automatically to kiss his lips. "Yes. Not until later, just in case he wants to talk or something. I'll text you."

"Promise me you won't be alone with him." His fingers slide through my hair, along my scalp.

I want to stay with him so badly, but at least there's a tangible end to the separation. I don't even want to be away from him again. It's like I finally found my home and now I have to leave. And somehow, I have this feeling like we won't see each other again.

"Jer wouldn't hurt me."

He blows out an irritable puff of air. "Let me know when it's over."

WHAT IF I SAY MOO?

MIA

A few hours later, Jer slides the last of our small bags into his trunk under an overcast gray sky. We hug Caesar and Erica goodbye.

The clouds huddle sullen and swollen above us. Maybe it will snow later in the day.

I let Danny have the front seat and sit in the back next to Penny. Jer is mostly silent on the drive home. He didn't wake up when I slipped into our room and climbed straight into the shower, but he's been quiet all day.

He probably thinks I'm annoyed with him for the way he handled my writing.

Or maybe he's angry because he saw my tattoo again when I was getting dressed this morning.

His gaze keeps slithering past me like he can't quite bear to look at me.

Everyone else is hungover, sunglasses on, drinking coffee like zombies. Each of them must have gotten more sleep than me, but I feel better than I have in my whole life, like I've just been set free after a long dark imprisonment. There's just one final set of shackles built of guilt left to be broken.

I need to tell Jeremy. It won't be easy, but he'll be happier in the end, with someone other than me.

And... Annie, I'll have to tell her too.

The thought burns thick in my stomach.

I text her now, as Jer drives down winding roads banked by gray-stained snow toward the highway.

> Mia: How are you, friend?

She answers fast. Breastfeeding maybe. She always is.

> Annie: The twins slept four hours straight last night. The SAME four hours. So that's good.

> Mia: Is four hours a lot?

> Annie: Yes. Usually they both wake up every two to three and not the same two to three. I almost never get to sleep more than an hour and a half at a time. This was huge.

> Mia: Then I amend my prior statement and say YAY! Woohooo! Four hours is awesome!

> Annie: Ha. How was Finger Lakes?

> Mia: Jer and I got into a fight.

> Annie: Why?

> Mia: He doesn't like my writing. We all drank too much, and he played blackjack and it just… I don't know.

> Annie: Jer gambled? How much did he lose?

> Mia: Whatever was in his wallet. A few hundred, not sure.

There is a long pause on her end. So long I put my phone down and watch the frozen landscape slide by. Danny and Penny talk about bands they want to see. I nearly drift asleep when the phone buzzes and it's her.

> Annie: You're having cold feet. These doubts are normal. Jer has no problem with your writing. You've always written. It will be okay.

I don't answer. I don't know what I'd say. It's not cold feet. But I'm trying to warn Annie. I don't want our break-up to shock her.

> Mia: How are you doing? Depressed?

> Annie: I'm not sure. I've never been depressed before. Mostly I just want sleep. But at least my nipples aren't bleeding.

Mia: Sigh. That's good. I think we can all agree that life is better when your nipples aren't bleeding.

Annie: Word.

Mia: Can I come by tomorrow night? I'll sleep over. Wake up with the babies. Let you sleep.

Annie: Are you a cow?

Mia: Not last time I checked.

Annie: Then you don't have milk. I'm the only one who can do it. Thanks though.

Mia: What if I say moo? I could bring the babies to you?

Annie: Greg does that. I don't even get up. He's started sleep walking.

Mia: Then I could let him get some sleep?

Annie: Nah, we'll muddle through. You'd never forgive me for the things I say in the middle of the night. I'm such a bitch. I don't even know how he's managing work.

Mia: Annie, I'd forgive you anything. Let me come by this weekend. You can go take a nap.

Annie: Deal.

My eyes well up. She may not even want to see me by then.

Jer's phone rings just as we hit the highway.

"Hey, Mom," he says, voice still a little rough from his hangover.

"Jer?" Even Penny, who's never met Jer's mom can tell something is wrong. Her voice has that warning tone people get when they're about to tell someone bad news.

"Mom? What is it?"

"It's your father." She pauses as if she's gearing herself up for something, and I reach forward to touch his shoulder.

"What's wrong with him?"

"We didn't want to tell you until after Thanksgiving."

"You're scaring me, Mom. Just tell me."

He hunches over the steering wheel like a beaten man, like he already knows whatever she's going to say isn't going to be good.

Danny touches his shoulder. "You need to pull over, man. Let someone else drive." He raises his voice. "Hang on, Mrs. Dixon. We're on the highway. Just let Jer pull over."

Jer is shaking, but he gets the car to the shoulder, and he and Danny switch places.

"We're back in the car, Mom. What's wrong with Dad? Is he dead?"

"No, sweetheart. Nothing like that." She takes in a deep breath, and I can picture her bird-like hands clutching tissues, her face tight with concern. "I didn't want to scare you. And I think he was embarrassed. It was little things at first. He was sick sometimes. Lost his appetite and then he lost weight. The doctor ordered some tests done. We thought it might be an ulcer but..."

Oh no. I squeeze Jer's arm.

She's silent for a long moment. Probably letting that sink in. I know what's coming, and my selfish heart sinks, because it means I can't possibly break it off with Jeremy now, and no way will I be able to see Stranger tonight.

Instantly after, shame sets in at my selfish heart. Poor Jer. Poor Annie. This will be so hard on them.

"Your dad has cancer, honey. I'm so sorry."

Jer reaches up and squeezes my hand. "How bad is it?"

"Pretty bad. Stage four."

I'VE ALWAYS BEEN A COWARD

STRANGER

Mia still hasn't texted me that it's over.

It's nearly mid-afternoon. They should be close to her parents' house in Newport by now.

James is in the living room.

I'm pacing.

Gogo's staring at me with brown, morose eyes. She still hasn't forgiven me for leaving her with a pet-sitter in town last night. Every time I look at her, she blinks at me like I've abandoned her. I'd reassure her, but someday I really will abandon her, maybe it's good for her to get used to it.

Back and forth I go, watching the hills in the backyard through the windows, and checking my phone incessantly.

Ender contacted me again.

I keep reading the message over and over again.

> Ender9551: I'd like to take out a second hit. Same time? Same place? Jeremy Dixon. Name your price.

Guess that means Jeremy didn't hire me.

"Stop pacing," James says.

"No."

He drops his book on his chest. "What's bothering you?"

I blow out a breath.

A woman I increasingly think of as mine is driving home with another man. We just had sex for the first time—my dick is still sore, as are the muscles of my ass and thighs, and I'm sure she's not so comfortable herself—and instead of spending the day together, cementing that bond, she's driving away from me, toward an unknown person who wants her dead. And I can't be there to help her. Even if I could, what would be the point? I can't keep her.

Gogo flops her head on the wood floor next to James, who tilts his head at me.

I can't keep any of this. This isn't the life I get to have, the brother, the dog, the house, the woman.

So I turn back to the barren trees outside.

"Don't..." James clears his throat. "Don't shut me out again, Stranger. What happened?"

Is that what I've done? Shut him out. When did I stop? Things have been easier between James and me for a while now. Maybe he's right, maybe since we started working together to find out who's trying to kill Mia, I've been sharing more with him. Talking to him more. I thought it was Tasha, or maybe just time. But maybe it's also me. Between him and Mia, they're forcing me to be human again, and I don't like it.

I tuck my hands into my pockets. "Ender took out a second hit."

He leans forward. "For who?"

"Dixon."

Oddly, he doesn't comment on that, instead asking, "Did you fuck her?"

"Yes." I turn away from the frigid mountain.

"She going to end it with him?"

"Says she will." I cross the room, drop down on the sofa, and finally Gogo seems to relent. She approaches me slowly, staring up with forlorn eyes.

I scratch the top of her head and her eyes roll back. When I smile, she rests her head on my thigh. Someone once told me dogs can't read our facial expressions. They were wrong. Gogo reads my face just fine.

James is still by the window. "Are you in love with her?"

In love with her? What would be the point? Even if I were, it wouldn't change anything. But I don't say any of that. I just stand there wondering what my life would look like if I were some other guy. A guy who got to have a life. I let it play out in my head... I'd buy a plot of land. There's an empty lot next door. Build a house. Let Mia fill it up with all her colorful shit. Maybe start my own business doing private security contracting. Designing systems and details. I've thought about it. There are enough people in New England who need custom security packages. On weekends, I'd be with Mia, write with her, laugh with her, maybe even have a family if that's what she wants.

"No."

James sends me a knowing look but doesn't argue. "So I guess Dixon isn't Ender."

I shake my head. "Unless he's suicidal, but given the timing–he was driving south with a car full of people today–I can't see it."

"Who then?"

I shrug helplessly.

My phone lights up. Finally.

> Mia: He just found out his dad has cancer. I can't do it now.

I blow out a breath. Before I can respond, she texts again.

> Mia: I'm sorry. I'll tell him. Please don't be upset.

Worry. This is what worrying feels like. I hate it.

> Stranger: I'm not upset. You're Mia. I wouldn't like you so much if you were the type of person who'd break up with a guy a few minutes after they got news like that. You okay?

> Mia: I'm fine. Just wish I could see you again.

> Stranger: Soon

When I toss my phone onto the couch beside me, James threads his hands together behind his neck. "I have an idea."

Thank fuck. Because I've got nothing. "Shoot."

"Say yes to Ender. Name a price. We'll watch them. See who's moving money around."

I shake my head. "We already did. The money comes from that account in Cayman. It's a dead end."

James nods. "Yeah, but somebody is moving the money to the account."

That's almost impossible. "We'd need access to every single account they have. Everyone we think might be behind it. And what if we've missed someone."

"Yeah."

I run my thumbs over Gogo's soft ears, think about Mia's electric pink thong. I'm starting to like her colors.

"We need help," I say.

I should have done this a long time ago. It takes a brave man to admit he needs help and I've always taken the coward's way out. With Mom after Dad died, with James after Mom left, with Mia.

I turn back to my phone, shoot off a fast email with everything relevant I know about Mia and the various suspects, and text the one person I know who's got the skillset to help with this. We haven't spoken in over a year, but we worked together for a long time. She'll answer.

> Stranger: I need you.

Her response comes back almost instantly.

> Lex: And here I am. Handy, isn't it?

> Stranger: How long would it take you to get financial details on a handful of people?

> Lex: Depends who they are.

> Stranger: Check your inbox. I'll pay whatever it costs.

> Lex: Eager much?

> Stranger: Very. Can you do it?

> Lex: For you, I can do anything. Kiss kiss.

> Stranger: Bang bang. Read my email, get back to me.

We wait while she reads them, James and Gogo and I silent. She's fast.

> Lex: A woman, Stranger. Didn't take you for the type.
>
> Stranger: The type who likes women?
>
> Lex: The type who falls in love. She's cute.
>
> Stranger: I'm not in love. We're going to reverse track a transfer. How long will it take?
>
> Lex: For all these people? Two, maybe three weeks.
>
> Stranger: That's too long.
>
> Lex: Have you noticed Christmas is less than a month away?
>
> Stranger: You're Jewish.
>
> Lex: The rest of the world isn't. I'll be as fast as I can.
>
> Stranger: How much?
>
> Lex: 10k plus expenses, family discount.
>
> Stranger: No problem.

20 - I TRUST YOU

MIA

I wait an hour and text Annie when we are almost at my parents' house. I keep it non-committal in case she hasn't heard yet. Everyone in the car is silent. No one knows what to say.

> Mia: You okay?

> Annie: You know about Dad?

> Mia: Yes. I'm so sorry.

> Annie: My poor mom. I can't believe I didn't realize something was going on. She was so distracted when she came up to see the babies. I actually got mad at her.

> Mia: You've had a lot going on. Don't blame yourself.

> Annie: And poor Jer. How's he holding up? I'm so worried about him with everything else with the company. It's just so much. I'd hate for him to have a relapse.

I frown at my phone, then out the window. The snow is gone down here, but the day is still gray. A relapse? She obviously thinks I know something I don't know. And if she realizes I don't know, then she won't tell me anything. Annie, close as she is to me, will always choose her family over anything else.

> Mia: I wouldn't worry. He's doing okay.

I pull a face. That better be true. What the hell could he be struggling with? We've been dating for a long time, so it has to have been before me. I glance up at Jer, slouched in the passenger seat, his forehead pressed against the passenger window.

He and his dad have always been close, but a distance has grown between them lately. I thought it was just Jer being busy with work, but now I'm not so sure.

Maybe his dad withdrew because of the illness?

I scale through the past few years, but I can't think of a single thing Annie could be referring to. A relapse?

Drugs? I've never seen Jer do anything more than smoke a joint, though I knew he did a lot of cocaine in college.

Alcohol? Maybe. He certainly drinks plenty, but I've never known him to go on benders, or drink and drive. I've never seen him act like an alcoholic, however alcoholics act.

Sex? The thought almost makes me laugh. Definitely not.

What else do people even become addicted to?

> Annie: Hmmmm. I thought we'd moved past it. But he's under so much stress with the business struggling, and the board, and now Dad. It would be so easy for him to fall back into his old ways.

Old ways? What 'old ways?' If he had 'old ways', I'd have seen them by now, right? What the hell is she talking about?

> Mia: I would know, Annie. He's been fine.

There's a pause so long, it becomes ripe with unspoken words. I'd give anything to be with her in person right now, so I could read her face, guess her thoughts.

> Mia: Unless you know more than me? Has he been falling back?

Hopefully, that's sufficiently vague and intelligent-sounding.

> Annie: I'm not sure. But I know he asked Mom and Dad for money a few weeks ago. And there's only one reason I can think of for that.

> Mia: Did they give it to him?

> Annie: No. Mom cried for days. She was convinced he'd taken out a second mortgage, that the board is suspicious. She even looked into his trips and found Macau and went ballistic. He says it was just business development, but who can say.

Macau? All I know is that it's off Hong Kong and people go there to party. So, I open the browser and google Macau.

My mind is busy with worries about prostitutes and STDs.

But the first thing that pops up are casinos.

People go to Macau to gamble.

The look in his eyes during poker last night comes back to me.

Who the hell am I engaged to? All this time I've thought Jer was nothing but kind and gentle and perfect, and I was the lying, cheating monster. But he's been gambling? His company is failing? They're suspicious of him? What else has he been hiding?

I text Stranger with a sinking heart and let him know I can't tell Jer now. His response makes my heart soar. He is becoming a single bright and shiny spot in my life. The hope to which I cling.

We drop off Penny and Danny, and I find myself tearing up as I hug them goodbye.

I've known Penny for only a few brief days, and yet I've come to truly care about her. "I'm going to miss you," I tell her as we say goodbye at the steps of my parents' house.

"I'll miss you too."

There's something about Penny that makes me feel like I knew her in another life. An old soul, my mom would probably say. "Tell Mom I'll call her tomorrow. But with Jer,"–I gesture his way–"I just can't come in."

She nods and just as I'm about to climb into the drivers' seat of Jer's car and take us home, I hesitate. "Hey Penny. You can trust my brother. Tell him. He won't disappoint you."

She smiles, wide and bright. "I will. You should tell your mom your secret. She won't disappoint you."

I grimace. Mom would make such a face if I told her, all blinky and repulsed. "I'll think about it."

"She might surprise you. That woman loves you so much."

Her eyes are a pure clear blue. It makes me wonder for a second, maybe I don't see Mom as clearly as I think I do. I obviously don't see Jer clearly either.

I climb into the car and the silence of Jer's grief is oppressive.

We don't talk much at all. He moves like an old man, like he's the one who's sick, like he's carrying the weight of the world on his shoulders. I have a million questions, but I bite my tongue.

Finally, when I can't stand it anymore, when we're inside, and he's sitting on my bed, facing away, staring out the window into the darkness of my own backyard, I open my mouth. "Are you okay?"

His shoulders bunch. "I hate when people ask that question. I'm not going to die, Mia. So sure, I'm okay. But my dad's dying."

"Fair enough." I pull my shirt over my head and tug down my pants, wincing as the tattoo over my shoulder stretches and burns.

He doesn't look back at me. "I don't know what I'll do without him. How the hell will I run the business without his help?"

"He's taught you what you need to know." I pull a nightgown over my head. It's a good lead in, though. Too good. I can't resist. "Annie mentioned the board was running an investigation. That you'd been under suspicion of embezzlement."

He glances back at me, his face turning red. "Annie talks too much."

"She seemed to think I already knew."

His rubs his neck.

"It's a reasonable assumption. I mean... most people would tell their fiancé something like that."

"I didn't want you to worry."

I toss my shoes in the corner, taking a deep breath to keep myself calm. "It's not about worrying. Don't you think I have a right to know if the man I'm going to marry is in debt? Might lose his job?"

"Everyone is in debt, Mia."

"Not me."

"Not everyone lives with a trust fund. Not everyone's parents pay for them to go to school."

"I know that. But I also think I should know what kind of debt you've got before I marry you."

He cocks his head. "So, you wouldn't marry me if I had debt?"

"I didn't say that."

"Then why does it matter?"

I find my own fists bunching. "Because if we got married, your debt would become mine. I'm not sure I want to take on debt without knowing how much debt there is."

"*If?*"

"How much debt, Jer?"

He sucks on his cheeks. "I don't know. My parents covered my school. I've got a mortgage."

I expected that. "Go on."

"Some credit card debt. I financed the car."

"What kind of credit card debt?"

"A few thousand on a couple different cards."

"How many thousands? How many cards? What's the total?"

He stands up and paces, his feet swishing on the blue patterned rug. "A couple hundred thousand dollars. Not too much. I'll pay it off as soon as I get the company back in the black."

I lower down onto the bed.

He keeps pacing across the room. I can't look at him. I stare at the wall behind him, listening as he talks about interest rates and greedy bankers.

He took out a jumbo loan on his house. Put down a few hundred thousand dollars. I remember how proud he was. A million-dollar loan. The car, call it another sixty thousand. A few hundred thousand dollars of debt. I bet he's lying. A few means three to me, but I bet it means five or six to him.

He's got debt ranging from one to two million dollars. The interest on that alone is crippling.

"Do you gamble?" I ask.

He stops pacing. The silence stretches. "A little."

"How much do you owe?"

"A few thousand. Not much."

"Who do you owe?"

"Jesus, Mia. This isn't a movie. What? You think I owe some mob boss a bunch of money?"

I can't stir up any words, because... yeah... that's pretty much exactly what I'm worried about.

He makes a scoffing sound in his throat. "Grow up."

What the hell do you say to a person when they say that. I *am* grown up. I don't have any debts. I don't gamble or steal or... cheat.

Oops.

I say nothing. My soul is hardly pure.

Jeremy stalks to the bathroom. "I'm going to shower and go to bed. Can we save the money talk for a day when I didn't find out my dad was dying?"

The door slams. I sit there for a long time.

Finally, I go back to my phone. There's a new text from Stranger.

> Stranger: Are you sad?

Mia: I'm sad for Jer, and for Annie, and in general for him. He's a nice man. But I'm fine. Mostly, I'm just frustrated because it means I can't tell Jer today.

Stranger: I don't like it but I get it.

Mia: I will tell him. I promise.

Stranger: When?

Mia: As soon as the dust settles, and he's okay.

Stranger: Is he spending the night with you?

I drop back on the bed, trace my palm over the flowery surface of the bedspread, look around my vibrant pink and blue room. This was where I lay the first time I spoke to Stranger.

We've come so far... and yet nothing is really different. Here we are with a pair of phones, a hundred miles and a fiancé between us.

I wonder where he is. Maybe in his spartan room on the leather sectional, picturing me alone with another man. I'd hate that if I were him.

Behind me the pipes in the wall rush with the sound of Jeremy's shower, and beyond that I hear the splash and splatter of the water against the tiles. What a tangled web I've woven. Now it feels like I'm cheating on Stranger.

Mia: Nothing will happen.

> **Stranger:** I don't like another man being in bed with you.

> **Mia:** It's not like that. We just got into a fight. We aren't speaking.

> **Stranger:** You belong in my bed. With me.

> **Mia:** Soon. Trust me.

> **Stranger:** It's not a matter of trust. I don't like another man being anywhere close to my woman. That… and I really want to watch you cum on my cock again. You make the best faces.

A dark thrill races through all my secret places. My whole body clenches, remembering the feel of him deep inside. I'm tender. Still hot for him. And the basest parts of me preen and rejoice at being claimed by him that way.

> **Mia:** Give me a week.

> **Stranger:** I fucking hate this. Every single goddamned thing about this situation.

> **Mia:** Me too.

> **Stranger:** One week.

I hold my breath, wondering what he'll say next. If he'll say anything at all. If he'll ask if I'll have sex with Jer. I won't. I wonder if he knows that, if he worries, if he trusts me. He doesn't say anything though.

Just as Jer turns off the shower faucet I text Stranger.

> Mia: Nothing will happen between him and me. Nothing has happened for a long time. You don't need to worry.

> Stranger: I trust you, Mia.

21 – HEAVEN SMELLS LIKE PEACHES

STRANGER

> Stranger: Did you do it?

I don't hold my breath, just toss my phone onto my bed and head toward the weight room.

James is there. We sweat together in a silence studded only by the clank of metal on metal.

His torso is deadly strong now, and what's left of his thighs.

"You know, I thought of something."

I glance his way. "What's that?"

"When I get the prostheses, I'll be back to being taller than you."

"By half an inch." I carefully set the hand weights back in the tree.

"Still," he pants, in the middle of a series of triceps lifts. "That's the worst thing. Having to look up at everyone. Even Tasha."

It's the first time he's mentioned her to me in any kind of a way that recognizes her as a woman. "She's cute."

He makes a face I can't quite interpret. Like he's agreeing and disagreeing at the same time. Like he thinks she's out of his league. A year and a half ago, he'd have said no one was out of his league. Now... I want to tell him something meaningful, like 'legs don't make the man', or something, but everything I can think up just sounds too stupid.

"Did she do it?" he asks, breaking my line of thought.

"Who do what?"

He rolls his eyes. "Mia. Did she end it?"

"No." My phone hasn't buzzed.

Her silence is enough of an answer. It's been seven days since she told me a week was all she needed.

And in that time, I have been busy. And so has Lex.

There is no one better.

The waiting creates a yawning chasm. Mia is in Providence with her grieving boyfriend. I am here, spying on her, stalking her, invading her privacy like a disease.

Secrets pile up between us like blocks in a wall that keep getting thicker and more impenetrable. Secrets I can never share with her.

They cloud my conscience. Anyone watching from the outside would condemn me. I have spied on her, stolen mail, read her phone messages and emails, spied on her friends and family. I've violated so much trust, that every time I think of it, a suffocating weight seizes my chest.

The evidence bloats my computer.

So many secrets.

Everyone has them.

Me.

Even Mia.

A little piece of her soul that she keeps only for herself. That's what would upset her parents, that she kept part of herself from them, the vibrant colorful part of her she gives only to me.

After another hour James eggs me to push harder than normal, until my whole body is shaking. Sweat pours down my back, and finally my phone buzzes.

> Mia: I can't tell him now. He's leaving for China to meet with a client. When he gets back.

I flop back on the bench.

> Stranger: You're delaying.

> Mia: No. Maybe. Can you imagine getting dumped before a 14-hour flight?

> Stranger: It's going to suck no matter when you do it. You think he'll be happier when you dump him as soon as he gets back?

> Mia: At least then he won't have to do a pitch to a client.

> Stranger: No. It will be Christmas next week. And then New Year's and then Valentine's Day. You're delaying. Own it. Don't lie to yourself Mia. Ask yourself why you're delaying.

> Mia: I hate you when you're right.

> Stranger: I'm always right.

> Mia: …
>
> Stranger: Ask yourself, why are you delaying?
>
> Mia: I'm delaying… because I don't want to hurt him. And because I know Annie will be upset.
>
> Stranger: Then tell Annie now. That's the hardest part. Then tell Jeremy when he gets back.
>
> Mia: … ugh… fine… yeah. Okay. I'll do it. I'll call her now.

We'll see. I'm not sure I believe her.

Gogo and I sit down and pay bills. Well, Gogo naps and drools on my feet, while I pay bills. Tasha isn't cheap. I pay her employer $140 an hour.

I'm going to need to take on a new job soon. The thought… bothers me for some reason.

When my phone rings a few minutes later, I'm surprised to see Mia's name on the caller ID. I didn't expect to hear from her for a while.

"Hey."

"I did it." Her voice is thick with tears.

I push away from the computer. "How did she take it?"

"Not good. She said I'm selfish, this is just pre-wedding jitters. She couldn't believe I decided to do it now, right before Christmas." There's a pause with a soft wet laugh. "She said she'd never talk to me again. I should think about other people instead of myself all the time. She started crying. She hung up on me."

I grit my teeth. "She'll come around. And if she doesn't, she wasn't as good a friend as you think she is."

She sniffles. "I think she was just surprised, mostly. I don't know if she'll come around. Annie is very loyal. She'll see this as a betrayal of her as well as him."

"You have other friends."

"She's been my best friend since high school. We went to college together. She knows me better than anyone."

"Then she knows you aren't selfish." I'm trying to make her feel better, but I think I'm just making it worse. "She'll calm down once she has time to process it."

She's quiet for a long minute. "Can I come over?"

Sometimes Mia surprises me. This is one of those times. "Now?"

Another wet laugh. "I mean, it will take me three hours or so to get there, but why not? I don't want to be alone. I want to see you."

"I can come to you."

"I want to drive. I'd just pace while I waited for you."

"Gogo will be excited to meet you. So will James. What do you want for dinner?"

She hums thoughtfully into the phone. "What were you going to eat if I didn't come?"

"A protein shake, a frozen chicken breast and some broccoli."

"Barf. That sounds awful. Is there a restaurant you like in town?"

"Lots."

"Pick one. Take me on a date, Stranger."

I look out over the mountain, past the empty land next to the farmhouse. Maybe it's worth it, the pain when I leave, to enjoy this life now, for the time I have left with it. "Drive safe. No panties."

She laughs, not sad now, just bright.

"Deal. Text me your address."

I spend three hours cleaning, showering, pacing, enduring James' mockery.

This place is empty. It's just a holding place for when James no longer needs me for anything. That's what I always planned. He'll get his prostheses in just a couple weeks now, and I'll take off, get far away… But now?

I keep on thinking thoughts I've got no business thinking.

But then she's there, climbing out of her car, all blonde hair, gold bracelets and a pair of black jeans so tight, I stop thinking about anything except how badly I want her.

James makes himself scarce, wheeling silently away without me even noticing.

I open the side door and Gogo and I step into the cold day to welcome her home.

She reaches into the car and grabs a small black duffel bag, and I instantly love every single thing about this moment.

She's come to me. She's bringing her things here. She's safe. And tonight, I'll sleep beside her, and in the morning, we'll have breakfast and spend the day together.

She's not crying, for which I'm grateful, because it lets me snag the bag, and then snag her and back her up against her car, get my free hand on her ass, squeeze it tight as I touch my lips to hers, feel her tongue on mine.

Fuck it. The closest neighbors are a mile down the road. James won't bother us. I drop the bag to the drive, get two hands on that ass, lift her up, and she doesn't miss a beat, she climbs me like a vine, rocking against my cock so hard I see stars.

Dimly, I become aware of Gogo, barking like mad, loud, insistent, determined. I know that bark. She thinks Mia's hurting me.

Mia leans back in my arms, her eyes unfocused.

"Gogo," I grunt.

"Huh? Oh," she says. "Oh!" and wriggles out of my arms.

Reluctantly, I let her get away from me. She bends over, rummaging through her bag, wiggling that fine round ass at me. "Where is it? There! Got it."

When she stands up, she's holding something behind her back where Gogo and I can't see.

I take her hand, and gesture toward Gogo. "This is Gogo. Gogo, Mia."

Gogo sniffs, her tail dragging low, her ears going back.

"I brought you something." She crouches down in front of Gogo.

I stroke Gogo's warm, brown ears.

She looks up at me and whines.

I touch Mia's slender shoulder. "It's important to be nice to Mia. She's special."

Gogo grumbles. Mia touches her gently on the neck. "I have a present for you, Gogo." She smiles her big wide smile and holds the present out before her, toward the dog.

A stuffed gray bunny. She squeaks it. Smart.

Gogo takes it gently between her teeth, backs away, struts past me for the open door, the bunny held high, to her favorite corner, where she will, no doubt, rip the bunny's fluffy white guts out.

Still crouched, Mia stares at up me. I stare down at her, tug her back to standing.

I start breathing hard. So does she.

We are barely even touching, but the air is already thick with whatever it is that lies between us. Electricity, chemistry. It's palpable.

I yank her body against me. It's five strides to move her inside the house, another fifteen to get her into my bedroom, back her up against my dresser.

I flip her over so she's facedown, her arms spread out, fingers splayed out wide over the surface.

I have to stroke that ass. The jeans are tight over a pair of ass cheeks so round, I don't even think, just smack them.

She squeals, half in laughter, half turned on, and the stupid grin on my face doesn't even bother me. I've been smiling since she showed up. I'm not even embarrassed.

She looks at me over her shoulder, wiggles her hips. "Do it harder."

"Yeah? You want me to spank you, Mia?"

Her lips twist in the sexiest half smile I've ever seen. She nods breathlessly. "Yeah."

"Hard?"

Classic Mia face scrunch, nose wrinkle, gear up, dive. "Leave handprints on my ass, Stranger."

"Motherfucking perfect." I shove a hand in the small of her back. "You asked for it. Face to the table, Reed. Don't move a muscle."

Her breaths are ragged, but she obeys.

I nudge her legs apart with my foot, still grinning like a giddy fucker. I've become someone I don't recognize, someone carefree, someone laidback, someone happy. Someone who plays sex games and makes jokes. And for this once, I'm just going to let myself enjoy this. Someday, when she knows the truth and hates me, I'll look back and remember this feeling.

I stroke her back with reverence, memorizing the curves of her, the lean elegance of her body. So soft and delicate, in comparison to my harder, bulkier form.

I pull my hand back. This time it's a full-on spank. Four of them. Two for each cheek. Hard enough to make my hand sting and the room ring with the hand-to-jeans echo.

She flinches, but I doubt it hurt too badly.

I let myself get into the fantasy of it. I call her a bad girl, laughing as I say it, but I'm only half amused. The other half is loving playing it out with her.

She rolls her head back and forth, tossing honey hair and peachy air my way.

I unbutton her jeans slowly, gently, softly. Lull her down with meandering, loving touches. Then I yank them down to her knees in a burst of controlled violence.

She yelps.

She didn't wear panties, just like I told her.

"What color were they?"

"Huh?"

"Your panties, the ones you took off to come here."

"You've got a serious thing for panties."

"Just yours. Color?"

"Fire-engine red."

"Hmmm. Did you bring them with you?"

"Yes."

"Good. I love your ass." I get handfuls, palming it like fruit I'm considering buying, touch every single part of her except that smooth, pink pussy, my final destination. "You've got a seriously nice ass, Mia."

When my thumb grazes over her asshole, she pants, her shoulders rising and falling. Her bracelets chatter like bells as she moves restlessly.

I land a hard spank on her right cheek. Then another. Smack. Her ass jiggles.

"I said don't move. Don't make me spank you even harder."

She laughs. "God, please spank me harder, Stranger."

"You think I'm kidding?" I hiss in mock anger.

"No."

"You're not afraid of me?"

"Not at all."

"You should be."

She goes still, angles an arched brow. "Why? You won't hurt me."

"Wanna bet?" I spank her left cheek three times in fast succession. Her eyes squint up, her body bucks, and pink marks bloom on her pale skin. Her pussy is pinker now. I swear it's pouting at me. A bead of moisture tosses light my way.

She sputters and squeals. Her eyes glisten with unshed tears, but she doesn't ask me to stop.

I slide a finger along her wet slit, dip lightly into that well, remembering all the times we texted about this. The reality is so much better. "Soaking. You like it, you dirty fucking slutty little girl."

A few more spanks, and I can't take it anymore. I open my pants, letting out a sigh of relief.

My poor dick has been so cramped. I bend over her, draw my teeth along her jaw, let her feel the weight and heft of my cock head bumping against her ass.

"You like being spanked."

She makes what I'm learning is the thoughtful Mia face. Anyone else would have laughed or ignored the question. But she's seriously analyzing her own response to this.

"Sort of. It's the time between spanks, the waiting, the feeling of being at your mercy, no idea what you might do next. I think that's the part I like."

I tug her shirt up so I can drag my tongue down the bumps of her spine, sink my teeth into the firm skin of her ass, trail my nose over her obliques.

I get a grip on her knee, lift a foot, tug off her shoe. Then the other. Then wrench her jeans off her calves, so she stands naked from the waist down, her chest down on the table, her arms splayed wide.

I step between her thighs, trail the head of my cock up and down her wet flesh, grunting at the contact. My body wars with my mind. My body just wants to fuck her, conquer her, take her rough and fast, get my cum inside her as fast as humanly possible. But my mind wants to pick her apart, open her up, take her to the edge and back so many times she's so limp and so broken nothing and no one can fix her but me.

I slide my hands under her body, close them on her breasts, and flip her over. I peel off her shirt, and the jungle green and sunflower yellow bra. Find her mouth, but only for a minute. Because what I really want to kiss, what I really want to taste, is further south, past the soft and tender skin of her neck, past her small, firm tits with their hard, tan nipples, her slender ribcage, navel, hipbones, over the smooth taut skin of her abdomen.

She exposes herself to me, unabashedly, rocking against me, splayed out wide. Mia like this is shameless.

I make my way down to lap my tongue up and down her clit, making tiny circles around it. She gets her fists in my hair, tugging on my scalp, rocking her hips, setting her own rhythm, her soft thighs scissoring around my cheeks. I fuck her with my tongue, devour her. She tastes like she smells. Like peaches and pussy.

I get two fingers inside, which makes her squirm. I get my other hand up to grip her tit, my thumb strumming a bit on the stiff peak which earns me a long breathy squeal. She rocks against my face.

I increase the tempo, as her squeals change to animalistic grunts, and her motions grow jagged.

Mia may look like a lady when she's all dressed up, but naked with my tongue in her cunt, she looks like what she is, a grunting human animal whose primary drive is procreation. Manners and kindness go away and she becomes wild and selfish and demanding. Perfect. That's the Mia I like best, the one I want for my very own, the bird that didn't just escape her cage, the bird that destroyed it.

She sags against the dresser, pushing my face away like she's too sensitive, like all she wants to do is sleep, like she can't take anymore.

But she will.

I heft her off the dresser with my hands under her ass, letting her sag against my chest, and toss her on my bed.

She tries to roll onto her side, but I stop with her with a hand on her chin. "Where do you think you're going?"

"So sleepy," she breathes, her eyes blinking open and closed.

"I'm not done with you yet." I open her mouth with a thumb on her chin, stroke her tongue with mine, use my knees to spread her thighs wider, fit my dick into that slick spot, and shove in balls deep.

She wriggles her hips, dreamy sighing, like a purr. "You feel good inside me."

I do.

And I've been to heaven.

It isn't white with flutes and gold horns and clouds.

It's hot and wet and feels like velvet. It smells like peaches, and looks like honey.

Heaven is my dick in Mia, her arms around me, and her tongue in my mouth.

Her eyes open wide, her hands go around my shoulders, and her legs lock me in a hug so tight my eyes burn.

"I'm on the pill. Don't pull out."

Sweeter words, I've never heard.

22 – WHAT'S YOUR REAL NAME?

MIA

Stranger's place is nice. Shockingly clean actually, for two single men.

Jeremy's place is stark and full of random things I've always promised myself I'd get rid of as soon as we were married. Framed tickets to college concerts, a signed hockey jersey tacked to a wall, a framed poster of a shiny red sports car. With ultra-modern furniture he so clearly purchased en masse, all chrome and black granite and red leather.

Stranger's is nothing like that. His place is comfortable, unpretentious. An old farmhouse he told me he'd had renovated. But he didn't cut corners. The glimpse I had as he backed me through the main space was of high ceilings, lots of windows, a massive stone fireplace, a big open kitchen. He's got money, enough to support himself—and his brother—in a life of comfort.

How?

He grew up poor. He was a Marine. How does he have the money to live like this?

I stretch sleepily under his warm body.

The bedroom we're in is at the back of the farmhouse, on the far-right side. It's got big windows, and blank walls the color of slate, empty surfaces, crisp white sheets on a big soft bed. It feels like a place I want to snuggle under a blanket and write.

Suddenly, I want that so badly and so clearly, all the lethargy leaves my body in a jolt, and I bolt upright. Or rather I try to.

He's still on top of me, breathing hard and pressing my body into the bed. I don't get far.

He grunts.

"Stranger?"

Grunt.

"Will you write with me?"

Grunt. "Right now?"

Why not? It's mid afternoon.

Even his grunts make me smile. I stroke my fingers through his hair.

"Yeah. We could light a fire, put our feet up, cuddle under a blanket." I wriggle underneath him. "Write until one of us gets bored or hungry or whatever."

It sounds like heaven, like all I've ever wanted.

"Two minutes," he whispers, running his nose along my temple. "I'm not ready to leave you."

He means physically leave my body, and my heart just melts. He's so achingly sweet, my Stranger, when he wants to be.

I stroke his hair and listen to him grumble. After a few minutes he gets off me and helps me up.

When I bend over to pull up my pants, he strokes my bottom. "Pink. Just barely."

My spank-marks.

"Then next time…" I grin, sinking my teeth into my lowerlip. "You can spank me harder." I pull up my jeans and button them.

His eyes burn into mine for just a beat too long, then he turns away and pulls on clothes with fast, brusque motions. "I'll go get your bag."

It's still outside.

He goes barefoot in the cold, in nothing but jeans and a flannel shirt. Kicking myself for mentioning the future like that, and a little embarrassed that he didn't respond, I pad along behind him, barefoot, but wearing my jeans and shirt, looking around for James.

But he's nowhere to be found, and there's nothing to do but stare at Stranger. All wrinkled and rugged and so hot I want to grab him and ask *why! why! why! why do you want me?*

He could have anyone.

And I'm just…me.

And what did that look mean? Surely, he isn't doing this just on a whim, he must know I want more than a fling.

He comes back and sets my bag down on the dining table. "I've never written with anyone before."

"Me neither." I dig out my laptop, trying to remind myself that it's just him. The same guy I've been talking to all this time.

But still, every time I look at him as he builds a fire, and gets a couple glasses of ice water, I feel a little prickle of fear.

He moves like a predator. And he's huge. I'm not used to the intensity of his physical presence yet.

We settle into the massive leather sectional together, side by side, my feet propped up on the coffee table beside his long ones, and the only sounds are the tapping of our keyboards, the crackling of the fire, and Gogo's occasional grumbling as she guts the little bunny I bought her.

He gets up from time to time to toss a log on the fire, feed Gogo, bring over a bowl of carrots—he's a health nut. Or I do, to get water, go to the bathroom, check my phone.

We pass three hours this way. Quietly working side by side. It's magic. It's the way I always imagined it would be between us, only better because my nose is full of his delicious manly, soapy, foresty smell, and my body still aches in all the right places.

I glance over at him. He's typing away, his brow furrowed, his beautiful full lips slightly pursed, the hollows of his cheekbones showing, his flannel rolled up to his elbows, the tattoos over his muscled forearms rippling. Jesus, he's like a romance novel hero come to life.

This is real now. And if we're really going to try this... Then... some of the secrets need to go.

"Stranger? I need you to answer a question for me."

He murmurs, fingers still moving on the keys.

"What do you do?"

"I'm a contractor. You know that."

We've talked about it briefly, but it's always been really vague. "Yeah, but what kind?"

He sucks on his lip, still focused on his computer. "Security."

"Private?" I cock my head. "Like a bodyguard?"

He closes his laptop, finally looking up at me. "Not really. It was a natural shift from the military to go to working for private individuals. Designing their security detail. I don't actually do the leg work, I just design the system and poke holes in it."

"So you protect people?"

The fading light through the windows glints in his eyes. "Sometimes."

"So... you're saying you are entirely perfect."

He rubs the back of his neck and his biceps bunches and ripples. "I have this one really awful flaw."

I hit save, close my laptop, and set it to the side. "Hit me with it."

"It's bad, Mia. Really bad."

"Oh god. Is this a deal breaker? Don't tell me you insist on hard-boiled eggs every day or something. I can't take it."

He takes a deep breath. "It's worse."

I make a big show of grimacing. "What could be worse than hard-boiled eggs? Oh god, please don't tell me you snore."

"This is worse. Especially for someone like you..."

I squeeze my eyes shut like I'm terrified. "Okay, tell me. I can handle it."

"Mia..." He lets the word linger in a long, dramatic pause. "I'm a terrible golfer."

I laugh, push at his laptop, so he'll move it, and crawl into his lap.

He pulls me over so I'm straddling him.

"What's your handicap? Twenty-two?"

He laughs, this man who once told me he never smiles, all white teeth and dimples. "Worse."

I fake shock. "A twenty-*three*?"

"It's so bad, I don't even have a handicap." He pulls me closer so our bodies fit together tightly.

"I can handle that. I'm pretty good, actually. I can teach you."

His face tightens and I realize what I just said.

Shit. I squeeze my eyes shut. I just did it again. And this time, I can't pretend I didn't see the way he pulled back.

I'm already imagining my life with him in it. And he's... clearly not thinking the same way.

I start to pull away, but he stops me, with a hard grip on my hips. "I'll make a deal with you. I'll let you teach me to golf, if you let me teach you to shoot."

I pop open my eyes. "Shoot? Like... guns?"

"Yes. Guns, Mia. It'll be fun."

I'm not so sure about that, but I shrug. "I have another question."

He takes a deep breath. "Hit me with it."

"Why do you like me?"

His grip on my hips tightens. "Hmmmm... you made me smile before I ever even heard your voice. You made me laugh through messages on that dumb website. You smell like peaches. I love peaches."

I drop my head onto his shoulder, so he can't see my face, feeling uniquely uncomfortable. I miss the darkness, the safety of distance, when all I had were words and I didn't have to face the intensity of his physical being.

He presses a kiss to my temple. "You put your every nasty, filthy thought down on paper and all I had to do was read it to know we'd be right together."

His hands slide up to cup the back of my head, pulling my face back so I'm forced to meet his eyes. "You're a good person, and you make me want to be better. I don't deserve you, but I want to. Your pussy is my heaven, and somehow, you're becoming my home."

My eyes burn, and I don't have the first thing to say. That sounded a lot like Stranger just said he loves me.

I'm not ready for that. I'm still technically engaged.

I tuck my hair behind my ear, wanting to give him something back, but I don't have his magic, so I just say one simple, true thing. "I didn't know how much fun life could be before you."

And then, because I don't want us to keep going down this path, I say something else that's true. "I'm hungry, and I want to meet James."

Stranger drives a big black SUV.

It smells like leather, and that more subtle Stranger-scent. We drive together to the local grocery store and back. I didn't want to go out to dinner and share him, plus he said James wouldn't come and third wheel it. So we decided to cook something together and eat at his house.

We get everything we need for chicken noodle soup, and head back. It feels so homey, sitting in the front seat of his car. He holds the wheel loosely, and I keep sneaking peeks at his painfully handsome profile.

I'm staring so much on the way home, he'll think I'm crazy if I'm not careful, so I get out my phone and check in.

Annie is still not talking to me.

Penny wants to know how my tattoo looks.

Mom wants me to come down for lunch to discuss her and Dad's thirtieth anniversary, and... I got twelve new reviews today.

I scan through them as Stranger's car bounces down a rutted road, and my heart plummets.

The rest are good. But one is... not. It's anonymous. That's not unusual at all. Half the reviews come from anonymous reviewers. But the tone sets my teeth on edge.

> Anonymous: This woman writes garbage. Go to hell Mia Reed. Quit sullying the planet with your crappy filthy boring work.

I cringe. Most reviews, even ones that give me lower stars, tend to be polite. This isn't for me. I couldn't connect. Way too racy. It's very rare for someone to hit at the author directly. It hurts.

I don't want to taint this day with Stranger. It's been so perfect so far. So, I dump my phone in my bag.

He slides his hand over the gear shift, and his broad palm settles on the top of my thigh. His hand is so big his fingertips reach all the way down nearly to the seat. His thumb strokes up and down. "You okay?"

"Yeah." It feels so normal. So homey. So natural. I wrap my hands around his forearm and stroke my own fingers up and down the springy hair on his forearms, trace the tattoos. Study them up close.

They are a work of art. Patterns in tiny details, fine as black lace, filled in with a rhythm of colors.

"Who does them?"

He shifts, his jeans rubbing against the leather. "An old Army friend. He opened up shop in Manhattan. I go down once a year or so, add, change, brighten. They take maintenance. You'll have to get yours redone in five years or so."

We pass another car but then we're alone, the road stretching in front of us, a ribbon of black in wide white fields.

"That feels like so far in the future I can't even worry about it now. I just want to get through the next month."

He squeezes my thigh. "Telling Annie was the worst part. You love her. You don't love Jeremy."

"That's true." I don't love Jeremy. I'm not sure if I ever did.

We lapse into silence. My mind keeps going to that horrible review. Go to hell.

Stranger pulls into his garage. "You okay? Are you feeling weird about all this?"

"No. Not at all."

He swallows so loud I can hear it. "It feels like you've gone quiet."

I should have known I wouldn't be able to hide it. "I got another shitty review."

His jaw ticks, and he presses the button to turn off the ignition. The car stills around us. "From who? Read it to me."

I get out my phone and read it, right there in the dark garage, trying very hard not to add a biased inflection to the words. They speak for themselves.

Stranger shrugs when I'm done. "Fuck them. It's some idiot."

I don't answer.

He takes my hand. Stranger is a hand holder. I love that. "Do you have any enemies, Mia? Anyone who hates you?"

I raise my brows. "You think it's personal?"

The corner of his mouth deepens. "It sounds personal."

I still don't answer.

His thumb strokes up and down the back of my hand. "You're a good writer. This is a case of a crazy reviewer, not your work being garbage."

My stomach untwists. I needed to hear that. I needed him, this beautiful, smart, wonderful, fun man I'm falling head over heels in love with, this man I'm learning to trust and respect, I needed him to tell me exactly that.

He opens his door and hops out, so I do too.

He takes the bags out of the trunk and meets me by my door. "Tell me about grudges. Anyone who hates you?"

I think for a while as we go inside and unpack the bags.

I'm a nice person, or I try to be. Mostly. I've never done anything wrong. No one hates me. "The only person I can think of is this one girl who really didn't like me in college."

Stranger looks up from the sink where he's washing carrots, but doesn't comment.

I like that he doesn't press. And I like that he doesn't scoff at me. Jer would have believed the review, implied that I did write garbage.

I tap my fingers on my plate. "Funky Amy. She wanted to write romance novels. I ran into her at a convention a few years ago. She said my work was stale."

"Funky Amy?"

"Annie used to call her funky because she smelled. Funky Amy Weldon? Warton? Annie was just talking about her the other day. Her husband died. He ran a pharmaceutical company or something. She's a billionaire now."

My shoulders sag because I miss Annie more in that moment than I ever have before. If she didn't hate me, I'd just text her. She'd say the same thing Stranger said. Ignore the bad review. They're stupid.

Stranger reaches across the island counter, closes his big fingers over mine, sucks in a long breath. "What did she smell like?"

I cover my mouth with my free hand, smothering a laugh. "Like onions. Always. It was so weird. At the time, I just thought she didn't shower enough, but now I wonder if she was ill or something. Kids are cruel."

He turns off the tap, sets the carrots on a cutting board and lifts a knife deftly. "Were you cruel?"

"No. Yes. Not really. She wanted to work on a project with me. I took one creative writing class. Annie and I did it together."

As I talk, I rummage through the cabinets and find a big pot, set it on the stove.

"Amy wanted to partner up with me, but I was already set to work with Annie and I said no. In the end the professor assigned partners and I ended up working with a guy named David who didn't finish his half until two hours before the piece was due."

I pour in some olive oil.

"So you weren't mean at all."

I turn on the gas range. It looks like it's barely been used. "I don't think Amy ever got over me saying no. David and I won. Our piece was published in the school's newspaper."

He's silent, chopping carrots in even swipes as smooth as any Michelin chef.

The packet of chicken thighs clicks as I slice it open, and drop them one by one into the pot to brown.

I can't stop a smug smile. "David works for NPR now. Our piece was really good."

He raises a brow, and I know sex is on his brain suddenly. He likes when I'm confident.

"Did Annie always like your writing?"

I swallow. "Always. I wouldn't be writing without her. She wanted to be a journalist. She pushed me to write so we could take classes together. Without her, I'd have probably actually become an accountant."

I'd have been terrible at it, and miserable.

"And Dixon?" He's done with the carrots, so he moves on to an onion. He slides the tip of the knife into the top with a deft flick. I've never seen anyone cut as evenly or fast as he does, at least not in person. You see it on TV all the time. He's like a chef, like he spends all day holding a knife. Deadly sharp. Deadly precise. *Slice, slice, slice, slice, slice.*

I shake salt and pepper into the pan. "Jer didn't know until a couple years after we started dating. He liked it being a secret."

Stranger just stares back at me, all dark eyes, stubbled jaw, hard edges and still so many questions. For every layer I unveil, a new one emerges. I walk to the sink, and fill up a bowl with warm water.

"Stranger... I just realized something. I don't know your real name."

He pauses in the middle of the second onion. "No one's called me by it since I was four, except doctors and assholes."

"I won't use it. You're Stranger to me. Always."

He sends me a baleful glare. *Chop. Chop. Chop.* He crosses to the pot, and swipes the onions and carrots in. "Henry."

"No." It comes out long and low.

"Yes."

My hands come up to cover my mouth.

He cocks his head, mocking my shock. "My brother's name is *James*. What did you expect?"

"I don't know. Something mysterious and awesome. Something really badass... like..."

"Stranger?" His eyes crinkle up, and he elbows me away from the sink to wash celery. "You can laugh, Mia. I can handle a little Mia laughter."

"Why did your dad call start calling you Stranger?" I pour the water into the pot.

He's quiet, rinsing the celery, then chopping.

"He was afraid of strangers as a kid."

I turn. The voice that spoke wasn't Stranger. It was James. I never heard him come in.

I smile. "James."

He smiles too, and finally, finally, I can do what I wanted to do the last time we met. I rinse my hands at the sink fast, go to him, and kiss his cheek.

His hands close around my upper arms. "Thanks for keeping him human," he murmurs in my ear.

I pull back to meet his gaze, hazel, just like Stranger's. I whisper, "I was going to say the same to you."

He clamps his lips between his teeth for a second, shakes his head at me, then says, "He kept pointing at people and saying 'stranger.' So Dad thought it would make him less afraid of strangers if he was one too, so he started calling him Little Stranger. It stuck. Then he wasn't little anymore... so he dropped that." James raises his brows. "Just so you know, I'm bigger."

"Alright, alright, alright," Stranger grouses, dumping celery into the pot.

James wheels his chair into the kitchen.

I picture them as kids, dark hair, hazel eyes. Young and scared.

"Did it work? The nickname."

"Yeah," James says, pulling open the fridge, and grabbing a bottle of wine.

"He was a good dad," I say, fishing blatantly.

Stranger's silent though, done chopping.

"The best." James' eyes harden like it hurts to think about him. He tilts his head to the side, working the cork into the bottle caught between his thighs. "Hey, remember that show we were watching?"

His words are clearly directed at Stranger, so I quiet up. Dump tarragon and Dijon mustard into the pot at random.

"Just finished it. You know who sent the money? Forgive me for being rude, Mia. We've been into this old mystery."

"No problem."

Stranger sets down the knife, face as intense as I've ever seen it. "Who?"

"The father."

The kitchen is silent for a long moment. What show are they talking about? I try to think about old mysteries, but then James sets a glass of white wine in front of me. "Ask me one thing you've always wanted to know about Stranger."

I don't even have to think. "What's your real last name?"

Silence stretches before us. Stranger's big thumb taps the counter. Up and down. Up and down.

James glances at him.

Stranger looks back. He cocks his head to the side. And it's him who answers. "Revin."

23 — MAYBE I CAN BE THAT GUY

STRANGER

James occupies Mia for me.

We've developed an understanding, James and me. Maybe it was always there, just shoved beneath the layers of guilt and shared history, but it's come to the surface in these past months, as we've worked together.

He knows what I need without speaking. And I know the same.

We're becoming a team. It's happening whether I want it or not, and I'm starting to doubt I can go back to the way it was, seeing him once or twice a year for an hour or two at a time.

I walk quietly down the hall toward the bathroom and slide my phone from my pocket. By agreement, he's been checking my email for me hourly, anticipating Lex's response as much as I have. With Mia here, I haven't been able to.

I pull open Lex's email.

> Lex: Your lure worked. Money was just moved to an offshore account in the Caymans. Broxman, Telker and Shone. Guess who?
>
> Papa Whitten.
>
> Yeah, boo. You read that right.
>
> So far haven't been able to find out anything about B, T & S except it's registered in the Caymans as a P corporation, meaning it's privately owned. Pulling some contacts there. Should have more soon. In the meantime, keep an eye out. The money will move to your account soon.

Jesus.

I rest my shoulder against the wall outside the bathroom, reading it over again. It makes no more sense on a second read.

Mia laughs at something James says, and I shut my eyes as the sound washes over me. She's so happy right now. I picture her face when I sit her down. *I have to tell you something. Mia, your dad hired me to kill you. I'm not going to do it though. Want me to kill him for you?*

There's no way to make that not a soul-crusher.

I tuck my phone back into my jeans. It doesn't make sense. Lex already looked into his accounts. The guy's got plenty of money, liquid and holdings. Why the hell would he want to kill his daughter?

When I get back from the bathroom, James is facing Mia across the island counter. She's perched on a barstool.

For a second, I'm not sure if I can touch her in front of James. I don't do relationships, never have, so I don't know what's expected.

But then she smiles at me, and he pushes a beer across the counter, and I don't even have to think.

I take a seat beside her, pick up my beer and relax while the soup simmers.

For the rest of the night, I put Ender out of my mind. I pretend I'm the guy who gets to keep this, the guy who gets to have a woman, a brother, a dog, a house, a job, a life.

It's nice.

That guy's lucky.

"I should go," Mia says, the next morning.

We're in the kitchen. I'm slicing a mango for her. There's a right way to do it, you slide the knife along the meat, just outside of the stone core. Then score the flesh in an even grid, keeping the tip just shy of breaking the skin. Flip the skin inside out then, and it practically slides off on its own.

"Why?" Tidy cubes of mango slide to the plate in a pile under my hand. "Do you have somewhere to be?"

She casts me a furtive look, shuffling her bare feet, toying with the end of my t-shirt. "No."

Gogo's feet tick as she crosses the wood floor and presses her nose against Mia's bare thigh. I need to trim her toenails.

"I don't want to overstay my welcome."

I cock my hip against the counter, set down the knife and wipe my hands on a dishcloth. "There's no welcome to overstay. You belong here. For as long as you want to stay."

She blinks up at me through her lashes, almost coy. That's unlike her. "I didn't pack enough stuff."

I study her. She doesn't look like she wants to go, particularly. Whatever's bothering her, I'm missing it. But it feels like she's asking me for something.

"Then wear my clothes." I push the plate to her. "They look better on you anyway."

"Won't James mind me being here?" She picks up a piece, licking her fingers, still avoiding my eyes.

"No. He wants you here." We both do. She's safe here.

"I need to check my mail."

I tilt my head to the side. Maybe she's trying to tell me something. Is this her way of ending it? I don't know enough about actually being with a woman. "Your mail can wait."

I turn away from her, look out the window so I won't have to see her face when she says whatever she's about to say. The empty land next to ours sits there. Nothing but a crumbling wooden fence and a broken barn on eight odd acres.

She's silent.

"Do you not want to be here?"

"No, I do," she says. "I just don't want to be in the way."

"You aren't."

She comes up behind me, her slender hands wrap around my waist, her warm breasts press against my back. A hug. I can't remember the last time anyone hugged me. "I... just... Stranger, what are we doing?"

I cover her hands with mine. I could tell her right now. I wouldn't even have to mention the dad part. Just the Ender part, ease it in slowly. *I'm a killer, Mia. Or I was. I think I don't have to be anymore. You make me want to be something more.*

Instead, I turn her in my arms, look down at her warm honey eyes. "Getting to know each other. Starting something real. Seeing where it takes us."

Her lips part, she leans up and kisses me, light as a butterfly's wing on the jaw.

I take a deep breath. There's just one thing you should know...

"Want to go for I hike?" I ask, almost surprised by the words as they come from my mouth.

Gogo starts to prance, recognizing the word.

"Yes," Mia says.

And like that, we find a rhythm.

I don't know how to be with a person like this, so I follow her lead.

She's everywhere, all the time. And so is her crap. Pots of various lotions cover the vanity in my bathroom. Along with a purple and orange striped bag full of makeup, they take over my bathroom. A book appears on the side table in my bedroom. Tubes of handcream appear in the living room and the kitchen.

It doesn't bother me. I take perverse pleasure in reading the labels. Healing chamomile and ginseng hand butter. Nighttime aloe and cucumber quenching eye serum. Orange blossom neck paste. It all sounds like shit I want to eat, or drink, or rub on her myself.

For five days, I get to see what my life could be. Showers with Mia. Hikes with Mia. Sleeping with Mia. Fucking with her, cuddling with her, eating with her, too. I like it all. I want it all.

It starts to feel possible.

A new hope forms in my mind.

Maybe I can be that guy, the one James described the day Mia came into my life. A normal writer guy.

There's just one thing in my way now.

Her father.

Well, two things. Me. If I'm going to be with her, I need to tell her the truth.

And I can't do that until I understand it myself.

24 – THE LIFE I WANT

MIA

It's December 21st when I pull up in front of Jer's apartment, park my car in the guest parking lot, and ride the elevator up to the penthouse floor.

I had to leave Stranger this morning. I didn't want to. I'd have stayed forever if he'd let me. In the five days I spent living with Stranger and James, I had a glimpse of a life I could have, one I want.

So, step one toward getting that life: end it with Jer.

It's time. He's back from China. I can't put it off any longer.

The door is ajar.

Jer's making pasta, barefoot at the stove wearing jeans and a wool sweater. The homey smell of carbonara wafts through the air, garlic and onions.

Two glasses of red wine sit on the counter.

He hands me one. "I opened a San Giovese."

Seven months ago, this would have been my idea of perfection. That was before Stranger though, and before I realized I could connect with someone the way I do with him, could trust someone so completely to respect my feelings, to be honest with me, to care about the same things as me.

Jer's not all bad, but he's not good for me either.

I take the wine glass but set it down on the counter. "We need to talk."

"So you said. What's up?" He turns back to the stove, stirring the sauce.

Long, deep breath. "I don't think I'm ready to get married."

His back is to me, so I can't see his face, but his shoulders square, and after a long pause he sets down the spoon on a plate nearby. "That's crazy."

"Not really. I've been thinking about this for a while."

He takes a long sip from his glass. "You never said anything."

"I did, sort of. You know I wasn't happy with your attitude about my writing."

He turns now. "This is about your writing? I don't care what you do. Write, don't write. It doesn't matter."

I drag my fingers through my hair. "It does matter. To me, it matters so much. I want to be with someone who's supportive of me, not merely tolerant at best."

"Fine. I'll be supportive. What do you want me to do? Go to a book signing with you? Do you even have those?"

My heart sinks because he struck a nerve. No, I'm not famous. My fans are loyal, but there aren't that many of them. And he did that on purpose. He wanted to hurt me. Remind me that my writing is small potatoes. "Not yet."

He turns back to the stove.

I twist the ring off my finger, set it on the counter, pick up my purse and walk quietly to the door.

It's only when I open the door that he leaves the stove. "Mia, you can't do this. We've set a date. You've got my ring. It'll be so embarrassing. We put down deposits on the venue. Sent out save-the-dates. You've got a dress."

"The ring is on the counter. Maybe you can use it to pay off some of your debts."

That wasn't nice, but I'm not perfect.

"Is that what this is about? I won't be in debt forever."

"It's not about the debt."

His shoulders sag. "What can I do?"

I lean my hip against the door, touching the straps of my purse with my fingers, looking at the floor so I don't have to see the shock and panic on his face. "I just don't think we're a good fit."

"Of course, we are. We've been together for so long." His voice rises. "I love you."

No. He can't really love me, if he kept secrets from me. After all this time, there's so much about him I don't know. And if I'm honest, there's a lot about me that he doesn't know. I've never been truly honest with him. Only with Stranger.

I look at Jer's face for a long time. He looks tired. There are lines around his eyes. Gray at his temples. A pair of wrinkles between his brows. We met when we were in college, just kids. I see him like he was, hopeful and happy, and my heart turns over. We were happy. Once.

"We've just grown apart."

"No." The muscle in his jaw ticks a beat. "It's Christmas. Let's just get through the holiday, reevaluate when we've both cleared our heads."

I don't need to clear my head. I don't need the holiday. But maybe it will help him get used to the idea.

He pulls me into a tight hug that smells like cologne and wine and detergent.

"I'm not coming to Florida." I pat his shoulders, pulling away.

"That's fine. I'll stay here with you. We can open presents in our pajamas like we did in college."

"You need to see your father. You can't stay on my behalf."

He sighs. "You have terrible timing."

"Yes. I'm sorry. I should have done this months ago, maybe years."

He backs away, looking broken and defeated. "We'll talk about this when I get back."

Talking won't change a thing. I'm in love with another man. I don't say that, though.

So instead I say, "Have a nice trip. Hug your father for me, and your mom. Merry Christmas."

His face twists at that, like he's thinking about my bad timing again, but he just shrugs and drops his hands in his pockets.

The look on his face stays with me as I take the elevator to the lobby and walk to my car. It looks the way I imagine a man looks when he's standing on the edge looking down.

Before I climb into my seat, I text Stranger.

> Mia: I did it.

> Stranger: How did he take it?

> Mia: I think he thinks it's temporary. That I'll change my mind.

Stranger: You okay?

Mia: I'm fine.

Stranger: Can I come down?

Mia: Yes.

Stranger: Now?

Mia: Want to stay for Christmas?

Stranger: Feliz Navidad.

Mia: Say it in Hawaiian.

Stranger: Mia Kalikimaka.

Mia: lol. The island way.

Stranger: I'm going to fuck you in a Santa hat.

Mia: Me in the hat? Or you?

Stranger: Both. Light up your tree, put on a red bra and some green panties. I'll be there in a couple hours.

Mia: What about James?

Stranger: He'll be happy for me.

Mia: Bring Gogo?

Stranger: You sure? I can leave her

Mia: Don't forget her dog food and a bed.

Stranger: Who's dog is she?

Mia: I just want you to be able to stay without worrying. Drive safe.

Stranger: Get ready.

25 – GARDEN VOMIT

STRANGER

Being with Mia—living with Mia—is like sliding into a warm pool.

I've never lived with a woman—always pictured it would be like on TV, her nagging me about bills and garbage, and me bitching about never getting laid. But this isn't like that at all. We share chores, empty the dishwasher together, cook together, do laundry together.

It's fun. She's fun. With her, I'm fun.

Having her in my home was perfect. I liked it better than living inside this kaleidoscope of potent colors, and if I have my way, she'll move in at some point, but if she insists, if it's important to her, if this place matters in some significant way, I guess I can live here.

I roll over on a pillow case that looks like garden vomit, and watch as the pool of light streaming in through the window makes its way across her hair, turning it from dark honey to bright gold.

She's asleep, her lower lip jutting forward in a slight pout, her eyebrows drawn slightly together.

Maybe she'll let me switch out the sheets.

My gaze settles on the magenta and ivory geometric wallpaper.

I sigh.

Maybe she'll let me take down the wallpaper.

Gogo grunts on the rug.

The rug is emerald green. The dresser is white and gold. The lamps are still parrots.

I'll learn to live inside her happy rainbow bubble.

I can't resist it, so I stroke my finger down the length of her long, narrow nose. If she didn't smile so much, she'd look almost haughty. She gets that from her mom, but her eyes are all her dad.

Her dad. He can't really be Ender. Lex is certain about the transfer though.

She stirs in her sleep, and her eyes pop open.

"Morning, Stranger." Her voice is hoarse and muffled with sleep. She does this thing in the morning, I think it's because she's worried about her breath, but she barely parts her lips as she speaks. It makes her look like a ventriloquist.

"Do you like it here?" I ask her.

"Don't you?"

"I like being anywhere you are."

Her lips curve. "But you miss your mountain?"

I kiss her. I don't care about her breath. I doubt mine is any better. "I miss being able to let Gogo out the backdoor so I don't have to get dressed first thing in the morning."

Gogo's tail thumps against the floor at the mention of her name, and probably the word out. The dog speaks English well.

"Do you want to go?"

"Will you come with me?"

She shakes her head. "Why don't you go back and be with James tonight. I have to go to my parents anyway. Danny and Penny got in last night. I can come up tomorrow."

"I'll wait." I wish I could come up with a decent reason to keep her from going to her parents' house tonight, but it seems unlikely her father will murder her in front of her mother and brother. "We'll leave tomorrow morning."

"Deal." Her hands slide down to the small of my back. "I wish you could come. I want you to meet them."

"There's no rush." I cup her firm, round ass. And in that moment, I make a choice. I'm going to be the guy with the house, and the job. I'm going to start that private contracting business. "We have the rest of our lives."

That is, assuming she doesn't hate me when I tell her the truth.

She leaves at 3pm.

The second she's gone, I settle in at her desk and call Lex.

She answers immediately.

"Happy Hanukah." The street sounds blur the noise around her. A bus and a pack of loud people pass her by, obscuring her words.

"Back at you, Lex. You spending time with family?"

"No family but you."

That stirs something in me. I'd be like that too, without James.

And now Mia.

She's become my family now, too.

I picture Lex alone in LA. "You should come east for a while. Come visit. Meet James. Meet Mia. I'm starting a business. We could do it together."

"You serious about her?"

"Yes."

"I'll come visit then. We can discuss business."

I push a pillow with an embroidered gold and pink tiger out of my way, and sit on the sofa, pulling open my computer. This is the first time I've been able to talk to her completely openly. "Talk to me about the dad."

"He moved the money to that account," she says bluntly.

"I know. But the question is why."

"You're thinking it's a coincidence? That's a serious coincidence."

I stare at his face on my screen. The kind eyes, the proud face. "I'm just thinking maybe there's another explanation. It doesn't feel right. All this time, I've been thinking it was someone who hates her. Why would the dad hate her?"

"Her mom's cheating. Maybe it's not the first time. Maybe Mia's not his kid?"

I'm quiet for a long moment. "She looks like him."

Another bus comes by and she's quiet for a minute, waiting for it to pass. "He doesn't need money."

"What if he's doing it for the brother?"

"Danny?" Lex asks. "I think he's on the level. He's in the red, financially speaking. Bought that agency I told you about, used up the last of his savings. But he's got value there. A good staff, a solid line up if he doesn't fuck it up. I wouldn't put down my last hundo on him, but I think he's a good bet. Doesn't seem desperate. Just hardworking."

That was basically my read. No real motive. Seemed like a good guy. Good guys don't take out hits on their sisters.

Gogo flops onto her side, her head resting on one of the pillows I displaced. She seems to like all Mia's stuff.

"And the girlfriend?"

"Penny. She's got her past. But why go after Mia? She has steady work out here. Zen shit. She organizes people's homes and isn't doing half bad at it. She has her past that she wants to keep buried, but no reason to take out her boyfriend's sister. She's got steady earnings, and she's saved up well."

My read too. "What's your gut say, Lex?"

Mine says it's not the dad. I just don't buy it.

There's no sound for a while but her breathing. I picture her walking fast down the city street, her brows lowered, face tight. Muscled but not thick. People get out of her way. She's no-nonsense. It's why we always worked so well together.

"My money is on the fiancé. If not him, Greg. They've got motive and need. Maybe it's their offshore account. Maybe the dad's getting conned by someone. Mia ever ask her dad for help on behalf of anyone?"

"Not that she's mentioned to me." That's an interesting idea though. I'll have to ask her about it. I picture Greg asking Mia for her dad to invest. Or going through Annie. If Annie asked Mia for money, I bet she'd try to help.

"Their finances are shitty enough," Lex adds. "They had a ton of money. Annie gave three hundred thousand to Jeremy two years ago, in cold cash. Liquidated their savings. They're living above their means, big house, two cars, country club membership, second mortgage. She had to stop working."

"You read his file?"

"Yeah."

"Curbsiding is no joke."

"That shit..." Lex hums again. "That shit's really fucked up. That's not natural to most people. It takes a certain kind, even drunk or stoned, to do that."

I run it through my head, play it out, play it against what I know about Greg. "I agree. My gut says he's got the biggest motive, too. Kids and a depressed wife."

Mia's insane spindly-ass hot pink desk chair groans as I shift to rise. "Thanks, Lex."

"Later, Stranger."

I hang up and take Gogo for a long walk.

I spend the evening alone, drink a protein shake for dinner, start thinking of business names. Stranger Danger keeps popping into my mind, so ridiculous it almost works, but I'm thinking Revin Securities, LTD. I make a to-do list. The hundred things I need to do to open a business in the state of New York. But I spend most of my time thinking about Mia.

I'm bored and considering turning on the TV, when my phone pings.

> Lex: Dixon just bought tix for a flight home tomorrow morning. I'm thinking he's going to try to get her back. Arrives 9:10

> Stranger: So he'll probably get in around 10-10:15, right?

> Lex: If he's coming straight for her? Yes.

26 – YOU PLANNED IT THIS WAY

MIA

Mom is wearing a red sweater with a green Christmas tree on the front. Stitched all over the tree are enamel and gold ornaments smaller than peas. I wish Stranger were here. He'd have something to say about that sweater. And Dad's pants. They're green and red plaid.

Lights all around the house glimmer in soft hues. It's a couple days before Christmas, but we got together early to celebrate.

Penny laughs on the sofa at something my brother said. He's beaming like he just won the lottery. My heart clenches seeing him so happy. Mom, ever-so-slightly tipsy after her second glass of champagne, snuggles up against my dad on an opposing sofa. Dad rubs her back and smiles into her eyes. I love the way he smiles at her.

Let someone smile at me that way, after all our time together.

They look so happy.

And I sit alone on a single side chair, and try not to think about Stranger, because it makes me want to leave. All I want is to go home, beg him to come here, and introduce him to my family. I want them to know him. I want them to know me when I'm with him.

I want him to belong to me and I want to belong to him, before everyone we know.

I want there to be no more secrets.

Instead, I shift awkwardly, sip my wine, and force myself to be social and make conversation. "When is the cruise?"

Mom preens. "February eleventh."

"To the islands?" asks Penny.

"Miami to Trinidad and Tobago and back again. Nothing but the sun and the sea."

Dad ruffles Mom's hair. "And golf."

She sends him a weird look. "And spa."

Again, I picture Stranger. He'd lean in and whisper in my ear. *Your parents are aliens.*

I smile.

"Where is Jeremy?" Dad leans forward. "Is everything okay?"

Mom tilts her head to the side, her face pinching up with disapproval.

I take a deep breath. "We broke up."

Dad leans back.

Danny whistles.

Penny's brows draw together with concern.

Mom lets out a long, pissy huff. "Oh, Mia. What are you doing?"

Like that, I feel about six years old again, scorned by my mother's disapproving frown.

I set down my glass. I am twenty-seven years old. I am an adult. "I don't want to marry Jeremy."

Dad stares at the carpet a few feet in front of my toes. "What did he do?"

"I'm not really ready to talk about it. It's not just about Jer. It's about me too. We aren't good together."

Mom waves her hand through the air. "Oh pooh. Of *course*, you are. It's been years. You've been together for so long. You *know* each other."

I thought so.

And that's not something I'm prepared to discuss with everyone, not right now. So, I clear my throat, glance at Penny. "There's something I need to tell you all." I don't meet anyone's eye. Just rush on before I lose my nerve. "I'm a writer."

Danny smiles at me and sends me a covert thumbs-up.

My mom nods happily. "Of course, you are, honey. We all know that. You wrote wonderful stories in college."

Dad leans forward, resting his elbows on his knees.

"No, I mean, I write novels. That's my job. I don't work in accounting. I write."

Mom sits up, back hot-poker straight. "That's wonderful! Why in the world would you keep something like that secret?"

I swallow. "I write romance novels."

She blinks. Once. Twice. Then a whole flurry of them fast. Her mouth tightens for just a second. Then she tosses a hand through the air, takes a quick sip of her champagne and says, "I wish you'd told me. I'd have been bragging to all the ladies in book club and tennis club that my daughter was a published novelist. You should *hear* what Patty Simmons says about her son—he's an analyst. Pah."

"I don't think you'd brag mom. I write erotic paranormal romance novels."

Mom blinks.

Danny laughs.

Penny raises a glass. "Really *good* erotic paranormal romance novels."

Mom sends a calculating glance her way. "Still sounds more interesting than working in publishing," Mom says firmly. It kind of sounds like she's trying to convince herself, but that's okay. She's not angry. I'm impressed.

"But you hate romance novels, Mom."

She lifts a shoulder. "Not if my *daughter* writes them."

It's my turn to blink. Danny raises his brows in an I-told-you-so way.

"Anyway, that's one of the reasons... Jer doesn't like that I write them. He doesn't like that I write at all."

Dad holds my gaze, long and level. Mom bubbles away about how maybe he doesn't understand that it matters, and I should talk to him, give him a chance, but Dad's gaze is understanding.

"Do your books sell?" he asks.

I grin. "Pretty well, actually. I'm solvent. Officially earning profits. I'm working on my eighth book. I have fans, real fans."

Dad's quiet for a long moment. "I'm proud of you."

My cheeks hurt, I'm smiling so big.

Mom tops off everyone's champagne. "I can't wait to tell Patty that. My daughter, the author!"

Penny clears her throat. She's chewing her lip. "I have a secret too."

Now Mom's smile fades. She sends me a quick glance. Danny shifts in his seat.

Penny clutches her hands on her lap. "I lied about having a big family because... the truth is... thatihavenofamily."

Danny grips her hand, pulling it into his lap.

I stand and go sit next to her. She isn't crying, but she's on the edge.

Silence fills the room.

"My dad... had issues. He... he and my mom ... died when I was little. I grew up in the foster system."

Mom's lower lip comes forward like it always did when I was little and I cried about something. "That's awful. Thank you for telling us the truth."

Dad trails his thumb up and down the stem of his glass. "Getting through high school must have been hard enough, but going to college too. How did you manage it?"

Now it's me who might cry. I've never been more proud of my family in my life. Mom may be a snob about some things, but they are all kind and caring and good.

This is who I want to be. A good, honest person with a loving family.

No more secrets.

Well, I'll tell them about Stranger next time.

The night passes in a blur, and before I know it, I'm back home with my Stranger who is less and less stranger and more and more everything.

We celebrate Christmas by drinking champagne in our underpants—he's got a serious thing for my colorful thongs—and somehow, when I go into the kitchen to refill our glasses, I end up bent over the cheese drawer with my face inside the fridge, my nipples rock hard in the icy air. There's something about being hot and cold, laughing, surprised and aroused all at the same time.

In the morning, Stranger and I wake up leisurely. He goes for his run with Gogo. I plug my nose but make eggs for him, and toast for me.

"Shower?" he asks when they come back.

I smile. "Tempting, but I have this scene in my head."

He kisses me lingeringly enough that I nearly decide the join him after all, but what I really want is to put the intensity of our lovemaking last night on the page. I need to write it out before I lose it.

I make my way to my desk. Stranger sometimes works there when I'm not using it, so it's not anything out of the ordinary to find his computer there. What is unusual is that the screen is open.

Usually, he keeps it closed.

I push it to the side, and open up my own, enter in the password and start to write.

But it's there, just staring at me. His computer. The password bar open.

I've been asking to see what he's working on, tapping away while I write, but he won't let me read it.

I just want a sneak peek.

I'm terrible. I know. One try. Just one, like a game. See if I can guess the password. His brother's favorite beer, he told me once. There's no way it's so simple.

It's what they were drinking at the farmhouse.

Heineken.

I type it out fast before I can change my mind.

When the screen opens, I'm almost disappointed. I can't possibly look. I shouldn't. I'll close it. I lift up my hand, touch the back of the screen, but what I see there, stops me.

Greg's face stares back at me from a PDF file.

Greg?

It's his social media photo. A picture of him holding the babies. Hadley and Hart's sweet sleeping faces.

What the hell? Why would Stranger have photos of Greg in his laptop? I read the text under the photo.

Curbside?

What does that even mean?

I google it and flinch.

Assault? Greg? He's a rough and tumble guy, sure, but all I've ever seen of Greg is joviality. I know he never has more than one drink.

I minimize the PDF, and a new face looks at me.

Jeremy, his Facebook photo too, of him and me on a boat.

Now my stomach twists.

I cringe as I read about gambling, massive debt, illegal loans from suspicious persons, embezzlement, prostitution?

My hands start to shake.

Why does Stranger have these files?

I nearly rise to stand, but Gogo drops her head in my lap. I stroke her head with one jittery hand and with my other, I minimize the file.

Penny's face. A father who killed her mother in a fit of temper, and then himself.

My brother? Broke due to a secret business acquisition and career as a PR rep? Danny? Really?

Annie's face. *Unemployed.*

I keep on clicking.

Jeremy's dad. Dying of terminal abdominal cancer. *Diagnosed three years ago?* Why did he only tell Jer and Annie now?

The last two pictures though, they freeze my blood.

My mom. There's a picture of her kissing a man I've never seen before. A younger man. And the notes. *Having an affair with her golf instructor.*

This information isn't even right. She's not having an affair. My blood boils.

Click.

And finally, my dad's handsome face with his salt and pepper hair. *Suspicious payments to an offshore holding company.*

My heart pounds so hard it blocks out all sound.

I click on his email. The latest one is from someone named Lex.

> Lex: Dixon just ordered an uber. Destination…Mia's place.

> Stranger: ETA?

> Lex: 10:11

I push back from the chair. Oh my god.

Jeremy's coming.

And Stranger knows.

And he didn't tell me.

Whatever is going on here, Stranger isn't who he says he is. He's been lying to me. About everything.

I yank my robe closed, belt it tight at the waist.

If Jer comes here, sees me like this, sees Stranger, it will break his heart. I can't even process the prostitution or what any of it means, but I do know one thing, it will destroy forever any hopes for a relationship with Annie.

And Stranger—what the hell is he trying to do?

I can't even keep a single thought in my head.

Is he a stalker? An FBI agent? A member of the mafia? Who is he?

I should never have messed around online. Mom was right. This is what I deserve for cheating and being stupid and trusting.

I turn toward the bathroom, thinking I should go kick Stranger out, a thousand questions circling around in my brain, like will he even go? Does he have a gun? Why is he here? Who is this man?

I have no idea what I'm planning, and I'll never find out, because there he is.

Stranger is standing in the middle of the hallway, a towel looped around his waist, his skin still wet from the shower, the tattoos standing out in all colorful glory. I used to see them as a sign that he is unique, intense, vibrant... Now I just look at them and wonder at the type of man who would willingly submit his body to so much pain.

Tattoos *hurt*. And he has so many. What was he punishing himself for?

He's still, frozen, his eyes are on his open computer.

His hands come up in front of him like I'm the police and he's just committed a crime. "Hang on, Mia. I can explain."

I'm breathing too hard to answer. I'm furious. I want to throw his laptop at him. I want to hit him. I want to scream at the top of my lungs and never stop until the whole building is leveled. I wish I'd never seen him.

No more secrets, I thought last night.

But that's not true. He has secrets. So many secrets.

"Everyone has secrets, isn't that what you always say?" My voice comes out low and cold and so deep I barely recognize it. I've never been so angry in all my life. "And you have more than anyone."

He opens his mouth. His knees are bent slightly, like he's waiting for me to attack.

"I was happy," I whisper. "I was so happy before I met you. You've ruined my whole life."

He flinches like I've hit him physically, like it's a blow he feels with his whole body, like it matters. But that's the secret magic of Stranger. That's been his secret magic all along. He reacts like a human. But he isn't. He's something else.

"Who are you?" I wail.

At exactly that moment, a key sounds in the door, and Jeremy walks in. "Mia?" His voice is soft, cajoling, like he's ready for a fight. "Are you okay?"

Then he stops. His body goes still as a statue. He takes one look at me, and one look at the half-naked stranger standing in my apartment, and his shoulders slump.

He spins on his heel and leaves without another word.

Tears fill my eyes. Whatever Jeremy has done, we've been together for years, we've supported each other through so much. And now we've been reduced to this. And for what?

I round on Stranger. "You *knew!* You planned it this way."

His lips part, but no sound comes out.

Now, I really do pick up his computer.

I hurl it straight at his lying face.

27 – AN ARM ON HER

STRANGER

I have no idea how much she saw, how much she read, how much she knows.

I don't usually fuck up. I'm not that guy. I don't make mistakes.

But this, right now... Jesus.

I fucked everything up.

I scrub my hands through my hair and stare at her gobsmacked face. She looks like she's just been hit by an airbus, skin pale, mouth drawn in. She must be thinking things like stalker and crazy.

But killer is so much worse.

She rocks back on her heels, her eyes wide, her shoulders rigid, her fingers clenched at the belt of her robe.

There isn't a single thing about this situation I like, least of all the guilt. The shame. The self-loathing.

I fucking hate emotions. It's so much better to ignore them.

But Mia doesn't let me. She never does. It's like she woke me up to everything, a whole world of shit I want and need and feel, and now I can't silence it anymore.

And I see it so clearly, what I allowed myself to become, a contract killer, a heartless asshole, a guy who insinuated himself into her life and liked it so much, he stayed, soaked in lies and drenched in secrets.

I don't want her to know that side of me. I want her only to know the me that laughs and hikes and cooks with her. The me that's fun and happy. The me who smiles and writes and makes love with her and plans for a ridiculous future he has no right to want.

This is my fault. All of it. Everything. I should never have gotten this close to her. I should have left her alone when I felt myself getting involved.

Gogo paces, her nails ticking out an anxious beat on the floor. She senses the wrongness of this.

I close my eyes. My subconscious is sabotaging me. I left the computer out, forgot to close it up, put it away. I told her my fucking passwords long ago. It's like I wanted this to happen, wanted Mia to know the truth, dare her to love me anyway. I set these dominos in motion, and with every click, I brought us here. Right now.

Sink or swim, Stranger.

For a minute, it's like I'm right back in the group home, facing down a pack of kids bigger than me, stronger than me. Fight or flight?

I'm in basic, haven't slept in days. The sergeant is screaming at me, spit flying, and I'm tired. So tired. Lift your weapon, soldier. What are you going to do?

Whatever you have to do.

Now, soldier.

And then later, I'm there, facing my first hit. A five hundred-yard shot with a long-range sniper rifle. Now, soldier. The mark fell with a spray of red. How did I get here?

I shake my head.

I got here the same way I've always gotten anywhere. I sink or swim.

"You knew!" she screams. "You planned it this way."

I can't deny that. I did set Jeremy up to see me naked in her apartment. For what? A chance to rip him from her life for good?

Yes.

So, she'd have no one else but me?

I don't know. Maybe?

It was nothing but selfishness.

And I'd do it again to keep her away from that useless shitbag.

Even if the price is her trust.

Because I care. I care so fucking much my chest tightens and I can't breathe.

Her hands rise from the belt to touch her cheeks. Her chest is rising. She stares at me like she's never seen me before.

The door slams. Dixon is gone.

I shake my head, try to clear away visions of bodies piling high, blood and guts and shame. So much shame.

And under it, despite everything, I'm still ass enough to feel a moment of satisfaction. Dixon, that pathetic fuck will never come near her again, making her feel bad about herself, preying on her sympathies, using her.

She had two assholes in her life.

Now... she has none.

I glance back at her just in time to see my computer come flying at my face.

I catch it before it hits me smack in the nose. Barely.

She's got an arm on her.

"Mia..." I hesitate. Mia what?

What the fuck can I say?

Sink or swim. Fight or die.

Speak.

But I don't.

Gogo hides behind the sofa, cowering. She isn't used to shouting or loud noises in general. She isn't used to seeing me so off kilter.

Mia's face twists, like a kid trying to decide whether or not to cry. After a second she spreads her hands wide. "Mia what? What were you going to say, Stranger? It's not what it seems? You've got it wrong. Trust me?" Her lips shake, her chin wobbling, but her voice is strong and firm and powerful. "I think it's exactly what it seems. You wanted Jeremy gone from my life. And now he is."

I nod tightly.

"Why?" she whispers it, and my chest clenches.

I stare back for a long time, going through my options. Because he might want you dead? Because someone wants you dead. Because he sucks. Because I don't fucking want him near you. Because I can't let you die. I can't live without you.

Jesus. When did that happen.

I settle on the truest statement of all. Hopefully the only one that really matters, words I'm not sure I've ever said in my whole life. "Because I love you."

Her nostrils flare. Wrong thing to say.

"You *love* me? You don't *love* me. You're a liar."

I can't argue.

It's true. I am a liar, but lying is the least of my sins.

She steps toward me. "Who the fuck are you? A lying, conniving, manipulative, stalking, crazy, kinda hot internet stranger?"

Yes. Yes. Yes. Yes. Maybe. Maybe. Yes.

I've never seen Mia in a temper. She is a force to be reckoned with. She's confident, undeterred, erudite in her rage, and if she's afraid of this man she suddenly doesn't trust, naked in her home—she isn't showing it.

I'm proud of her.

"Were you even in the military?"

"Yes."

She doesn't make a move toward the wallet. "And now? What are you?"

For a moment, her eyes fill with something that looks like hope.

"Are you undercover FBI? Looking into Jeremy?" Her voice breaks, and her face crumples. "Mafia? Are you crazy, Stranger? Are you stalking me?"

I take a deep breath. "I know it looks bad, Mia. I'm not crazy. And I'm not trying to hurt you. I'm trying to protect you."

"From who? Why? What the hell do you do?"

I can't answer that. Or maybe I could. But I don't, I just sink into a silence so thick I'm drowning.

She must feel it too, because after a long pause, she slides down into the silly pink chair. "Just go."

I squeeze my eyes shut, take a long deep breath. "Please. You don't understand. It's not safe. I can't leave you alone."

She laughs, short and hard. There's an edge to Mia I haven't seen before. She's sweet, but she's so much more.

And there is nothing I can say.

I'm a contract killer.

Someone hired me to kill you. Maybe your dad.

I won't do it though, I promise.

I need to find them.

So, I settle for another truth. "I just want to keep you safe."

She turns her back on me. "Leave."

Short of tying her up and holding her hostage until I find Ender—and I'm not willing to do any of those things—I don't have any choice.

I grab my shit and walk out the door, Gogo close on my heels.

I close the door gently and listen on the other side. Maybe I expected to hear screaming or crying or ranting, but I don't.

I hear nothing. So I dress in the hall, yanking on my pants and stepping into my boots, tuck my computer under my arm and leave. What choice do I have?

Striding down the hall, I pull my phone from my pocket and call James.

Mia doesn't have to be with me.

I can handle that.

But she does have to be alive.

CHERRY ON THE MISERY CAKE

MIA

I suppose I deserve this.

Mom warned me.

She was wrong about his weight and his teeth though.

But he is... a what?

A psychopath? A stalker? A deranged maniac?

How could he hide it from me? All this time, all these months of texting, and talking, then the time I spent at the farm house, the time he spent here.

How could I not see?

Because I'm an idiot. A blind, trusting, stupid idiot.

I didn't see the truth behind Jer's façade either, and we were together for years.

I sink into the sofa, pull the throw blanket up over me, and just let it all marinate. I wish Gogo was here. She'd rub her wet nose on my arms and let me pet her velvety ears.

It just keeps on spinning. A thousand thoughts at once.

It's too much. Danny has a secret business? Why didn't he tell me? I knew about Penny. She told me, most of it. Not about how it happened. My heart hurts for her, thinking of a child going through all that alone. But why is Stranger looking into my family? Who is he?

What does he want with me?

It's humiliating. I fell in love with the perfect man, trusted him, believed in him... and all along he was lying to me, faking it, pretending.

And now my life is in ruins. No fiancé. No best friend. No godbabies to spoil.

My face crumples.

I was so happy before he came into my life. I was in love, engaged, had a best friend and a good family. I was literally thinking about how smug and happy I was when I opened that first message from him. And now? It's just a mess. Not that I can hold him responsible for Jer's lies, or the mess with my parents...

Maybe I can fix things with Annie. I have to try.

I grab my phone and start a text to her, but before I can hit send, a message comes through. It's her.

> Annie: Seriously Mia? You were cheating on Jer? It's like I don't even know you. It's like someone replaced the kind, thoughtful, generous Mia with a selfish bitch who thinks of no one but herself.

My eyes well up at that.

Me selfish?

I toss the blanket aside. I can't yell at Stranger, but I can sure as hell yell back at Annie.

> Mia: Either you care about me as a friend or you don't. We've known each other for nine years. We've been best friends that entire time. You think I'm selfish? Look in the mirror. If I weren't Jer's ex-fiancé, if I were just Mia, your best friend, what would you ask me now? Have you even thought about me?

> Annie: I'd have been way harder on you. I'd have asked you to take a long hard look at your life and ask what the hell you're thinking of. Did you even think about the future you just destroyed? It was all so perfect and you just fucked everything up. For what? Some freak with tattoos?

I guess Jer told her about Stranger. He'd been standing in the hallway wearing nothing but a loose towel. His brightly tattooed chest, all hard and rippled, his hair still wet.

Poor Jer.

It's like that scene from a movie where the woman comes home to find her husband in bed with a hotter, harder, prettier, younger woman wearing red lace lingerie.

Jer came home to find a taller, harder, hotter, tattooed, bristly, rugged, naked man in his ex-fiancé's apartment.

My heart sinks. I get why Annie is mad. I understand. I would be angry too if someone broke Danny's heart, shamed him that way, maybe more so if she was my closest friend, someone I trusted, because I'd feel betrayed too.

> Mia: My choice to end it with Jeremy has nothing to do with the man he saw me with.

> It has everything to do with the lying. He was cheating on me, gambling and drinking and lying about it. He didn't tell me about the debt, about any of it.

I leave out the prostitutes. Annie doesn't need to know that.

There's a long pause. Long enough that I wander through my apartment, gathering all of Stranger's things. The book from the side table. The phone charger from the living room. The toothbrush. A pair of briefs, a t-shirt from the bedroom. The unopened Christmas present he brought with him. I didn't get him anything.

I bring the t-shirt to my face, bury my nose in it and inhale. Soap and Stranger. My eyes burn, my nose prickles, and the tears do come now.

I shove all his things in a bag and drop it by the door like it's on fire, climb into the shower, lay down on the tile and cry.

I cry for Jer, the boy he was and the man he's become. For Annie and the loss of a friend. I cry for Danny and Mom and Dad. I cry for Stranger, and myself, and all the dreams I had when I was a kid and none of them involved an internet crazy person. I've never been so humiliated, so ashamed, so degraded. I cry for all the things.

I bared my soul to a man. I gave him every single little part of myself I'd ever hidden from anyone. I let him see inside me, the good, the bad and the shameful.

And all along he'd been playing me.

I feel so ... stupid.

I don't know how long I cry, but at some point, my fingers turn to prunes, the water runs cold, and I have no tears left, so I get out of the shower, dry off and climb into bed without even brushing my hair.

I do grab my phone though.

Annie didn't bother responding.

And I got three new reviews.
All bad.
I just hit rock-bottom.
It's official.
Each review is worse than the next.

An insult to the word book. A catastrophe. I'd ask for a refund, but no one can refund my time.

> This is trash. Trite and utter nonsense.

> Only read this book if you are dangerously stupid or masochistic.

Last time, Stranger made me feel better, but this time, I have no Stranger, no wild distraction, no desperate hope.

And just because it wasn't bad enough, I also have an email from Wet Panty.

> Linda@wetpanty.org: We regret to inform you that due to personal reasons, we can no longer offer an interview to you.

That's the cherry on the misery cake.
I hate my phone.
My personal life is a disaster.
My professional life is in collapse.
Tomorrow is Christmas Eve.
And I am all alone.

I hole up. Text Mom and Penny, tell them I'm sick. Then ignore my phone entirely. Nothing good happens on that nasty black-magic device of evil. Occasionally it lights up in the corner, casting an eerie glow around my darkened bedroom. Eventually I think—I hope—it dies.

Mom shows up on Christmas around noon. I don't open the door.

She bangs on it for a while, shouts through the door about ungrateful daughters, deep betrayals on the holidays, maternal guilt and making her worry, and leaves.

When I open the door, there's a bag containing my Christmas stocking. Santa still visits their house. Beside the bag is a Tupperware containing leftovers from Christmas brunch.

I eat it in my pajamas watching Christmas movies, crying into gingerbread men and the little peppermint cookies Mom makes every year.

I would have been with Stranger right now, naked but for Santa hats, probably having mind-blowing sex. Or maybe just talking, joking, laughing... beyond conned.

I wake in the early evening, drooling on the couch, to someone knocking at the door.

I peer through the peep hole.

Penny.

She looks... perky, with her long black hair, a red sparkly sweater. She has makeup on.

I look down. There's a mystery stain on my gray sweatpants, and I'm wearing Stranger's t-shirt. It's covered in crumbs.

"I see you, Mia. Open up."

I dust off the crumbs but make no move to open the door. I didn't bother with deodorant or a brush after my cryfest in the shower yesterday and I've barely gotten out of bed since. "I think maybe I smell."

"Then let me in. You can go shower while I unpack," her voice comes through the door.

She holds up a brown paper bag. "I brought wine."

"Fine," I grumble, pulling open the door. "Don't look at me. I'll be back in ten."

I round on my heel, take the fastest shower known to man, and come back a few minutes later, squeaky clean, in a pair of yoga pants and sweater.

Penny cleaned up while I was gone. The place looks a bit better. But the bag of Stranger's things still sits by the door, a gross reminder of my own failings, my thousand mistakes, my insane arrogance in thinking a man who looks like an enormous tattooed god could actually want me for... me.

I suck in a long and painful breath.

I was so smug once, before him.

I thought my life was so perfect.

She's sitting at the dining table. I try not to remember how Stranger and I had sex right there, but it's impossible. He wore the Santa hat, and went down on me for so long I cried for him to stop. The memory sends a sex-flashback straight to my vagina so sharp and so hard I wince.

Penny sits placidly with two glasses of wine and a plate piled high with Christmas ham and all the fixings. "Sit down and tell me what's going on."

I chew on my lip, toy with the naked finger that once wore Jeremy's ring.

She cocks her head to the side, her dark hair glimmering under the lights of my tree. "I won't tell anyone anything, Mia. I'm really good at keeping secrets. Trust me."

She is indeed..

And I'll have to tell someone at some point. Why not Penny?

"Promise not to judge me? You can laugh, I don't mind being laughed at..." I have to suck on my lower lip for a minute because the tears threaten to come back. "I just don't think I can handle judgment right now."

"I would never judge you. Or laugh at you."

I take my seat, sip my wine, and spill... everything, starting right from the beginning, the very first message.

Penny listens in a silence that is truly impressive. Not very many people can keep their mouths shut and just hear. I certainly can't.

But she does. She just listens to me talk about the mystery, the excitement, the fear, the doubt. Then the sex and the trust and the love. And finally, the heinous truth. Lies, darkness, secrets, so much shame.

When I finish, she pours the last of the bottle into our glasses.

"He was good, celebrating when you were accepted to the Wet Panty thing. He knew what you needed."

I nod. "So good. A real con artist."

She lifts a shoulder. "Maybe you're too quick to judge."

I tuck my feet under me, tugging at the fleece socks. "I don't really see any other reasonable explanation."

She rolls her wine glass back and forth between her hands. "Well... like with your mom, you just assume the worst possible explanation is the only one."

"What else could it be?"

"Maybe your dad can't get it up. Maybe she needed sex. Maybe your dad knows. People have... understandings sometimes."

I make a face. "Not people like my parents."

"Maybe... she's not sleeping with that guy."

"I can't see any world in which she'd cheat. They're so in love."

"I guess my point is... your mom loves you, and she loves your dad. Maybe you could give them the benefit of the doubt."

I play out a few different versions. I like all of them better than the reality. "It's wishful thinking though. That's what I keep doing with Stranger, trying to paint it all pretty pink and happy. I've done that my whole life. Avoided the ugly, the real, the hard. Sought out the happy, the sexy, the fun. It's easier to pretend not to see it. And that's exactly the type of thinking that brought me to this dark place. I didn't see the truth when it was right in front of me. Jer was lying to me. Stranger was lying to me. Neither of them actually loved me at all."

"What do you think Stranger wanted?" Penny asks.

I toss my head back, blow air up at the ceiling. "Depends on who he really is. I've had some insane ideas. Ones that I'd cook up for a book. The most obvious, the most simple explanation is that he's deranged. Some kind of sadistic maniac who was stalking me."

She nibbles on a peppermint cookie. "That doesn't seem simple or obvious. That seems really hard to believe. He didn't seem deranged or sadistic up in Finger Lakes."

I nod. "He was a good actor."

"To be honest," she says. "That seems like ego talking."

I make a face.

"I'm serious, think about it." She plops her foot up on my coffee table, between a sculpture of horses I got in Beijing, and a hot pink gorilla Erica got me in San Diego. "You're biased, determined to make yourself the center of the mess, it has to be your fault for not seeing the truth. What if it's not about you?"

I rub my eyes. "Nothing makes any sense."

She takes a long thoughtful sip of her wine. "I mean... I think you're saying the simplest explanation is that he's a maniac, because then all you can do is blame yourself. Then it's about you and your own mistakes. But what if it isn't? What if it's about Jeremy? If he's really been gambling, embezzling, drinking, seeing prostitutes... I don't know. What if Stranger was investigating him and he got close to you in order to get information on Jeremy?"

"That seems so dramatic though, like a book or a movie."

"Maybe." She wrinkles her nose up. "It just seems easier to believe that, than that Stranger was some creepy stalker guy. He doesn't look like a creepy stalker guy."

I laugh, because I've had that same thought so many times. "How do you know? How many creepy stalker guys do you know?"

"None. Did he offer an explanation?"

I shake my head.

"Did you ask for one?"

"Not really."

We sit in silence for a minute, before she says, "What do you need to do?"

"What do you mean?"

"You just canceled a wedding. You must have a to-do list."

Ugh.

"So much. I need to send out emails to vendors, the band, the venue, the guests." I look down at my wine. It's almost gone. I need more. "I have to send back so many presents."

Her face lights up. "That's my specialty."

"What? Sending back silverware?"

She laughs. I love her already. "No. Helping people declutter, get a grip on their lives. Tomorrow, we'll print up return labels and pack everything up. We'll send out an email to your guests so they can cancel their plans. Then we'll reorganize your entire house and get your life as organized as we possibly can. And soon, you're going to have to turn on your phone."

I just stare at her. It's too much.

"And the day after that, you will speak with your mother. But tonight... we're getting drunk and watching a chick movie. We'll eat the rest of those cookies and we won't talk about Stranger at all... unless you want to. And if you need to cry, that's cool too."

"You're going to marry my brother, right?"

She nods. "That's the plan."

"Good."

We find The Bodyguard on Netflix, and stay up too late, and drink too much wine, and eat too many Christmas cookies.

It takes a real friend to blow their diet with you. And an even better one to belt out along with Whitney Houston with you.

29 - PONY UP

STRANGER

There are men out there who bumble through life. You see them on the news, in movies and books. Hapless guys who drop their keys or fall off curbs, hit their women, get arrested, get drunk, lose their money, don't pay their taxes.

That's not me. I'm not that guy. I do not do things spontaneously or emotionally. I plan. I'm careful. Cautious. Deliberate.

I take my time, calculate everything before I go after a mark. Emotion has nothing to do with it. I run on logic, clean and cold and always without mistakes.

Except I'm pretty sure I just made the biggest mistake of my entire life.

The thought haunts me through my drive home, down every stretch of salted asphalt flanked by exhaust-covered snow between Mia's home and mine.

I fucked it all up. All of it, right from the beginning.

It would have been so easy to tell her. Months ago.

I have to tell you something, Mia. Sit down. Someone wants to hurt you. She'd have been scared, yes. But she'd have come around. Right?

No, even pissed off, I know that's not what would have happened.

She'd have gone to the police, she'd have thought I was crazy, and she'd never have spoken to me again.

But I could have told her last night. Or when she asked what I did. I could have told her.

It wouldn't have ended well then either.

In the garage now, I turn off the car but I don't get out.

I hit the remote and the garage door slides shut behind me, leaving me in the dark.

Still, I don't get out, just sit there with my hands wrapped around the wheel.

I'd love to write it off, say she turned me into a woman after all, but that's not it. She turned me into a man. She woke me up. I was dead before her. She brought me to life one text at a time.

And without her? I'll be dead again, living in a void. I don't want that.

My hands start shaking on the wheel, so I gather them into fists. An all-too-familiar weight settles in my chest as hard and cold as stone.

I could go back.

Knock on her door.

Explain. Beg her to listen. Tell her that I'm a hitman, not a stalker. That I contacted her so I could kill her, not just because I'm a pervert. But that's worse. So much worse. It might actually be better to be a pervert than what I truly am.

Gogo whines in the passenger seat, shifting restlessly, her nails dragging on the leather. She's confused that we're still here. She probably needs to pee.

I scrub my hands up and down my face. My beard has grown too long now. It's itchy on my skin. But Mia liked it, liked when I ran it down the small of her back, along her neck, the pads of her fingers. I liked that she liked it. The mild irritation of the beard on my face was nothing to the sounds she made when I dragged it over the soft skin of the insides of her thighs.

Slowly, I unbuckle my seatbelt and circle the car and open the passenger door.

Gogo throws herself bodily at me.

I catch her, lower her to the ground. Her nails click frantically as she runs to the trio of steps that lead into the mudroom. I still haven't cut them.

I follow her, letting grim resolve work its way through my veins.

Nothing has changed. Not really.

I let Gogo out and walk through the barren, silent house.

James is in the weight room.

His gaze flicks behind me, smile fading. "Where's Mia?"

"She found the files in my computer."

He turns away from me. "I'm sorry, man. How much does she know?"

I sink into the sofa. "Too much. Not enough."

"What do we do now?"

"I don't know." I resist the urge to stand up and shove my fist through the wall. At least when I was with her, in her physical presence, I knew no one could hurt her.

Now though...

She's all alone.

I slide my thumb across my screen of my phone, a little beat of excitement coursing through me when I see I have a message. It's not her though.

> Lex: Call me, Stranger.

> Stranger: Ring ring.

The phone rings and a second later, Lex is there. She doesn't say hi, just launches straight into it.

"There's been another transfer."

"From who?"

"The dad. Keith. He just transferred another three fifty."

"Thousand?"

"Yup."

That's exactly the amount of money they owe me for the second hit on Dixon and Mia.

"To the same offshore account?"

"Broxman, Telker and Shone."

"That makes no sense. Why would he send that money preemptively? March is a long way away."

I put Lex on speaker phone, so James can hear too. "Because you were right," she says. "He's an investment guy. He's not going to leave that kind of money sitting around for three months. No, I think Ender asked for more money, and he's dumb enough to pony up."

James and I lock eyes. "Who though?"

"Whoever decided to do it isn't making much sense. If they need money, why not just take the money from the dad. It's got to be personal. Whoever did this wants Mia dead."

That's the thought that's been lurking in the back of my mind from the beginning It feels personal. It's not logical. Need money, borrow from that dad. Why kill anyone?

This whole time we've been looking for a motive and assuming it was all about Mia's money. What if it was something else?

James rocks back and forth in his chair, his brows drawn together like they always do when he's thinking. "That fits with the timeline too. I've been annoyed by that from the beginning. Who orders a hit seven months early? That's crazy."

"Someone who's got no idea what they're doing?"

That doesn't feel like Greg. I play out the kind of person who curbsides someone. They have to plan it out, even while enraged. They have to line the person up, even as their victim cries, resists. It's not the move of pure rage-born violence. It's calculated, despite rage. It's ice cold.

"I don't think it's Greg."

"Me neither," says Lex.

"Nor me," says James.

"Then who?" I ask. "Look into that woman again. The rich lady whose husband died. She hated Mia in school."

James makes a face. "She's been busy, traveling all over the place. It's not her."

I open the find-me app in my phone, check on Mia. She's still at home. Good. "Has she been to the Caribbean? Doesn't take more than a minute to send an email."

"I don't remember, but I'll find out."

"Thanks, Lex."

"You bet. Look after your lady."

My chest does that annoying confusing thing again. Mia isn't mine anymore.

But Lex doesn't notice. "Whoever is behind this, is unpredictable. And probably impulsive."

For the next six hours, James and I reread every shred of information I've got on everyone in Mia's life. I try to focus, but I'm distracted. I keep checking the find-me app. She went dark two hours ago.

I keep on pacing. Did her phone die? Or was it turned off on purpose?

James gets me a beer, sets it down in front of me, but I don't touch it.

"Fuck it," I say. "She already thinks I'm a crazy stalker. I'm going to go check, just to make sure. Watch Gogo?"

He nods, and off I go, driving south again, hating myself with every mile. I should have done this all differently.

When I get there, I park a few streets up, just in case she looks out the window. I don't want to dig myself an even deeper hole.

I slide through the bushes in a dark shadow and peek through her window. She's on her sofa in a pile of colorful pillows. Penny is with her, their faces lit in the blue glow of a TV. As I watch, Mia laughs at something Penny says, covering her mouth with her hands the way she does when someone says something unexpected.

It makes my stomach tighten.

I miss that laugh, but I'm glad to see it.

She'll be fine.

She's not broken inside like me.

That seems fitting.

I walk back to my car. I'll get a hotel room nearby so I'm close, just in case. I have a bad feeling, an itch at the back of my neck, something I can't ignore.

I send her another text.

> Stranger: "I miss you."

30 – BE SELFISH

MIA

Two days later, right on Penny's schedule, I go home. She was a blur of activity, taping up boxes, slapping on labels. She even helped me load everything into my car and carry it all into the local post office.

My place has never looked better. She helped me declutter drawers, clean out closets, donate things to Goodwill. It's still colorful and busy and bright, it's just not cluttered. I feel... lighter.

But now, it's time to go home. I can't keep hiding from Mom and Dad forever.

It isn't fair.

Dad's in his office when I get there.

"Where's Mom?"

He glances up from his computer, an irritable scowl on his face. "She just got in. Probably in the kitchen or her room."

"Where was she?"

He shrugs, still staring at his computer screen. He looks... almost alarmed.

I hesitate in the doorway. "You okay, Dad?"

He nods, then sends me a distracted look. Then it's like he actually sees me. "We missed you at Christmas. What's going on, peanut?"

There are things you just don't tell dads. Stranger and our torrid affair is definitely one of them. "I'm fine."

He narrows his eyes, tilts his head like he has since I was a little girl. "You can talk to me... you know, if you need to."

I pat the door jam. "I know Dad, thanks."

When I leave, he's staring back at his computer again, and I can't help but wonder about the transfers mentioned in Stranger's file. What was that for?

I find Mom, in the mudroom, sneaking up the back steps. She looks like she fell off the front page spread of Golf Weekly magazine, all glowing and happy, her hair pulled back in a careful, fluffy ponytail.

My heart sinks.

My whole life Dad, Danny and I went golfing, while Mom stayed behind and did something else. Usually she read a book, or went out to lunch, got a massage, spent some time on her own, but she never golfed.

Golf was always Dad's thing. He tried. He asked a million times if she'd come. *There's no shame, hon. Everyone is bad when they start. Never too late to learn.*

But she'd never come.

So why now? Is she having an affair? Was Stranger right?

"Mom?"

She jumps when she sees me and freezes half way up the back steps like a cartoon villain. "Oh, Mia! You scared the hell out of me."

I swallow. "Why are you wearing golf clothes?"

She makes a face. "Don't you dare tell your father. I've kept this secret for over a year!"

I suck in a breath. "What would I even tell him?"

"That I was golfing," she whispers.

"It's the middle of winter. Where would you golf?"

"Lower your voice." She holds her finger over her mouth. "He can't see me dressed like this, it would spoil everything. I'll be right back. Go wait in the kitchen."

She skulks up the steps, and I head in to wait for her.

I get out two glasses and fill them with water, slouch into the counter stools and wait.

"You swear you won't tell him?" she hisses a few minutes later, when she comes back wearing her more normal attire of black pants and an ivory sweater.

"Are you having an affair?"

She freezes mid stride, her mouth dropping. "Where in the world did you get that idea?"

I study her face. Mom doesn't lie. At least, I don't think she does.

I realize suddenly how little I actually know my parents. They're a unit. Like I just pigeon-holed them at some date in my childhood and never saw them as anything else.

Mom is just *Mom* to me. The woman who didn't like romance novels and liked Jeremy and expected me to act a certain way. She wasn't a woman with a distinct personality all her own.

And same with Dad. I saw him as just... my dad.

I pick up the water. "Seriously, Mom. Just tell me, are you cheating on Dad?"

"No." She sends me a hurt look. "I wanted to surprise all of you. Danny too. I thought maybe if he came out this summer, when you all went golfing, I'd surprise you at the club by joining in. I've been taking lessons. The club got this indoor simulation. It's like a computer game, but I swing a real club."

I try to picture that and fail. "Why?"

"The cruise. Your dad always wants to golf when we go on vacations, but he doesn't love joining other groups or going alone. He always wants me to go. So I've been taking lessons for the last year." Her eyes stare into mine, that hurt look making my stomach clench with shame that I doubted her. "I've been learning so I can play with him."

See.

I want to call Stranger on the phone, shout at him that not everyone is a horrible liar. Sometimes people have secrets that hurt no one. Like me and Danny and Penny and Mom.

We have our secrets, but they're innocent.

Not like him. Or maybe like him?

I don't even know his secrets.

Mom's staring at me like I just peed on her carpet.

Might as well get it all out there. "I got a tattoo."

She doesn't even blink, so I turn around, and tug my sweater down so she can see my back.

If she sees it, she doesn't say anything. "I just want you to be happy, Mia. That's all I've ever wanted."

Me too. I take a long deep breath. I've only ever really truly been happy with Stranger. I don't know if it was real, though.

"I was proud of you with Penny, Mom."

"What did you expect? Me to spit on her?'

"I don't know. I didn't think you liked her."

She finishes her water. "I didn't like her because I thought she was lying to Danny, not because I'm some heartless ogre who can't sympathize with a woman who lost her family as a kid. It's like you don't know me, Mia. Thinking I'd cheat on your dad. Keeping your writing from me? Not telling me about Jeremy? Why?"

"I don't know."

"Maybe it's time you practice trusting people."

I stare at her face. It's like looking into the future, we look so much alike. She just has a few more lines on her face, a little more wear. I hope someday I look like her. She's still beautiful.

All this time I thought the problem was that I'd been too trusting. But maybe she's right. I kept everyone at arm's distance, not trusting them to accept me as a writer.

"Annie says I'm being selfish ending it with Jer."

Mom laughs. "I'd expect better from a woman who just had kids. She knows the truth. Before you have kids is the last time in your life you get to be selfish. Once you're married, once you have a baby, your selfish days are gone. You be selfish, Mia. This is your time. You decide who you want to spend your whole life with."

I take a deep breath.

"Is that this internet man?"

Maybe? If he's got a decent explanation. Maybe I owe it to both of us to ask him.

"Mom?"

"Yes?"

"Can I borrow a phone charger?"

31 – THE ORANGE DOT

STRANGER

I flip over on scratchy sheets. My feet hang off the bottom of the bed. I cracked a window, and the air blows in icy and damp, but it beats the heater.

To be fair, the hotel isn't that bad.

But it has no garden vomit, or ladyscented pots and tubes of lotion. And it has no lamps shaped like parrots or spindly pink desk chairs.

It's nearly 11am. I probably got about three hours of sleep. I check my phone reflexively.

It's weird not being in contact with Mia. For months I've checked my phone every few minutes just to see if she's texted. Now, it's like I got dumped in a silent frozen lake.

She hasn't answered. I check her location again. Her damned phone has been off all day.

I hop in the shower, scrub down fast and grope for my phone as soon as I get out. My thumb is too wet to open it right away and I fumble a few times.

There's a text. It's probably James. I click on the icon.

It's not James.

It's her.

> Mia: You were wrong about my mom. She's taking private golf lessons to surprise my dad. That was the golf pro in those photos. He's gay. Which made me think, it's not always the worst possible explanation. Maybe it isn't with you either. I'm willing to listen if you want to talk.

I could almost sigh. I rest my hip against the counter. Something strange and warm moves through my chest.

> Stranger: Can we meet?

She doesn't answer though. I stare down at my phone for a few foolish minutes before I realize whatever she's doing, she isn't staring at her phone like I am.

I set the phone down. It buzzes almost instantly. I lurch for it, drop it, grab for it, knock it high, fumble again. When I finally get it face-up and answered, it's James.

"What?"

"Morning to you too."

I don't answer. Just glare at my own face in the mirror. My beard has gotten even thicker, I have bags under my eyes, I've lost weight. I look like shit. "What do you want, James?"

"I found something last night. None of us asked what the mom's name was."

"Her name is Shelby."

"No. Not Mia's mom. Dixon's mom."

I frown at my reflection. I know her name. "Bunny Dixon."

"Her maiden name is Bernadette Telker Snead."

I frown. The name of the Caymans fund. Broxman, Telker and Shone. "What's Broxman and Shone then?"

"I don't know. They're old money. It's a family fund."

I'm still frowning. Bunny is sixty-three. She lives in Florida. "You think Jeremy's mom is Ender?"

James makes a noise like he's waiting for me to catch up. "Who would Mia's dad be willing to give money to?"

I don't even have to guess. "Annie."

"Exactly. Let's say she runs the fund, we know she's got her hands in the business and the family finances. What if she sees the business tanking. She and Greg are flailing, strapped for cash. She can't work. Two kids on the way. She sees her brother steadily ruining her family business, but he's getting married, and Mia won't give him unlimited money... unless she's dead and he has the money in his own name. She takes out a hit on Mia for after the wedding. She knows how to contact you... somehow. But she needs money so she hits up Mia's own dad, tells him her sob story. Of course he wants to help. It's the best friend of his baby girl. Then Jer starts spiraling, spinning out, gambling. He's a liability. Costing more than he's worth. So she takes out a second hit. Guess who's his beneficiary."

I lean forward, wrapping my fingers around the edge of the granite vanity. That feels right. It explains the long wait time, the strange word use. "Mia said she's got bad post-partum depression."

I check Mia on the find-me app.

She's on the highway, headed north, headed toward my house. The warm feeling grows at seeing her phone back on, at knowing I'll see her again, that she's giving me a chance. She wants to see me. Bad enough to hear me out, let me explain myself ... and what the fuck will I say? I picture her, the moment she sat on the edge of decision, chewing that lip, wrinkling that nose, doubting, unsure, then taking the risk. For me.

Except... I'm not there.

She's driving north for nothing.

I call her.

She doesn't answer.

I start gathering my things fast, yanking on jeans, a shirt, socks, my Glock .26, a knife. Stuffing things in my pocket, my toothbrush still in my mouth, doing everything one handed, I keep watching that tiny orange dot on my phone's screen.

She's coming back to me and I need to get there first, which means I need to get on the road too.

I make it to the door, remember the toothbrush in my mouth belatedly, and toss it into the waste basket in the bathroom, spitting in the sink.

I'm in the hallway, stalking toward the elevator when Mia's orange dot makes an abrupt exit, getting off the highway.

The tiny orange dot does a U-turn.

What the hell?

As I watch, the dot ambles down a small side road, headed west of the city, out toward farm country.

I know who lives out that way.

Annie and Greg.

She's not coming to me. She's going straight for Annie.

32 – WHAT ABOUT WET PANTY?

MIA

There is so much freedom in honesty. My parents know the worst now. My engagement is over. My career is in the dumps.

I have nothing to lose really. And everything to gain. I can get Annie back, I have to believe that. I will get my career back in order. And Stranger...

As Penny said, it's not really any better assuming Stranger is insane and stalking me. I'd rather know. Just in case he is crazy, I send out a text message to Penny, Danny, and Mom letting them know that I'm going to see Stranger Revin outside Albany. I even include his address at the end just in case.

Penny sends back clapping hands and a heart.

> Danny: That tattooed guy?

> Mom: Oh, well then, good luck. Love, mom.

> Dad: What 'tattood guy'?

I picture mom having a silent aneurism explaining the tattooed guy. She's trying. And Dad? God knows what he'll think. That's his problem I guess.

I feel... light.

The guilt over Jer, the shame over betraying Annie, the fear of how they'd react, the embarrassment over ending the wedding... it's still here—but honestly, it's not all that bad. I don't have to worry about it anymore. The build-up before ripping off the band-aid is so much worse than the reality.

In the aftermath, I feel hope.

I turn the radio up, sing along at the top of my lungs, hit the gas and head toward Stranger, and hopefully a damned good explanation.

I make it about six miles up the freeway, when I glance down at my phone.

Annie texted.

I pull over fast, swerving and narrowly missing a red Honda. The driver lays on the horn. I deserve it.

Please let Annie be feeling forgiving!

> Annie: I feel horrible about everything. I don't have enough people in my life to throw away a friend and you're my oldest and closest. I don't want to lose you. Can we meet?

My heart soars.

> Mia: Yes! I could be at your house in ten minutes? Can I come?

> Annie: Perfect.

I hit the gas, and get off at the next highway.

Stranger can wait.

I'm so happy, my chest feels like it might explode. I don't want to lose Annie. I'll do anything to avoid losing her.

The snow is thick on the long drive up toward Annie and Greg's house. Someone has plowed it and salted. Greg probably. Or Annie maybe, if she was desperate enough for a break from the babies.

I picture one of them waking in the dark, getting out their old bobcat and moving the snow around, thick gloves and a thermos of hot coffee. It reminds me of Stranger.

When it snowed at his place while I was there, he left while I was sleeping. I didn't even hear him go. And by the time I woke up, it was all done. James was wheeling around the drive sprinkling sand and salt over the areas Stranger had cleared with the shovel. They worked together with the ease of two people accustomed to sharing tasks. It looked peaceful. I didn't mention it, but I got the impression they both enjoyed it.

The memory feels off to me, like a sore tooth.

At the time it felt so homey and warm. Tasha had pulled up shortly after, and she and James had disappeared into the gym, and Stranger and I curled up on the sofa and wrote. But now, I can't help but wonder, was he really writing? Is he really even a writer?

I pull my car over the final rise and pull around the circular drive, parking under the porte cochere. Annie's family has owned this place for three generations. It's a big house, old, historic. It breaks my heart that they've mortgaged it so much they'll have to pay the bank when they sell it. At least, if Stranger's information was right.

I leave my purse in the car, not even bothering to take in my phone.

I want my whole focus on Annie. One hundred percent. She needs to know how much she means to me.

I lift the big iron lion doorknob, but before I can even bring it down, Annie's there at the door, pulling it open.

It's dark inside. The old wood paneling and oriental carpets seeming to suck all the light from the room. Annie's face is wan, drawn, aged in a way I can't describe. We're the same age, twenty-seven, but she looks old.

"Let's go for a walk," she says, turning her back on me to pull open a paneled door beside the entry way. "I need to get out of here."

"What about the babies?"

She hands me one of Greg's coats, and pulls out two pairs of snow boots. "Greg's working from home. He's got them." Her jaw tightens. The muscles and bones in her face are so clear, pressing against her skin. She looks gaunt.

Maybe she sees me looking at her painfully thin legs, because she says, "my milk quit. The doctor thinks I've lost too much weight."

I take the coat without argument. I tug it on, and slide into the snowboots.

"You want a hat?" She shoves one at me.

"Sure."

Shoulders rigid, her body pulled tight as a bow, she jerks her head at the door. "Let's walk around to the pond. Greg says it still hasn't frozen all the way."

The house and grounds are nearly two hundred years old. Originally there were kitchen gardens, a groundskeeper's cottage and a formal rose garden, but mostly it's been overrun. I thought that was a strategic choice on the Dixons' part, even found it charming in an unpretentious sort of way, but now I wonder.

We pick our way through the snow, sticking vaguely to the old brick paths we know are there only through memory.

I think maybe neither of us knows where to start, or maybe we're both scared of saying the wrong thing, but we walk mostly in silence. There's something so brittle about her, so edgy that I'm scared she'll lash if I make a misstep.

I assume she's thinking about what she wants to say to me.

My mind keeps drifting to Stranger. I can't help but wonder if he's seen my text. If he even wants to see me, talk to me, if he even cares. My stomach clenches. And if he does want to see me, what will he say? What can he possibly say that would make any sort of sense?

The pond is about half a mile from the house. We leave the clearing of the old formal gardens and cut through a path in the woods.

It's not until the trees open up and the pond comes into view maybe fifty yards ahead of us that Annie finally turns to me. "Are you with that tattooed guy now?"

"I don't know."

She doesn't even blink. "Do you want to be?"

"I don't know."

When she's frustrated, she has this face she makes. The same one Jer always makes. It must be hereditary or maybe just learned. Maybe it's the face Bunny always made. But they wrinkle up their chin and scrunch up their lips, scowling with their brows.

"Can we talk about us instead? Our friendship?"

She pinches the bridge of her nose. "No. Yes. I guess... I need to understand first what's going on with you. How are things?"

I look across the pond. It isn't frozen all the way. Greg was right. Only small patches. It's slushy more than frozen, with squashy white piles of snow amid the darker black of the water. A sad canoe, half rotten, sits in a mess of slush.

"Pretty bad, Annie. I won't lie. I don't want to lose our friendship."

She's quiet, so I glance back at her.

A ghost of a smile flickers across her face. "How're sales?"

"Sales are okay. I got another slew of bad reviews."

"The stalker?"

"I don't know. They're the least of my worries to be honest. How's Jer?"

That frustrated look takes over again, and her mouth draws inward. "The board asked him to resign. He's bad."

Because she's starting to look like she blames me again, I lift my shoulders. "Annie, if you found out a month before your wedding that Greg was cheating on you, gambling, lying, would you have married him?"

Her gaze slides past me, along the tree line behind us. "No."

"So can you honestly blame me?"

Her eyes narrow, but she turns away and keeps on walking toward the pond. "Who says I blame you for ending the wedding?"

I follow her, picking my steps carefully in the overly large snow boots. "You were pretty angry."

"How about Wet Panty? The blog?" She sends me a look I can only describe as sly. It's unlike her. She looks up at me through her lashes, slipping her hands in her pockets, and facing me fully for the first time since we left the house.

There's something about the look on her face that makes me step back. "What about it?"

One of her dark brows lifts. "Did they tell you why they canceled your booking?"

I stare at her. I didn't tell her they canceled on me. "How did y—"

Her mouth quirks in, a small smile. "The owner is Jewish, you see. I just sent her a copy of a paper you wrote in college defending the Third Reich."

"What are you talking about? I never wrote a pape—"

"But your name was on it." The small smile stretches, her nose wrinkling. "Mia Whitten. Anti-Semite."

I shake my head. "You wrote an anti-Semitic paper, put my name on it and sent it to her? Why?"

She grins now. "I didn't have to actually write it. I found one online. You'd be amazed what you can find online now."

"Why would you—"

"You can find a killer online. You can... hire people to write fake reviews, you can learn to open untraceable email addresses."

I'm still stuck. She ruined Wet Panty for me? Killer? Bad reviews? *What?*

I hold up my hand in front of me. "You wrote the bad reviews?"

She licks her lips, steps toward me. "Most of them."

That hurts. Deep down in my chest. "Why? Why..." I step back. Jesus, is there anyone in my entire life I've ever seen clearly? "Why would you do that?"

The smile clears off her face lightning-fast. "Because you had no right to take up a career as an author." She's shaking now, breathing fast through pinched nostrils. "You wanted to be an accountant. You only signed up for writing classes because I pushed you into it."

I can't keep up with her. She's so angry. I've never seen her like this. The look on her face is pure hatred. "I know that, Annie. I've always been grateful to you for that. I'd have ended up crunching numbers and bored without you."

"And then you came in and got better grades, you got that internship with Melinda Hatchwin, you won an award, you got a fucking fan base." Her voice rises to a shriek. "And I got nothing. Nothing. A shitty truncated journalism career. A brother who's destroying my family's empire piece by piece. A husband who got passed over for partner again. Twins? Who the *fuck* has twins? I never get to sleep. Ever. And you... it's all sunshine and success." She lets out a wild laugh. "And *tattoos* apparently."

"Annie..." I clear my throat. "I think you need to talk to your doctor. This isn't you. This isn't who you are."

She laughs again, a hyena cackle that echoes across the pond, bounces around in my ears. Her eyes flash. "Trust me, Mia. This is exactly who I am."

I step back, turning toward the path back to the house. I wish I had my phone on me. The look in her eyes is left of sane, and if I could only call Greg, he'd come and help with her. I don't know what to say.

"I'm not going to listen to this." I turn my back on her, and take a single step toward the tree line. I need to go back toward the garden, toward the path leading to the house, toward my car, my phone. But I pause when I hear a click.

I'm not a gun person. Never held one. Never even seen one in real life except on the belts of police officers. But I know the sound of the safety being removed. I'm not even sure how. It's a quiet, dull metallic snick. Maybe I know it from movies. Or maybe there's something baser, some instinct of prey that tells me she just raised one on me.

33 – ROCKS

MIA

"Not one more step, Mia."

I freeze, lifting my arms slowly. My heart pounds in my ears.

"I have a gun," she says. "I realized something last night, the best way to get something done, is to do it myself. Plus, then I get to keep the money. I've only paid a modest deposit."

I turn, slowly, rotating on my feet, and come face to face with the barrel of an ugly black-metal handgun.

I know nothing about guns.

But I'm pretty sure that big black thing projecting off the front of it is a silencer. I suck in a long breath.

Sometimes I see things really clearly, like everything just makes sense. My place in the world, the things around me, the people. This is not one of those times. Nothing makes any sense. Annie—Annie—has a gun and she's pointing it at me?

I look around frantically. A stick? A branch I can hit her with and run to the woods? Hide in the trees? It's too far. Not a decent plan, and besides, there are no handy branches lying just within arm's reach. Just snow dusted rocks and earth. Annie could shoot me before I got my hands on anything even halfway useful.

I need time. To think. To plan. To wait for a miracle.

"What money?" I ask.

"Oh, I keep forgetting!" she says in a happy voice, like we're just hanging out chattering about good times. "You don't know. I hired someone to kill you."

"You hired a hitman?" I round on her, spitting out the words.

She laughs, a self-indulgent chuckle, deep in her throat, that stops me cold. This isn't a fight between two friends.

She's not the Annie I've known all my life. Or maybe she is and she's just shed her skin, but she's different.

She's crazy.

"No, Mia. You're talking to me. You know me. I only hire the best. I hired the best hitman on the planet. I came across him when I was a journalist. Totally by accident. I was at a party at Senator Trahern's house, near your parents' actually. Anyway, I had to use the bathroom, but I got turned around, ended up in her office. Dropped something under her desk and got stuck when she came in with someone. Never knew who. They didn't know I was there. They were talking about some black ops in Africa. Some guy, an assassin."

I'm only listening with half an ear, still looking around frantically, searching for something, anything I can use as a weapon. A slight movement at the edge of the tree line just over her shoulder catches my eye.

A man. With black hair and slashing eyes, shoulders for days. He's tall, with beard bristle, and I can't see them because his fleece isn't rolled up, but if it was, I'd see tattooed forearms. And if I was closer, I'd see hazel eyes.

I've missed him so much it makes my eyes burn.

Stranger.

He has such great timing. I don't even care how he knew to come here.

I see him for only a second, then he's gone, evaporated into the trees around him.

"He was too expensive though." Annie prattles on, as easily as she used to chat about breastfeeding and funky Amy. "Luckily, I know someone with too much money. Three guesses who?"

I shake my head trying to clear it.

"Oh, you're no fun Mia." She tilts her head, the smile wavering, her eyes flashing. "Guess!"

"What... what..." I take a step away from her. "What are you talking about?"

"Turn around and walk toward the pond."

I study the trees, but don't see anything. Not even a flicker of movement. My breath is coming so fast my head spins.

"Turn AROUND!" Annie screams.

It freezes my blood—this woman she's become bears no resemblance to the woman I've known, the woman I've loved, for so long.

It's a wasted effort, but I have to try. I lick my lips, try to remember how much history we share, tilt my head, let her see I'm no threat to her. "What are you doing, Annie? Put that away."

She shakes her head slowly back and forth. "I want you to bend over and pick up some of the rocks on the shore."

That's so random I scowl. "What are you talking about? This is nuts, Annie. I'm your best friend."

She lets out a long caustic scoff. "Rocks, best friend. Now."

"Why?"

Her nostrils flare, and she steps closer. The gun is level with my heart. "Pick up some rocks, Mia. Now. And fill your pockets with them."

Then it clicks. The comment about the lake only being half frozen. She plans to shoot me and sink me in her pond. "No."

She sighs dramatically, shrugs. "Okay. I'll shoot you right here then. I was hoping to avoid it. I suppose the blood will wash away in the spring rain. Hmmmm... I don't want to get any on myself. What did the internet say? Ten to twelve feet to be safe."

She purses her lips, waggles her head back and forth studying the space between us and steps back a couple feet. "Alright, you ready?" She raises her brows and grins at me.

"No!"

"Then pick up the goddamned ROCKS!" Her voice bites across the freezing air, so loud a bunch of birds in the woods take off, squawking and flapping into the sky.

Where are you, Stranger? I'm half expecting her to shoot me in the back as I bend down and pick up a smooth stone, then another. There's an idea forming in the back of my mind, one that terrifies me even more than Annie and her gun.

The rocks in my hand are smooth, cold enough to make my bare fingers ache.

"In your pockets. Fill them full."

I stuff the stones in the pockets of Greg's old coat. Moving as slowly as I think I can get away with. I wonder what he'll think when he hears I'm gone, when his coat is missing, when the police come. There's no way they won't interview my best friend when I disappear. And my mom will notice when I disappear. Dad will notice. They won't let this go.

"Now walk over to the canoe," she says when she's satisfied.

I move slowly, passing her, so I stand between her and the canoe. Her back is to the tree line... and Stranger. Wherever he is.

"This is stupid, Annie. My mom and dad are going to miss me disappearing. They'll call the police. They'll figure out we're friends."

She makes a weird strangled noise. "Seriously, Mia. You can barely look at me. You think when I open the door with my leaking tits they'll bother looking at me twice? Most they can do is get a warrant and search the property. You'll be at the bottom of the lake by then."

Charming. Jesus, when did she get so cold?

I scan the edge of the woods.

He's there, a finger held over his lips. He's holding something in his hands. A gun like Annie's, only longer, and scarier. My eyes fill with tears. I have no choice now.

I have to trust someone.

I screw up my face, perched on the edge of indecision. I think I get it now, all of it. Who Stranger really is, what he wanted from me all along, why he's here.

He's the killer.

She hired him.

I stare at his face for a long minute.

That's what he wanted all along. Why he bothered with me.

He fucking joined the writers' website to kill me.

I've been wrong about everyone, always trusting the wrong person.

For once, I'm going to trust myself.

"Go on," Annie says. "Get in the canoe."

Jesus. Her plan is to send me out in the canoe, with my pockets full of stones and let me sink to the bottom. The canoe will get me out into the water, and not much more.

The pond isn't enormous, but it's not tiny either, and no one comes down here. With the stones in my pockets, I may never be found.

I peel my gaze away from Stranger.

The canoe didn't look good from far away, but up close it looks worse. It's swayed and buckled, the wood wet on the bottom and warped, but dry and cracked on the top.

To get to it, I'll have to step in the slushy bank of the pond. My pants and boots will get wet, and then I'll be slow and freezing.

I cast her a dubious glance.

But I'm not alone. I have a hitman on my side. Maybe? What if this is the end and he shoots me and keeps the money?

Stranger's behind her, a finger still held over his lips, his eyes locked on mine, begging me, daring me, I can practically feel him screaming at me silently.

I know him so well. After all this time, all the chats and the phone calls and the texts and the days we spent in each other's pockets. The look on his face screams at me that he's real, demands that I trust him.

I remember James and Gogo, the farm house. The expression he made when I threw the computer at him, like he was finally getting what he deserved.

Something must flicker on my face, because Annie's shoulders twitch as she starts to turn to follow my gaze.

I don't even think. Just move by pure instinct. I raise one of my too-small river rocks and hurl it through the air right at her face.

It connects with her cheek bone.

I'm screaming.

She's screaming.

I think.

I don't know.

There's no cover. If she sees Stranger, she'll probably start shooting at him, but if she looks at me, she'll definitely shoot at me. The canoe is my only hope. And that Stranger will stop her.

I take a running jump, stomp through the slush and dive into the canoe.

My motion sends it gliding out into the water, pushing through slush, until I'm out over frozen black water. Ice water like a thousand tiny blades flows over the edges of my boots, tangles in my pants, weighs me down.

I barely hear the soft popping of the silenced gun, but I hear the wood of the canoe splinter. Not once, but twice. The old buckled bottom shifts under my feet.

It starts to fill with water so icy cold my hands stiffen instantly. I move clumsily to my feet, trying to keep my balance in the topsy-turvy canoe, arms held out wide. There are no paddles.

Shore is more than fifteen feet away. Fifteen feet of black water thickening with strands of ice and patches of slush.

Stranger shoots, shouting, but I can't hear him.

There's a bang so loud my teeth chatter and my ears ring, and a fine puff of pink cloud that erupts in the air around Annie. She collapses to the ground.

I check myself for new holes or blood spouts. But the bullet didn't hit me. Never even aimed for me. He didn't shoot me in the end.

He stands over her, gazing down with a face I've never seen on another human before. Ice cold.

He looks up at me.

I shout, or rather I try. Nothing comes out of my mouth but a hoarse, chattery whisper.

I yank off the stupid, rock-filled coat, tug off the boots, and dive into the water.

34 – WHO IS THIS GUY?

STRANGER

My bullet hits Annie in her right bicep.

Drops of blood as fine as dust fan across the air like pink fog around her, marking the snow.

Her handgun drops to the snow with a dull clank and lands four feet to her right.

She looks up at me, her mouth quirking, maybe with surprise, before her knees buckle, and she hits the ground.

In the aftermath of the gun's report, my ears ring, the sound warping and stretching.

Mia shouts something from the water, the flimsy excuse for a canoe she's in shooting out into the lake like a rocket, collapsing under her weight. What the fuck was she thinking diving into it like that?

We've only got a couple minutes before she freezes.

I stalk to Annie. I should kill her.

But the last thing I want after everything is to be the guy who kills Mia's best friend, even if that friend is a deranged killer.

Annie crawls awkwardly across the frozen mud and slush and stones toward her gun, using one elbow and her knees, her feet scrambling to get purchase. She's close, her fingers only a few inches from the gun, when I kick her in the arm, smackdab in the center of the bullet hole, sending her flopping onto her back like a fish belly-up, hissing and grunting.

Her mouth screws up like she's getting ready to talk, to say a whole bunch of shit I'm sure I don't want to hear. I pull back and connect the toe of my boot with her temple in a blow I hope will knock her out but not knock her stupid forever.

Her eyes roll back, and she goes still.

I grab the gun and tuck it into the back of my jeans.

"Stay there, Mia," I shout.

Maybe I can tow the boat in before she gets too wet.

I turn back just in time to see her hurl one of her boots in the water, and dive in after it, fully submerging herself in water that's only a degree or two from frozen.

Jesus. We're still a full half mile from the house or a car or anywhere I can get her to keep her warm.

"Fuck." I leave Mia floundering in the water, and jog back to Annie, yank off her coat, and tug down her sweatpants, leaving her slack, pale skinny body in the snow, on a slowly spreading bed of red.

Mia's made it about half way to shore, splashing slush and keeping up a steady stream of shouts. Her words are meaningless over the rest of the noise.

I dump Annie's jacket and pants by the edge of the water, and make my way to Mia, stomping into the slushy water to just above my knees, and fuck it's cold. Blinding, burning cold.

Mia's teeth chatter, her lips bold blue in a deadly white face.

She keeps shouting at me as I haul her wet body against me. "The ba-ba-ba-beeees," she sputters through her lips, her voice high-pitched and desperate. "Don't hurt her."

I drag her up the bank. Her clothes and the cold have weighed her down so much that her feet don't work, and she's stumbling so much I have to lift her into my arms.

Before we're even all the way out of the water, I yank at her sopping wet coat, then peel her out of a shirt so cold and wet my fingers get stiff. When I tear her jeans down, she falls into the snow and lands on her ass, still shouting at me. "The ba-ba-beees. The babies. C-can't hurt her."

It worries me that she's not even shivering anymore.

I pull the dripping jeans from her ankles and snatch Annie's pants from the snow, start shoving Mia into them, cursing when they stick to wet skin.

She's not helping me, still shouting, so finally I pause.

"She's fine," I snarl. "I shot her in the arm. And kicked her in the head. She's unconscious. Now stop fucking fighting me."

Her brows snap together, but finally her shoulders relax, and she's unnaturally still as I finish bundling her into Annie's dry coat.

I heft her fireman style over my shoulders and get to my feet. I need to get her inside, get her warm. I make it half way to the tree line when she starts bucking on my shoulders, twisting and writhing and generally making it impossible to hang on to her.

I trip on a log and stumble, nearly dropping her, my own feet starting to get sluggish in my waterlogged and frozen boots. "Mia, let me get you back to the house."

"Annie," she shouts. "We can't leave her there. She'll freeze to death."

"She just tried to kill you."

She nods, her pale eyelids drooping. "I know, but still. Get her. I'll walk."

I want to shout at her that I'm trying to be a hero here. I'm trying to do the right thing for her, save her life, and if she'd only cooperate it will be fine, but she's right. Annie will probably die if we leave her half-naked and bleeding in the snow for as long as it will take for me to get Mia back and warm. Not to mention the inherent risk of leaving a deranged woman hell-bent on murder unsupervised and unimpeded.

So I don't bother arguing, I simply turn back on my clumsy freezing feet, march back to Annie's prone body, and sit down in the snow, with Mia on my legs so her bare toes don't touch the snow. Her teeth are finally chattering, but her fingers aren't working well enough, so I have to yank Annie's boots off for her, and shove her feet into them.

It's the last thing I want to do, but I lift Annie's scrawny body over my shoulders and stand up. Mia sways but keeps her balance in Annie's shoes, and together we set off toward the house.

It takes too long, but the movement seems to help Mia's body warm up a little. She's still deathly white, her lips an ugly purple, but she's moving. As long as she's moving, she'll be fine.

She opens the front door for me. It swings wide, slams into the wall with a crash that shakes the house, and echoes around the foyer. It's one of those old houses with black and white marble floors, wood paneling, and oil paintings on the walls. All it's missing is a coat of armor in a wall niche under the stairs.

"Everything okay?" A man shouts from somewhere inside. Greg, I assume.

A minute later he appears, eyes round in his square face. He takes in Mia, then me holding is nearly naked bleeding wife thrown over my shoulder. "The fuck is going on?"

Mia's shaking so hard and sputtering, her fingers shivering as she manages to shut the door behind us.

I glance at Greg. "Get Mia upstairs. Now."

"What's wrong with Annie?"

Too many things wrong with this guy's wife to name, so I just send him a dark glance, and start walking up the stairs. "Upstairs Mia, now. I want you in the shower, getting warm."

She doesn't argue, but does send a long look at Greg.

Greg glares at me. I'd rather not do this, but he's not exactly cooperating and while I'm fine with letting Annie bleed out in his foyer, I'm not fine with Mia's purple lips. So I slide my gun from my pocket, level it at his face. "Up the fucking stairs. Now."

His jaw drops.

"Move."

With a long, steady breath, he glances at the living room, where I'm guessing the babies are, and follows Mia up the stairs. "Is Annie okay?"

"She's better than she deserves to be," I say when we get to the top of the landing. The house has a pair of hallways that stretch to the left and right.

Blood drips from Annie's fingers and lands on the carpet.

"Mia? What's going on?" Greg stares at his wife on my shoulders, glares at my gun. "Who is this guy?"

Mia staggers down the hallway, her feet clumsy, and we follow. Annie's light, but she's starting to get heavy on my shoulders, forcing my neck to jut forward, and the way Greg keeps glancing at me, I half expect him to bum rush me any minute now.

I tap my finger on the side of the gun. "Don't try anything, Greg. In a minute I'll put your wife down, we can take a look at her arm. Mia can take a warm shower, and we can discuss what just happened. But for now, your only job is to stay alive for your kids, and the only way you're going to do that is if you don't fuck with me."

He takes a deep breath, his mouth tightening, but his shoulders relax slightly and he follows Mia down the hallway.

35 – TOO MANY THINGS

STRANGER

"Stop," I say, gun still trained on Greg.

He shoots me a grim glare, his shoulders bunching, fists tightening, but does as I say.

"Back against the wall."

He steps back until his shoulder blades bump against the wall... begrudgingly. "I need to check on the babies."

"Couple more minutes. Don't move."

He doesn't.

I listen for the sound of infant crying but hear none, so I dump his wife on the bed, dropping her over my shoulder. She lands with a thump. Her skinny limbs bounce, but her eyes don't even flutter. She looks bad, skin gray and pasty.

I roll my shoulders. "Mia, go shower. Ten minutes. Start with luke-warm water. Transition to hot slowly."

She sags against the door, her fingers fumbling with the zipper at the front of her coat. Keeping my eyes on Greg, I tuck the gun into my jacket pocket and tug on her zipper.

Those big eyes blink up at me, and I can't resist it.

I press a quick kiss to her shaking lips. It's good that she's shivering again. Her body is working to warm itself. There's so much I want to say, so much still between us, but she needs to get warm first. "Go."

She shuts the door with a click.

Greg shifts in his bare feet. "Can I go to my wife yet?"

I nod, but pull my gun out again.

He touches Annie's neck, checks her pulse. "What happened?"

"She tried to shoot Mia." I sit down on the foot of the bed, watch as he shifts Annie into a more comfortable position. "So I shot her."

"How bad is it?"

"She'll be fine."

He doesn't move. It's normal. Freezing like this in the face of unpredictable and sudden changes. Inability to make a quick decisions. "Who are you?"

"Mia's friend. You need to stop the bleeding."

The water turns on in the bathroom. There's a glassy click and I picture her stepping under the spray, the water dripping down her skin. I hope she listened to me about the temperature.

"The tattooed guy." Greg's still staring down at Annie, his face stony as he wads an end of a sheet up against her bloody biceps.

"One and only."

"You know anything about gunshot wounds?"

I know some. The bullet passed through. I don't think it hit the bone. "Probably more than you."

His jaw ticks. "Can I go check on my kids?"

"If you try anything, I'll kill her."

"Can I take her to the hospital?"

"Not unless you want her to go to jail."

He walks to the doorway, hovers, ear cocked toward the stairs. I'm guessing he's listening for crying and doesn't hear anything, because he pads back in on the carpet. "What do I do now?"

Not that I want to help Annie, but I'm certain Mia would say it's the right thing to do. "Get gauze or something to wrap around it. Iodine if you've got it. Trust me, if you bring police in, she'll end up in prison. You don't want that. But just in case, give me your phone."

He says nothing, hands it over, pauses for a minute like he's gearing up for something. Then rises, and leaves the room.

He comes back a few minutes later with his arms full. I can't help but like the guy in a weird way. He doesn't waste time with questions. He feels like a hundred other guys I worked with in the Marines. Makes me wonder what the guy did, the one he curbsided, but I don't ask.

We work together in silence.

When Mia comes out, her hair wrapped up turban style, wearing a robe of Annie's, her cheeks are pink. She doesn't come to me though, just leans against the door jam.

We've cleaned Annie up. She's on the bed, the bloodstained clothes gone, a fresh bandage around her biceps, blankets tucked around her to keep her warm. She's just waking up.

Greg's sitting next to her.

The babies still haven't made any noise.

We all stand around awkwardly, watching as Annie blinks, and shifts her feet, moans.

"Did you know?" asks Mia from the door, her eyes on Greg.

"Know what? I still have no idea what's going on."

Mia clamps down on her lips. "She tried to kill me."

"I only see one person who got shot."

I pull Annie's gun from the back of my pants. It's an old Beretta 8000 from the 90s. The silencer makes its weight off balance. I press the magazine release and it clicks out into my palm. I stuff it in my pocket, pop the slide. Someone's been keeping it oiled and clean. It's in decent shape. It slides out clean, revealing the bullet in the chamber. The cartridge ejects, and I tuck that into my pocket with the magazine, lock the slide back and engage the safety, before unscrewing the silencer. I set it down on the bed beside the gun. "Recognize this?"

Greg stares at it. "It's Annie's dad's."

Her boney, pale hand lifts up weakly and touches her bandage, there's a small smile hiding on her lips.

I want to smack her so bad my fingers twitch.

"She made me put rocks in my coat." Mia yanks on the belt of the robe like it personally offended her. "She was going to shoot me and sink me in the pond." It comes out fast, like she just passed some threshold. Her gaze flits to me and back to Annie's face. "We played in that pond as kids."

No one says anything. Those words hang in the air, and suddenly I can picture it. Mia as a child, innocent, carefree, the bird not yet caged, laughing, playing make-believe around that pond. I shake the image from my mind, stare at Annie, who's still unmoving, that sick little smile still lurking on her face.

"You hired someone to kill me?"

Annie's throat bobs. "Where are my babies?"

Greg pats her thigh awkwardly over the covers, then pauses, his hand hovering over her in the air like he's not sure he should touch her. I try to imagine how I'd feel if I suddenly found out a woman I cared for, a woman who'd had my children, was a murderer. I fail.

"They're still asleep downstairs. Did you..." He clears his throat, and runs his hands through his hair like he can't quite believe he's about to ask this question. "Fuck. Did you hire someone to kill Mia, Annie?"

She gives a jerky nod.

Two babies, a wife who's batshit, a slew of debt he took on for her family. This guy's got problems longer than smoke.

Mia's lip starts to wobble.

I know that face. I want to go to her, but she wouldn't like it. So, I just stand there taking up space.

"Why?" she whispers.

Annie lifts a bony shoulder, then clutches her arm and winces. "We sunk the last of the money we had into the business and Jer just pissed it away. But you." Her voice goes ugly, the darkness inside her bubbling to the surface. "You have plenty of money. If you hadn't insisted on the pre-nup it would all have been fine, but then you had to go and force Jer to sign it. It was you or the babies. I needed the money back for them."

Greg presses his knuckles to his lips, his brows drawing together.

Mia squeezes her hands together, nods tightly, and it's almost proof of their shared history, their friendship that she walks right over to the dresser opposite the bed, roots around and pulls out a pair of black stretch pants and a gray sweatshirt. She knew exactly where they were. "I'm taking clothes from you."

Annie just rests her head back on the pillows. "Be my guest."

"Where did you get the money?" I ask. I need Mia to hear all of it. That way she'll know, every last bit. She won't be able to tell herself it wasn't so bad later on, forgive this bitch.

She pulls the pants on under the robe.

Annie laughs, but the sound lacks any real joy. "That's the best part. From your own dad."

Mia's gaze flits my way before she turns her back to us, drops the robe. I have a quick flash of her perfect smooth back. The new tat on her upper right shoulder blade. Then she whips the sweatshirt on and shoves her damp hair out of the way.

When she turns around again, she's not crying. There's no wobble to her lips. Her eyes are blazing. She knows. She's known since she saw me at the pond with my finger to my lips.

Greg looks at me. I think he's connected the dots too.

Annie's the only one who hasn't figured it out yet. She glares at me.

Part of me wants to thank her. If she hadn't found me, I'd still be a stone man, an island. Now I have a brother, a dog, a life.

We stare at each other, Mia and me. Greg and Annie, sitting on their bed, an ocean of shit between them, their tiny newborn babies downstairs, they fade away. I hope she can see it on my face, the truth, all of it, no lies.

I want to reach for her but I can't. So I shove my hands into my pockets. "When did you figure it out?"

Annie says something, but we both ignore her.

"At the pond." Mia swallows. "I had to make a choice. Trust you or not. I didn't even really have time to think about it. Just went with my gut. I guess I trust you."

I remember the moment. Her face frozen, mouth open as I walked across the bank toward Annie. Her eyes had gone wide. She threw the stone... jumped toward the only place there was any cover from Annie and her bullets.

That's Mia.

For me, she jumps.

Something uncurls inside me, some tightened cord I've been holding since she saw my computer. I think it's hope, I'm not sure. For the first time, I can actually believe there might be a chance for us, despite everything.

I cross to Mia and do what I've wanted to do since the morning she threw my laptop at my face. I get one hand on her jaw and the other around her waist, my fingers on the swell of her ass, and I kiss her. There's the Mia taste, honey and peaches. Her fingers hook into the top of my jeans, but she doesn't hug me.

The kiss is over fast, but I keep her body pressed against me, reassured by the warmth of her.

"What happens now?" Greg asks, voice thick. He's still slumped forward like he can't quite wrap his head around the sudden change of his entire life. An hour ago, he was a happily married, new dad, now he's the husband of a would-be-murderess.

I take Mia's hand, look down at her, raise a brow.

Her lower lip pushes out. "Can we get my dad back his money?"

I nod. Lex can do it. Or we can make Annie run the transfer.

"What do we do?" she asks, her voice cracking.

"It's up to you."

She looks at Annie.

Annie's feet move under the covers on the bed, the white bedspread shifting like clouds in a stormy sky.

"You can't tell the police," Greg says.

Mia's big honey-gold eyes move to me.

"That's not true." I squeeze her shoulder. "We could, but I'd have to leave. Disappear. It's your choice."

I don't want to leave. I want to stay in New York, with James and Gogo and Mia. I want to be the guy who gets to have a life. But for her, I'll go. If that's what she needs.

Mia pulls her hand from mine. "Do you want that?"

The old temptation to avoid the emotions is there, tell her it's not my choice, what I want doesn't matter, take the coward's way out, make sure I don't let anyone see that I care. Instead, I grit my teeth. No more lies. I tell the truth, take a stand, try to reach toward the life I want instead of the life I have. "No. I don't."

For the first time in my life, I don't want to leave. Not at all.

She doesn't answer. For a long, long minute, she just stares at me, something moving across her face. Fear, hope, regret. Finally, she presses her face against my chest, her nose resting right between my pecs. I slide my fingers through her hair, breathe in the smell of mint shampoo, whatever detergent Annie and Greg use, and somewhere under it all, the peaches.

Then she pulls back, stepping away from me.

"I'll start a college savings plan for the babies," Mia says suddenly. "With my own money. Not much. I'll add to it each year." She blinks a couple times, the corners of her mouth deepening. "Give my dad back the money. But don't ever contact me again."

I splay my hand across her back, wondering if she'll say that again, only at me instead of Annie.

"Know this," I say, turning to face Greg and Annie on the bed. "If anything happens to Mia, I'll come for you." I let Annie see my face, the darkness in my eyes, I let her read the depths to which I'd go for Mia, written there as clear as day. All the assholes I've killed, none of them were personal. For Mia, it would be personal. "The babies too."

I'm not even sure if I'm lying as I say the words, but they have to be said either way. Annie may not care about much, but she does care about those babies.

She flinches, her eyes sliding away from mine.

Mia pulls even further away from me.

Greg sits up straight. "Nothing will happen to Mia." His shoulders bunch. "Or the babies."

"Then get your wife some help."

Mia walks to the door, and I follow her out, not bothering to spare either of them another glance.

She's moving fast. Too fast.

I jog down the steps behind her, skidding to a stop when she rounds on me in the foyer.

Her feet are bare, and I step up close enough the tips of my boots, still wet and cold, nearly touch her small, pink-nailed toes. Just like in the bathroom at the winery. Only this time, her eyes are clouded.

I touch her cheek, and she closes her eyes.

"When?" she whispers.

"When what?" I ask, though I'm pretty sure I know what she means.

"When did you decide you weren't going to kill me?"

A cry rings out across the house. One of the babies has woken. Greg says something from upstairs and comes running down the steps.

A second cry joins as he hits the bottom, and he sends us both a wary glance. We should go. But first...

"You asked me if I could trust you," I say. "I was walking in the woods, about to swim in a waterfall."

Her eyes drift out of focus like she's scrolling through memories. "The day you said you liked peaches?"

"Yeah. I said you could trust me. I knew then. I'd been doubting already."

She takes a deep breath, steps back from me, walks to the closet and digs out a pair of boots that must be Greg's. She yanks them onto her feet. "I need some time. I can't... I can't make any sense of this."

I follow her through the door, into the cold, watch her slide into the front seat of her car. "Can you drive?"

She sends me a sidelong glance. "Yes."

I'd rather she didn't. What I really want is to drive her home, feed her hot soup, fuck her until we both know she's alive and safe and that we belong to each other, but I can see on her face that's a non-starter.

So instead, I ask, "How long?"

She shakes her head, a tight little move, mouth grim, eyes drawn. "I don't know. I'll be in touch... if I... when... I don't know. I didn't..." She twists in the seat, punches the ignition button, grips the wheel with her fingers, looks ahead so our eyes don't meet. "I considered a lot of options, but that you were trying to kill me wasn't one of them. And Annie... there's been a lot of revelations this week. I just... I just need some time."

I drop my hands into the pockets of my jacket. "Fair enough."

She doesn't look back. Just switches the car in gear. I close the door for her and try to ignore the sullen thunk that echoes across the still gray day.

I stand there a long time, watching as she turns her car, and drives away from me, out of sight.

Then I get in my own car, drive home to James, home to Gogo, home to start a new job, one that doesn't involve killing anyone, and I wait for Mia.

36 – WE ALL HAVE SECRETS

MIA

I don't drive to my home.

There's nothing there for me right now but confusing memories, unopened presents, and questions.

Instead, I drive for the coast, to the gray Atlantic, for the place I spent all my summers. Watch Hill. My grandparents' house. I drive past the gray-shingled town along the marina, the wintered boats, the vacant closed-for-winter buildings, ice-cream shops, pizza parlors, souvenir stores, and I remember summers with my parents, with my grandparents.

We used to have dinner there, and Danny and I did swim team at the club pool. My mom had her forty-fifth birthday party overlooking the marina. We cracked lobsters until our hands cramped.

I turn left along the coast and wind my way uphill, turn past the thick boxwood hedges that line the edge of their property. The drive winds down again, toward the shore, and the house rises into view. Clapboard facing, a widow's lookout, dormer windows, hydrangea bushes dormant for winter, grassy dunes. Memories flood back. My mom and dad, Gigi and Papa, Danny and me. Later, Jer and Annie too.

Everything was so simple back then, all those sunny summers on the water. When did everything change? When did everyone start lying? Why?

I shake my head as I pull up to the front drive.

The place is mostly empty now. Mom or her sister, my Aunt Tabby, come up every few months and check on it, make sure it's doing okay, have someone in for maintenance, and every summer we try to come here for a bit, but it isn't the same.

It hasn't been since Gigi and Papa died.

I open the door with my key, walk into the empty foyer, and the tears start to fall.

I don't know when they stop, but eventually they do. I shower, get dressed in some of my grandmother's old clothes, go to the store, unpack my laptop, and start working.

I sit most days on a window seat overlooking the icy water and sleet raining down on the beach. Sometimes I go for walks in it, watch the waves slosh cold and gray on the shores, but mostly, I write, drink tea, and try not to think.

I call the host of Wet Panty, explain as much as I can without lying. Strangely, she believes me. She reinstates my interview.

Mom comes up briefly. Erica comes down. I talk to Penny and Danny on the phone, but mostly, I spend time alone.

Eventually, my hands stop shaking when I get dressed. I stop seeing Annie's face in my dreams, hearing the click of her gun. I stop thinking of her, wanting to talk to her, tell her things like I used to. I stop reliving every moment we spent together, wondering what I missed and how I couldn't see. And when I bolt upright in bed in the middle of the night a few weeks later, the sheets aren't soaked in sweat for the first time since I got here.

Staring up at the ceiling, at the old wooden beams of the attic bedroom I've slept in since I was a kid, listening to a frosty wind blow in the rafters, I know one thing to be incontrovertibly true.

Stranger said it right from the beginning.

We all have secrets.

He wasn't lying.

Me. Him. Everyone.

And that's okay.

It's not so much what we say or don't say.

It's what we do.

And Stranger saved my life.

I reach across the dark, grope around on the side table for my phone. Its blue light fills the room so bright I squint.

> Mia: Can I come up tomorrow?

> Stranger: Always.

> Mia: 10am?

> Stranger: I'll be here.

As soon as the sun rises, I get in my car, drive home and collect the unopened presents, then I get back in the car and drive north.

I have so many questions, and finally, I'm ready for some answers.

37 – A KINDA HOT EX HITMAN WRITER GUY

MIA

The sun slides from behind the clouds when I'm about five minutes away.

That seems fitting somehow. Its light sprawls over the sparkling snow lumps that will melt into fence posts and bushes in the spring sunshine. Pastures that I'm sure house cows in warmer months, spread over the hills where he lives. I bet in a few months there will be flowers here, wild grasses, deer in the paths he described to me on the phone.

I turn into the freshly-salted drive.

The door opens before I even make it to the driveway. Gogo races out, jumps over a few snow piles, spins a few circles, squats down and pees, her tail penduluming back and forth like mad.

She remembers me.

That makes me grin, as I look back to the man in the doorway.

As always, my breath hitches at my first glimpse of him. He folds his arms across his chest, nothing but a Henley from the cold, but he looks like he could stand there all day.

The corners of his eyes crinkle. His lips spread, white teeth, dimples, smile lines. I never had a chance anyway.

I slide the gear shift forward into park, open my door, step out. Gogo prances up and dances around me, her tail wagging so hard her butt moves with it. I squat down and stroke her ears, hum to her until she loses interest in me and darts off into the snow after something only she can hear.

When I rise, Stranger's still there. Waiting. I can read it on his face. Your move, Reed.

I had a long time to think about what I'd say to him. He meets me at the edge of the front steps that lead up to the porch. I stop, one step below him, stare up into those warm hazel eyes. There's a touch of orangy-gold in there, mixed with the green and gray flecks.

"Hello, Stranger."

His brows lift and his mouth quirks. "The whole drive to think about it, and that's your line."

"Stole it from this guy I knew."

The smile fades. "You don't know him anymore?"

I look out over the white fields, at Gogo, nose to the ground now, tracking something with her tail down, a girl on a mission. "Not as well as I thought. But I'd like to."

The muscles of his neck tighten, his Adam's apple dips. "Hello, Mia."

I reach up, slide my hand into his. "No lies?"

"No lies." He whistles for Gogo, and she races back to us, her tongue lolling. We dry her off in the entryway together, checking between her toes to make sure there's no ice there.

"Hey, Mia." It's James.

I turn happily to say hi to him and freeze, my mouth hanging open like a sitcom star. He's standing in the kitchen. And I mean standing.

I can't see them, because he has on jeans and a pair of sneakers, but clearly his prostheses arrived.

I hug him. Unlike with Stranger, it's an easy and uncomplicated hug, like hugging Danny. "You look good." I glance back and forth between him and Stranger. I point at James. "You're taller than Stranger."

For some reason that makes them laugh, and like that, I feel like I've come home. James makes an excuse a few minutes later, pegs me with a glare that makes me promise not to go anytime soon, and leaves us alone.

Stranger rubs the back of his neck like he isn't sure what to do with me.

"Invite me to your room?" I say.

His shoulders lift momentarily, I can see his brain working, itching to tease me for sounding like a kid in her parents' house. But all he says is, "Want to come with me to my bedroom?"

I nod.

He steps closer, and finally, those big hands settle on my waist, burning hot through my sweater.

"First, I've got to be honest with you about something." He backs me up a step toward his room.

"Oh?"

His head cocks. "Mia, I'm not a vampire."

That surprises a laugh out of me, but his face stays grave.

He backs me up another step, and our bodies are closer now. Close enough that his hips bump against my belly as we move.

"I can live with that."

He blows out an exaggeratedly relieved sigh. "I'm also not an alien. Or a warrior. Or a shifter."

I grin and let him guide me backward into his room. "Ah. I see what you did there."

"I don't have a thirteen-inch minotaur cock, or a magic stone, or any superpowers." He kicks the door shut behind him and keeps on walking me backward until my legs bump against his bed. One hand slides down to cup my ass, the other rising up my back, to cradle my head. He leans in closer. "And I can't cum buckets."

My breath hitches and everything inside me goes all melty and dumb like it always does, and when I talk it comes out all silly and breathless and pathetic. I'm so far gone it's not even funny. "So, you're saying you aren't a hero in a romance novel? Then what are you?"

"I'm a kinda hot ex-hitman hobby writer guy."

I screw up my face like that's not quite enough, even though it is. And he's not kinda hot. He's a super hot ex-hitman hobby writer guy. It's the ex part I needed to know most, that it was over, no more killing. "Hmmm..."

"Not enough?"

"I'm thinking."

"Okay, I've got one thing that might tip the balance." He lowers his lips to mine.

"What's that?"

A slight pause while he swallows, and his thumb strokes my cheek. "I love you."

I close the distance between us, touch our lips, taste his perfect, special Stranger taste, make that same stupid whimper he always pulls out of me, and I just melt into him.

"I love you too." I slide a hand under his shirt, touch hard, hot skin. "But you're done with killing now, right?"

He nods.

I need the words though. Out loud. "You're not going to kill anyone else are you? It's really over?"

"You were my last hit." His breath feathers along my cheek as he presses kisses there, moving toward my temple, sliding past my ear.

I shiver, helping as he pulls my shirt over my head. "So what do we do now?"

My shirt pops free, and he stares at my bra, and groans. "Recycling bin blue."

It takes me a minute. The color of my bra. "The color is cerulean."

"Whatever." He tugs open the button on my jeans. "I'm starting a business with James and an old friend named Lex who you'll love. Revin, Inc." He slides down my jeans and groans. "Green. Perfect."

I tug at his shirt. "What kind of business?"

He pauses, half crouched as he tugs my jeans down my thighs. "Personal defense contractor. And I bought the land next door."

I nearly fall over when he yanks my jeans off one foot and they get stuck on my boot, but I catch myself on the bed, rise up on my elbows. "Why?"

"Because I want a life, a normal one. I want you to move in with m—"

I must make a face at that, because he stops tugging on my clothes and glares at me. "Not right away. But eventually. I want to do this. With you."

There's a part of me that wants to push it away, skirt the subject, brush it off for another time, but that was the old me. This one says what she wants and doesn't lie, especially not to herself.

"I want that too." I kick off my other boot, and laugh when Stranger yanks off the jeans and crawls up the bed on top of me, his big body all prowly and hard, my mind skips to the moment I saw him in the woods and I knew, deep down in my bones, in the fibers of my soul, that I was safe because I wasn't alone anymore, my Stranger was there, a stranger no longer.

His lips are soft, but his beard stubble is rough, and so are his calloused palms as they move up my bare skin. My heart skips in my chest, and for once my brain's not focused on sex so much, but on hope, because our future looks so bright and shiny I can't even wait for it. I want it all, a man I can laugh with about crackers, share my every horrible thought with, plan with, feel safe with.

"I'll move in when the house is ready." My fingers glide over the smooth, bunched muscles of his back.

He freezes for a second, and then his whole body relaxes into me, he wraps his arms around me in the biggest, warmest bear hug of my life.

"Perfect, Mia."

WANT MORE SEXY DIRTY STORIES?

Thank you for reading!

Book 2 is Lex's super sexy story about a trip to Iceland, a cabin in the snow, and a mysterious stranger without a name. More secrets, more lies, a secret billionaire badass and way more dirty talk.

Turn the page for a sneak peek.

If you liked this, sign up for Immy's VIP room for a FREE BOOK and to be the first to know about giveaways, sales and new releases:

www.imogenkeeper.com

Fight Dirty with Me
Sneak Peek

LEX

Note to self: when traveling to Iceland in February, confirm in advance that you've reserved a car that actually works.

The sky over Reykjavik is full dark, a blizzard's rolling in, and I'm tired. I've been standing at this rental counter, holding my cool with, I think, admirable patience for over two hours.

"The car's heat doesn't work?" I ask, too exhausted to even drum up any surprise. "We're like a hundred miles from the arctic circle. How is that even possible?"

The double doors of the rental car office open on a frigid blast of wind, and a family walks in. A friendly-looking couple—probably exhausted from a long flight like me, with a kid barely old enough to walk.

The rental car guy and I both look over.

"I'm so sorry, again," he says. "I can bring out another one?"

I sigh through my nose loudly.

He keeps disappearing for fifteen minutes at a time and bringing out new cars. He does it all with a smile pasted on his face, his blond hair bouncing with every profuse bob of his head as he makes noises that sound like genuine apologies, but nonetheless I'm pretty sure he gives zero shits about my time.

The first car didn't have snow tires.

The second had a broken seat. The driver's seat.

The third one had a window that didn't roll all the way up—he offered me duct tape.

The little girl rubs big dark eyes the shape of buttons and presses her face into her mom's shoulder. The mom's practically swaying on her feet.

Waiting for me means more waiting for them.

And, according to every travel blog I read, the south highway to Vik closes the second the snows get bad, and by then, I need to be full-on snow-tires-to-macadam or I'll be stuck in Reykjavik until the storm passes. And that cannot happen.

A room in Vik has my name on it. A sexy black-walled, white-sheeted, glass-walled room with a view of iced-over water, mountains and skies, six stories up from a sleek, modern-as-sin dining room with a table for one set for yours truly.

I even know what I'm going to order at dinner. Arctic char with pureed cauliflower, sturgeon caviar, cornichon pickles, and whatever fancy overpriced wine the server recommends.

And if a tall blond Viking-looking Icelandic man works up brass balls big enough to hit on me, I may just take him to my room and fuck him like a porn star.

Why?

Because this is my trip.

This is for me. I earned this vacation, working for my douchenozzle thundercunt of a boss—and yes, I did just call my dad a thundercunt. He's my boss and my dad, and I love him, but he's an asshole.

"Do you have cars that aren't broken?"

He nods so earnestly it's hard not to believe him, even on this fifth round. "The next one was just returned today. It's in good shape. I checked it myself."

I want to ask about the other cars. Why he didn't check those? But I bite my tongue, glancing back at the family behind me. I don't want them driving without heat or without snow tires or a seat that works.

I hold up my hand.

Vik is calling.

I'm not wasting any more time on this.

"I'll take the car without heat. It's only a three-hour drive." I'll bundle up. How bad can it be?

He smiles blandly. "Very good, ma'am."

"But," I hold up my hand, leaning forward, lowering my voice, so he can hear me but the family behind us won't. I let my face show every ounce of basic-training that had me running until I fell asleep mid-stride, followed up by specialized training that taught me how to kill a man with my bare hands, interrogate insurgents and basically be a person you really don't want to mess with. I'm not physically imposing, but I have a resting bitch face that makes grown men shudder. "You will give them a fully-functioning car."

He gulps.

"You won't waste their time."

"Yes." He nods.

I narrow my eyes.

"I mean no, ma'am."

An hour later, music blaring out euro rap, my GPS directing me along the Ring Road that skirts the southern coast, I'm questioning my decision. Hard.

It made sense at the time. Why else did I buy a full-body snowsuit, a balaclava, sub-zero rated gloves, snow boots, fleece socks and long underwear if not to make use of them? I'll never need them in LA, that's for damned sure.

If I even go back to LA.

It'll be an adventure, something to remember when I'm old and gray. That wild trip with that crazy heatless car I drove from Reykjavik to Vik. Fun. That's what normal people who don't spend all their time digging up dirty little secrets think is fun.

Right?

Wrong.

Vik is still ninety minutes in front of me, my fingers are half frozen to the steering wheel despite the thick gloves I'm wearing, and the windshield's half fogged over.

I figured the engine's heat would help keep the car warm.

It doesn't.

Not even a little bit.

The road to Vik was clear according to Google maps when I left. Weather showed the storm holding until nearly midnight.

I should have been fine.

I am not fine.

The clouds are dumping down snow so vengefully you'd think I personally pissed them off. The roads keep on getting slushier and slipperier.

The wipers are going full-blast with a manic wompwompwomp.

My speed keeps dropping. I'm creeping along at just north of 20 kilometers per hour, my headlights jutting uselessly ahead of me, twin cones of speckled white. The road is invisible, blending into the landscape on either side. There's not a street light in sight. Road signs are rare.

I've driven in snow once before—on a mission with my unit in Georgia, the country not the state. I understand the logistics of driving in the snow. No sudden moves, no aggressive turns, no slamming on the breaks or the gas—basically you drive like a geriatric sitting on a phonebook.

I'm doing everything right, but something goes wrong anyway.

I hit a slick spot on a downhill turn.

The tires lose their grip on the pavement.

The car careens wildly.

I try to adjust. Not hard. Not overly-aggressive. I just nudge the car back toward where I think the road is, but the car completely ignores me. I may as well do nothing.

It picks up speed, writhing like a snake downhill and slams into a...something.

My arms flap upward like a crash test dummy, knuckles rapping the ceiling. The air bag explodes in a violent blast of noise, hits my face so hard it burns and my vision goes to spots.

My arms flap down, and the airbag deflates and dies with a lingering whistle.

Snow dumps down on the windshield. The wipers have stopped their manic wiping.

As silence settles in like a shroud, I take a few seconds checking on my senses.

Blinking my eyes. Checking my ears. Wiggling my fingers. Nothing hurts. Except my face burning from the airbag and my broken pride.

Physically, I'm fine. Though my neck may disagree with me later. I ricocheted off the airbag like a jack-in-the-box.

I shift the car into reverse and touch the gas. Unsurprisingly, the engine doesn't respond.

Fuggety shitballs.

I try turning the key a few more times, pumping the pedals. Just in case.

The car coughs once, sputters twice, then whimpers like a dying calf, and that's about it. The ignition doesn't catch. I'll have to call the rental agency for a tow. Or maybe the hotel can send a car to meet me. I'm past halfway.

I pull my glove off with my teeth, open my phone's email to find the number for the rental car, and…I have no service.

Of course, I have no service.

Why would I have service?

I'm in the middle of nowhere.

In Iceland.

I waste some time tapping the screen and trying, but it's useless.

And then, as if it were mocking me, my phone's battery light downgrades from a thin green line to a thinner red one. Perfect.

The engine, which was providing the minimal heat in the car, rapidly cools, any lingering warmth leaching away through layers of metal and glass.

Through the windows, nothing but snowflake-spattered darkness surrounds me. The vastness of that black settles in, raising my hackles like someone just set their sights on me, my forehead in their crosshairs.

I'm dressed for the weather, but that doesn't mean I can stay in this car. For one thing, all I have is half a bottle of water and half a pack of starbursts—only the gross orange and red left over. For another, depending on the blizzard, I could end up buried alive here.

I'm not sure the Icelandic police force allocates funding to poking errant snow piles on the off chance an idiot tourist is trapped inside one. But I kind of doubt it.

So...looks like I'm probably not going to make it to Vik in time for my Arctic char.

I can practically hear my old unit laughing at me, their voices in my head. Yo, Lex, you're so fucked.

This just got serious.

Yeah. Basically.

Lex, you gotta move, girl.

That too.

There has to be something somewhere somewhat close.

I pull up the map app on my phone, preloaded so the lack of service hasn't affected it. I can see where I am. The nearest town, a string of letters I can't even attempt to pronounce, is four, maybe five, miles up the road.

I'm in good shape. Once I get up to the road, I can cover that distance, on this terrain, in this weather in about ninety minutes.

I'll leave my suitcase here in the trunk and come back for it when the storm ends. I never pack anything essential in there anyway—though the girliest parts of me feel genuine sorrow leaving behind all the sexy new threads I bought for this trip. A new wardrobe for the new me.

I pull my balaclava on over my mess of too-curly hair. Tuck the small hunting knife I packed in my checked-bag into the right-hand pocket of my parka where I can grab it if needed. Then don my snow goggles, my gloves, and shifting in my seat, my carry-on backpack, with the computer I never leave behind, the water, the starbursts, an extra scarf, and open the car door.

A blast of wind attacks it, nearly wrenching it from my grip. Damn. Wind-chill minus a thousand.

I muscle it closed behind me and lock the door with a lonesome beepBEEP.

Fat snowflakes swirl all around me, the wind whips at my clothes, howling like werewolves in the night.

I pull the hood up over the balaclava.

Some amount of moonlight backlights the clouds. They swell above me like great dark pillows.

My snow boots have never been worn before. They're factory-slick on the snow as I scrabble my way up the hill. Total rookie move, setting off for Iceland with untried-gear, I know, but I didn't expect to crash-land in the tundra.

With a great deal of effort, my breath puffing inside the balaclava, I make my way to the road, and stay in the shoulder—or what I think is the shoulder.

There's a fence that runs along the edge, nothing but wooden posts linked together with wire, sticking up just above the snowline.

I can't see the road, but the fence makes me reasonably confident that I won't wander somehow into one of Iceland's many springs, rivers or lakes, and the ground here has better purchase. It feels like snow packed down on highway.

I move at a steady speed. Enough to cover ground, but not enough to break a sweat. The last thing I want is to freeze inside my suit if I stop and rest.

At the bottom of the first hill comes a second hill. I climb it, check for a signal. There isn't one.

But what there is—is a light.

A single flickering light in the not-too-far distance. Lights mean people. Lights mean buildings. Lights hopefully mean heat and water.

I'll take it.

I grin into my balaclava. It can't be more than a hundred yards.

It takes about eight minutes to get to the light, which sits in a forest of fir trees, set back from the main road by about fifty feet. A single bulb with a small black metal roof above it, posted to the right of a single black door with a number 5 painted on it in white. The door sits in the middle of a small building with no windows. At least, not on the front.

It's a shack at best. Raw wood siding, a sloping metal roof, just the one rinky-dink light.

I frown.

Iceland has statistically low rates of crime—but I can't tell you the last time I knocked on the door of an isolated building with no idea who was on the other side.

Please don't let me have just survived an icy crash in the Icelandic wilderness only to have arrived at a murdershack.

I blow out a breath, tuck my hand in my pocket near my knife and knock on the door. My glove muffles the sound. So I knock harder.

KnockKnock.

Nothing.

I take off my glove, and instantly regret it. The wind sucks the warmth from my hand so fast, my fingers instantly prickle and burn.

Knock. Knock. Knock.

Nothing.

Shit.

My hand hurts too bad. I put the glove back on and kick the door a couple times.

Nothing happens. Which is pretty appropriate, considering the luck I'm having tonight.

I spin in a slow circle.

There are no lights anywhere. I'm not even sure I'll be able to find the car at this point.

It's cold out here. Not in a toss another log on the fire, Bob or gee, I'd really love another sweater cold. No. It's cold, like I might die out here if I don't get inside cold.

The wind is high, and I can truthfully say that hike up and down two hills to here was not easy. I won't make the full five miles in ninety minutes.

It might take two hours or three?

And if the fence posts end, what then? If my phone completely dies, I'll have no light. I could get lost and wander onto a frozen lake and end up nowhere, walk off a cliff, break an ankle.

That's a really shitty and stupid way to die.

I'll circle around. Maybe there's a window I can break, climb in, pack some snow in a bottle, let my body heat melt it for water, spend the night here. I'm sure the owners will understand. I'll reimburse them.

I'm just about to take a step toward the side of the shack, when a hinge creaks behind me, and a rectangle of warm light floods from the doorway.

I whirl, air-pumping my fists, not even caring how stupid I probably look. Suck it, death-by-blizzard!

My victory dance is met by unamused silence.

What, or should I say who stands in the doorway has my arms lowering to my side, my one hand shifting closer to my knife.

He's big. Well over six feet. Broad shoulders. Probably two-thirty, maybe more. The kind of guy made big both by nature and experience. Bare feet. Jeans. A flannel shirt. A sort-of-handsome-but-not-quite face, unshaved jaw, brows raised, eyes narrowed in an unimpressed kind of way.

His bearing doesn't say military but it does say tried. "What do you want?"

Wait? Is he speaking English?

Still bundled up in the balaclava, I pull my chin back and study him afresh. He's totally speaking English. With an American accent.

"You're American," I say.

He blinks, shifting to look over my shoulder like he's trying to figure out how I managed to materialize out of the night without a vehicle. His eyes narrow. "So are you."

"Yes," I say.

He folds his arms across his chest, sizing me up, and leans a wide flannel-encased shoulder against the door jamb. "What do you want?"

I gesture vaguely at the road behind me. "My car crashed. Well, to be fair, I crashed it."

"Okay."

I blink behind my snow goggles. This should be obvious to him. It seems like a pretty simple walk from point a: my car crashed, to point d: I need shelter from the storm. "There's a blizzard."

"I'm aware."

"I have no cell service."

He doesn't react to that. Just nods like I'm boring him.

"The heat in the car doesn't work."

"So?"

I'm not much of a people person. I have a few good friends and while my family and I love each other a lot, we also drive each other batshit. Generally, I like individuals, but loathe people. I'm no social butterfly, but I do know it's not a good idea to let sarcasm taint my words when I'm begging for help from a larger human. So I speak very slowly, so even the least personable, least perceptive human on the planet can understand. "This is the only light for miles around."

"Yeah." He shifts, the pointer finger of the hand resting on his impressive right bicep straightens, indicating southeast. "Town's four point eight miles that way."

Now, this is where I pause. He's not stupid. He's precise. He knows where he is. He's not missing my point because he can't connect the dots. He's refusing to connect the dots. Because he's seriously willing to let me die? He's just establishing pecking order? He's bored?

Which places me at the mercy of a dick-face-in-flannel, no-heat-sharing ass of Olympian proportions.

I fold my arms together, mimicking his posture like we're two cowboys prepping for high noon. It's like rubbing two marshmallows together with the thick insulated puffer sleeves of my parka. "Well, that's handy. You can walk to town if you want."

His brows draw together, a perfect, man-scowl forming between them, and shakes his head. "You're not coming in here."

Fight Dirty with Me Sneak Peek

LEX

"So, you're cool with a dead body on your front stoop?" Though, I guaran-damn-tee, if a body's going to lie on a stoop, it won't be mine.

He's quiet for a long time. So long, I map out how I'll handle him if he's serious. I shift my stance so I'm only two feet from him and the doorway. It's closer than people would normally stand, but given the context, he might assume I'm trying to get closer to the heat, the light, the safety. I'll get the rubber of my boot sole between the door and the lock. Which will give me time to surprise him, keep that latch from closing. An upward ram of my snow-pant wrapped knee to his groin. I doubt I'll land a blow to his gonads. Men are freakishly good at blocking that. But as he shifts his mass to block, I can get behind his knee, knock him forward with my foot. Get my knife to his bare throat. The plus side of my padded outfit—I'll be able to take some hits, even from this muscle-bound fucker, if needed.

I pull my gloves off, slide my hand into my pocket, grip the handle of my knife. Just in case. Fuck, that's cold.

He sucks on one cheek, his mouth pulling sideways. "You chew gum?"

Huh? "No."

"Smoke?"

"No."

"Snore?"

Okay, okay. I see where he's going with this. I release the knife, but keep my hand in the pocket, out of the biting cold. "I don't think so."

"Are you annoying?"

I bobble my head a little. "I don't think so."

If the blasting cold is bothering him, he's showing no signs of it. "On a scale of one to ten, ten being so annoying people run away when they see you coming, and a one being you don't ever open your mouth, how annoying are you?"

That feels like a trick question. Sometimes people run away, and I frequently keep my mouth shut. "Neither." I shrug. "Or both? Who's counting?"

"So a five, maybe?" he deadpans. "You're half annoying."

"Yeah, that sounds right. I'm half annoying, and you're fully an asshole, so we're even. Now let me in."

The shadows at the corner of his lips darken slightly, his arms drop from their crossed position, and he turns his back on me, leaving the empty doorway behind him. "I catch you taking pictures of me, I will fuck your phone up."

"Trust me, I have no interest in taking pictures of you." Asshole, I whisper to myself as I bolt inside and shut the door behind me.

Disaster averted. Shelter acquired. Still breathing through my breath-dampened balaclava, I spin on my boots and see...everything. And nothing.

I peer to the right.

I peer to the left.

And see a whole lot of non-space through the wide yellow-tinted bug-eyes of my snow goggles.

"What are you doing?" he asks from where he's sat on a low white duvet-covered bed in the rear right corner of the room. The wall above him boasts a set of empty raw pine shelves built into the headboard.

I'm not getting a house vibe from this place. He doesn't live here.

"Looking for the rest of it."

He crosses his hands behind his head, leaning back. "You're looking at it."

I'm kind of understanding his reticence now. Sharing a house with a stranger is one thing. Sharing one small room is another.

The place is tiny. Twelve by twelve at the most. The wall with the door where I stand has white flat-face cabinets on all sides and a handy row of wall hooks. The left facing wall boasts still more white-faced cabinets, a low horizontal fireplace, and more cabinets. The third wall has the full-sized bed he's reclining on, a side table and a lamp. The last wall has a single massive window looking out into a dark wildness and a single door. I hope that single door leads to a bathroom.

The ceiling though. That's a thing of beauty.

That's the point of the white cabinets and walls, the sterile white-pine floors with nothing but a lone furry hide on the floor before the fire.

It's a clear spread of glass, an unimpeded view of the snowy sky above.

I pull off my goggles. Warm air hits my eyes. I peel off the balaclava next. The snow I accumulated has started to melt. Cold drops of water spray over me. My hair's a half-damp, half-frozen mess. I unzip my parka next and take it off, then my fleece, hanging each item on the wall hooks beside his. He has good gear. High quality, factory-slick like mine. Pricey but unused. He's a tourist, too.

Without the parka or fleece, all I've got is the thin long-sleeved black top I wore on the plane. A simple, unadorned cotton-rayon blend that clings with a plunging neckline I'd have died before wearing six months ago.

That's what this trip is supposed to be. A chance for me to not be…well…me.

Or rather to be the real me. Not Lex, the daughter who does what she's told. The Marine who takes orders. Me. The real me. Lex who's got tits and isn't afraid of them.

I like my tits. They're not huge, but they look good in this shirt. I bought this shirt because of my tits.

My boots are caked with snow, making half-melted piles everywhere. I shake them off on the entry mat.

He's still sitting on the bed, watching me with no apologies or reservations. It's a bold look for a man who knows damn well he's stuck with me for the unforeseeable future.

"What are you looking at?" I ask, straightening, meeting bold look for bold look, establishing some pecking order of my own.

"You."

At least he's honest. "Why?"

His lips quirk. He's totally looking at my tits. "There's nothing else to look at."

Fair enough. "No books?" There's one on the shelf over his head.

His big shoulders move in a shrug.

"TV?"

He gestures at the tiny room around us. No TV.

Okay. You want to watch, jackass? Fine. I unbuckle the shoulder straps and my snow pants drop in a rustle of water-resistant, wet black.

I step out carefully. Under the snow pants, I've got on the short black skirt and the black tights I wore on the plane. I smooth the skirt down over my thighs.

His head tilts to the side slightly, his gaze traveling up and down my body as I hang the snow pants up on a hook beside my parka.

I turn away, arch my neck and stare up at the glass roof above, let him get a good long look.

Fat flakes still come down fast. I check my phone. Still no service.

"Did you read the weather report?" I ask him.

"It's Iceland." This guy talks like pops from a carbine gun. Staccato. Efficient. Each syllable given almost equal weight. It's—Ice—land.

"So?"

"The weather changes every ten minutes." Pop. Pop. Pop. Pop. Pop. Like he's weighed out every word before he says it. All grit, no silk. No mistakes. It's oddly attractive.

"Anyone ever tell you you've got a way with words?" I grab my carry-on and squat in front of the fireplace to warm my tingling fingers and dry my hair. It puts me closer to him. He's only a few feet away on the bed.

He doesn't say anything.

"Thanks for letting me in, by the way." I meet his eyes over my shoulder. "I mean that."

He says nothing.

There's not much for me to do. And I'm going to be here for a while.

I have a book—a sexy romance covered in bare-naked man chest—a spontaneous purchase at the airport I'm thoroughly enjoying.

I dig it out of my bag and settle in, leaning against one of the cabinets beside the fireplace, legs stretched out in front of me.

He's still staring.

I clear my throat. "I'm Lex."

"Okay."

"A normal person would tell me their name now."

His brows pull together in a scowl, his chest rising in a silent sigh. Not an angry one. A puzzled one. "Does my name matter?"

I twist my lips. He would say that. I just met this guy and already I know that much.

He's one big contrary bastard. "No, I'm serious. Does my name really matter?"

"Guess not." This is going to be a long blizzard. "What brings you here?"

"Northern lights."

I look up. Too bad about the blizzard. I can almost picture it on a clear night. I came to Iceland for the lights too. Classic bucket list filler. "It's an Aurora Borealis viewing shack."

His mouth moves slightly, lips pursing out, either to hide a smile or a frown. "They call them cabins."

"I bet they do." The point of this whole place is to lie in that bed, stare up into space above and watch nature paint the night sky in greens and blues, and if you're very lucky, some purples and pinks.

A part of me turns to jelly. With another man, a less weird, less antagonistic man, this could have been so romantic.

I lift my book up high, and don't even allow myself to feel embarrassed by the rippling abs on the cover, though I can feel his gaze lingering, taking me in, drawing conclusions of his own.

I have no complaints. My situation is massively improved over twenty minutes ago. Then I had: no roof, no fire, and the distinct possibility of dying. Now I have: everything I need. This willing-to-let-me-die-in-the-blizzard jackass can do what he likes, stare at me all night, or go to hell wearing a speedo made of gasoline.

Keeping half an eye on him, I immerse myself in a world of sex and romance, but eventually my body takes over.

I'm hungry and I have to pee.

I get up, ignoring him, and walk toward the only door in the place other than the entry.

"What are you doing?"

I send him a look and decline to answer. It's a stupid question.

The bathroom's a shocker. It's big. As big as the other room. A whole entire wall of glass—I can see nothing now, but anticipation for morning prickles through me. I bet there's quite a vista out there. A massive black marble shower, a toilet, inset shelving, a tub the size of a Volkswagen, a small sink.

Fancy.

I do my business, wash my hands, and find a glass sitting on a shelf. I drain and refill it six times at least. Hiking in blizzards is thirsty work, and these Icelanders like they're glasses small.

My stomach growls.

This place is isolated on purpose. Distance from city lights increases Borealis visibility. They'd have marketed it as having food, or at least food storage. And this guy doesn't seem like the type to get caught with his pants down.

When I get back to the main room, he's still in his position on the bed, arms crossed, unperturbed. I walk to the empty cupboards flanking the side of the fireplace, open one experimentally. Hit the jackpot.

"What are you doing?" he asks again, more belligerently this time.

"I'm hungry."

"That's my mini-bar."

"As I said, I'm hungry." I poke through a basket of fancy packaged nuts and dried fruits. Lingen berries. Acai berries. Mango. "A dried selection of global offerings. What a world."

"Stop, he says.

I look back and pointedly tear open a pack of dried mango.

His eyes go wide.

It makes me laugh. He's such a control freak.

It's exactly the expression of shock my dad used to make when I was disobedient as a child. The perfect you-wouldn't-dare face of a person who's used to being obeyed.

I'm developing ideas about this guy. Expensive clothes. Solo trip to a fancy Icelandic Aurora Borealis viewing cabin that stocks dried acai berries. Accustomed to giving orders. There's an iPad, an iPhone and a silver-and-gold watch—no way he's basic enough for it to be Rolex—on the shelf that passes for a nightstand beside the bed. No ring.

A single guy with money. Big, but not military. A guy used to giving orders. He's a business guy of some sort. So what the hell is he doing here?

What the hell am I doing here?

I smile at him, pop a piece of dried mango in my mouth and turn back to the other sleek cabinet doors.

There's a fridge, I discover, paneled in glossy-white. Bubbly water, champagne, wine, orange juice. Cheese, jam, cured meats, smoked trout dip, caviar, sour cream, carrots, cucumber, apples. I was so wrong about this place. "It's not a murdershack at all," I breathe and pull out a bottle of sparkling water.

He stalks the three feet across the room toward me.

"Stop." His hands close on my hips, biting into my skin through my clothes, and pulling me back. He shoves me with a hand to my gut.

I let him.

My knees hit the bed, and I fall backward on my butt, dried mangoes clutched in one hand, bubble water in my other. Sitting on the bed beats sitting on the floor anyway.

I now have: a seat, an empty bladder, bubble water and dried mangoes.

My situation improves exponentially with every minute. I'll probably be a billionaire in an hour.

I grin up at him. "So you're saying you're territorial about your snacks."

"They're mine."

"Can you share? Or do you intend to eat your delicious array of globally-sourced goodies in front of me while I grow increasingly hungry and unpredictable?"

He takes a breath, lets out a long-beleaguered sigh and opens the fridge again. "Jesus, is this you when you're not unpredictable?"

I shrug. "This is me at my most rational and well behaved. You do not want to see me when I'm hungry."

With a morbidly blank face, he pulls out cheese and meat and jam, and, like a magician pulling things from a non-existent hat, he materializes a loaf of bread from a cupboard I didn't find.

It's my turn to narrow my eyes. "Why are you being nice all the sudden?"

"You said you were hungry. It's not nice to give food to hungry people."

That's confusing. "It's mean to feed hungry people?"

He frowns. "Are you always binary? It's neither. It's human."

Whatever. "That's deep, man," I say, letting my voice tinge toward sarcastic, and pop another dried mango into my mouth.

He turns his back to me and a minute later, I hear a pop. He's opened a bottle of wine.

"Giving people wine is nice," he says.

I'm still not sure if that was a taunt or an elaborate set up. It would actually be pretty funny if he turned back with one glass and deadpanned, I'm not nice.

There's a guggle guggle guggle as he pours.

Not once, but twice.

Which makes me feel rude and ungrateful. "I can pay for my share of all this stuff." I take a bite of cheese so creamy it melts on my tongue.

"I don't doubt it." The flannel shirt shifts with every move of his shoulders and arms. He's been making opinions about me, too. Recognizes my clothes are like his. "But there's no need."

Because he's loaded? Or he's genuinely a decent guy and I read him wrong? Because he thought I was someone else when I knocked on the door? Someone who wanted to take his picture? Who is this strange secretive man?

"What am I supposed to call you if you won't give me a name?"

He shrugs.

"You won't give me a name, I'm going to have to give you a nickname. I dub thee, Flannel Man," I say, chewing happily. "Thank you for sharing your tiny abode and your exotic snacks."

Predictably, he doesn't react. When he turns, he holds out a stemless glass of red wine.

He's towering over me. I'm about even with his belt buckle.

He lifts the glass. "Wine?"

I suck a blob of cheese off my thumb, and take the glass from his hand. "Yes, please."

The bed bounces when he sits down at the head of it.

"Thank you."

He ignores that, pointedly picks up his book. Conversation, evidently, is over.

He reads his book, leaning against the head of the bed. A nonfiction with a picture of an old white guy on the cover. I curl up against the double-paned glass that separates me from the blizzard outside, make a nest of his bedding and read mine.

We sip our wine in silence.

It's actually—if I take away the bizarreness of his behavior—kind of nice. The gas fire tosses up warm shadows, the snow glitters in the glass above. Silence, a rare thing in LA, broken only by the occasional tinkle of his glass when he sets it on the table beside him after taking a sip, or the turning of our pages. I eat the cheese and bread and dried mangoes with all the stealth and patience of a ninja librarian, lest I annoy him by loud-chewing.

At some point, he gets up. The wine has settled a nice warm burn in my belly. My brain is hazy. In my book, my hero's just traded his life for the heroine.

I pull uncharacteristically dreamy eyes from the book, to see Flannel Man standing at the cupboard again. The wine bottle looks like a toy in his hand. He's rolled up the sleeves of his shirt. Thickly corded forearms, dusted with dark hair. Thick chest muscles. A flat belly, probably ridged in all the right places. Narrow hips.

Flannel Man, despite being a raging asshole, is hot.

If he's pouring wine, I want some more. I scoot forward, so my feet are on the floor, my ass on the edge of the bed.

He swallows, all jutting adam's apple and muscular throat.

Even his neck is hot. How can a neck be hot? There's a distinct bulge behind the zipper of his jeans. I bet he's big. He's a big-dick kind of guy. I trail my tongue along my upper lip, contemplating that thought.

"What are you looking at?" his voice yanks at me.

I tear my gaze up to his eyes and borrow his line from before. "You."

His lips curve. "Why?"

I spread my hands. "Nothing else to look at."

"You know what it makes me think when I see a woman looking at me like that?"

I lean back on the bed, taking my weight on my elbows. "Probably the same thing it made me think when you were looking at my tits earlier."

He sets down the wine bottle. "You took off your parka earlier. Your tits nearly spilled out of your shirt. You know what I was thinking?"

"What were you thinking?"

The intensity in his eyes ratchets up a hundred percent. "I was thinking I'd never have imagined them hiding under that parka when I opened the door and saw a bug-eyed snow blob dancing in the wind on my stoop. I was thinking I wanted to see them. They look soft. Smooth. Warm."

His gaze probes into me. Probably looking to see if he's scared me. He hasn't. Probably wondering if I'm interested. I am.

"I was wondering how your body moves when someone trails their teeth over your nipples. Do you buck your hips? What face do you make when you come? I was wondering what you'd do if I told you to take your shirt off and show me your tits, right then and there."

"Impressive orations, Flannel Man." I don't move a muscle. I don't even blink. "That's the most words you've said since I got here."

He cocks his head to the side like an entomologist studying a very rare and unusual bug. "Is that what you were thinking about my dick when you were looking at me like that?"

Suddenly, it's way too hot in here. My skin feels flushed.

"Were you wondering how big it is? What it would feel like in your mouth. Against your bare thighs. Inside your body? If I grunt or sigh when I come. If I'm a good kisser?"

I certainly am now.

I say nothing. What the hell is there to say? I'm not afraid of him. I don't know his past or his training or his skill set, but I know mine. I'm not in any likely physical danger. What I feel is something else—challenged. Goaded. Tested. Dared.

His eyes rove over my face like it's a book written in a language he knows perfectly well. He tips his chin my way. "Show me your tits."

My mouth smiles against my will, my tongue toying with my upper teeth in my surprise. "N—"

He holds up a massive calloused hand, five fingers spread wide. "I'm going to stop you right there. You've got two options here. You can say no, and I'll hand you a second glass of wine, sit down on the other side of the bed, and we can go back to our books. We'll spend the rest of this blizzard in polite, semi-uncomfortable silence. And in a month or two, we'll barely remember that totally-forgettable stranger we met in a murdershack in Iceland."

A hint of a smile curls his lips at the sarcastic word. He's teasing me. Not in a mean way. Just in a way that lets me know he's been paying attention and he's liked what he saw.

I take a long sip of my wine. "Or?"

"Or..." He rests his hand on his hip. "You can show me your tits. And, because you have beautiful tits, my dick will be very hard. I'll walk closer to you. My pants will be too tight, so I'll unbuckle them."

I smile. "Naturally."

He nods, face deadly serious. "I'll show you my dick and it'll be level with your soft pink lips. I'll get up really close to you. You'll open wide.

It won't be planned out or intentional, it's just what would happen in that moment. I'll slide across the velvet of your tongue. I haven't had sex in a while, so I probably won't last that long."

His tongue curls over his upper lip like he's imagining it all in his mind's eyes. "And you'll give me really good head because you'll be feeling daring. Sexy. Because this isn't what you do, is it? Not normally."

My throat tightens. He's read me well.

"And I bet you don't normally give blowjobs. This isn't who you are, but for this blizzard, it's who you want to be. You're going to suck me long and hard and deep, and when I come, you'll swallow it."

I swirl the last sip around in my glass. "I don't swallow."

He grins. A full on white-toothed, dimpled-cheeks, rough-jawed grin that makes my chest thump. "I bet there's a lot you don't do. You'll do it for me."

He lets that hang in the air. A threat. A promise. A lure. All three.

"And then, because my dick will still be hard, I'll stand you up and strip you bare. I'll lay you down on that carpet in front of the fire, open your thighs and fuck your pussy with my tongue until you scream so hard your voice goes sore, until your whole body's sweaty. When that's over, I'll fuck you until you can barely walk. And because by then, there will still be nothing else for us to do, we'll fuck again. I'll be gentle, don't worry. And tomorrow, too. We'll do every nasty, crazy, unheard of thing we've ever imagined and are mutually willing to do with each other, because we know this—" he gestures all around us, "this is a chance for us to do whatever the hell we want to do. And when we leave here, we can look back for the rest of our lives at the wild blizzard we spent in Iceland fucking like tomorrow won't ever come. I bet we'll both go to our deathbeds remembering it with a smile on our wrinkled-up faces."

Pop. Pop. Pop.

I'm breathing as hard as if I've been running even though I haven't moved. He's staring at me like this matters. And I have no idea what his story is. But he's like me—I'd bet the contents of my 401K on it. Trapped. Desperate for something that belongs to no one and nothing but himself.

It resonates.

I've spent my whole life doing things because someone else thinks I should.

This time, I want to do something for me.

"So, I'm going to tell you one final time." His eyes burn into me with a raw intensity that is nothing short of carnal. "Show me your tits, Lex."

Check out a sneaky peek of GenesisKeys' dark paranormal romance.
Not for the faint of heart